The Q Chronicles

For orders other than by individual consumers, Pocket Books grants a discount on the purchase of **10 or more** copies of single titles for special markets or premium use. For further details, please write to the Vice-President of Special Markets, Pocket Books, 1633 Broadway, New York, NY 10019-6785, 8th Floor.

For information on how individual consumers can place orders, please write to Mail Order Department, Simon & Schuster Inc., 200 Old Tappan Road, Old Tappan, NJ 07675.

The STAR TREK® SCRIPTBOOKS

Book One: The Q Chronicles

POCKET BOOKS
New York London Toronto Sydney Tokyo Singapore

POCKET BOOKS, a division of Simon & Schuster Inc.
1230 Avenue of the Americas, New York, NY 10020

ISBN: 0-671-03446-4

First Pocket Books trade paperback printing January 1999

10 9 8 7 6 5 4 3 2 1

Printed in the U.S.A.

CONTENTS

The Q Chronicles

STAR TREK: THE NEXT GENERATION

Encounter at Farpoint

#00000-721

Written by
D. C. Fontana
and
Gene Roddenberry

Directed by
Corey Allen

STAR TREK: THE NEXT GENERATION

Encounter at Farpoint

TEASER

FADE IN:

1 EXTERIOR SPACE—STARSHIP (OPTICAL)

The *U.S.S. Enterprise* NCC 1701-D traveling at warp speed through space.

PICARD (voice-over)
Captain's log, stardate 42353.7. Our destination is planet Cygnus IV, beyond which lies the great unexplored mass of the galaxy.

2 OTHER INTRODUCTORY ANGLES (OPTICAL)

On the gigantic new Enterprise NCC 1701-D.

PICARD (voice-over)
My orders are to examine Farpoint, a starbase built there by the inhabitants of that world. Meanwhile . . .

3 INTERIOR ENGINE ROOM

Huge, with a giant wall diagram showing the immensity of this *Galaxy*-class starship.

PICARD (voice-over)
(continuing)
. . . I am becoming better acquainted with my new command, this *Galaxy*-class *U.S.S. Enterprise.*

4 CLOSER ON VESSEL DIAGRAM

Showing the details and size of this enormous starship.

PICARD (voice-over)
I am still somewhat in awe of its size and complexity.

5 INTERIOR LOUNGE DECK

With its huge windows revealing the immense span of the starship's outer surface.

PICARD (voice-over) (continuing)
. . . my crew we are short in several key positions, most notably . . .

6 INTERIOR BRIDGE—WIDE ANGLE

PICARD, TROI, and DATA seated in the command area. Starfleet LIEUTENANT WORF, a young Klingon, is at the Ops station and a SUPERNUMERARY is at conn.

PICARD (voice-over)
(continuing)
. . . a first officer, but I am informed that a highly experienced man, one Commander William Riker, will be waiting to join our ship when we reach our Cygnus IV destination.

7 ANGLE EMPHASIZING PICARD AND DATA

As Picard turns to Data:

PICARD
You will agree, Data, that Starfleet's instructions *are* difficult?

DATA
Difficult . . . how so? Simply solve the mystery of Farpoint Station.

PICARD
(smiles)
As simple as that.

TROI
Farpoint Station. Even the name sounds mysterious.

PICARD
The problem, Data, is that another life-form built that base. How do I negotiate a friendly agreement for

Starfleet to use it while at the same time snoop around finding how and why they built it?

DATA

Inquiry . . . the word *snoop* . . .?

PICARD

Data, how can you be programmed as a virtual encyclopedia of human information without knowing a simple word like *snoop?*

DATA

Possibility . . . a kind of human behavior I was not designed to emulate?

It is all Troi can do to keep from smiling.

PICARD

It means "to spy, to sneak" . . .

DATA

(interrupting; delighted)

Ah! To seek covertly, to go stealthily, to slink, slither . . .

PICARD

(wanting to cut it off)

Exactly, yes . . .

DATA

. . . to glide, creep, skulk, pussyfoot, gumshoe . . .

Data trails off his words, finally becoming aware of the annoyance registering on Picard's face. Troi cannot keep back the smile now . . . *then suddenly her face is contorted in pain.*

TROI

Captain . . . I'm sensing a . . . a *powerful* mind. . . .

Interrupted by the sound of a BRIDGE ALARM.

8 WIDER ANGLE

All checking their consoles, puzzled at readings they're getting.

WORF

Something strange on the detector circuits . . .

OVERLAPPED by an ever more compelling SECOND BRIDGE ALARM (similar to the old naval HONKING SOUND) begins to sound. At the same time, the main viewer FLICKERS and *an unusual SHINING, SPARKLING GRID SHAPE APPEARS stretching across the whole of the galaxy ahead of them.*

9 EXTERIOR SPACE—*ENTERPRISE* AND GRID (OPTICAL)

Emphasizing the incredibly SHINING GRID which the *Enterprise* is approaching. Seeming impossibly large, yet in some ways as delicate as a spiderweb, it is composed of interlocking geometrical shapes.

10 INTERIOR BRIDGE—VARIOUS ANGLES

Data is looking up from his command position console, showing as much alarm as we'll ever see on his face.

DATA

It registers as *solid,* Captain. . . .

TROI

Or an incredible powerful force field. But if we collide with either . . .

PICARD

(to conn)

Go to Yellow Alert. And shut off that damned noise.

Conn turns OFF honking sound. Picard is taking time to check all readings *but we're now coming very close to the strange grid.*

WORF

Shields and deflectors, up, sir.

Milking the drama of approaching collision. Then, conversationally:

PICARD

Reverse power, full stop.

CONN

Controls to full stop, sir.

The strange shimmering GRID on the viewer is now very close to us as *Enterprise* movement stops.

CONN

Now reading full stop, sir.

Overlapped by something akin to a ROLLING THUNDERSTORM accompanied by a BRILLIANT AND SUSTAINED FLASH OF LIGHT ON THE BRIDGE to the side of Picard. The light burst physically shakes all bridge crew for an instant, *then RESOLVES ITSELF INTO A HUMAN-SIZE FIGURE standing at that point on the bridge.* As the bridge crew's eyes adjust, it does indeed appear to be a human . . . but one dressed and posturing as *an Elizabethan-era sea captain wearing Sir Walter Raleigh–type "court dress," complete with neck ruffles, lace, leg stockings, ceremonial sword, etc.* Now and later, we shall know this life-form as Q.

11 ANOTHER ANGLE (OPTICAL)

As Q (Elizabethan) makes a formal bow (of that same era) to Picard. At which the turbolift doors snap open and TWO SECURITY CREW members start to ENTER, led by Security and Weapons Officer NATASHA YAR. However, Q merely gives a nod in that direction and a miniature of the space grid outside APPEARS AT THE TURBOLIFT ENTRANCE, barring the security team's entrance, and CLOSES THE TURBOLIFT DOORS. Then Q turns toward Picard.

Q (ELIZABETHAN)

You are notified that your kind has infiltrated the galaxy too far already. You are directed to return to your own solar system immediately.

12 ANGLE TO INCLUDE OPS AND CONN

We will see conn stealthily, carefully reaching to the small phaser on his belt.

PICARD

That's quite a directive. Would you mind identifying what you are?

Q (ELIZABETHAN)

We call ourselves "the Q." Or you may call me that; it's all much the same thing.

(indicating costume)
And I have presented myself to you as a fellow ship captain so that you will better understand me.
(indicates)
Go back from where you . . .

13 ANOTHER ANGLE (OPTICAL)

Interrupted by conn drawing his phaser. But Q barely nods toward conn at which a FLUTTERING ELECTRIC BLUE WAVE envelopes that bridge crew member, and we HEAR THE BRIEF BEGINNINGS OF A SCREAM as conn falls with the SOUND of a frozen hard object striking the deck. Picard comes to his feet, ignoring Q as:

Q (ELIZABETHAN)
Stay where you are!

14 EMPHASIZING PICARD

Who is clearly very angry as he kneels at the prone form of conn, who appears to have been instantly frozen solid. Troi hurries INTO SHOT kneeling too. There is even white evaporation vapor rising up from the body.

PICARD
Data, call medics!

TROI
He's frozen. Can you feel the cold?

Picard grabs up conn's phaser from the deck (reversing it, wisely), stands and puts it under Q's nose.

PICARD
He would not have injured you!
(indicates phaser)
Do you understand this; the stun setting?

Q (ELIZABETHAN)
Knowing humans as you do, Captain, would you want to be captured helpless by them?
(moves closer)
Now, *go back or you will certainly die!*

FADE OUT.

PART ONE

FADE IN:

15 EXTERIOR *U.S.S. ENTERPRISE* AND GRID (OPTICAL)

Appropriate THEME MUSIC with spaceship hanging motionless, still facing the mysterious SHIMMERING GRID that stretches in front of it from galaxy horizon to horizon.

16 INTERIOR BRIDGE—EMPHASIZING CONN'S FORM

In the background on a *floating stretcher* conn is being taken to the turbolift; advanced medical emergency aids are attached to his body.

PICARD

Is he still alive?

MEDIC

For now. We'll do our best, sir.

17 EMPHASIZING Q (OPTICAL)

Ignoring the previous, intent instead on inspecting his Elizabethan costume as Picard comes up to him.

Q (ELIZABETHAN)

Your little centuries go by so rapidly, Captain. Perhaps you'll understand this better.

The visitor moves his hand slightly. We hear the same ROLLING THUNDER SOUND. *Another BLINDING LIGHT FLASH and his body remains the same humanoid face and figure as with the Elizabethan dress, but now the green officer's uniform of the U.S. Marine Corps. Over his jacket pocket are three rows of medals, and his narrow garrison cap shows the bars of a captain.*

Q (MARINE CAPTAIN)

Actually, the issue at stake is *patriotism.* You must return to your world and put an end to the communists. All it takes is a few good men.

PICARD

What? That nonsense is *centuries* behind us!

Q (MARINE CAPTAIN)
But you can't deny, Captain, that you're still a dangerous, savage child-race.

PICARD
Most certainly I deny it. I agree that we still were when . . .
(indicating)
. . . humans wore costumes like that, *four* hundred years *ago* . . .

Q (MARINE CAPTAIN)
At which time you slaughtered millions in silly arguments about how to divide the resources of your little world. And four hundred years *before that* you were murdering each other in quarrels over tribal god-images. And since there have been no indications that humans will *ever* change . . .

PICARD
But even as far back as . . . !
(indicates)
. . . that costume, we had begun to make rapid progress.

Q (MARINE CAPTAIN)
Oh? Shall we review your ''rapid progress''?

18 ANOTHER ANGLE (OPTICAL)

The Q visitor moves a hand again to create THE SAME SOUNDS and the SAME BLINDING FLASH, producing the same human image but this time unshaven and with an UGLY AUTOMATION LOOK AND IN THE UNIFORM OF A MILITARY OFFICER FROM THE MID-21st–CENTURY WARS. Q's voice sounds a bit drugged now as he eyes his new costume.

Q (21ST CENTURY)
(interrupting)
Rapid Progress to where humans learned to control their military with drugs.

19 ANGLE INCLUDING OPS POSITION

As Worf gets a message and turns toward Picard.

WORF

Sir, sickbay reports that Lieutenant Graham's condition is better.

All have turned toward Worf, showing relief.

Q (21ST CENTURY)

Concern for one's comrade. How touching.

WORF

(indicates Q)

And now, sir, a personal request. Permission to clean up the bridge?

Picard shakes head, stares Worf down when he seems about to protest. Meanwhile Tasha has come to her feet too:

TASHA

Lieutenant Worf is right, sir. As security chief I can't just stand here and . . .

PICARD

Yes, you can, Tasha.

During this, Q has withdrawn a slender tube attached to his 21st-century uniform, makes an adjustment which lets a round pill roll into his mouth, and bites down on it with a "POP" SOUND.

Q (21ST CENTURY)

Ah, yes . . . *better!*

(deep breath, feeling it)

Then later, on finally reaching deep space, humans of course found enemies to fight out there too. And to broaden those struggles . . .

(indicating Worf and Tasha)

. . . you again found *allies* to permit still more murdering and *all over again the same old story.*

PICARD

(interrupting; angry)

No! The most dangerous "same old story" is the one we're meeting now! Those who go on misinformation, half-information, *self-righteous* life-forms who are eager *not* to learn but to *prosecute,* to *judge* anything they don't understand or can't tolerate.

Q (21ST CENTURY)

What an interesting idea. *Prosecute* and *judge?*

CAMERA CENTERS ON Q as he absorbs what Picard has said. He takes a step or two, turns.

Q (21ST CENTURY)

(continuing)

And suppose it turns out we understand you humans only *too* well?

PICARD

We've no fear of what the true *facts* about us will reveal.

Q (21ST CENTURY)

The *facts* about you? Splendid, splendid! You are a veritable fountain of good ideas.

(smiling; pleasant)

There are preparations to make, Captain, but when I return . . .

Q gives a 21st-century *salute* to Picard.

Q (21ST CENTURY)

(continuing)

. . . we will proceed *exactly* as you suggest!

A BLINDING FLASH OF LIGHT and the alien visitor is gone.

20 WIDE ANGLE ON BRIDGE

It takes a moment to accept the fact Q is really gone; then Worf turns to Picard.

WORF

Sir . . . respectfully submit our only choice is to fight. If we Klingons understand anything, it is the meaning of that kind of talk.

TASHA

My sentiments too, sir. Fight or try to escape.

21 ANGLE EMPHASIZING PICARD

Turning to Troi:

PICARD
Sense anything, Commander?

TROI
(shakes head)
Its mind is much too powerful, sir. And frightening. Concur we avoid further contact if possible!

22 ANGLE EMPHASIZING PICARD

Clearly he has to come up with something. He reflects for a moment more, then makes up his mind, turns to Troi.

PICARD
From this point, no station aboard, repeat *no station,* for any reason will make use of signals, transmission, or intercom.
(crossing quickly to ops and conn)
We'll try to take them by surprise.
(to Worf)
Inform engineering to make ready for maximum acceleration. We'll find out what this *Galaxy*-class can do.

WORF
Aye, sir.

As Worf stands and hurries off, Picard turns to Data.

PICARD
Records search, Data. Results of detaching the Saucer Module at high warp speeds.

Data quickly draws on his memory.

DATA
Inadvisable at any warp speed, sir.

PICARD
Search theoretical.

DATA
(thinking; then)
It *is* possible, sir. But absolutely no error margin.

Picard nods and stands, RAISES VOICE:

PICARD
Attention bridge crew!

23 VARIOUS ANGLES

Picard waits until all are turned toward him.

PICARD
(continuing)
Using print-out only, notify all decks to prepare for maximum acceleration. *Maximum,* you're entitled to know, means we'll be pushing our engines well past safety limits. Our hope is to surprise whatever that is out there, try to outrun it.
(looks around, then)
Our only other option would be to put tail between our legs and return to Earth as they demand.

24 INTERIOR ENGINE ROOM—TRAVELING WITH WORF

As he takes us into WIDE CAMERA ANGLE, aiming for a feeling of both the starship's *huge size* and its *enormous power.*

25 ANOTHER ANGLE (OPTICAL)

Worf nodding at a reading which an engineer shows him, then EXITING to return to the bridge. Meanwhile, engineering personnel work at their controls and a LOW-PITCHED WHINE quickly works itself up into a DEAFENING HIGH-PITCHED SHRIEK while ENERGY DISPLAYS APPEAR AT MAIN ENGINE CONNECTIONS.

26 EXTERIOR SPACE (OPTICAL)

Showing both the *Enterprise* and the mysterious grid.

27 INTERIOR BRIDGE—ANGLES INCLUDING MAIN VIEWER

Worf enters bridge from turbolift, crossing to his position.

WORF

Engine room ready, sir.

Picard stands behind Data, who is at the conn position.

TROI

The board shows "green," Captain. *All go!*

Picard moving back to his command position as:

PICARD

Stand by . . .
(takes his seat, checks bridge, then)
ENGAGE!

The entire bridge SHUDDERS under a SCREAM OF POWER as we

CUT TO:

28 EXTERNAL SPACE—ANGLE ON *ENTERPRISE* (optical)

Suddenly into maximum warp, the energy release momentarily DISTORTING BOTH THE ALIEN GRID AND THE STARS IN SIGHT AROUND IT. When the EFFECT is over, the starship has turned, seeming to almost brush against the mysterious grid, and is then racing away from it.

29 ANGLE EMPHASIZING GRID (OPTICAL)

With *Enterprise* in background at warp speed, escaping. Then the "grid" suddenly shrinks in size, growing brighter as it coalesces together INTO A BRIGHTLY COLORED SPINNING SHAPE which now races after the *Enterprise.*

30 INTERIOR BRIDGE—VARIOUS ANGLES

The faces of the bridge crew reflect the fact that *Enterprise* is at very high warp speed and continuing to accelerate into even higher warp.

WORF

Velocity warp nine point two.

DATA

Heading, three-five-one Mark one-one, sir.

PICARD

Steady on that.

TASHA

The hostile is now giving chase, sir. Accelerating fast.

WORF

We are now at Warp *nine point three,* sir. Which takes us past the red line, sir.

PICARD

Continue accelerating.

(to Troi)

Counselor, at this point I'm open even to guesses about what we've just met.

TROI

(considers, then)

It . . . it felt like something *beyond* what we'd consider a "life-form."

PICARD

"Beyond"?

TROI

Very, very advanced, sir. Or . . .

(considers)

Or certainly, very, very *different!*

WORF

(with emphasis now)

Sir, we are at warp nine point four.

TASHA

Hostile is now beginning to overtake us, sir.

PICARD

Are you sure?

DATA

Hostile's velocity is already warp nine point *six,* sir. Shall I put them on main viewer?

PICARD
(nods)
Reverse angle on viewer.

31 ANGLE INCLUDING MAIN VIEWER

VIEWER IMAGE SHIMMERS into reverse view, which is much the same as the forward view except for ONE BLINKING POINT OF LIGHT AT IMAGE CENTER.

DATA
Magnifying viewer image.

ANOTHER VIEWER SHIMMER with the CENTER POINT OF LIGHT BECOMING THE SPINNING COALESCENCE seen earlier. It's still far away, tiny in size, but will grow in size during later SCENES.

32 VARIOUS ANGLES

As needed.

TASHA
Hostile's velocity now at nine point *seven,* sir.

PICARD
Ops, inform engineering *we need more!*

DATA
Engine room attempting to comply, sir. But they caution us . . .

PICARD
(interrupting; to Data)
Go to *Yellow Alert!*

Data hits a control and the Yellow Alert ALARM SOUNDS FIVE TIMES. Then Picard turns to Tasha.

PICARD
(to Tasha)
Arm photon torpedoes, Weapons Station. Place them on *ready status.*

TASHA
Torpedoes to *ready,* sir.

Picard is aware of the concerned glances received from Troi and Data.

33 WIDE ANGLE

The entire bridge suddenly SHUDDERS HARD, and it brings startled looks to the faces of some of the bridge crew. Then the motion eases.

WORF
That was a design tremor, sir. A warning.

TASHA
Hostile now at warp nine point eight, sir.

WORF
Our velocity is only nine point five, sir.

DATA
Projection, sir. We may be able to match the hostile's nine point eight, sir. But at *extreme* risk.

TASHA
Now reading the hostile at warp nine point *nine,* sir.

Picard stands, raising his voice to carry throughout the bridge.

PICARD
Attention, bridge. Printout message, urgent, to all decks.
(selecting the right words)
All stations on all decks, make ready to detach ship's Saucer Module.

Some of the bridge crew is startled, but all are soon putting their consoles in order for the move. Picard turns to Worf at conn position.

PICARD
(continuing)
You will command the Saucer Module, Lieutenant.

Worf comes to his feet in protest.

WORF
I am a Klingon, sir. For me to seek escape while my captain goes into battle . . .

PICARD
(interrupts hard)
You are a Starfleet officer, Lieutenant.

WORF
(hesitates, takes seat)
Aye, sir.

PICARD
(to bridge again)
Note in ship's log that at this startime, I am transferring command to the Battle Bridge.
(to Data)
Make the signal, Data.

Data touches a control and we HEAR (still preserved from surface-ship days) the BUGLE CALL "BEAT TO QUARTERS" which continues REPEATING as all bridge crew members (except Worf) begin leaving their posts. While SUPERNUMERARIES arrive on the turbolifts, our bridge crew begins exiting the bridge.

FADE OUT.

PART TWO

FADE IN:

34 EXTERIOR SPACE—THE *ENTERPRISE* (OPTICAL)

Still at high warp. We cannot see the image of the following "hostile" (which is not magnified in this ANGLE).

PICARD (voice-over)
Captain's log, stardate 42354.1. Preparing to detach Saucer Module.

35 INTERIOR BATTLE BRIDGE

As the turbolift doors snap open, Picard and the others ENTER the smaller, sparce and functional Battle Bridge.

PICARD (voice-over)
. . . so that families and majority of the ship's company . . .

36 INTERIOR MONTAGE OF SAUCER SETS

Families, children, science technicians, etc., moving into safe areas.

PICARD (voice-over)
(continuing)
. . . can seek relative safety while our vessel's stardrive, containing our Battle Bridge . . .

37 INTERIOR BATTLE BRIDGE—VARIOUS ANGLES

Acquainting us with the smaller and more severe Battle Bridge, its configuration and positions. Picard is speaking the balance of his log entry to the microphone at his command position.

PICARD
(continuing)
. . . and main armaments, will turn back and confront the mystery that is threatening us.
(turning to Tasha)
Lieutenant, your torpedoes *must* detonate close

enough to the hostile to blind it at the moment we separate.

TASHA

Understood, sir.

PICARD

Worf, this is the captain . . .

38 INTERIOR BRIDGE—EMPHASIZING LT. WORF

The young Klingon at the captain's command station now.

WORF

Yes, Captain?

PICARD'S INTERCOM VOICE

Begin countdown . . .

(touches panel control)

Mark!

39 EXTERIOR SPACE—THE *ENTERPRISE* (OPTICAL)

Traveling through space for a moment, then photon torpedoes blasting out of the starship's aft tubes. The torpedo pattern disappears into the distance behind the vessel.

40 INTERIOR BATTLE BRIDGE

All intent on what is happening as:

TROI

All decks acknowledging, sir.

DATA

Starship separation . . . *six,* five, four, three, two, one . . .

41 EXTERIOR *ENTERPRISE*—ANGLES ON SEPARATION MECHANISM (OPTICAL)

As we see the largest of the assemblies begin to move, yawning open. Other mechanisms are doing their jobs too . . . and THE MONOLITHIC STARSHIP DIVIDES INTO ITS TWO SECTIONS . . . STARDRIVE AND SAUCER MOVING APART.

PICARD (voice-over)

Ship's log, exact moment of separation, stardate 42354.22.

As the stardrive section gets safely clear of the saucer, it begins turning, doubling back to face the Q menace. And now in the direction of that threat, we begin to see PHOTON EXPLOSIONS in the far, far distance.

42 INTERIOR BATTLE BRIDGE—INCLUDING MAIN VIEWER

On which we see a tiny but SOMEWHAT LARGER IMAGE OF THE HOSTILE VESSEL in front of which the last few PHOTON DETONATIONS HAPPEN AND FADE AWAY.

TASHA

All torpedoes have detonated, sir.

PICARD

(to Data)

Reverse power and hold this position.

DATA

(gives a surprised look)

Reverse power . . . decelerating.

TROI

That will bring them here in just minutes, sir.

TASHA

Will we make a fight of it, Captain? If we can at least damage their ship . . .

PICARD

(indicating viewer)

Lieutenant . . . are you recommending we fight a life-form that can do all those things?

(as Tasha hesitates)

I'd like to hear your advice.

TASHA

I . . . spoke before I thought, sir. We should look for some way to distract them from going after the saucer.

DATA

All forward motion stopped, sir.

PICARD

(to Troi)

Commander, signal the following in all languages and on all frequencies: *we surrender.* State that we are not asking for any terms or conditions.

TROI

Aye, sir. All language forms and frequencies.

43 ANGLE ON MAIN VIEWER

Where the IMAGE OF THE HOSTILE is rapidly growing in size.

44 EXTERIOR SPACE—*U.S.S. ENTERPRISE* (OPTICAL)

As the HOSTILE IMAGE rushes down on the starship, THE COALESCENT SHAPE OPENING UP INTO SOMETHING LIKE THE SHIMMERING GRID WE'VE SEEN, but now as if to enclose (and perhaps crush) the starship. A FURY OF SOUNDS like CLANKING—SCREAMS OF METAL BEING STRESSED BEYOND ITS LIMITS.

45 INTERIOR BATTLE BRIDGE—VARIOUS ANGLES

As the bridge and the entire stardrive section is SHAKEN ALMOST ANGRILY as the same CACOPHONY OF CLANKING-SCREAMS continues. All bridge crew cling to their seats until the SHAKING AND SOUNDS *REACH A PEAK.* As when Q first appeared, FLASHES OF LIGHT BLIND US and become:

46 INTERIOR Q COURTROOM—EMPHASIZING PICARD, DATA, TROI, TASHA

It is an immense courtroom meant to reflect strength and power. (We'll discover that it dates back to the mid-21st-century post-atomic crisis era.) Both decor and legal procedures reflect the time when a desperate humanity, still wounded and bleeding from nuclear war, sought answers to its pain and problems through the merciless strength of a new form of dictatorial government representing neither capitalism nor communism. Our three starship people are in old, ragged and stained uniforms which "demean" them as criminals. In comparison with the gleaming steel and glass of the rest of the courtroom, the prisoner's dock at which our people sit is made of rough-hewn, hard, and ugly wooden benches. Suddenly, our Starfleet group is CAUGHT IN A HARSH GLARING SPOTLIGHT. Data, looking around with great curiosity, is the first to speak:

DATA

Historically intriguing, Captain. Very, very accurate.

PICARD

(nods)

Mid-21st century, the post-atomic horror . . .

Interrupted by the SOUND OF A BELL, and CUT TO:

47 ANGLE INCLUDING MANDARIN BAILIFF

Important, the MANDARIN BAILIFF is not a fun figure. Despite the Asian robe and accent, he is an important authority figure—and his expression and actions underscore this. He carries a slim, portable viewscreen, the face of which contains scrolled information he will occasionally refer to. Now he nods to a court functionary who uses an ancient, oriental bell, DOLEFULLY CLANGING to gain attention.

MANDARIN BAILIFF

All present, make respectful attention to honored judge!

48 ANGLE EMPHASIZING SPECTATORS

Some still arriving, chattering in excitement, having to be intimidated into silence by 21st-CENTURY SOLDIER, heavily armed. Picard waves in a way indicating Data and Troi should *not* stand.

TROI

(quietly to Picard)

Careful, sir. This is *not* an illusion or a dream.

PICARD

But these courts happened in our past . . .

TROI

I don't understand either, but this is *real.* I can *feel* that!

49 OTHER ANGLES AS NEEDED

A 21st-century MILITARY OFFICER moving to our Starfleet group, leveling his automatic weapon toward them.

FUTURE MILITARY OFFICER

Get to your feet, criminals!

Our people ignore him too. The Mandarin Bailiff is CLANGING THE BELL again. Data sees something, indicates:

DATA

At least we are acquainted with the judge, Captain.

50 ANGLE ON JUDGE

The "judge's bench" (an appropriate 21st-century design on Chapman camera crane) comes floating into the courtroom. Seated in it is Q (JUDGE), which gives "his Honor" physical access to every part and corner of this courtroom. As he floats serenely over spectators' heads, *suddenly there's the RATATATTAT of an automatic weapon.*

51 ANGLE INCLUDING MILITARY OFFICER

Just completing FIRING a warning burst at the feet of Picard.

MILITARY OFFICER

(screaming angrily)

Attention! On your feet, attention!

But Tasha is pivoting in fast, taking the weapon and throwing the officer crashing to the floor. Judge's bench (camera crane) brings Q INTO SCENE fast.

Q (JUDGE)

You are out of order!

But he's speaking to the downed military officer, not to Tasha. Which turns out to be a sentence of death—carried out by a pair of soldiers who step in, raising their automatic weapons, FIRING at the officer lying on the floor. Spectators break into APPLAUSE as the officer slumps and lies unmoving.

Q (JUDGE)

(continuing)

The prisoners will *not* be harmed . . .

(a glance at Picard)

Until they are found guilty, of course.

Still hovering over the fallen officer, Q indicates the body.

Q (JUDGE)
(continuing)
Dispose of that.

Picard has taken the automatic weapon from Tasha.

PICARD
Can we assume you mean this will be a fair trial?

Q (JUDGE)
Yes, absolutely equitable.

Picard hands the weapon to Bailiff. Q (JUDGE) swings his bench to CENTER FRONT of the courtroom.

Q (JUDGE)
(continuing to Mandarin Bailiff)
Proceed.

MANDARIN BAILIFF
(refers to his portable viewscreen)
Before this gracious court now appear these humans to answer for the multiple and grievous savageries of their species.

Judge's bench swings Q (JUDGE) in literally nose-to-nose with Picard.

Q (JUDGE)
How plead you, criminal?

DATA
If I may, Captain . . .
(gets a nod)
Objection, your honor. In the year 2016, the New United Nations declared that no Earth citizen could be made to answer for the crimes of their race or forebears.

Q (JUDGE)
Objection denied!

Followed by CLANGING OF BAILIFF'S BELL and CHEERS FROM THE SPECTATORS.

52 ANGLE EMPHASIZING Q AND PICARD

Q (JUDGE)
(continuing)
This is a court of the year 2049, by which time more "rapid progress" had caused all "United Earth" nonsense to be abolished.

At which point Tasha comes to her feet *very* angry.

PICARD
Tasha, *no* . . .

TASHA
I must . . .
(to Q)
. . . because I grew up on a world that allowed things like this court. *And it was people like these that saved me from it. I say that this so-called court should get down on its knees to what Starfleet is, what it represents* . . .

53 ANOTHER ANGLE (OPTICAL)

And Q (JUDGE) flies INTO SCENE, gesturing toward Tasha as he did earlier to the conn on the bridge . . . resulting in the same FLUTTERING ELECTRIC BLUE WAVE THAT ENVELOPS HER. As Tasha goes rigid, frozen, Data supports her, lowers her form gently to the floor as:

TROI
(shouting to Q)
You *barbarian!* That girl . . .

Q gestures and the same FLUTTERING ELECTRIC BLUE WAVE ENVELOPS HER TOO. Picard leaps in, keeps her frozen, rigid form from crashing down.

MANDARIN BAILIFF
Criminals keep silence!

54 ANGLE ON PICARD

Bending over Tasha, then to Q:

PICARD
You've got a lot to learn about humans if you think you can torture us or frighten us into silence.

(to Data)
Are they still alive?

DATA
Uncertain. Lieutenant Graham was, when our medics thawed him out.

Q (JUDGE) glides in closer on his bench.

Q (JUDGE)
You will answer the charges!

PICARD
Or *what?* Or *this,* or *worse?* Or *death?* I suggest you take a better look at human history.

Spectators have begun GRUMBLING over Picard's failure to answer Q.

Q (JUDGE)
You are charged, criminals. How plead you?

PICARD
Just a moment ago, you promised "the prisoners will not be harmed." We plead nothing so long as you break your own rules.

LOUDER GRUMBLING from the spectators now.

Q (JUDGE)
I suggest you center your attention on the trial, Captain. It may be your only hope.

PICARD
And *I* suggest you now may be having second thoughts about this trial! You're considering that if you conduct it fairly, *which was your promise,* you may lose.

Q (JUDGE)
(laughs)
Lose?

PICARD
Yes, even though you're judge, *and* prosecutor . . .

Q (JUDGE)
(nods)

And jury.

PICARD
(considers it; nods)
Accepted . . . so long as you keep to your agreement.
(indicates Troi and Tasha)
And assaulting prisoners is hardly a fair trial.

55 OPTICAL ANGLE ON Q (OPTICAL)

Seems to be considering it. Then he looks downward, indicates.

Q (JUDGE)
This *is* a merciful court.

Q waves his hand DOWNWARD TOWARD TROI AND TASHA AND A RIPPLE OF LIGHT plays over the two women, UNFREEZING THEM.

ANOTHER ANGLE Q (JUDGE)

The court very disorderly now with some spectators standing on their benches SHOUTING as an annoyed Q brings his bench up hovering over the heads of everyone.

Q (JUDGE)
(greatly AMPLIFIED)

SILENCE!

The order is so LOUDLY AMPLIFIED that it comes near to shaking the entire courtroom structure. The spectators bite off their words and sink frightened into their seats. We notice Q throwing a glance toward Picard to see if the captain is properly impressed. Then the bench is lowered to allow Q to face Picard again.

Q (JUDGE)
(continuing)
Continuing these proceedings, I must caution you that legal trickery is not permitted. This is a *court of fact!*

PICARD
(same words; same time)
. . . court of fact!

(nods)
We humans know our past, even when we're ashamed of it. I recognize this court system as the one which agreed with Shakespeare's suggestion—"Kill all the lawyers."

Q (JUDGE)
(nods)
Which humans did.

PICARD
Which led to the rule: "Guilty until proven innocent."

Q (JUDGE)
Of course. Bringing the innocent to trial would be unfair.
(leaning in; voice amplified)
YOU WILL NOW ANSWER TO THE GRIEVOUS SAVAGERY CHARGE AGAINST HUMANITY.

PICARD
We'll be happy to answer specific charges. "Grievous savagery" could mean anything.

Q (JUDGE)
(interrupting)
Obviously it means causing harm to fellow creatures!

PICARD
Such as you did when you froze a member of our bridge crew? Will you be joining us in the dock here?

Q (JUDGE)
You fool. Are you certain you want a full disclosure of human ugliness?
(to Mandarin Bailiff)
So be it! Present the charges.

Mandarin Bailiff refers to his portable viewscreen, then steps forward and presents it for Picard's examination.

MANDARIN BAILIFF
Criminal, you will read the charges to the court.

Picard takes the parchment, glances through some amount of it. Then he looks up.

PICARD

I see no charges against *us,* your honor.

Q (JUDGE)

(pounds bench top)

Criminal, *you are out of order!*

Soldiers move in, unslinging automatic weapons; the barrels of two of them are now placed against Troi's and Data's heads.

FADE OUT.

PART THREE

FADE IN:

56 INTERIOR Q COURTROOM—WIDE ANGLE

Action continuing from where it ended. The gun barrels are now pressing even closer to Troi's and Data's heads as:

Q (JUDGE)
Soldiers . . .
(indicates guns)
. . . you will press those triggers if this criminal answers with any word other than "guilty" . . .

57 CLOSER ANGLE

The soldiers CLICKING FIRING ACTION TO FULL COCK. Q turns to Picard.

Q (JUDGE)
Criminal, how plead you?

Picard takes his time, looking to his people, the soldiers holding the guns at their heads, then to Q. He seems to be taking too much time, and one of them shifts his weight, the other begins grasping his weapon even more firmly. Then:

PICARD
Guilty . . .

Picard's people can't help showing relief, and even the soldiers lighten up their stance and their grip on the weapons, until:

PICARD
(continuing)
. . . provisionally so.

Surprised by this add-on, the soldiers begin bringing their guns in close again, looking for guidance to Q, who looks as if he could decide either way. After considering it for a moment:

Q (JUDGE)
The court will hear the provision.

PICARD

We question whether this court is abiding by its own trial instructions. Do I have permission to have Commander Data repeat the record?

Q (JUDGE)

If this is legal trickery . . .

PICARD

Your own words, your Honor.

(to Data)

Exactly what followed his Honor's statement that the prisoner would not be harmed?

58 EMPHASIZING DATA

Taking a moment to consult his memory, then:

DATA

Yes, sir. The captain has asked the question . . .

(in Picard's VOICE)

"Can we assume this will be a fair trial?"

(in Data VOICE)

And in reply, the judge stated . . .

59 OTHER ANGLES

As Data goes on.

DATA

(continuing in Q's VOICE)

"Yes, absolutely equitable."

Q (JUDGE)

Unacceptable testimony, entirely unacceptable . . . !

PICARD

If your Honor pleases, there *is* a simple way to clear up this disagreement.

(waits until he has Q's attention)

We agree there is evidence to support the court's contention that humans have been murderous and dangerous.

(moves in closer to Q)
I say *"have been"* . . . and therefore we will respectfully submit to a test of whether this is *presently* true of humans.

Q (JUDGE)
(suddenly alert)
I see, I see.
(an idea forming)
And you petition the court to accept you and your comrades as proof of what humanity has become.

PICARD
There should be many ways we can be tested. We have a long mission ahead of us. . . .

Q (JUDGE)
Another *brilliant* suggestion, Captain. But your test hardly requires a "long mission."
(LAUGHS)
Your immediate destination offers more challenge than you can possibly imagine. Yes, yes, this Farpoint Station will be an *excellent* test of human worth.

Picard, like the others, is now becoming just a bit concerned. What *does* lie ahead of them on Farpoint Station?

60 ANGLE INCLUDING MANDARIN BAILIFF

With Q nodding to him as the Bailiff stands, raising his voice.

MANDARIN BAILIFF
Stand respectfully. All present, respectfully stand!

61 WIDE ANGLE

Spectators standing. Picard and his people coming to their feet too.

62 EMPHASIZING Q AND PRISONERS (OPTICAL)

As Q moves his bench into position.

Q (JUDGE)
This trial is adjourned to allow the criminals to be tested.

The Mandarin Bailiff LOUDLY CLANGS HIS BELL.

MANDARIN BAILIFF

This honorable court is adjourned!

There is a smile coming onto the face of Q as he turns to Picard.

Q (JUDGE)

Captain, you may find you are not nearly clever enough to deal with what lies ahead for you. It may have been better to accept sentence here.

Q WAVES TOWARD THEM, PRODUCING THE BLINDING LIGHT EFFECT we've seen before—and the EFFECT BECOMES:

63 INTERIOR BATTLE BRIDGE

Picard and the others now in their normal garb and at their regular stations, all beginning to register their realization of where they now are.

64 ANGLES EMPHASIZING DATA, TROI, AND TASHA

Reacting to where they now find themselves. Data turns to the ops position.

DATA

Uh . . . what is present course, Ops?

The OPS OFFICER looks at Data, surprised.

OPS

(to Data)

It's exactly what the captain ordered, sir. Direct heading to Farpoint Station.

Data has reviewed his console readings during this, turns to Picard:

DATA

Confirm we *are* on that heading, sir.

OPS

(to Data)

Know anything about Farpoint? It sounds like a fairly dull place.

PICARD

Actually, Ops, I've heard just the opposite.

Picard, Data, Troi, and Tasha exchange looks, then settle back.

65 EXTERIOR SPACE—LONG SHOT—PLANET (OPTICAL)

Moving in on a yellowish ball of a planet glowing against the black backdrop of a starry space in the reflected light of its sun. There is some cloud layer. At this distance, the planet's land masses are vague and indistinct.

RIKER'S VOICE

Personal log, Commander William Riker, stardate 42354.4, at Farpoint Station.

66 CLOSER—ON THE PLANETS AND THE *U.S.S. HOOD* (OPTICAL)

An older class starship (the *U.S.S. Hood*) lies in geosynchronous orbit above the planet.

RIKER'S VOICE

. . . *U.S.S. Hood* has dropped me off at Farpoint Station where I await the arrival of the new *U.S.S. Enterprise*. . . .

67 CLOSER—ON THE OLD CITY/STATION (SPECIAL EFFECTS)

AN AERIAL VIEW of the small, obviously old Bandi city connected to the modern sprawling spaceport/station, both set in the middle of a harsh and forbidding landscape. This is Farpoint Station. CAMERA PUSHES IN on the Old City portion.

RIKER'S VOICE

. . . To which I have been assigned as first officer. Meanwhile . . .

68 INTERIOR OLD CITY CORRIDOR—PANNING RIKER

Commander William T. Riker approaching the door leading to the office of Farpoint's administrator.

RIKER'S VOICE

. . . I have been asked to visit the office of Farpoint Station's administrator.

69 INTERIOR ZORN'S OFFICE—OLD CITY—DAY—ANGLE ON RIKER AND ZORN

Riker ENTERING, crossing to an elegant, unusually shaped desk where ZORN, the station Groppler (administrator) rises and (unused to handshaking) at first offers the wrong hand, then gets the procedure straightened out with MUMBLED APOLOGIES. Like all the Bandi, Zorn is tall, skinny, rather gray-looking—appears to be sixtyish (as do all the Bandi, including the young ones.)

ZORN

I thought you might like to know, Commander Riker, that we've still no word from your vessel. But, I trust we have made your waiting comfortable?

RIKER

Luxurious is more like it. Would it seem ungrateful if I ask for some information?

ZORN

Anything!

RIKER

Fascinating how in the midst of an old city like this, you've built a completely modern tritanium and duraglass space station. Your energy supply must be as abundant as I've heard.

ZORN

Geothermal energy is the one great blessing of this planet. I'll have all the details of that sent to your quarters.

RIKER

Thank you. But it still seems incredible how you've built this station so rapidly and so . . . so perfectly suited to our needs.

Pushes a desktop bowl of fruit toward Riker.

ZORN

Would your care for an Earth delicacy, Commander?

RIKER

Well, if there's an apple there . . .

There isn't and we can SEE that this disappoints Zorn.

RIKER
(looking up; continues)
It doesn't matter . . . what I was saying was . . .
(sees something out of SCENE)
Well, I'll be damned!

70 CAMERA PANS RIKER

As he steps to the far end of Zorn's desk where ANGLE REVEALS a second bowl of fruit. Riker picks an apple from it.

ZORN
Ah . . . ah yes, there was another selection here. . . .

RIKER
(perplexed)
Zorn, I would have sworn it wasn't here a moment ago.

ZORN
And does your failure to notice it make it unwelcome?
(smiles)
The same with Farpoint Station, Commander.
We hope a few easily answered questions about it won't make Starfleet appreciate it less.

Riker eyes Zorn thoughtfully, then takes a bite out of the apple. He chews, then:

RIKER
I'm sure it won't, sir.
(raises apple)
And this is delicious. Thank you.
(crossing to door)
Good morning, Groppler Zorn.

He is EXITING even as Zorn levers himself out of his own chair.

ZORN
Good morning.

The door closes behind Riker, and Zorn turns around angrily.

ZORN
(continuing)
You've been told not to do that. *Why* can't you understand? It will arouse their suspicions.

As he speaks, CAMERA ANGLE WIDENS TO REVEAL clearly that there is no one else in the room; nor does he appear to be speaking into any sort of communication device. He seems to be talking to the walls.

ZORN
(continuing)
. . . and if that happens, we will have to punish you. We will, I promise you. *We must!*

No reply that we can hear. Is this man mad?

CUT TO:

71 INTERIOR FARPOINT FOYER

In considerable contrast to Zorn's Old City office we just left, this structure has a ''starbase'' look with its dazzling tritanium and glass construction. The few people in sight are Starfleet personnel. ENTERING FOREGROUND are DR. BEVERLY CRUSHER and her fifteen-year-old son, WESLEY.

Like most other humans of this century, she doesn't look her age. Although forty years old, she looks hardly more than thirty. Her attractiveness is underscored by a naturally provocative walk—the woman can't help it. This is counterbalanced by her quick intelligence and her professional knowledge and skill as a physician. Her son, Wes, has that same quick intelligence, multiplied by four. That lively brain is ensconced in the body of a perfectly normal boy with moderate good looks and a cheerful personality, but with considerable maturity for someone his age.

72 ANOTHER ANGLE

Riker ENTERS SCENE behind them and hurries to catch up. He calls:

RIKER
Doctor Crusher . . .

WESLEY
Mother, it's Commander Riker.

Beverly slows, lets Riker walk along with them. We see that despite her attractive face and form, she is naturally dignified and a bit reserved with new acquaintances like Riker.

RIKER

And hello to you, Wesley. Enjoying Farpoint Station?

WESLEY

(happily)

Yes, *sir.*

Riker smiles at the boy. It's clear he approves of this polite and likable kid. Then he becomes aware that Beverly has answered his greeting and is waiting.

RIKER

Saw you and thought I'd join your stroll, if I may.

BEVERLY

Actually, we're about to do some shopping.

Riker throws her a look. Is she rejecting the offer of his company?

RIKER

I've been meaning to visit the mall myself. If I'm welcome?

BEVERLY

Of course.

She moves toward an exit door. Wes has been looking from one to the other of them, interested in what they've said . . . and not said.

73 INTERIOR FARPOINT SHOPPING MALL—DAY

The ANGLE suggests a covered, airy mall with flowers and trees—many of them Earth types but with a scattering of alien vegetation too. It is a spacious walkway with a number of pleasant shops and booths. In background we SEE Bandi natives of this world, a tall and grayish life-form, quiet and overly polite. Beverly, Wesley and Riker move down a line of shops.

74 CLOSER—BEVERLY, WESLEY, RIKER

As they walk, Wes continuing to eye the two adults. Then:

WESLEY

If you're wondering about Mom, Mister Riker, she isn't actually unfriendly. She's just shy around men she doesn't know.

Beverly is startled; Riker amused.

BEVERLY

Wesley . . . !

(swallows her annoyance; to Riker)

I believe that means he would like us to be friends.

RIKER

(grins)

I'm willing, Doctor.

(more serious)

And although we're not officially part of the *Enterprise* yet, I thought there might be something useful we could do while we wait.

Beverly stops at a table in front of a shop selling exotic materials. The modest selections of cloth are lined up on the table, some draped for best effect. Beverly looks over them critically, feeling weight and texture. The Bandi SHOPKEEPER has stayed at the rear of the booth.

BEVERLY

"Useful"? How and what, Commander?

RIKER

Investigating some things I've noticed here, Doctor. The last was a piece of fruit. . . .

Beverly has frowned over a particularly pretty piece of material which she holds up for the shopkeeper to see.

BEVERLY

Would this be available in emerald green?

The Bandi merchant smiles, nods and takes the bolt of cloth INTO A SMALL CLOSED-OFF AREA BEHIND. Wesley watches the merchant go as Beverly turns to look at Riker appraisingly.

BEVERLY

(continuing)

I'm sure, Commander, there are reasons for a first

officer to want to demonstrate his energy and alertness to a new captain. But since my duty and interests are *outside* the command structure . . .

The Bandi merchant comes quickly with the bolt of cloth—now emerald green—and interrupts Beverly by holding it up for her approval.

RIKER

Isn't it nice he happened to have the right color?

Beverly glances sharply at Riker, suppressing a somewhat chagrined look.

BEVERLY

(to Merchant)

Thank you. I'll take the entire bolt. Charge it to Beverly Crusher, chief medical officer, *U.S.S. Enterprise.*

The merchant nods, ticks the information off on a flat little gadget that dangles from his belt, and hands her the bolt of cloth.

75 ANOTHER ANGLE—DOLLYING WITH BEVERLY, RIKER, WESLEY

As they walk away, Riker enjoying the look that's come onto her face over this incident.

RIKER

Let's see, where were we?

BEVERLY

I was accusing you of inventing work in order to curry favor with your new captain. I apologize.

WESLEY

Finding the exact right color took him only about twelve seconds, Mom.

They stop a little distance off and look back toward the shop.

BEVERLY

Maybe this *is* something Jean-Luc Picard will want looked into.

RIKER

Jean-Luc? You know Captain Picard?

WESLEY

(proudly)

When I was little, he brought my father's body home to us.

Riker is startled, but Beverly only smiles, fondly pats her son's head.

BEVERLY

Yes, Wes, long, long ago.

(to Riker)

Shall we continue the walk? I'd like to know you better, Mister Riker.

CUT TO:

76 INTERIOR FARPOINT LOUNGE—DAY—ON GEORDI AND MARKHAM

LT. GEORDI LA FORGE and ENSIGN SAWYER MARKHAM are in the small, comfortable lounge area. Markham is a likable young man, enthusiastic, energetic. He is still inclined to shoot from the hip rather than consider before speaking, but he is a capable (and very new) graduate of the academy. We SEE Geordi at first only from behind, and we may routinely register the fact he is black.

MARKHAM

Where is she? They say she's never late—not since the old burrhog took over the captain's chair.

RIKER'S VOICE

You wouldn't be talking about the *Enterprise,* would you, Ensign Markham?

77 WIDER ANGLE

The two young men turn around sharply to find Riker has come up behind them. The most important thing we notice about Geordi is that he wears a strange flattish device (like futuristic goggles) over his eyes. Although he is technically blind, his head always turns toward the person speaking to him because he can, in fact, see as well as or better than anyone, through the use of the visual prosthesis. As they realize that Riker is a senior officer, both young men straighten to attention.

GEORDI/MARKHAM

Sir. Yes, sir.

Riker smiles at the ingrained and traditional response of the recent academy graduate.

RIKER
You can stand at ease, gentlemen. We're not on the *Enterprise* yet.

MARKHAM
You know we're assigned to her, sir.

RIKER
(extending his hand)
Riker. I'm slated to be first officer.
(they shake hands)
I read the service records on all new personnel on the trip out. Excellent academic record at Starfleet Academy, Mister Markham.

MARKHAM
Thank you, sir.

RIKER
And you, Mister La Forge. Captain Dreyer praised your performance on the *Hood.* Why did you request transfer to the *Enterprise?*

GEORDI
Who wouldn't, sir? The biggest, newest, fastest starship in the fleet—

RIKER
Commanded by the best burrhog in the fleet. Right, Mister Markham?

MARKHAM
(sheepishly)
Yes, sir.

RIKER
(grins)
I've already forgotten who used those words.

GEORDI
Shouldn't we have heard something from her by now, sir?

A BANDI WOMAN approaches:

BANDI WOMAN

Commander Riker?

RIKER

Yes?

BANDI WOMAN

The *Enterprise* has been picked up on our monitors, sir. I should tell you, sir, it is only the stardrive section.

All three crew members are surprised to hear this.

RIKER

(to Woman)

What about the Saucer Module?

BANDI WOMAN

We've received no explanation, sir. But the captain signals that you're to beam up immediately.

GEORDI

(to Markham)

Our new captain doesn't waste time.

RIKER

A good rule for all of us to follow, gentlemen.

Riker touches his communicator. His VOICE is now ''treated'' to indicate he is transmitting. (This will be standard communicator format.)

RIKER

Enterprise, this is Commander Riker on Farpoint. Standing by to beam up.

TRANSPORTER EFFECT (OPTICAL)

FADE OUT.

PART FOUR

FADE IN:

78 EXTERIOR SPACE (OPTICAL)

The *Enterprise* stardrive section in orbit of the Farpoint planet.

79 INTERIOR STARDRIVE TRANSPORTER ROOM—ANGLE ON PLATFORM (OPTICAL)

As Riker BEAMS IN. Lieutenant Tasha Yar of security is there, waiting until Riker is fully materialized, then:

TASHA

Lieutenant Yar of security, sir. Captain Picard will see you on the Battle Bridge.

Riker was prepared to shake hands, but Tasha is already leading the way toward the turbolift.

80 INTERIOR TURBOLIFT

As Riker follows her inside, she speaks quietly toward the controls:

TASHA

Battle Bridge.

The doors snap closed and the lift moves. Riker looks Tasha over, waiting, then:

RIKER

With the saucer gone, can I assume something interesting happened on your way here?

TASHA

I'll let the captain explain, sir.

81 INTERIOR BATTLE BRIDGE—ANGLE ON PICARD

He is seated in the command chair with Data, Tasha, and a couple of other crew members at their stations.

DATA

We are cleared into the standard parking orbit, sir.

PICARD
(nods)

Make it so.

The bridge turbolift doors open; Riker ENTERS the bridge after Tasha, follows her to Picard.

TASHA

Commander Riker, sir.

RIKER

Riker, W. T., reporting as ordered, sir.

Picard takes his time, looking Riker over and then offering his hand.

PICARD

I really didn't expect to welcome you to half a starship, Riker.

(to Tasha)

Is the viewer ready?

TASHA

All set up, sir.

PICARD
(to Riker)

We'll first bring you up to date on a little . . . "adventure" we had on our way here, Commander. Then we'll talk.

TASHA
(to Riker)

This way, sir.

True, Picard does *not* waste time. Tasha is already leading Riker toward a viewer at the aft section of the Battle Bridge.

82 ANGLE ON AFT VIEWER

As Tasha motions Riker to the seat, turns the VIEWER ON. The VIEWER SHOWS A SHOT FROM EARLIER WHEN Q (ELIZABETHAN) HAD APPEARED AND IS TALKING TO Picard. The VOICES ARE FAINT and Riker leans in, riveting attention to the bridge record.

83 ANGLE ON PICARD AND DATA

As the android officer turns toward the captain.

DATA
(interrupting)
Message from the Saucer Module. It will arrive here in fifty-one minutes, sir.

PICARD
Inform them we'll hook up as soon as they arrive.

Picard stands, crosses past Tasha on his way to the turbolift.

PICARD
(to Tasha)
Bring him to my ready room when he's done there.

Picard EXITS via turbolift.

84 ANGLE ON RIKER

Where VIEWER SHOWS ANGLE ON THE Q GRIDWORK STRETCHED OVER THE HEAVENS, THEN SHOT OF Q (21st CENTURY). Riker TURNS AWAY FROM VIEWER TOWARD CAMERA as he looks at the crew members on the bridge. He speaks to no one in particular.

RIKER
He calls that "a little adventure"?

85 INTERIOR BATTLE BRIDGE READY ROOM

Picard at a viewer going over a rather complex screen of formulas. A KNOCK at the door; he turns the viewer off.

PICARD
Come.

Riker ENTERS, crosses to where the captain indicates he's to sit. He does so, looking at Picard. Then:

RIKER
Wow!

PICARD
(laughs, nods)
Exactly.

RIKER

This Q, sir . . . is he crazy? I mean, *seriously?*

PICARD

Seriously, does it really matter how we judge them? We're dealing with something that can juggle starships as if they were pebbles.

RIKER

It's a rather astonishing "little adventure" you've had, Captain.

PICARD

(snaps)

The issue isn't what we call it, Commander. The important thing is we can be dead certain . . . accent on *dead* . . . that Q wasn't joking. We're alive only because we were placed on "probation," a very serious kind of probation.

Over which we have heard a CHIME SOUND.

PICARD

(continuing)

Go.

DATA'S VOICE

The Saucer Module is now entering orbit with us, sir.

PICARD

Acknowledge. Commander Riker will conduct a manual docking. Picard out.

RIKER

Sir?

PICARD

You've reported in, haven't you? You are qualified?

RIKER

Yes, sir.

PICARD

Then I meant *now,* Mister Riker.

Riker jumps to his feet, EXITS. CAMERA PANS to Picard, whose expression now relaxes. He's not too unhappy with what he's seen of his new first officer so far.

86 EXTERIOR SPACE—SAUCER SECTION, STARDRIVE SECTION (OPTICAL)

As before, the Saucer Module is above and ahead of the stardrive section. The stardrive section is *SLOWLY* moving ahead toward the Saucer Module for linkup.

87 INTERIOR BATTLE BRIDGE—FULL SHOT

Riker at the conn, concentrating. Tasha and Data are studying him, privately evaluating this new man.

DATA

You say you will be doing this *manually,* sir? No automation?

RIKER

As ordered.

88 EMPHASIZING RIKER

He's making a couple of calculations, glancing up at the viewscreen.

89 ANGLE ON VIEWSCREEN (OPTICAL)

The rear end of the saucer is moving closer, but it is still high.

90 EMPHASIZING RIKER

RIKER

(to Data at conn)

Two percent rise. Up angle adjustment three degrees. Maintain docking speed.

Ops and conn positions AD LIB repeats of Riker's orders.

91 EXTERIOR SPACE—SAUCER AND STARDRIVE SECTION (OPTICAL)

The stardrive section is seen rising, angling forward slightly, still moving slowly toward the saucer.

92 INTERIOR BATTLE BRIDGE—EMPHASIZING RIKER

Glancing at the offscreen viewscreen, works his console again.

RIKER

Level her out. Maintain docking speed. Docking crew, prepare for reconnection.

93 EXTERIOR SPACE—ANGLE ON SAUCER AND STARDRIVE SECTION (OPTICAL)

The two are level now, quite close together, the stardrive section still moving slowly forward.

94 INTERIOR BRIDGE—ANGLE ON RIKER

Riker looks up at the viewscreen again.

95 ANGLE ON VIEWSCREEN (OPTICAL)

The saucer looms in the viewscreen—everything is level, the docking section is dead ahead—we are still moving forward.

96 CLOSE ON RIKER

He makes a couple of quick entries on his console.

RIKER

All stop. Her inertia should do the job now.

97 EXTERIOR SPACE—SAUCER AND STARDRIVE SECTION (OPTICAL)

The two glide together smoothly.

98 INTERIOR BRIDGE—WIDE SHOT

Riker hits a couple more tabs on his panel as:

RIKER

Rejoin lock-up . . . *now.*

99 EXTERIOR SPACE—FINAL HOOKUP (OPTICAL)

The reverse of disconnecting SHOTS we saw earlier—huge STARDRIVE SECTION and SAUCER MODULE MECHANISMS MAKING FINAL HOOKUP.

100 EXTERIOR ENTERPRISE IN ORBIT (OPTICAL)

The docking complete.

101 INTERIOR TURBOLIFT

Riker with Data, Tasha, and others. The time this takes is indicative of the size of this new *Enterprise.*

RIKER (voice-over)
Enterprise log, first officer entry. Ship's modules rejoined, stardate 42354.71, with command now transferred back to the main bridge.

Riker looks up to see Tasha is watching him. Then:

TASHA
Neatly done, sir.

RIKER
I don't imagine many mistakes happen under Captain Picard.

TASHA
No sir, they don't.

102 INTERIOR BRIDGE

As the turbolift arrives. Lt. Worf crosses toward it, intercepts Riker.

WORF
I am Lieutenant Worf, sir. Captain Picard requests you come immediately to his quarters.

Having had little more than a glance at this main bridge, Riker turns and reenters the turbolift.

103 INTERIOR PICARD'S CABIN

Much larger and more comfortable than the small Battle Bridge ready room we were in earlier. Picard is there, turning as he hears a KNOCK:

PICARD
Come!

Riker ENTERS.

PICARD
(continuing)
A fairly routine maneuver, but you handled it quite well.

RIKER
Thank you, sir. I hope I show some promise.

An exchange of looks between the two. Clearly, Riker is annoyed by this ''faint praise'' kind of welcome. Picard leads the way to a setting for coffee.

PICARD
Some coffee.

RIKER
No thank you, sir.

PICARD
(pours himself a cup)
And now I have a kind of ''what sort of second-in-command have I inherited?'' question.

RIKER
Yes sir, I thought you might.

There's nothing disrespectful in Riker's tone of voice, but he does leave an impression that he's not to be walked on either.

PICARD
I noticed in your envelope that Captain DeSoto thinks very highly of you. One curious thing, however: you refused to let him beam down to Altair III?

RIKER
In my opinion, sir, Altair III was too dangerous to risk exposing the captain.

PICARD
I see. A captain's rank means nothing to you.

RIKER
Rather the reverse, sir. A captain's *life* means a great deal to me.

PICARD

Let me postulate something here, Mr. Riker. Isn't it just possible that you don't get to be a starship captain without knowing when it's safe to beam down or not? Isn't it a little presumptuous for a first officer to second guess his captain's judgment?

RIKER

Permission to speak candidly, sir?

PICARD

Always.

RIKER

You've been a first officer yourself. You know that assuming that responsibility must, by definition, include the safety of the captain. I have no problem with following the rules you lay down. But under no circumstances will I compromise your safety. If you have a problem with that, sir, you can put me back on the *Hood* before she leaves.

PICARD

You don't intend to back off that position?

RIKER

No, sir, I can't.

Picard takes another beat to study him carefully, then:

PICARD

One further thing . . . a special favor I have to ask of you.

RIKER

Anything, sir.

PICARD

Using the same kind of strength you showed with Captain DeSoto, I'd appreciate it if you can keep me from making an ass of myself with children.

RIKER

Sir?

PICARD

I'm not a family man, Riker, and yet, Starfleet has given me a ship with children aboard.

RIKER

(nods)

Yes, sir. And families . . .

PICARD

And I don't feel comfortable with children. But, since a captain needs an image of "geniality" toward the little monsters, you're to see that's exactly what I project.

RIKER

Aye, sir.

For the first time, Picard smiles, extending his hand. We see he's surprisingly warm when he wants to be. Riker takes Picard's hand for a firm and friendly handshake.

PICARD

Welcome to the *Enterprise,* Mister Riker.

104 INTERIOR ENTERPRISE BRIDGE

As Riker steps out of the turbolift. He stops, takes in the size of this compared to the Battle Bridge. The Klingon lieutenant is at the conn position. He turns, seeing Riker:

WORF

Yes sir, Commander?

Riker crosses in, shakes hands.

RIKER

Thank you, Lieutenant. Is Commander Data on duty?

WORF

Commander Data is on a special assignment, sir. He is using our shuttlecraft to transfer an admiral over to the *Hood.*

RIKER

An admiral?

WORF
He has been aboard all day, sir, checking over medical layout.

RIKER
Why the shuttlecraft? Can he just beam over?

WORF
I suppose he could, sir. But the admiral is a rather remarkable man.

105 INTERIOR ENTERPRISE CORRIDOR—ANGLE AT INTERSECTION

DATA'S VOICE
But, sir, the transporter could have you on the *Hood* in a matter of seconds, Admiral.

Data and the admiral ENTER SCENE at the intersection. The admiral is very old with an almost transparent look.

ADMIRAL
Have you got some reason to want my atoms scattered all over space?

DATA
No, sir. But at your age, sir, I thought you should not have to put up with the time and trouble of a shuttlecraft.

The admiral stops. Facing Data, he draws himself up as straight as he can. His voice is crotchety and trembly—and fiercely stubborn.

ADMIRAL
My age? Hold it right there, boy, what about my age?

DATA
Sorry, sir. If that subject troubles you . . .

ADMIRAL
Troubles me? What's so damned troubling about not having died? How old do you think I am?

DATA
One hundred forty-seven years, Admiral. According to Starfleet records.

ADMIRAL

Explain how you remember that so exactly.

DATA

I remember every fact I am exposed to, sir.

The admiral peers at him closely, scowling.

ADMIRAL

I don't see any points on your ears, boy, but you *sound* like a Vulcan.

DATA

No, sir. I am an android.

ADMIRAL

(snorts)

Almost as bad.

DATA

(at a loss, but still respectful)

I thought it was generally accepted, sir, that Vulcans are an advanced and most honorable race.

The admiral stares at him a moment, his severe blue eyes gentling and his feisty scowl fading. He pats Data's sleeve and nods slightly.

ADMIRAL

They are, boy. They are. And also damned annoying at times.

DATA

Yes, sir.

As they move away, Data gently assisting the old man:

ADMIRAL

This is a new ship, boy, but she's got the right name. Remember that.

DATA

I will, sir.

ADMIRAL

You treat her like a lady.

(beat, quietly)

She'll always bring you home . . .

FADE OUT.

PART FIVE

FADE IN:

106 EXTERIOR SPACE (OPTICAL)

Both the *Enterprise* and the *Hood* in orbit close together. CAMERA ANGLE shows how much LARGER the *Enterprise* is.

107 INTERIOR SICKBAY

Beverly is wearing medical ''blue''—or whatever color—science personnel are going to be assigned. She steps toward a LARGE VIEWSCREEN which comes on, showing readouts indicative of the status of the ship's medical facilities.

BEVERLY

Show me the results of Captain Picard's most recent physical examination.

The screen promptly BEGINS TO FLASH UP PRINTED INFORMATION, followed by X-ray-type shots, etc. Beverly studies it for a while.

PICARD'S VOICE

Already at work, Doctor?

108 ANOTHER ANGLE

As Beverly turns to find Captain Picard ENTERING. She nods in answer to his question.

BEVERLY

Yes, on a subject that's very important to this mission, Captain.

(unhurriedly to computer)

Screen off.

The screen GOES DARK.

PICARD

I wanted to say ''welcome aboard.''

109 CLOSER ANGLE—BEVERLY AND PICARD

As if they're appraising each other, then:

BEVERLY

Thank you, Captain.

PICARD

And I thought I should talk to you very personally about your assignment here.

110 CLOSER TWO-SHOT

As Beverly nods, waits for him to continue.

PICARD

(continuing)

I wanted you to know I protested your posting to the *Enterprise.*

BEVERLY

Oh? Do you consider me unqualified?

PICARD

Hardly. Your service record shows you exactly the kind of CMO I'd want.

BEVERLY

Then you must object to me personally. Has it to do with our last meeting?

PICARD

I'm trying to be considerate of your feelings, Doctor Crusher. For you to serve with a commanding officer who would continually remind you of such a terrible personal tragedy . . .

BEVERLY

(annoyed; snaps)

If I *had* any objections to serving with you, I wouldn't have requested this assignment, Captain.

PICARD

You requested this posting?

He turns to exit. Beverly stirs, and her next words stop him.

BEVERLY

Captain. My feelings about my husband's death will have no effect on the way I serve you, this vessel, or this mission.

Picard gives it a moment's thought, extends his hand.

PICARD

Then, welcome aboard, Doctor. I'm pleased to have you here.

Beverly allows only a perfunctory handshake.

BEVERLY

Thank you. And now, if I can return to my duties . . .

It is clear that Picard wanted to say more, but she has neatly blocked any further conversation.

PICARD

(uncomfortably)

Well . . . as I said, "Welcome aboard."

She doesn't respond further and he has no choice but to turn and exit.

111 EXTERIOR SPACE—*ENTERPRISE* AND *HOOD* IN ORBIT (OPTICAL)

Again, EMPHASIZING the considerable difference in the sizes of the two starships as we SEE that the *U.S.S. Hood* is PULLING AWAY, LEAVING ORBIT.

112 INTERIOR BRIDGE—ANGLE ON RIKER

He is standing before the huge viewscreen. Behind him is the young Klingon, Worf, at the conn position with the rest of the bridge stations only nominally manned. Set in geosynchronous orbit over the planet, the *Enterprise* requires minimal monitoring at this time.

113 ANGLE ON TURBOLIFT DOORS

They OPEN, and Picard steps out onto the bridge.

PICARD

Have you signaled the *Hood,* Mr. Riker?

RIKER
(nods)
Your exact message.
(in French)
Bon voyage mon ami. Aye, sir.

114 ANOTHER ANGLE—TO INCLUDE MAIN VIEWER

As Picard smiles and steps toward it.

PICARD
And what was my answer, computer?

MAIN VIEWER FLICKERS, then startles us with an ugly FLASH OF LIGHT that becomes an IMAGE OF Q (JUDGE) who is in LIMBO, but looking directly at Picard. His VOICE BOOMS LOUDLY, annoyed in tone:

Q (JUDGE)
DO YOU EXPECT ME TO WAIT PATIENTLY THROUGH ALL THIS NONSENSE? OR DID YOU THINK I WAS GONE?

Picard is as startled as Riker. The young Klingon, Worf, comes tumbling out of the conn position, drawing his phaser and placing himself protectively between Picard and the threatening Q image.

PICARD
Do you intend to blast a hole through the viewer, Lieutenant?

Worf apologetically puts his phaser away, lets Picard wave him aside.

PICARD
(continuing)
If the purpose of this is to test human worth, your honor, you *must* let us proceed in a normal human way.

Q (JUDGE)
YOU ARE DILATORY! YOU HAVE TWENTY-FOUR HOURS! ANY FURTHER DELAY AND YOU RISK SUMMARY JUDGEMENT AGAINST YOU, CAPTAIN.

A FLASH OF LIGHT and the main viewer returns to an image of the planet below.

115 ANOTHER ANGLE

WORF
Sorry, sir . . .

RIKER
No criticism. You reacted fast . . .

PICARD
. . . but in a completely useless way.

WORF
I will learn to do better, sir.

PICARD
Of course you will. We've a long voyage ahead of us.

Picard dismisses Worf with a flicker of a smile, which takes the sting out of what he just said.

RIKER
(lowers voice)
Hope you're right, sir. About the long voyage ahead.

Picard looks to main viewer as if checking that Q is truly gone.

PICARD
I hope so too.

RIKER
What do we do, sir? With them monitoring every move, every word . . .

PICARD
S.O.P., Mister Riker.

RIKER
Standard Operating Procedures?

PICARD
(nods)
We do exactly what we'd do if this Q never existed. If we're going to be damned, let's be damned for what we really are.

Riker is suddenly very pleased with this captain. He nods emphatically.

FADE OUT.

PART SIX

FADE IN:

116 EXTERIOR SPACE (OPTICAL)

U.S.S. Enterprise in orbit of planet Cygnus IV.

PICARD (voice-over)

Captain's log, stardate 42372.5. Of the twenty-four hours Q allotted us to prove ourselves . . .

117 INTERIOR BRIDGE—ANGLE INCLUDING MAIN VIEWER

Minimum bridge crew on duty.

PICARD (voice-over)

. . . eleven have now passed without incident. And yet I cannot forget Q's prediction that we will face here some critical test of human worth.

118 INTERIOR BRIDGE READY ROOM

Picard and Riker comparing notes.

RIKER

This planet's interior heat results in abundant geothermal energy, sir. But it's about all this world *does* offer.

PICARD

And it's your belief that this is what made it possible for them to construct this base to Starfleet standards?

RIKER

Yes, sir. We have to assume that they've been trading their surplus energy for the construction materials used here. According to our ship's scans, many of the materials used are not found on this world.

PICARD
(smiles)
Perhaps it's like those incidents you describe in your report as "almost magical" attempts to please us.

RIKER
Those events *did* happen, sir.

PICARD
And in time we'll discover the explanation. Meanwhile, none of it suggests anything threatening. If only *every* life-form had as much desire to please Starfleet.
(stands)
Ready to beam down? I'm looking forward to meeting this Groppler Zorn.

Picard is leading Riker to the cabin door.

RIKER
I'm convinced there's more to it than just "pleasing us," sir.

PICARD
(as they exit)
Like something Q is doing to trick us?

119 INTERIOR BRIDGE

As Picard and Riker enter from the adjoining ready room. Troi is just arriving in the turbolift, and Picard calls to her.

PICARD
Over here, Counselor!
(to Riker)
I've asked her to join us in this meeting.
(indicating)
May I introduce our new first officer, Commander William Riker. Mister Riker, our ships's counselor, Deanna Troi.

120 TWO-SHOT—RIKER AND TROI

He's obviously stunned to find her here, although she isn't at all surprised.

TROI'S VOICE
(carrying her thoughts)
Do you remember what I taught you, *Imzadi?* Can you still sense my thoughts?

Then, she holds out her hand formally.

TROI
A pleasure, Commander.

RIKER
(nervously)
I, ah . . . likewise, Counselor.

121 ANGLE INCLUDING PICARD

Studying the two of them with some curiosity now.

PICARD
(to Riker)
Have the two of you met before?

RIKER
We . . . we have, sir.

PICARD
Excellent. I consider it important that my key officers know each other's abilities.

TROI
We do, sir; we do.

Meanwhile, Picard has indicated the turbolift and is leading them toward it.

122 EMPHASIZING TROI

As she looks back toward Riker serenely.

TROI'S VOICE
(her thoughts)
I, too, would never say good-bye, *Imzadi.*

123 EXTERIOR FARPOINT STATION (OPTICAL)

ESTABLISHING SHOT as:

PICARD'S VOICE
My crew and I need a bit more information. . . .

124 INTERIOR ZORN'S OFFICE

Where Zorn sits behind his desk, his posture and attitude indicating some nervousness. Seated facing him are Picard, Riker, and Troi. We see that Zorn's attention is on Troi.

PICARD
(continuing)
. . . before we make our recommendations to Starfleet.

ZORN
No objections to that, but . . .
(eyeing Troi again)
. . . but I'm puzzled over your bringing a Betazoid to this. If her purpose here is to probe my thoughts, sir . . .

TROI
I can sense only strong emotions, Groppler. I am only *half* Betazoid; my father was a Starfleet officer.

ZORN
I have nothing to hide, of course.

PICARD
Good, since we admire what we've seen of your construction techniques. Starfleet may be interested in your constructing starbases elsewhere too.

125 ANGLE EMPHASIZING TROI

As her expression begins to indicate an awareness of something distressing, something painful. During which:

ZORN
Unfortunately, Captain, we are not interested in building other facilities.

126 ANGLE EMPHASIZING PICARD AND RIKER

This stumps Picard for a moment, during which:

RIKER

If I may, Captain . . .

(gets a nod)

Then a trade, Groppler? Some things you need in return for the loan of architects and engineers who can demonstrate your techniques.

127 EMPHASIZING ZORN

ZORN

We Bandi do not *wish* to leave our homeworld. If Starfleet cannot accept that small weakness, then we will be forced, unhappily, to seek an alliance with someone like the Ferengi, or . . .

Zorn interrupted by a small GROAN coming from Troi. Her eyes are now closed over a strong distress she's sensing.

128 VARIOUS OTHER ANGLES

As appropriate.

PICARD

Counselor . . . ? What is it?

TROI

(glancing toward Zorn)

Do you want it described here, sir?

PICARD

Yes! No secrets here if we're all to be friends.

(to Zorn)

Agreed, Groppler?

ZORN

We ourselves have nothing to hide, but . . .

TROI

(another GROAN, grimacing)

Pain . . . pain, loneliness, terrible loneliness, despair . . .

(indicates Zorn)

I'm not sensing him, sir. Or any of his people . . . but it's something very close to this location.

PICARD
(to Zorn, demandingly)
The source of this? Do you have any idea?

ZORN
No!
(stands)
No, absolutely not. And I find nothing helpful or productive in any of this!

PICARD
(stands, to Zorn)
That's it? No other comment?

ZORN
What do you expect from us? We offer a base designed to your needs, luxurious even by human standards . . .

Riker and Troi come to their feet, too, as Picard interrupts.

PICARD
. . . while refusing to answer even our simplest questions about it.
(to Riker)
We'll adjourn for now . . .
(to Zorn)
. . . while we all reconsider our positions.

The three CROSS toward the exit.

ZORN
Captain, the Ferengi would be *very* interested in a base like this.

PICARD
Fine. I hope they find you as tasty as their other past associates.

Picard and his people EXIT.

129 EXTERIOR SPACE (OPTICAL)

The *U.S.S. Enterprise* still in orbit over Cygnus IV.

130 INTERIOR HOLODECK CORRIDOR

Riker moving as if seeking someone. He intercepts a YOUNG ENSIGN who is passing, and the junior officer sees Riker's emblem of rank and snaps to attention.

RIKER
Ensign, can you help me find Commander Data? I was told he's somewhere on this deck.

YOUNG ENSIGN
This way, sir.

131 ANGLE AT CORRIDOR WALL

As the ensign steps to a black surface of the corridor wall.

YOUNG ENSIGN
You must be new to these *Galaxy*-class starships, sir.
(puts hand on the black surface, saying)
Tell me the location of Commander Data.

At the touch and the words "Tell me" the black surface comes alive with light patterns showing appropriate information.

COMPUTER VOICE
Lieutenant Commander Data . . . now located in holodeck area four-J.

YOUNG ENSIGN
(indicating readout)
And as you see, sir, it's pointing you that way.

RIKER
Go that way? How far?

YOUNG ENSIGN
(smiles)
You'll know, sir.

Riker AD LIBS a thanks, goes in the indicated direction.

132 PANNING RIKER

Moving off in the indicated direction. Then the black surface there comes alive with a FLASHING DIRECTION SIGNAL.

COMPUTER VOICE
This way, please. The next hatchway on your right.

RIKER
(responding automatically)
Thank you . . .

COMPUTER VOICE
You're more than welcome, Commander Riker.

Which startles him a bit, but he walks on and turns right at a sophisticated looking holodeck hatchway.

133 EXTERIOR PARKLAND

The Parkland hidden at this moment by a WILD SECTION OF CORRIDOR WALL AND HATCHWAY which, when the hatch is opened, will REVEAL PARKLAND.

COMPUTER VOICE
(continuing without delay)
And if you care to enter, Commander . . .

RIKER
(snaps; interrupting)
I do.

Immediately, the hatch slides open and we SEE THE PARKLAND (LOCATION). It looks (and is) *real,* including land contours, trees, and even a small stream nearby. Beyond that the Parkland stretches off for what appears to be miles and miles away to the horizon.

134 ANGLE BACK TOWARD HATCHWAY

As Riker ENTERS through it and stands inspecting the Parkland scene with genuine appreciation and then HEARS SOMEONE WHISTLING A MELODY, but doing it rather badly and laboriously.

135 ANGLE PAST RIKER INTO PARKLAND

As he MOVES AWAY, seeking the source of the WHISTLING, which will begin to grow LOUDER now.

136 ANGLE AT STREAM

As Riker crosses, stepping from rock to rock. He makes a misstep, almost falls, then recovers and gets across. He looks back at the stone that caused it.

137 CLOSER ON RIKER

As he walks, the WHISTLING is nearby now. He stops, calls:

RIKER

Hello!

The WHISTLING has continued without pause, Riker cocks his ear, corrects his direction slightly.

138 EXTERIOR WOODLAND GLEN

Riker ENTERS SHOT through shrubbery, sees something and stops.

139 ANGLE ON DATA

Lying there, cushioned by deep grass. He's totally absorbed in certain melody notes he's attempting—and keeps missing.

140 PANNING RIKER

Moving onto TWO-SHOT where he stops, and WHISTLES the same melody, hitting the correct notes. A startled Data looks up blankly, then comes quickly to his feet, but Riker waves him back down, sits beside him.

DATA

Marvelous how easily humans do that, sir. I still need much practice.

Riker, acting uncomfortable, avoids the subject. He hesitates, then:

RIKER

There are some puzzles down on the planet that Captain Picard wants answered. He suggests I put you on the away team I'll be using.

DATA

I shall endeavor to give satisfaction, sir.

Riker hesitates, wanting to say something but not sure how to begin.

RIKER
Uh, yes. And when the captain suggested you, I, uh, looked up your record . . .
(hesitates)

DATA
Yes, sir, a wise procedure always.

RIKER
Your rank of lieutenant commander, I assume now must be honorary.

DATA
No, sir. Starfleet Class of '78; honors in quantum mathematics and exobiology.

RIKER
But your files . . . they say you're a . . .

DATA
(waits, then)
Machine? Correct, sir. Does that trouble you?

RIKER
(hesitates)
To be honest . . . yes, a little.

DATA
Understood, sir. Prejudice is very human.

RIKER
Now *that* troubles me. Do you consider yourself superior to us?

DATA
I *am* superior in many ways. But I would gladly give it up to be human.

RIKER
(studies Data, then)
Nice to meet you, Pinocchio.

Data seems confused by this.

RIKER
(continuing; explains)

A joke.

DATA
(straight-faced)

Ah! *Intriguing.*

RIKER
(big grin)

You're going to be an interesting companion, Mister Data.

FADE OUT.

PART SEVEN

FADE IN:

141 EXTERIOR PARKLAND—RIKER AND DATA

We HEAR A VOICE (Wesley) and Riker gets to his feet, looks off in that direction.

DATA

This pattern is quite popular, sir. Perhaps because it duplicates Earth so well, coming here,

(apologetically)

Makes me feel as if I am human too.

RIKER

(taking it all in)

I didn't believe these could be so real.

DATA

Much of it *is* real, sir. If the transporters can convert our bodies to an energy beam, then back to the original pattern again . . .

RIKER

Yes, of course.

(indicates)

And all these have much simpler patterns.

142 EXTERIOR PARKLAND AT STREAM

Data leading the way, then indicates.

DATA

The rear wall.

RIKER

(peers)

I can't see it.

DATA

You will.

PANNING RIKER TOWARD US

He's squinting hard now. Then he stops, reacts at something he can now make out.

RIKER

Incredible!

143 INTERIOR STAGE HOLODECK—ANGLE PAST RIKER (OPTICAL)

As he hurries toward where we can now SEE the holodeck wall (REAR PROJECTION SCREEN) on which we can now SEE that the PARKLAND soil, rocks, and vegetation blend with the PROJECTED IMAGE there. Astonished, Riker backs away from this, squinting again.

144 EXTERIOR REAL PARKLAND—RIKER'S P.O.V.

Where, of course, the wall blend is no longer visible.

WESLEY'S VOICE
(calling)
Mister Riker, isn't this great?

MEDIUM ON RIKER

Turning, then grinning, waving.

RIKER'S P.O.V.—THE ROCK CROSSING AT STREAM

Where Wesley Crusher is hurrying toward us, bouncing from rock to rock.

WESLEY

This is one of the simpler patterns, Mister Riker. They've got *thousands* more, some you just can't believe.

ANGLE TO INCLUDE RIKER AND DATA

Moving down the stream.

RIKER

Careful, that next rock is loose . . .

WIDER ANGLE

As that rock moves underfoot, tumbling Wesley into the stream.

PANNING DATA IN

Demonstrating his enormous strength as he easily lifts Wesley completely out of the water. An amazed Wesley looks at Data.

WESLEY

Wow!

145 EXTERIOR PARKLAND—ANGLE ON WILD HATCHWAY AND CORRIDOR SECTION

As the hatchway smoothly SLIDES OPEN AGAIN. Through it is REVEALED THE PARKLAND, through which Riker, Data, and a very wet Wesley make their way to the HATCHWAY. As they MOVE THROUGH HATCHWAY, the bulkhead BEGINS CLOSING.

146 INTERIOR HOLODECK CORRIDOR—ANGLE ON CAPTAIN PICARD

The captain walking with a senior officer when he sees Riker and the others. He motions the senior officer to continue on by himself, stops and waits.

VARIOUS ANGLES—AS APPROPRIATE

As Riker, Data, and Wesley move INTO SHOT with Picard. Wesley is instantly aware that his soaked clothing is dripping water onto the starship deck. He'd like to remove himself but knows that Picard has already seen his puddle forming on the deck.

RIKER

Mister Data has agreed to join my away team, Captain.

PICARD

(with another glance toward Wesley's puddle)

Very good.

WESLEY

Sir, maybe I should get something to wipe this water up.

PICARD

(coolly)

Good idea.

Picard turns and EXITS.

147 INTERIOR SICKBAY—BEVERLY AND WESLEY

Wesley is wiping himself dry now. He is enthusiastically trying to explain his adventures.

WESLEY
—and there's a low-gravity gymnasium, too. It would be hard to get bored on this ship.

148 CLOSER TWO-SHOT—BEVERLY AND WESLEY

As he wipes, he's been turning something over in his mind.

WESLEY
Mom . . .
(beat)
could you get me a look at the bridge?

BEVERLY
That's against the captain's standing orders.

WESLEY
Are you afraid of the captain, too?

BEVERLY
I certainly am *not!*

WESLEY
But Captain Picard *is* a pain, isn't he?

BEVERLY
Your father liked him very much. Great explorers are often lonely, . . . no chance to have a family . . .

WESLEY
Just a *look,* at the bridge, Mom. From the turbolift when the doors open. I wouldn't get off. I promise.

BEVERLY
You're looking for trouble, Wes.

He shuts up. Beverly looks at him and can't ignore the very real *want* in his eyes.

BEVERLY
(continuing)
Let's see what we can do.

On Wes's delighted grin:

CUT TO:

149 EXTERIOR FARPOINT STATION/CITY—DAY—EMPHASIZING STATION

TO ESTABLISH our location.

150 INTERIOR STATION SHOPPING AREA—DAY ON AWAY TEAM

Which is made up of Riker, Data, Troi, Tasha, and Geordi. There are a number of people in the mall area, some in identifiable *Enterprise*-type uniforms. The others are in various civilian clothes. They are taking in the Bandi shops, booths, food, and drink offered by Bandi vendors.

TASHA
Recommend that someone could begin by examining the underside of the station, sir.

TROI
Our sensors do show some passages down there, sir. Perhaps you and I?

Troi glances at Riker with just a shade of archness, perhaps the lift of an eyebrow. Riker glances away, troubled.

RIKER
Tasha, you and the counselor.

Troi and Tasha move off. Riker turns to Geordi.

RIKER
Let's us start with the topside. Have you noticed anything unusual?

Riker and the others move out of scene, examining everything they pass.

DISSOLVE TO:

151 INTERIOR ANOTHER STATION AREA

ON GEORDI as he looks around the area, moving slowly and scanning carefully. Then he shakes his head.

GEORDI
Well, I can't see through solid matter, sir, but the material so far looks very ordinary.

DATA
Confirmed by the construction records, sir. Almost exactly the same material that Starfleet uses.

Riker reaches to his insignia, to switch on his communicator.

RIKER
Riker to Tasha, Troi, come in!

We milk the next few moments, Riker growing apprehensive. Then, finally, with Riker showing relief:

TASHA'S VOICE
(from communicator)
We were about to call you, Team Leader. We've found something interesting.

152 INTERIOR UNDERGROUND PASSAGEWAY

Not at all what one would expect of a "service tunnel," if this is indeed that. These are smooth, rounded, glistening wall whose GLOW lights up the entire passageway. (We'll see something similar later on a mystery vessel.) Tasha is activating her communicator.

TASHA
We're in a passageway directly under the station, sir. But the tunnel walls here are made from something we've never seen before.

RIKER'S VOICE
And Troi, have you sensed anything there?

Troi appears reluctant as she activates her communicator.

TROI
Sir, I've avoided opening my mind. Whatever I sensed in the Groppler's office became very painful.

RIKER
I'm sorry, Counselor, but you must. We need more information.

Troi complies . . . then her face contorts in agony and a SMALL SCREAM ESCAPES. She sinks to her knees, Tasha hurrying in to support her.

TROI
(continuing)
No, no, such pain. It's so close to us here . . . pain, pain . . .

RIKER'S VOICE
(overlapping)
Hang on, I'm coming . . . *Enterprise,* lock us onto her signal!

Tasha has her arm around Troi, whispering words of comfort.

153 ANOTHER ANGLE (OPTICAL)

After a moment, the familiar TRANSPORTER SOUND BEGINS. Riker, Data, and Geordi BEAM IN, SOLIDIFY. Then Riker hurries over to Troi while Data and Geordi examine their surroundings with great curiosity.

154 ANGLE ON TROI

Riker helping her very tenderly:

RIKER
I'm sorry. Close your mind from the pain . . .

TROI
It's also unhappiness . . . terrible despair . . .

RIKER
Who?

TROI
I don't know! No life-form anything like us.

Riker is looking around at the glowing walls.

RIKER
What in the hell kind of place is this?

(turning)

Geordi, what do you see?

Geordi has been inspecting the wall closely. He shakes his head.

GEORDI

It's of no material I recognize, sir. Or have even heard of.

155 EXTERIOR SPACE—*ENTERPRISE* (OPTICAL)

As before, in geosynchronous orbit.

156 INTERIOR *ENTERPRISE* BRIDGE—ANGLE ON PICARD

In the captain's chair. The bridge is nominally manned at this time. We will see Worf at the ops panel. Picard glances around as the SOUND OF THE TURBOLIFT DOORS OPENING COMES OVER, and he freezes.

157 PICARD'S P.O.V.—BEVERLY AND WESLEY

Standing just inside the turbolift door. Beverly is uncomfortable; Wesley is all eyes, taking in as much as he possibly can in this one limited look at his dream place. Beverly starts to step out, gesturing to Wesley to stay in the turbolift.

BEVERLY

Permission to report to the captain . . .

158 WIDER ANGLE—INCLUDING PICARD, BEVERLY

PICARD

(coolly)

Children are *not* allowed on the bridge, Doctor.

BEVERLY

Captain, my son is not *on* the bridge. He merely accompanied me on the turbolift.

PICARD

Your son?

BEVERLY

His name's Wesley. You last saw him years ago when . . .

She trails her words; Picard understands.

PICARD

Oh, back then.

He glances from Beverly to Wesley, clears his throat.

PICARD

(continuing)

Well—as long as he's here . . .

159 WIDER—INCLUDING WESLEY, BEVERLY, PICARD

Wesley looks to Picard hopefully. Beverly waits, then Picard shrugs, tries to sound friendly.

PICARD

I knew your father, Wesley. Want a look around?

Wesley is out like a shot.

PICARD

(continuing, quickly)

But don't touch anything!

Wes is in awe. To him, this is the equivalent of a devout Catholic stepping into the nave of St. Peter's Basilica. The turbolift is on the level of the "horseshoe," so the command positions are spread below him. Picard moves down to the captain's chair level, Wesley moving with him. He is careful to put his feet down just right so he doesn't even scuff the floor. Picard watches, steps aside to gesture toward the command chair.

PICARD

(continuing)

Try it out.

(as Wesley does so)

The panel on your right is for log entries, library-computer access and retrieval, viewscreen control, intercoms, and so on.

WESLEY

(nodding; pointing)

Yes, sir. And here, the backup conn and ops panels, plus armament and shield controls.

Picard looks closely at Wesley, perplexed.

PICARD

The forward viewscreen is controlled by the ops position . . .

WESLEY

Yes sir, which uses high resolution, multispectral imaging sensor systems . . .

PICARD

How the hell do you know that, boy?

Before Beverly or Wesley can reply, a VERY DISTINCTIVE SIGNAL SOUNDS (Captain's com signal) and Wesley, closest to the control, transfers the signal into audio as:

WESLEY

Perimeter alert, Captain!

Wesley is instantly embarrassed; Beverly is mortified; Picard is angry.

WES

I'm sorry. I didn't mean to . . .

BEVERLY

Wes! You shouldn't have touched anything . . .

PICARD

Off the bridge! Both of you.

Worf has come to his feet, not sure whether or not he should respond to the call. Beverly is hustling Wesley toward the turbolift.

WORF

You have a perimeter alert, Captain.

BEVERLY

(to Picard)

As my son tried to tell you!

She EXITS into the turbolift, the doors CLOSING behind her and Wesley. Picard, slamming his fist into his other palm, jumps for his command chair as:

PICARD

Picard. Go ahead.

SECURITY VOICE

Ship's sensors have detected the presence of a vessel approaching this planet. No ship is scheduled to arrive at this time.

PICARD

Have Mister Riker and his team beamed back up! Security, could that be the *Hood* returning here?

SECURITY VOICE

The vessel does not match the *Hood*'s configuration or I.D. signal.

PICARD

Put it on main viewer!

160 ANGLE ON VIEWSCREEN (OPTICAL)

Instantly, the image of a ship is flashed on the screen. It appears big, dark, ominous—even at far range—and it is approaching very swiftly.

161 ANGLE ON PICARD AND WORF

PICARD

Identification?

SECURITY VOICE

Vessel unknown, configuration unknown, sir.

PICARD

Hail it!

WORF

(works his panel)

We have been trying, sir. No response.

PICARD

Raise all shields, phasers at ready.

WORF

(works panel)

Shields up, sir. Phasers ready.

(turns to Picard)
Could this be that Q you mentioned, sir?

162 CLOSE ON PICARD

Staring at the viewscreen.

PICARD
I almost hope so, Lieutenant. We face too many "unknowns" already.

163 ANGLE ON VIEWSCREEN (OPTICAL)

The ship is closer now—looks menacing—and still coming fast.

FADE OUT.

PART EIGHT

FADE IN:

164 EXTERIOR SPACE (OPTICAL)

The *Enterprise* in orbit.

165 INTERIOR BRIDGE—WIDE ANGLE

All bridge positions are filled now, everyone watching the viewscreen intently.

166 ANGLE ON VIEWSCREEN (OPTICAL)

The mystery vessel approaching closer.

167 PICARD AND WORF

PICARD
Continue universal greeting on all frequencies. Get me Groppler Zorn.

There is a BEEP, a pause, then:

ZORN'S VOICE
This is Zorn, Captain.

168 INTERIOR ZORN'S OFFICE—DAY—ON ZORN

He is seated at the desk and speaks into a small portable communicator grid, shaped to fit the palm of his hand.

PICARD'S VOICE
There is an unidentified vessel moving into orbit with us. Do you know who it is?

169 INTERCUT BETWEEN ZORN AND PICARD AS NEEDED.

ZORN
There are no ships scheduled to arrive until—

PICARD

I asked if you know who it is, Groppler. You mentioned the Ferengi Alliance to me.

ZORN

(very nervous)

But we have had no dealings with them. It was only a . . . a thought.

PICARD

Are you very, very certain of that, Groppler?

ZORN

I promise you we were making an empty threat, Captain. I wanted your cooperation. Forgive me—

WORF

Definitely entering an orbital trajectory, sir.

SECURITY POSITION

It measures half again our size, Captain.

170 EXTERIOR SPACE—ANGLE ON MYSTERY VESSEL/*ENTERPRISE* (OPTICAL)

The mystery vessel approaches and settles into geosynchronous orbit. It is positioned slightly above and to the side of the *Enterprise*—and it is a great deal larger than the *Enterprise.* Suddenly, A GLOWING PULSE OF LIGHT throbs out from the mystery vessel toward the *Enterprise.*

171 INTERIOR *ENTERPRISE* BRIDGE—FULL SHOT

The LIGHT GLOWS OVER EVERYTHING AND EVERYONE ON THE BRIDGE. They are startled by it, but no one is hurt. As the GLOW FADES AWAY:

PICARD

All stations, give any damage reports.

The others are looking at each other, shaking their heads. No problems.

DATA

I would guess we were being scanned, sir.

172 INTERIOR UNDERGROUND PASSAGEWAY

Troi is leaning against the strange, smooth, and shining tunnel wall as if still feeling pain. Riker, obviously still concerned for Troi, is examining the strange tunnel walls with the tricorder while Geordi moves his "eyes" inches away from the surface to examine it closely. Data is testing his communicator, and we'll HEAR him trying to get a signal back from the *Enterprise.*

TASHA
(to Troi)
Pain again?

RIKER
(turning; sharply)
Troi, you've been at it enough!

TROI
No, I feel close to an answer of some kind.

DATA
(interrupting)
Commander, something down here is shielding our communicators.

TROI
(comes to her feet)
Yes, that's *exactly* the feeling I've been reading. As if someone doesn't want us to be in touch with our ship.

RIKER
Come on . . .
(leads the way)
. . . let's get to the surface.

173 EXTERIOR SPACE—*ENTERPRISE* AND MYSTERY VESSEL (OPTICAL)

The mystery vessel *clearly larger than the Enterprise* and moving near it in orbit.

174 INTERIOR BRIDGE—INCLUDING MAIN VIEWER (OPTICAL)

On which is featured an IMAGE OF MYSTERY VESSEL.

OPERATIONS POSITION
There is no computer record of any such vessel, sir. Not even close.

SECURITY POSITION
Still no response, sir. We've done everything but threaten them.

PICARD
Sensor scans, Mister Worf.

WORF
Our sensor signals seem to just bounce off.
(bites off words; indicates to viewer)
Something is happening, sir . . .

175 FULL ON MAIN VIEWER (OPTICAL)

As a beam of something STRIKES DOWNWARD TOWARD THE PLANET SURFACE. (It doesn't not look exactly like the *Enterprise* phasers but is the same sort of thing.)

176 EXTERIOR SPACE—ANGLE ON MYSTERY VESSEL (OPTICAL)

As another phaser-like BEAM STRIKES DOWN AT THE PLANET.

177 INTERIOR BRIDGE

Excitement.

178 ANGLE ON OPS POSITION

WORF
They are firing on Farpoint, sir . . .!

PICARD
(toward Security position)
Bring phasers and photon torpedoes to ready!

WORF
No, hold it, sir. They are hitting the Bandi city, not Farpoint Station.

179 INTERIOR UNDERGROUND PASSAGEWAY

Riker and his team racing to where the rounded, smooth, and shining walls of the tunnel begin to give way to a more ordinary-looking rectangular corridor of mixed stone and tile walls.

180 ANOTHER ANGLE—INCLUDING STAIRWAY AHEAD

Riker pulling to a halt in order to examine with curiosity the blend where the unknown-type tunnel walls give way to stone and tile construction similar to what we've seen in the Bandi Old City. Ahead is a stone block stairway leading up to that Old City. Geordi has hurried in, peering closely at the more familiar kind of wall surface.

TROI
(indicates ahead)
Those stairs are where Tasha and I entered down here, sir.

GEORDI
At this point, it becomes ordinary stone and tile, sir.
(turns, puzzled)
Matching what's above.

Followed by a LONG RUMBLING EXPLOSION ("PHASER HIT" type) WITH THE LONG FLASH OF IT REFLECTING DOWN THE STAIRWAY FROM THE UPPER LEVEL AHEAD. As this SOUND FADES, then we HEAR A FAINT DISTANT SCREAM which dies away too.

TASHA
My God! Was that a phaser blast?

DATA
Negative. But something similar.

Again, the SAME KIND OF EXPLOSION SOUND followed by similar LIGHT FLICKERS from the stairway ahead. Riker turns to Troi:

RIKER
You, Tasha, and Geordi will beam up to the ship from here. Now!
(to Data)
Come on, I want to see exactly what's happening.

Riker starts off to the stairway, Data following.

TROI
Don't. If you should be hurt . . .

A stern look comes over Riker's face as he turns quickly to her:

RIKER

You have your orders, Lieutenant! Carry them out!

TROI

Yes sir, I'm sorry, sir.

181 ANOTHER ANGLE (OPTICAL)

Riker and Data begin climbing the stairway, leaving the CAMERA CENTERED ON TROI, TASHA, AND GEORDI. Troi has already reached for her communicator control.

TROI

Enterprise, three to beam up.

After a moment, the familiar TRANSPORTER SOUND, followed by TRANSPORTER EFFECT ON THE THREE DISSOLVING INTO THE LIGHT SPARKLE. Then, they're gone.

182 INTERIOR COVERED VILLAGE SQUARE (OPTICAL)

OLD CITY IN BACKGROUND where FIRE RAGES in a smashed structure in that part of the Old City we can see. In CLOSER FOREGROUND is an entrance to the underground passageway, this entry guarded by thick, handworked metal door, locked. This village square is a connecting point between the Old City and Farpoint Station. A short distance in the OFFCAMERA DIRECTION lies Farpoint mall.

183 THE METAL DOORS (OPTICAL)

We HEAR a hand phaser HUM as a GLOW FLICKERS OVER THE METAL DOORS, which now spring open, and a CLASHING OF METAL SOUND. Riker and Data ENTER SCENE though those door, phasers in hand.

184 CLOSER—RIKER AND DATA

As Riker touches his communicator control.

RIKER

Enterprise, Riker. Come in.

185 INTERRUPTED BY THE CLOSER SOUND OF A PHASER-LIKE BOLT FROM THE MYSTERY VESSEL. Also from closer, THE LIGHT OF THE BLAST REFLECTS ON THEIR FACES and they whirl to see:

186 ANGLE INTO OLD CITY

Where a building is being BLASTED INTO STONES AND DUST.

187 INTERIOR ZORN'S OFFICE—OLD CITY

Filled with the dust and SOUNDS of a nearby BLAST. Zorn is working frantically with his communicator.

ZORN
Enterprise, Enterprise, help us! Come in, *please* . . .

188 INTERIOR BRIDGE—WIDE ANGLE (OPTICAL)

On MAIN VIEWER THE IMAGE OF THE mystery vessel, which as we watch will FIRE ANOTHER PHASER-LIKE BOLT DOWN TOWARD THE PLANET. The bridge crew are anxiously poised on the edge of their seats, waiting for Picard's next order.

ZORN'S VOICE
. . . what shall we do? Help us, *please.*

PICARD
(overlapping)
Tune him down!
(into transmitter)
Commander Riker, go ahead. Where are you?

189 ANOTHER ANGLE—INCLUDING TURBOLIFT

As the doors SNAP OPEN TO REVEAL TROI, TASHA, AND GEORDI, who hurry onto the bridge, take their regular positions (Geordi relieving ops). Meanwhile:

RIKER'S VOICE
With Data, on the edge of the Old City, Captain. It's being hit hard. Who's doing this?

PICARD
And Farpoint Station? Any damage there?

190 INTERIOR COVERED VILLAGE SQUARE—FARPOINT MALL IN BACKGROUND.

No indication that Farpoint Station has been damaged at all. Riker, standing with Data, is using his communicator.

RIKER
Negative on damage to Farpoint, sir. Whoever they are, it seems they're carefully avoiding hitting the station.

PICARD'S VOICE
It's from an unidentified vessel that's entered orbit with us here. No I.D., no answer to our signals . . .

During which there's another BLAST SOUND with the same kind of LIGHT FLICKERS.

191 ANGLE INCLUDING OLD CITY

As Riker whirls again in that direction, interrupting Picard:

RIKER
They're hitting the Bandi city hard, sir. Many casualties very probable.

192 INTERIOR BRIDGE—EMPHASIZING PICARD

Everything as we last left it.

PICARD
(into transmitter)
Understand, Commander. Would you object to a clearly illegal kidnapping assignment?

RIKER'S VOICE
No objection; anything you order, sir.

PICARD
Zorn may have the answers we need. Get Groppler Zorn and bring him here!

RIKER'S VOICE
Aye, sir!

193 ANGLE INCLUDING MAIN VIEWER (OPTICAL)

Picard looks at the IMAGE of the huge mystery vessel still in orbit nearby. Picard turns to Troi:

PICARD

They're forcing a difficult decision on me, Counselor.

TROI

(nods)

But I doubt protecting the Bandi would violate the Prime Directive. True, they are not actual allies . . .

PICARD

But we *are* in the midst of diplomatic discussions with them.

(turns to Tasha)

Lock phasers on that vessel, Lieutenant.

194 ANOTHER ANGLE (OPTICAL)

In background, Tasha touching panel controls.

TASHA

Phasers locked on, Captain.

Anything further INTERRUPTED BY OPTICAL EFFECT, the BLINDING LIGHT FLASH we've seen before and FADING TO REVEAL Q, *wearing the judge's* costume *from the earlier courtroom sequence. He is standing in front of Picard.*

Q (JUDGE)

Typical, so typical. Savage life-forms never follow even their own rules.

FADE OUT.

PART NINE

FADE IN:

195 EXTERIOR BRIDGE—EMPHASIZING PICARD AND Q

Rather than being nervous over the arrival of Q (JUDGE), Picard has become coldly angry.

PICARD

Get off my bridge!

196 ANOTHER ANGLE

Q stepping toward Picard, smiling sadly.

Q (JUDGE)

Also interesting, that order about phasers.

TASHA

(ignoring Q; to Picard)

Still standing by on phasers, Captain.

Q (JUDGE)

(turning to Picard)

Please don't let me interfere. Use your weapons.

PICARD

You're the one who has a lot to learn, Q. With no idea of who's on that vessel, my order was a routine safety precaution.

Q (JUDGE)

(breaking into LAUGHTER)

Really? No idea of what it represents? The meaning of that vessel is as plain as . . .

(then taps his nose)

. . . as plain as the noses on your ugly little primate faces?

LOUDER LAUGHTER.

Q (JUDGE)
(trying to control it)
And if you were truly civilized, Captain, wouldn't you be doing something about the casualties happening down there?

In answer, Picard touches the communications control on his uniform.

PICARD
Captain to CMO, are you reading any of this?

197 INTERIOR SICKBAY—ANGLE EMPHASIZING BEVERLY

But she's with a half dozen MEDICAL ASSISTANTS *very* busy preparing medical supplies, bringing portable medical equipment, etc.

BEVERLY
Medical teams already preparing to beam down, Captain.

PICARD'S VOICE
(relieved)
Compliments on that, Doctor!

198 INTERIOR BRIDGE

Picard turning back to Q.

PICARD
Any questions? Starfleet people are trained to render aid and assistance whenever . . .

Q (JUDGE)
(interrupting)
But not trained in clear thinking.

PICARD
Let's consider *your* thoughts. You call us "savages" and yet you *knew* those people down there would be killed. *You're* the one whose conduct is uncivilized.

WORF
Sir, they are firing on the planet again.

199 ANGLE INCLUDING MAIN VIEWER (OPTICAL)

Where we SEE the mystery vessel beginning to FIRE BLASTS down at the planet again.

PICARD

Force fields full on.

(to Worf)

Go to thrusters! Position us between that vessel and the planet.

WORF

Aye, sir, thruster power to . . .

Worf trails his words, perplexed. His panel is fading, GOING DARK.

WORF

(continuing)

We have no ship control, sir. *It is gone!*

200 INTERIOR CORRIDOR OUTSIDE ZORN'S OFFICE—DAY—RIKER AND DATA

They are headed toward Zorn's office door when the BLUE BOLT HITS beside the door, flooding the scene with a FLASH OF BLUE LIGHT. The corridor rocks, and the ceiling comes down partially. Riker and Data are flung down by the explosion. A beat, and then Data stirs, sits up. Riker is slower, but is managing to haul himself upright.

DATA

Are you undamaged?

RIKER

Yes. You?

Data's eyes glaze slightly as he seems to go into a sort of "trance" that lasts just a few seconds. Then:

DATA

All systems operating.

201 ANGLE INCLUDING ZORN'S OFFICE DOOR

It is hanging by its hinges, and debris-dust is drifting out of it. Riker and Data move quickly to and through the open door.

202 INTERIOR ZORN'S OFFICE—DAY—FULL SHOT

As Riker and Data ENTER. The office has been badly damaged, especially near the door. OFFSCREEN THE SOUND OF ANOTHER BOLT EXPLODING echoes. The room shakes under the impact. There is a MUFFLED SOB near the desk.

203 CLOSER ANGLE—NEAR DESK

Zorn is cowering under his elegant desk, shaking and sobbing in fear.

ZORN
Please. You can make it stop. Drive it away.

RIKER
Drive *who* away, Groppler?

Zorn reacts as if he knows he's said too much.

ZORN
I don't know.

DATA
Unlikely, sir.
(to Zorn)
Our records show that you supervised all Bandi contact with other worlds . . .

ZORN
We haven't done anything wrong!

RIKER
Then if we can learn nothing from you, perhaps we'll leave.

ZORN
(frightened)
No! No, don't leave, I'll try to explain some of . . .

204 EMPHASIZING ZORN (OPTICAL)

A kind of TRANSPORTER SOUND is heard, and then a TRANSPORTER EFFECT, somewhat different from the Starfleet variety, centers on Zorn. He begins SCREAMING as he FADES FROM VIEW.

205 ANGLE ON RIKER

As he keys his communicator.

RIKER
First officer to *Enterprise.*

PICARD'S VOICE
Go ahead, Riker.

RIKER
We've lost Zorn, sir. Something like a transporter beam, it snatched him out of here.

206 INTERIOR BRIDGE

Q still in the captain's seat, listening to:

RIKER'S VOICE
Question, sir, could it have been the Q character you met earlier?

Q (JUDGE)
(laughs)
None of you know who it is? You're running out of time, Captain.

207 ANGLE EMPHASIZING PICARD AND TROI

She's frowning, trying to "feel" something.

TROI
Captain . . . Suddenly I'm sensing something else. It's *satisfaction,* enormous satisfaction.

PICARD
From the same source as before?

TROI
No, that was on the planet.
(indicates)
This seems to be from here.

208 ANGLE TO INCLUDE MAIN VIEWER (OPTICAL)

And the image of the mystery vessel.

Q (JUDGE)
(to Troi)
Excellent, Counselor!
(indicates Picard)
He's such a dullard, isn't he!

INTERCOM VOICE
Captain from transporter room. First officer and Mister Data now beaming aboard.

Q (JUDGE)
Excellent also!
(to Picard)
Perhaps with more of these little minds helping, you'll . . .

209 EMPHASIZING PICARD

As he whirls suddenly on Q.

PICARD
(interrupting)
That is *enough,* damn it!

Q (JUDGE)
We have an agreement; have you forgotten . . . ?

In background, the turbolift doors SNAP OPEN but are unnoticed by Picard and Q as they continue their argument. Riker and Data appear, move onto bridge as:

PICARD
We have an agreement which you are at this moment breaking by taking over our vessel, interfering with my decisions!
(steps up nose-to-nose)
You are not welcome on my bridge. Now, either leave or finish us. One of the two!

Q stands, during which we have the impression that everyone is holding his breath. Then:

Q (JUDGE)
(gently)
Temper, temper, mon Capitaine. I am merely trying to assist a pitiful species. Perhaps I'll leave if Mister Riker provides me with some amusement.

PICARD
(to Riker)
Do *nothing* that he asks!

Q (JUDGE)
But I ask so little. And it is so necessary if you are to solve all this.
(turns; indicates vessel image in main viewer)
Beam over there with your . . . what is it called . . . your "away team"?
(to Picard)
You *should* already know what you'll find there. But perhaps it was too adult a puzzle for you.

RIKER
Captain, with all respect, I intended to suggest beaming over there.

210 EMPHASIZING Q (OPTICAL)

Amused at all this. He turns from Riker to look at Picard.

Q (JUDGE)
You show promise, my good fellow.

PICARD
But *you* don't. You should have long ago realized that *humanity is NOT a criminal race!*

Q (JUDGE)
YOU MUST STILL PROVE THAT!

A familiar BLINDING FLASH, and then Q is gone.

211 ANGLE EMPHASIZING PICARD AND RIKER

Realizing Q is gone, turning to look at each other. Riker checks a reading on his panel.

RIKER

Of the twenty-four hours Q gave us, we have less than one left, sir.

PICARD

(nods)

But I had a feeling you impressed him, Number One. That's hopeful.

RIKER

Thank you, Captain. That's the first time you've called me "Number One."

PICARD

(small smile)

I believe I'll enjoy getting to know you, Bill. If we live long enough.

FADE OUT.

PART TEN

FADE IN:

212 EXTERIOR SPACE—*ENTERPRISE* AND MYSTERY VESSEL (OPTICAL)

In orbit over the planet.

213 INTERIOR TRANSPORTER ROOM

Riker's away team moving onto the transporter platform. With him are Data, Troi, and Tasha. They carry the usual away team equipment, which they're now checking.

RIKER

Phasers on stun.

Everyone checks hand phasers. AD-LIB answers of "checked," "on stun," etc. Riker turns to transporter chief.

RIKER

Energize.

214 INTERIOR MYSTERY SHIP TUNNEL—WIDE ANGLE (OPTICAL)

TRANSPORTER SOUND, then the BEAMING EFFECT. Then, fully MATERIALIZED, Riker and the others look around to orient themselves.

DATA

Most interesting, sir.

TASHA

Much the same construction as the underground tunnel we saw.

Which describes it perfectly. The same rounded shape and GLOWING WALL of unknown composition. The "tunnel" is deserted; NO SHIP SOUNDS of any kind.

TASHA

(continuing)

But no sound of power; no equipment. How does this ship run?

Riker nods a direction. Tasha takes the point as they move out. Clearly, these are exceptionally well-trained people. Data is already using his tricorder to check the walls. He obviously gets nothing, shakes his head. Troi suddenly staggers, GROANS.

RIKER

Troi, what is it?!

(waits anxiously)

Is it the same as you felt down there?

TROI

No, this is . . . different. It feels much more powerful . . . full of *anger* . . . *hate* . . .

TASHA

Toward us?

TROI

No. It's directed down toward the Bandi Old City.

DATA

Most intriguing again. The place that this vessel was firing upon . . .

(abruptly stops; to Riker)

Sorry, sir, I seem to be commenting on everything.

RIKER

(small smile)

Good. Don't stop it, my friend.

215 EXTERIOR SPACE (OPTICAL)

Enterprise and the mystery vessel still in orbit.

216 INTERIOR BRIDGE—EMPHASIZING PICARD

Geordi and Worf at their positions. Picard is in the command seat, antsy.

RIKER'S VOICE

Enterprise, Riker. This is turning out to be a very long tunnel or corridor, sir. Still no sign of mechanism or circuitry . . .

217 INTERIOR NARROW MYSTERY SHIP TUNNEL—RIKER AND GROUP

Still led and followed by the security people, they're now moving along fairly rapidly although this tunnel is narrower here. Otherwise, its look hasn't changed.

RIKER
(continuing)
. . . or controls, readouts, nothing at all like any vessel I've seen before.

TROI
(interrupting)
Groppler Zorn, sir . . . in great fear . . .
(motions)
Just ahead.

218 INTERIOR TUNNEL CONNECTION

Troi and the team arriving, standing puzzled at what seems to be only a sharp turn where we SEE a strange indentation in the tunnel wall there. Troi, intent on this, steps closer, pushes her body against the indentation.

TROI
It's definitely Zorn, Commander. Here!

RIKER
(stepping in)
Careful . . .

But the tunnel wall is soft here—it gives perceptibly, as Troi pushes harder and then PLOP . . . she disappears through it. (NOTE: *Or* the ''wall'' opens to let her through and then closes behind her.)

RIKER
Troi!!!

Then he pushes, disappears through the same wall.

219 INTERIOR ZORN'S ''CELL''

Riker sliding through the pliable opening in the tunnel wall, joining Troi, who is standing there aghast at what is suspended in the center of this area.

220 ANGLE AT FORCE FIELD (OPTICAL)

Zorn is held suspended off the deck in the center of a cylindrical force field. The force field edges GLITTER SOFTLY to outline the shape of it.

221 ANGLE ON THE AWAY TEAM (OPTICAL)

As the other team members come through the "wall" too, stand, reacting at the sight of Zorn.

222 ANGLE AT FORCE FIELD (OPTICAL)

The FORCE FIELD SPARKLES, CLICKS, causing Zorn to writhe and twitch. He SCREAMS.

ZORN
No! Please! No more! Please, no more . . .

223 ANGLE ON AWAY TEAM (OPTICAL)

They move forward toward him, and are brought up sharply by the leading edge of the force field. Data has already started to scan with his tricorder. Riker calls to Zorn.

RIKER
(continuing)
Zorn. Can you hear me?

Zorn manages to lift his head, and WE SEE his pain-filled face, his features twisted into a grimace of intense agony.

ZORN
Make it stop the pain. *Please* . . .

TROI
Has the alien communicated . . . ?
(breaks off; then to Riker)
That's it, sir! It's just *one* alien that I'm sensing here.

ZORN
(another GROAN)
Please! I don't understand what it *wants.*

TROI
(studying Zorn; then)
Not true. He *does* know.

Data interrupts by holding his tricorder so that Riker can see the readings he's gathered. Riker registers surprise at seeing something unique as Data pulls out his phaser. Riker does the same and both of them concentrate on making some exact setting on their phasers.

224 ANOTHER ANGLE (OPTICAL)

As Data and Riker raise their phasers toward Zorn.

ZORN
(in terror)
No, no, please don't!

Data and Riker trigger their phasers and we SEE a SORT OF COLORED GLOW on the FORCE FIELD HOLDING Zorn, the GLOW SPREADING OVER THE ENTIRE FORCE FIELD. Then, suddenly the FORCE FIELD DISAPPEARS, GLOW AND ALL, and Zorn tumbles out onto the floor free of restraint.

225 EMPHASIZING "LIVE" PART OF CELL WALL (EFFECTS)

Where the wall seems to be "alive," undulating. Beyond it, Tasha is assisting Zorn to his feet, supporting him. Meanwhile, Troi looks around Zorn's "cell," sensing something troubling. Riker has turned on his communicator:

RIKER
Away team to *Enterprise* . . .

A TENDRIL OF PLASMA EMERGES FROM THIS PART OF THE WALL, swaying and moving toward Troi.

DATA
(interrupting; warning)
Troi . . . !

But the TENDRIL is already wrapping around her. Data tries to pull the TENDRIL from Troi, succeeds only in getting a NEW TENDRIL wrapped around himself.

226 ANOTHER ANGLE (EFFECTS)

The floor of the area suddenly going soft, away team members sinking into it while still ANOTHER SECTION OF WALL FOLDS ITSELF OVER

TASHA. (What we're seeing is this part of the mystery "vessel" becoming a living thing.)

RIKER
Enterprise, come in. Beam us . . .

Interrupted as his feet are YANKED OUT FROM UNDER HIM.

DATA
Enterprise, we need help . . .

Interrupted by the NEW TENDRIL WRAPPING ITSELF AROUND HIS HEAD.

227 INTERIOR BRIDGE

Picard speaking anxiously toward his command panel as we HEAR Riker's MUFFLED SOUNDS OF DISTRESS.

PICARD
Transporter chief, yank them back! *Now!*

WORF
Captain . . . !

228 ANGLE INCLUDING MAIN VIEWER (OPTICAL)

Toward which Lieutenant Worf is pointing. On it the IMAGE of the mystery vessel is BEGINNING TO CHANGE IN SHAPE. The firm, hard edges of the spaceship are giving way to something softer, very mysterious in nature.

229 ANOTHER ANGLE (OPTICAL)

In which we SEE a familiar BLINDING FLASH, and Q appears, now wearing the uniform of a STARFLEET CAPTAIN.

Q (STARFLEET)
Your time is up, Captain.

PICARD
Get off my bridge!
(into command panel)
Transporter Chief, *do you have their coordinates?*

230 ANOTHER ANGLE (EFFECTS)

Q stepping to the command position.

Q (STARFLEET)
He can't hear you, Captain.

Q gestures upward, at which Picard is suddenly lifted into the air and then to the side of Q's hand motion in that direction.

PICARD
Q, I've people in trouble over there . . . !

As Picard hovers above, Q steps up and sits in Picard's command position. Bridge personnel are coming to their feet angrily, then hesitate as:

PICARD
(continuing)
Everyone, *at ease!* That's an order!
(to Q)
My people are in trouble, *Q*. Help them; I'll do whatever you say . . .

As Q gives another hand signal downward, the captain is gently deposited onto the deck.

231 WIDE PORTION OF BRIDGE (OPTICAL)

As the same strange transporter SOUND that accompanied Zorn's "kidnapping" is heard and the same STRANGE TRANSPORTER EFFECT APPEARS, this time MATERIALIZING FIVE IMAGES—Riker, Data, Troi, Tasha, and Groppler Zorn.

232 ANGLE EMPHASIZING PICARD

Very surprised, looking from his away team to Q.

Q (STARFLEET)
You'll do whatever I say?

PICARD
(hesitates; nods)
It seems I did make that bargain.

TROI

The agreement isn't valid, sir. It wasn't Q that saved us.

Q (STARFLEET)

(quickly; indicating viewer)

Save yourselves! It may attack you now.

233 ANGLE INCLUDING MAIN VIEWER (OPTICAL)

On which the changed IMAGE of the mystery ''vessel'' seems to be floating in closer to the *Enterprise.*

RIKER

It was *that* which sent us back, Captain.

TROI

Yes sir. It's not a vessel, sir. It's *alive* somehow. . . .

Q (STARFLEET)

She lies! Destroy it while you have a chance.

(to Tasha)

Make phasers and photon torpedoes ready . . . !

PICARD

No! Do *nothing* he suggests!

ZORN

But that thing was killing my people, Captain . . .

PICARD

True, but *why?* Was there a reason?

Q (STARFLEET)

It is an *unknown,* Captain! Isn't that enough?

PICARD

If you had *earned* that uniform you're wearing, you'd know that the *unknown* is what brings us out here!

Q (STARFLEET)

Wasted effort, considering the human intelligence.

PICARD

Let's test that . . .

(to Zorn)

. . . starting with the tunnels you have under Farpoint, Groppler.

RIKER

Identical to the ones on that space vessel life-form, over there. Why was it punishing you, Groppler?

PICARD

In return for pain *you* caused to some other creature?

ZORN

We did nothing wrong! It was injured; we helped it. . . .

PICARD

(interrupting; to Zorn)

Thank you, that was the missing part.

(turns)

Tasha, rig phasers to deliver an energy beam.

TASHA

(puzzled)

Aye, sir.

Tasha steps to her panel, makes settings on controls there.

RIKER

Yes, Captain, I understand now. It has to be conceivable that somewhere in the galaxy there could exist creatures able to convert energy into matter . . .

PICARD

(nodding)

And into specific patterns of matter. Much as our transporters do.

TASHA

(indicating)

On the viewer, Captain!

234 ANGLE EMPHASIZING MAIN VIEWER (OPTICAL)

Where the vessel/creature IMAGE is SOFTENING FURTHER INTO AN AMORPHOUS, COLORFUL, AND LOVELY SHAPE. Picard turns to the Groppler, demanding:

PICARD

Zorn, you captured something like that, didn't you?

On main viewer, the IMAGE NOW SHOWS LOVELY FEATHERY TENDRILS, and it is BEGINNING TO MOVE DOWN TOWARD THE PLANET. Zorn reacts to this, shows panic.

ZORN

Warn my people, please! Leave Farpoint Station immediately!

Q (STARFLEET)

He's lied to you, Captain. Shouldn't you let his people die?

PICARD

(nods to ops)

Transmit the message. "Leave Farpoint immediately."

TROI

Then it was a *pair* of creatures I was sensing. One down there in grief and pain, the other up here, filled with anger . . .

DATA

(nodding)

And firing not on the new space station, but on the Bandi Old City.

PICARD

(to Q)

Attacking those who captured its . . .

(to Troi)

. . . its mate?

TASHA

Energy beam ready, sir.

PICARD

(to Tasha)

Lock it in on Farpoint Station.

Q stands in an annoyed manner, indicates the captain's position to Picard.

Q (STARFLEET)
I see now it was too simple a puzzle. But generosity has always been my weakness.

As Q moves aside, Picard takes his position, turning to Tasha.

PICARD
Let it have whatever it can absorb. Energize!

235 EXTERIOR SPACE—THE *ENTERPRISE* (OPTICAL)

in orbit, as a THICK, PALE BLUE ENERGY BEAM AIMS DOWNWARD.

236 EXTERIOR FARPOINT STATION (OPTICAL)

HIGH DOWNWARD SHOT SHOWING THE ENERGY BEAM terminating and being absorbed into Farpoint Station.

237 INTERIOR BRIDGE—INCLUDING MAIN VIEWER (OPTICAL)

Picard and others watching the energy beam terminating at Farpoint Station.

TASHA
Now getting feedback on the beam, sir.

PICARD
Discontinue it.
(to Zorn)
Groppler Zorn, there'll soon be no Farpoint Station if I'm right about this.

Q (STARFLEET)
A lucky guess!

ZORN
I know we deserve this loss, but please believe me, we meant not to harm the creature, but to use it.

TROI
Sir, a feeling of great joy. And gratitude.

238 EXTERIOR FARPOINT STATION (OPTICAL)

The city/station miniature—the Farpoint Station part of it GROWING SOFT, SHIMMERING, SLOWLY BECOMES A CREATURE OF GOSSAMER, FEATHERY LIGHTNESS—now gracefully rising up from its captivity.

239 ANOTHER ANGLE (OPTICAL)

Where what was once the "mystery vessel" but now an increasingly beautiful COLORFUL, FEATHERY TENDRIL SHAPE is descending closer and closer to what was once the Farpoint Station part of city/station (miniature).

THE TWO CREATURES (OPTICAL)

The smaller one rising up toward its mate. They touch—delicate matter/energy tendrils twining—and then together they move upwards out of sight.

240 EXTERIOR SPACE—THE *ENTERPRISE* (OPTICAL)

As the two creatures rise up past it.

241 INTERIOR BRIDGE—INCLUDING MAIN VIEWER (OPTICAL)

On which the two creatures are rising upward OUT OF IMAGE FRAME.

TROI

Great joy and gratitude . . . from both of them.

242 ANGLE EMPHASIZING Q (OPTICAL)

As Picard turns on him.

PICARD

And why? Because it furnishes entertainment to you! You use other life-forms for recreation.

Q

If so, you've not provided the best . . .

PICARD

Get off my ship, you smug hypocrite.

Q (STARFLEET)

Why not? We can also meet another time, another place.

PICARD

That doesn't frighten us at all! You accuse us of grievous savagery? No, the one proven guilty of that crime is you!

ANOTHER BLINDING FLASH AND Q DISAPPEARS. It takes a moment to realize that he is gone. Then:

RIKER

I trust this isn't the usual way our missions will go, sir.

Picard screws up his face in mock consideration of this, then nods.

PICARD

On no, Number One, I'm sure they'll be much more interesting.

FADE OUT.

THE END

STAR TREK: THE NEXT GENERATION

Hide and Q

#40271-111

Teleplay by
C. J. Holland
and
Gene Roddenberry

Story by
C. J. Holland

Directed by
Cliff Bole

STAR TREK: THE NEXT GENERATION

Hide and Q

CAST

PICARD
RIKER
BEVERLY
DATA
TROI
TASHA
GEORDI
WORF
WESLEY

Q
WOMAN (SURVIVOR)

Nonspeaking
CREW MEMBERS
SICKBAY STAFF
TWO SENTRIES
ANIMAL SOLDIERS
DOZEN SURVIVORS
CHILD (FEMALE SURVIVOR)

STAR TREK: THE NEXT GENERATION

Hide and Q

SETS

INTERIORS

U.S.S. ENTERPRISE
CORRIDOR
MAIN BRIDGE
CAPTAIN'S READY ROOM
TRANSPORTER ROOM

PLANET DISASTER AREA

EXTERIORS

U.S.S. ENTERPRISE

PLANET—QUADRA SIGMA III
PLAIN
THIRD RIDGE
BIVOUAC AREA

STAR TREK: THE NEXT GENERATION

Hide and Q

TEASER

FADE IN:

1 EXTERIOR *ENTERPRISE* IN SPACE (OPTICAL)

The great ship streaks through space at warp speed.

2 INTERIOR ND CORRIDOR

Two crew members, their arms loaded with supplies, race along the corridor. They pass DOCTOR CRUSHER in the corridor.

3 NEW ANGLE

Beverly checks her staff as they pass with emergency medical packets on way to turbolift.

BEVERLY

Include a burn unit with each kit. On arrival, identify the most critically injured and beam them up to cargo bay six . . .

PICARD'S COM VOICE

(interrupting)

Doctor Crusher, this is the captain.

BEVERLY

(touching wall panel)

Doctor Crusher here.

PICARD'S COM VOICE

Additional information. The number of colonists at the site is five hundred four—including thirty-eight children.

4 INTERIOR *ENTERPRISE*—MAIN BRIDGE

PICARD is in his command chair, TROI to his left. WORF at the aft station. GEORDI has the conn, DATA on ops. TASHA at tactical.

The tension level is very high. The mission is urgent. As Picard answers, RIKER ENTERS from the turbolift, CROSSES the bridge and takes his position.

PICARD

So far nothing more than the initial message. Explosion—cause unknown—many injured. Are you prepared, Doctor?

BEVERLY'S COM VOICE

We believe so, sir.

GEORDI

Captain, we are now at warp nine point one.

DATA

Which will bring us into the Quadra Sigma system in three point two hours.

Riker takes his position.

RIKER

Captain, I have a schematic of the explosion site. It suggests the cause as a methane-like gas seeping in underground . . .

TROI

(with alarm)

Captain, I am . . .

5 ANGLE ON TROI

Her face is full of apprehension.

TROI

I am sensing what we encountered months ago . . .

Interrupted by the SOUND of the BRIDGE ALARM.

6 ANGLE ON PICARD

He turns. KLAXON HONKING—LIGHTS FLASHING.

7 ANGLE INCLUDING MAIN VIEWER—PICARD'S P.O.V. (OPTICAL)

The main viewer SHIMMERS as an unusual SHINING, SPARKLING GRID SHAPE APPEARS, seeming to stretch across the whole of the galaxy ahead of them.

8 ANGLE ON PICARD (OPTICAL)

He recognizes the shape—he has seen it before en route to Farpoint Station.

DATA

The Q entity, sir? It is identical to the grid we encountered when . . .

WORF

It reads *solid,* sir. If we *hit* it . . . !

PICARD

Not now, damn it, Q . . .

(to Helm)

Emergency full stop!

GEORDI

Yes, sir.

TASHA

Shields and deflectors, up, sir.

The familiar SHIMMERING GRID on the viewer is now very close to the *Enterprise.* Forward movement stops.

8A EXTERIOR SPACE—*ENTERPRISE* IN FRONT OF GRID (OPTICAL)

8B INTERIOR MAIN BRIDGE (OPTICAL)

GEORDI

Now reading full stop, sir.

The words overlapped by something akin to ROLLING THUNDER, accompanied by a BRILLIANT and SUSTAINED FLASH which becomes RAPIDLY ROTATING, BLINDINGLY BRILLIANT, DIAMOND-BLUE LIGHT. While there is no hard-edged shape, it is of about the same volume of a very large man.

Q (voice-over)
(amplified and powerful)
Humans, I thought by now you would have scampered back to your own little star system.

PICARD
(waits, then)
If this is Q I'm addressing, our vessel and crew are on a mission of rescue where a group of badly injured . . .

Q (voice-over)
(interrupting)
We of the Q have studied our recent contact with you . . . and are impressed. We have much to discuss, including perhaps the realization of your most impossible dreams.

The expressions of the bridge crew reveal they are intrigued by this statement . . . and in the potential of the Q entity to do remarkable things, however annoying its actions in the past. Even Picard takes a moment to absorb this.

PICARD
(sarcastically)
However intriguing we may find that to be, we are now in the midst of an urgent journey. Once we have completed that . . .

Q (voice-over)
(louder; angrier)
You will abandon that mission, Captain. My business with you takes precedence!

9 INTERIOR MAIN BRIDGE—ANGLE ON BRIDGE CREW

Reflections of the BRILLIANT DIAMOND-BLUE LIGHT on their faces as they look ahead toward this newest shape of Q. They shield their eyes from it.

Q (voice-over)
If my magnificence blinds you, then perhaps something more familiar . . .

An explosion of sudden HISSING SOUNDS startles the bridge crew into expressions of mixed surprise, fear, and loathing.

10 OMITTED

11 ANGLE ON Q SERPENT

A WRITHING SNAKE with snapping fangs, continuing mixed HISSING, DARTS toward them from whence came the Q light-image.

12 REVERSE ANGLE

Both Worf and Tasha vaulting down onto the command deck, instinctively drawing phasers as they try to position their own bodies between the frightening snake-thing and the bridge crew, as we:

FADE OUT.

ACT ONE

FADE IN:

13 INTERIOR MAIN BRIDGE—ANGLE ON TASHA AND WORF

First one, then the other, discovers phasers inoperative. The snake head seems an instant away from fanging them . . .

WORF

Damn, the phasers are useless!

PICARD (voice-over)

Q, STOP THIS!

14 EMPHASIZING PICARD AND RIKER

On their feet.

PICARD

Stop this and we agree to talk for a moment!

At which WE SEE the reflection of a familiar BRILLIANT LIGHT FLASH, blinding Picard and Riker again. Then as they lower their protecting hands, they REACT at the sight of:

15 ANGLE EMPHASIZING Q

In the full-dress uniform of a Starfleet ADMIRAL.

Q (ADMIRAL)

Starfleet Admiral Q at your service!

PICARD

You are *not* a Starfleet Admiral, Q . . .

Q (ADMIRAL)

Neither am I an Aldebaran serpent, Captain. But you accepted me as such.

Riker nods, a hint of the irony of this on his features.

RIKER

He's got us there, Captain.

Q (ADMIRAL)
(nods)
The redoubtable Commander Riker, whom I noticed before. You seem to find this amusing.

RIKER
I might, if we weren't trying to rescue a group of suffering and dying humans who . . .

Q (ADMIRAL)
Your species is always suffering and dying. . . .

PICARD
(interrupting)
No, Lieutenant Worf . . . !

16 ANGLE TO INCLUDE WORF

Trying to ease himself into a clear line of fire toward Q. He freezes at Picard's order, eases his almost hidden small phaser back into his belt.

PICARD
You'll make no move against him unless I order it.

Q smiles toward Worf.

Q (ADMIRAL)
Pity. You might have learned an interesting lesson. Tsk, a macro head, a micro brain.

Worf is obviously unrepentant. Picard, thinking furiously, tries another direction.

PICARD
Q, you said you had the realization of "some impossible dreams" to offer us. Once this rescue is complete, I'll listen seriously to whatever proposal you wish to make and then, subject to it being acceptable . . .

Q bursts into what sounds like genuine LAUGHTER.

Q (ADMIRAL)
". . . subject to" your foolish human values? Picard, why do you people distrust me so?

Picard starts to open his mouth, shuts it.

DATA

Sir, if . . .

Picard shakes his head, forcing Data into silence . . . also clearly including the rest of his bridge crew in this.

Q (ADMIRAL)

Yes, Captain, it is best they don't answer that. But you . . . you, Picard, I grant the freedom to answer me honestly. Why do *you* distrust me so?

PICARD

Q, right now humans may be dying because you . . .

Q (ADMIRAL)

(angry now)

SPEAK! Why do you distrust me?

PICARD

(beat)

Why? On our first meeting, Q, you seized my vessel and condemned all humans as savages, and on that charge, you tried us in a post-atomic 21st-century court of horrors where you attacked my people . . . then you again seized my vessel . . .

Q (ADMIRAL)

How that angers you: "Seized my vessel, seized my vessel . . ."

PICARD

(without pause, ignoring this)

. . . and then proceeded to interfere with our Farpoint mission, threatening to convict us as ignorant savages if, in dealing with complex and powerful life-forms, we made the slightest error . . . and when you failed even there . . .

Q (ADMIRAL)

(interrupting)

At that point, the Q became interested in you.

(turns to include bridge crew)
Cannot some of you understand your incredible good fortune?!
(to Picard, mimicking)
"Seized my vessel, seized my vessel . . ." The complaint of a closed mind *too* accustomed to military privileges.
(to Riker)
But you, Riker, and I remember you well, what do *you* make of my offer?

RIKER
I stand with my captain.

Q (ADMIRAL)
(smiles)
Of course, you do. Commendable loyalty.
(indicating bridge crew; to Riker)
And what of these others? Since humanity now interests us, how shall we come to know them better?

RIKER
We don't have time for these games.

Q (ADMIRAL)
Ah, yes! A game . . . for interest's sake, a *deadly* game. *To the game!*

And, at a wave of Q's hand, the entire bridge crew except for Picard . . . DISAPPEARS, leaving Picard alone on the bridge.

17 EXTERIOR PLANET PLAIN (OPTICAL)

The bridge crew members are standing in approximately their previous bridge positions on a treeless planet plain. They have just been snatched from their ship; their captain and they are understandably confused and uncertain, except for Tasha and Worf, whose security orientation have them immediately combat-ready. This place is bright, hot.

18 EMPHASIZING RIKER

Looking up.

19 RIKER P.O.V.—TWIN SUNS (OPTICAL)

Close together (avoiding the necessity of twin shadows), apparently rotating about each other. Both suns are brilliant, but the smaller sun, about one-quarter the size of the larger, is not quite as brilliant as the large one.

20 BACK TO EXTERIOR PLAIN (OPTICAL)

Data and Geordi, looking up too, move in next to Riker.

DATA
Obviously a class-M world, gravity and oxygen within our limits . . .

GEORDI
. . . but a twin sun? Where are we?

DATA
Considering the power demonstrated by Q the last time . . . *Anywhere!* Assuming this place even exists.

RIKER
But this won't be boring. If Q's anything, he's imaginative.
(to the others)
Apparently the captain wasn't meant to be with us here.

TASHA
(overlapping)
Sir! Over here . . . !

21 ANGLE INCLUDING Q

Who stands where a rock formation has previously hidden him. He is now wearing a French MARSHAL'S uniform, circa the Napoleonic Wars. As Riker, very curious, moves toward Q, CAMERA MOVES AND PANS TO REVEAL also a headquarters-type campaign tent of the same era, complete with shade canopy and transportable field furniture. Q indicates two such chairs and a small table which holds a pair of tall, cool drinks.

Q (MARSHAL)
Join me, Riker. A good game needs rules and planning . . .

Riker hesitates.

Q (MARSHAL)
(continuing)
Wasn't it your own Hartley who said "Nothing reveals humanity so well as the games it plays"?
(smiles; nods)
Almost right. Actually, you reveal yourselves best in *how* you play.

Data has moved in next to Riker and speaks quietly.

DATA
Sir, what he has in mind could provide us with vital information.

Riker nods, moves toward the campaign tent. Q sits, waves invitingly toward the empty seat. He also picks up one of the tall drinks and WE CAN HEAR ICE CLINKING in it.

22 RIKER AND Q

As Riker inspects the remaining drink without sitting yet, picks it up and looks a question toward Troi.

TROI
(registering surprise)
What I sense is . . . pleasure, sir.

Riker sips the drink, registers surprise too.

RIKER
Incredible. I was just thinking of an old-fashioned lemonade . . .

Q (MARSHAL)
. . . and so it *became* that. An excellent thirst quencher; it becomes quite hot out on this plain.

RIKER
What about my people?

Q makes a waving gesture.

Q (MARSHAL)
Whatever they want, of course!

23 ANGLE INCLUDING OTHERS

REACTING to the fact they suddenly have tall drinks of various colored liquids in their hands. Hesitantly, a couple of them sip. Worf, however, tilts his glass, pouring the contents out onto the sand. Strangely, this pleases Q's sense of humor.

Q (MARSHAL)
The rigid Klingon code! Drink not with thine enemy!
(to Riker)
Which explains something of why you defeated them.

RIKER
Still arguing the human past? Perhaps you're *not* that original.

Q (MARSHAL)
Au contraire! It is the human *future* that now intrigues us . . . and should concern you most. Of all species, yours cannot abide stagnation . . . change is at the heart of what you are. But *change* into what? That's the question!

DATA
That is what humans call a *truism.*

Q (MARSHAL)
(annoyed)
Meaning 'hardly original' . . .

RIKER
(hint of humor)
You're the one who said it. And while we're at it . . .
(indicating Q's uniform, tent)
. . . this isn't part of any human future . . .

Q (MARSHAL)
True, I borrowed this from your stodgy captain's mind. It is dressing for the game we will play, and games require boundaries, dangers, rewards, familiar settings, that sort of thing.

Riker looks over Q's uniform, the tent, etc.

RIKER
It's not that familiar to me. . . .
(calls)
Data?

DATA
(stepping in)
It is from Europe's Napoleonic Era, sir, late eighteenth, early nineteenth centuries. This is a campaign headquarters tent, his uniform is that of a French Army marshal, the . . .

RIKER
(to Q)
And a *marshal* outranks even an admiral . . .

Q (MARSHAL)
Would I go from a Starfleet admiral to anything less?

RIKER
(hint of a smile now)
Of course, you wouldn't.
(indicates)
But Napoleonic equipment on an alien planet with dual suns . . . ?

Q (MARSHAL)
As you've said, I'm nothing if not *imaginative.* And the game should reflect that. Shall it be a test of strength? Meaningless, since you have none. A test of intelligence? Equally meaningless . . .
(eyeing Riker)
A game needs risk . . . something to win; something to lose.

RIKER
If we must play a game, what would we win?

Q (MARSHAL)
The greatest possible future you can imagine!
(beat; thinking)
Which, of course, requires something *totally* disastrous *if you lose!*

(thinking again)
The point of this game will be whether *any of you can stay alive.*

24 EMPHASIZING TASHA AND WORF (OPTICAL)

As the others react, Worf responds:

WORF
If your "game" is fair, we will.

Q (MARSHAL)
For shame, Lieutenant Worf. *Fairness* is a human concept.
(to Riker)
Think *imaginatively!* It will, in fact, be completely *unfair . . .*

TASHA
You've gone too far.

She is drawing her phaser, but Q is pointing his finger at her just as fast.

Q (MARSHAL)
Game penalty!

Visible even in this bright desert setting, a FLASH OF LIGHT in which Tasha DISAPPEARS. Reacting, Riker turns angrily to Q.

RIKER
Where is she, Q? You can forget your game if . . .

Q (MARSHAL)
To use a 20th-century term, Commander, she's in a . . . a "penalty box." Where she can remain unharmed unless one of you merits a penalty.
(smiles)
Unfortunately, there is only *one* penalty box. If any of you should be sent there . . . dear Tasha must give up the box to you.

GEORDI
And . . . where does she go?

Q (MARSHAL)
(to Worf)

Into ''nothingness.''
(looking to the others, individually)
I entreat you to *carefully* obey the rules of the game. The only one who can destroy your Tasha now . . . is *you.*

FADE OUT.

ACT TWO

FADE IN:

25 EXTERIOR SPACE—THE *ENTERPRISE* (OPTICAL)

But not in orbit of a planet. Instead, it seems to be traveling somewhere at what we know as normal warp speed. MUSIC only.

26 INTERIOR MAIN BRIDGE

Picard at a turbolift, touches the door, without effect. Then he tries to bang it.

PICARD
Turbolift control, do you read? This is the captain.

No response. Picard CROSSES to his bridge position, touches his panel controls.

PICARD
(continuing)
Engineering, this is the bridge.

No response.

PICARD
(continuing)
Security—this is the captain.

Again—nothing.

PICARD
(continuing)
Computer?
(waits)
Computer on!

The computer still doesn't respond. He's cut off. Isolated. Picard touches his insignia.

PICARD
(continuing)
Captain's log . . .

The SOUND is wrong, indicating that:

PICARD
(continuing)
Damn . . . I can't even make a log entry.

TASHA (offscreen)
I wish I could help you, Captain.

27 WIDER ANGLE

As Picard, startled, whirls toward the VOICE. It is Tasha who stands at her familiar position at security. Unusual for Tasha, she is showing some strain over what has been happening.

PICARD
What . . . what are you doing here?

TASHA
I . . . well, this sounds strange, but . . . I'm in the penalty box.

PICARD
You're *what?!*

TASHA
(tightly)
In Q's penalty box. As I said, it *sounds* strange but it definitely *isn't.* Somehow I know that one more penalty . . . by me or *anyone* . . . and I'm gone.

Curious and concerned, Picard moves toward her.

PICARD
Gone?

TASHA
(distraught)
Please do not keep reminding me . . .

PICARD
I'm sorry . . .

TASHA
(instantly)
No, *I'm* sorry. It's so frustrating to be controlled like this. . . .

There's a half-SOB in the ordinarily strong and controlled VOICE, and Picard REACTS to it.

PICARD
Lieutenant . . . *Tasha* . . . it's all right . . .

TASHA
(astonished and angry)
What the hell am I doing? *Crying?*

PICARD
Don't worry. There's a new ship's standing order.
(smiles)
When in a penalty box, some tears are permitted.

Tasha looks up warmly, comforted by this.

TASHA
Captain . . . if you weren't a captain . . .

Q (MARSHAL) (offscreen)
(interrupting)
Consorting with lower-rank females, Captain?

28 ANGLE TO INCLUDE Q

Seated in the captain's command position. He smiles, enjoys having startled Picard this way.

Q (MARSHAL)
Destructive to discipline, they say. But you are, after all, only human, eh?

Picard has made his way down to the command level where he now looks Q and the uniform over.

PICARD
A Marshall of France? *Ridiculous!*

Q (MARSHAL)

One takes what jobs one can get. For example, your log entries.

(looks up)

Starship log, stardate today . . . This is Q, speaking for Captain Jean-Luc Picard, whom we consider too bound by Starfleet custom and tradition to be useful in this activity.

PICARD

But who proved himself a resourceful opponent when he defeated you at Farpoint.

Q (MARSHAL)

(with "log" tone again)

The *Enterprise* is now helpless, stuck like an Earth insect in amber while its bridge crew plays out a game whose real intent . . .

(aiming this at Picard)

. . . is to test if their first officer is worthy of the greatest gift the Q can offer.

Picard takes a long moment to absorb this; then he nods.

PICARD

So, you're taking on Riker this time.

(smiles)

Excellent! He'll defeat you just as I did!

Q (MARSHAL)

A wager on that, Captain? Your command of this starship against . . . ?

PICARD

Against your staying out of humanity's path . . . *forever!* Done?

Q (MARSHAL)

Done!

(smiles)

And you've already lost, Picard. You see, Riker is to be offered something *impossible* to reject.

Q storms toward the ready room.

29 EXTERIOR THE PLANET

All but Worf are there, studying a point on the distant terrain.

RIKER
Geordi, can you still see Worf?

GEORDI
(nods)
I'd see the freckles on his nose, if he had them, sir.
He's at the third ridge now . . .

TROI
The *third* ridge . . . ?

GEORDI
Moving well.
(distracted)
Oh, oh!
(peers)
Good, he sees them. They look like sentries, sir.

30 EXTERIOR THIRD RIDGE

Worf—the trained warrior—approaches with caution. It is indeed a bivouac area. Worf can hear the unseen men SPEAKING IN FRENCH. He edges closer.

31 ANOTHER ANGLE

Worf pushes through the rocks, FREEZES.

32 ROCKS—WORF'S P.O.V.

Two sentries are walking a perimeter patrol. They are dressed as Bonapartist soldiers, carrying muskets. As they approach, WE SEE their uniforms look genuine enough . . . but then we make out their *faces!* Humanoid *but with fearsome, fanged, inhuman features.*

33 BIVOUAC AREA

Worf reacts at this. Then he moves as close as he dares. Those in the camp appear to be preparing for a battle. But where human troops would be yelling, these soldiers are GROWLING, SNARLING. Over that, the CLATTER of caissons—equipment being assembled.

34 ANGLE ON WORF

He hears a squad approaching—slips back among the rocks and DISAPPEARS.

35 INTERIOR CAPTAIN'S READY ROOM

Picard comes to the door. Q is sitting in the chair with his back to Picard.

PICARD
Q, listen to me. You seem to have some need of humans . . .

Q (MARSHAL)
Or concern regarding them.

PICARD
Whichever it is, why try to solve it through this confrontation with us? Why not a simple direct explanation, a statement of what you seek? Why these games?

Q turns, and WE SEE he is holding Picard's complete works of William Shakespeare. He indicates the books.

Q (MARSHAL)
I'm surprised you have to ask when your human Shakespeare has already explained it so well.

PICARD
Indeed he did, Q. But careful you don't depend too much on any single viewpoint he . . .

Q (MARSHAL)
(ignoring this; interrupting)
Why these games I require of you? A pity you're not familiar with the contents of your own library. Hear this, Picard, and reflect.
(lifts book, quotes from it)
"All the galaxy's a stage, and . . ."

PICARD
(interrupts)
"All the *galaxy*"? "All the *world's* a stage . . ."

Q (MARSHAL)

Oh, you know that one? Then how about, ". . . Life's but a walking shadow, a poor player that struts and frets his hour upon the stage, and then is heard no more. It is a tale told by an idiot, full of sound and fury, signifying nothing."

PICARD

And so you say, how we respond to a game tells you more about us than our real life, a "tale told by an idiot."

(still amused)

Interesting, Q.

Q (MARSHAL)

(lifts book)

Shall I quote from Hamlet?

PICARD

No. I know Hamlet. And what he said with irony I prefer to say with conviction.

(quoting)

"What a piece of work is man! How noble in reason! How infinite in faculty. In form, in moving, how express and admirable. In action, how like an angel. In apprehension, how like a god . . ."

Q (MARSHAL)

(upset; interrupting)

You don't *really* see your species like that?!

PICARD

I see us one day *becoming* that, Q. Is *that* what concerns you?

Q comes angrily to his feet, SLAMMING the volume down and DISAPPEARING in a FLASH. A startled and puzzled Picard watches him go, then turns to ponder the meaning of Q's anger.

36 EXTERIOR PLANET

The same plain. Riker, Troi, and Data watch as Geordi scans the distant desert ridges.

RIKER
Can you still see Worf?

GEORDI
(shakes head)
It's hard to keep him in sight, sir. But the soldiers there . . . they've formed a "skirmishing line," I think you'd call it . . . and they're headed this way.

RIKER
Carrying ancient powder and ball muskets?

GEORDI
That's what their weapons look like, sir.

DATA
Muskets are appropriate to the 1790–1800 French army uniform.
(shakes head)
But it is hardly a "weapon" by our standards, sir. A lead ball propelled by gunpowder one-hundred meters at most with any accuracy . . .

GEORDI
Against *phasers?* Just one of our hand phasers could finish off an entire regiment of them.

RIKER
Except for one thing . . .
(to Troi)
That hardly sounds like Q, giving us an advantage like that.
(puzzling; then REACTING)
Unless . . .

37 SPECIAL EFFECT ANGLE (OPTICAL)

Suspecting some kind of trap, Riker draws his own hand phaser. He checks its setting, aims it well away from everybody else . . . touches the trigger lightly for just an instant.

The PHASER SOUND precedes an EXPLOSION OF DUST AND DIRT at a point where Riker was aiming the phaser. It causes a hole at least the size of one caused by a howitzer shell.

38 ANOTHER ANGLE

It also produces another effect—the FORM of Worf, large phaser in hand, propelling itself INTO SCENE, rolling to a stop where the Klingon is aiming his phaser, seeking the away team's "assailant" that fired the phaser blast.

WORF
(growling it)
DROP YOUR WEAPONS!

He aims this way, then that, attempting quickly to spot who or whatever is menacing his friends.

RIKER
(exhibits hand phaser)
I'm afraid it was me, Worf. Making certain our phasers still operate.

Worf returns his own phaser.

WORF
A warrior's reaction.

GEORDI
Incredible, Worf! You came out of nowhere!

RIKER
(to Worf)
Report. What did you find?

WORF
Sir . . . what they are wearing may be old Earth uniforms, but what is inside those uniforms is not human at all. More like vicious animal things.

GEORDI
Oh, oh! Good old Q. But how can even the most savage animal forms threaten us if they're armed with the equivalent of popguns?

39 SPECIAL EFFECTS ANGLE (OPTICAL)

Geordi, who has been scanning the terrain, now turns to Riker.

GEORDI
They're moving in fast, sir.

40 ANGLE EMPHASIZING RIKER

Data's back is to him.

RIKER
Data, if you've got a theory on what's happening . . .

Data's FORM turns, REVEALING IT IS NOT DATA AT ALL, BUT Q—and using his own VOICE despite the Data clothing.

Q (DATA)
Think fast, Commander Riker.
(reacting; pointing)
And move fast . . .

Q is pointing at two of the fierce-looking Animal Soldiers in French uniform that have moved INTO SIGHT, aiming their "muskets" at Geordi, who jumps behind a rock. TWO PHASER BLASTS. The first hits a rock near Geordi. The second BLASTS A BROAD FURROW in the desert floor.

RIKER
That's no musket!

41 ANOTHER ANGLE (OPTICAL)

Q is REACTING to the uniformed Animal Soldiers, seeing them now, swinging their weapon in their direction. Riker spins, FIRES HIS PHASER, DEMATERIALIZING both his opponents.

RIKER
(anxiously)
Troi, Geordi, Worf . . . !

Q pulls him down as:

Q (DATA)
You have only one chance to save them, now. Send them to your ship!

RIKER
You'll let me beam them?

Q (DATA)
(shakes head)
Send them the same way I do. I have given you that power.

Geordi comes scrambling INTO VIEW.

Q (DATA)
(continuing)
Do you understand? I have given you the power of the Q.
(demonstrates with sweeping gesture)
Use it!

Worf and Troi come INTO VIEW too.

42 ANOTHER ANGLE (OPTICAL)

Riker becomes aware of someone scrambling toward him. *It's Data,* the real Data using his own body. Q has gone. CAMERA JIGGLES WITH ANOTHER MAJOR PHASER HIT.

Q (voice-over)
(echo chamber)
Use your power!

With little other choice, Riker makes a hand gesture—causing FLASHES OF BLINDING LIGHT in which Data, Geordi, Troi, and Worf DISAPPEAR. On Riker's stunned expression:

FADE OUT.

ACT THREE

FADE IN:

43 INTERIOR MAIN BRIDGE

The bridge is empty—the displays and readouts are still frozen. The ambient noise is still absent. SLOW PUSH IN to Tasha sitting on the bench beside Riker's position. Head in hands, she stares at the floor. Suddenly the room noise changes and on the SOUND her head comes up.

44 WIDER ANGLE ON THE BRIDGE (OPTICAL)

The display screens are alive. All the bridge's ambient SOUNDS are back. Tasha looks over to Picard's ready room.

45 READY ROOM DOOR

Picard STEPS OUT. He too has heard the change. He walks to his command position.

PICARD
Take the conn, Lieutenant.

Tasha rises.

46 ANGLE ON PICARD

He sits and touches his arm-panel.

PICARD
Engineering—this is the bridge.

ENGINEER'S COM VOICE
Engineering here, sir.

PICARD
Are all systems back on-line?

ENGINEER (com voice)
Back on-line, sir? They were never off.

47 ANGLE ON TASHA

At the conn position.

TASHA

Captain, you had better look at this.

Picard walks over to Tasha.

48 ANGLE ON TASHA AND PICARD

He looks at the readout.

TASHA

There has been no interruption in course or speed. Both have remained constant. Captain—it's as though we never stopped.

Picard straightens up.

PICARD

We never did. Q suspended time.

49 WIDE ANGLE—MAIN BRIDGE

FLASHES OF LIGHT and the members of the bridge crew REAPPEAR except for Riker. Alive and unharmed.

50 INTERCUT ANGLES OF CREW

All of them are naturally disoriented—the shock of the experience cannot be instantly thrown off.

TASHA

Where's Commander Riker?

They look around.

WORF

He was with us.

GEORDI

He must still be on the planet.

(to Picard)

We were under attack by . . . by Animal Things . . .

PICARD

Animal Things?

GEORDI

Animal Things in uniform, sir . . .

(quails at Picard's expression)

Which I think Data could probably explain better, sir.

As Picard turns to Data, the android decides he wants no part of this.

DATA

You may find it aesthetically displeasing, sir. I could just file a computer report on that . . .

TROI

(interrupting)

Sir, the *important* thing right now is *why is Commander Riker missing?*

PICARD

Understood, Counselor, but Will is almost certainly safe . . .

(troubled)

. . . at least "safe" in a physical sense. Q has an interest in him . . . in fact, Q's entire visit has something to do with our first officer.

DATA

And the reason for that, sir . . . ?

PICARD

I wish I knew. Q became interested in him at Farpoint.

(shakes head)

I've no idea what it means.

(to the others)

Meanwhile, we must proceed with our rescue mission . . .

51–52 OMITTED

53 EXTERIOR DESERT

Empty—no Riker. But there are footprints in the sand indicating a direction toward a jagged rock formation on the otherwise unbroken sandscape.

54 ANGLE AT ROCK FORMATION

REVEALING Riker, who has managed to find himself a little shade. He sits, leans back against a rock. Then, starts to laugh. It is a deep, satisfying laugh from one who has just been let in on a cosmic joke.

Q (offscreen)
Something amuses you?

Riker looks up.

55 ANGLE UP ON Q—RIKER'S P.O.V. (OPTICAL)

Standing on a ledge above Riker, heavily backlit by the *two* suns. (If possible, formed here by two brightly illuminated OUT-OF-FOCUS balls as described earlier.) We'll see more clearly in a moment also that Q wears rank and uniform identical to Riker's.

Q (COMMANDER)
Perhaps you would share the joke with me?

56 ANGLE ON RIKER

As Q moves down into TWO-SHOT. Riker eyes Q for a long beat, then:

RIKER
The joke is you, you silly son of a bitch.

Q glares at Riker, who now seems confident and at ease about something.

Q (COMMANDER)
Strange gratitude from one who has been granted a gift beyond any human dream. How can you not appreciate being able to send your friends back to their ship . . .
(the sweeping gesture)
. . . or sending the soldiers back to the "nothingness" from which they came?

Q takes a beat, sits on a piece of rock next to Riker, leans toward him confidentially.

Q (COMMANDER)
(continuing)
Certainly, you understand that at this moment you can send yourself back to your ship . . . or to Earth, or

change your shape and become anything else you want to be . . .

RIKER
(interrupting; strongly)
What do you need, Q?

Q (COMMANDER)
"Need"?

RIKER
You want something from us, Q. Desperately! What is it?

Q (COMMANDER)
Want something from you foolish, fragile, nonentities? Careful, Riker, you're beginning to sound like your captain.

RIKER
(grins)
Now *that's* a compliment, Q. But it's not an answer.

Stung by this, Q comes to his feet, raising a hand as if to make the gesture we've seen before . . . finds Riker still smiling up at him. He turns, walks angrily a few steps away, then a few back as if bringing his anger under control.

Q (COMMANDER)
(clipped; angry)
Riker . . . we have tried to offer you a gift beyond all other gifts . . . !

RIKER
. . . Out of the "goodness" of your heart?

They exchange looks for a long, long moment. Then Q seats himself again, and finally:

Q (COMMANDER)
After Farpoint, I returned to where we exist . . . the Q Continuum.

RIKER
Which means exactly *what?*

Q (COMMANDER)
(trace of annoyance)
The limitless dimensions of the galaxy in which we exist. We could hardly be capable of acting in ways that seem so astonishing to you . . . if we were limited to the primitive dimensions in which you live, dimensions which would make us prisoners of time and space.

RIKER
(beat; absorbing this)
What do you mean by *we?*

Q (COMMANDER)
(more annoyance)
In our Continuum the terms *we* and *I* mean much the same.

RIKER
I don't understand . . .

Q (COMMANDER)
Of course you don't, and you never will until you become one of us.

RIKER
(reacting)
Until? . . . Would you mind going over that again?

Q (COMMANDER)
(nods)
If you'll stop interrupting me. This really isn't the time to teach you the true nature of the universe.
(leans in again)
At Farpoint, we saw you as savages only, and thought to frighten you into scurrying back to your system. We discovered, instead, that you are an unusual creature in your own limited ways . . . ways which in time may not be so limited.

RIKER
(nods)
We're growing. Something about us compels us to learn, explore . . .

Q (COMMANDER)
(nods)
The human compulsion. And, unfortunately, for us, a force that will grow stronger century after century, eon after eon . . .

RIKER
Eons! Have you any idea how far we'll advance?

Q (COMMANDER)
Perhaps in a future you cannot yet conceive . . . *even beyond us.* And so, we *must* know more about the human condition. We have selected *you,* Riker, to become part of the Q . . . to bring that human need and hunger to us so that we may understand it.

RIKER
(ponders, then)
I . . . suppose you mean that as a compliment, Q . . . or maybe it's my limited mind . . .
(stands)
. . . but . . . to become part of you?! *I don't even like you!*

Q looks at Riker, seeming amused.

Q (COMMANDER)
You're going to miss me!

Q makes the sweeping gesture, and it produces the familiar BLINDING LIGHT FLASH in which Q DISAPPEARS. And almost immediately, the startled VOICES of the bridge crew, with Riker whirling in that direction:

TROI
Oh, no!

GEORDI
Come on, not again!

57 OMITTED

58 GROUP SHOT

Where the entire bridge crew, including Picard and WESLEY, find themselves facing a line of the French uniformed Animal Soldiers, who menace the *Enterprise* people, ATTACHING LONG AND DEADLY LOOKING BAYONETS ONTO THEIR MUSKETS, clearly intending to use them.

WESLEY
(totally confused)
What's happening, Commander Riker? I was sitting in school . . .

TASHA
(interrupting)
My phaser's gone. Worf, are you armed?

Worf checks, shakes his head, but nevertheless he and Tasha move to place themselves between the bridge crew and the danger. Picard has moved quickly to Riker.

PICARD
Where is Q? If you have any answer to this, Number One . . .

Interrupted by an Animal Soldier lifting a bugle, blowing the OLD FRENCH ATTACK CALL. A SNARL AND ROAR from an Animal Soldier with sergeant's stripes, and the line of soldiers advance, bayonets leveled at the bridge crew.

59 SPECIAL EFFECTS ANGLE ON WORF

Moving forward to take on the entire attack line. He moves fast, dodges a bayonet, trips, *then a second Animal Soldier slashes him in the back with a bayonet, and Worf goes down in a SPURT OF RED BLOOD.*

60 SPECIAL EFFECT ANGLE ON WESLEY

As he FREEZES, shocked.

WESLEY
Worf!

Then, the Animal Soldier who got Worf pivots fast, leaps at Wesley . . . *and skewers the boy* through the middle.

61 ANGLE ON RIKER

Shocked, wildly angered!

RIKER

NO! DAMN IT, DAMN IT TO HELL . . . !

He makes the sweeping gesture he's learned.

62 WIDE ANGLE (OPTICAL)

As Riker's gesture creates a smaller version of the METALLIC GRID. IT APPEARS between where the bridge crew has instinctively retreated and the advancing line of Animal Soldiers, blocking them completely. Picard REACTS strongly to what Riker just did.

PICARD

Riker, you . . . you did that?!

RIKER

And that's not all!!

Grimly, angrily, Riker makes the sweeping gesture *even more strongly, and the ENTIRE SCENE IS FILLED WITH BLINDING LIGHT.*

63 INTERIOR MAIN BRIDGE—TIGHT ANGLE ON WESLEY (OPTICAL)

Wesley APPEARS, suddenly feeling at his torso where he was just stabbed. He's no longer hurt. Worf ENTERS SHOT, also whole in body.

64 ANOTHER ANGLE—INCLUDING PICARD AND OTHERS

Picard looking at Riker almost disbelievingly.

PICARD

That grid, their wounds . . . only the Q could do that. . . .

He cuts off his words, becoming aware of the formidable expression on Riker's face.

FADE OUT.

ACT FOUR

FADE IN:

65 EXTERIOR SPACE—*ENTERPRISE* (OPTICAL)

With the Disaster Planet in far distance ahead of the starship—a small ball seen from here.

PICARD (voice-over)
Captain's log, stardate 41591.4. Twelve minutes out from Quadra Sigma III where the survivors of an underground disaster desperately need our help. Aboard the *Enterprise* . . .

66 INTERIOR MAIN BRIDGE

Riker, Troi, Data, Geordi, Tasha, and Worf at their positions. Riker's features showing the strain of what has happened, he makes little eye contact with the bridge crew and they appear equally uncertain of how to handle him.

PICARD (voice-over)
(continuing)
. . . First Officer William T. Riker needs help nearly as badly. But this is a subject so far out of my experience . . . out of *any* human's experience.

Riker has made for the captain's ready room, EXITS into it.

67 INTERIOR CAPTAIN'S READY ROOM

Riker CROSSING IN and coming to a halt in front of Picard's desk. Picard waves him to a seat, almost angrily.

PICARD
Will, how the hell do I advise you *what* to do?!

Riker looks up sharply at the angry tone . . . then understands it, nods.

RIKER
No one has ever offered to turn you into "God"?

PICARD
(snaps)
Don't joke with me! What the Q has offered you has got to be close to "immortality," Will. They're not lying about controlling space and time; we've seen it in what they can do. But . . .

RIKER
You've also seen it in what *I* can do.

Picard leans across his desk toward Riker, intent.

PICARD
Of all things, that troubles me most, Will. Are you strong enough to refuse to use that power?

RIKER
Certainly!

PICARD
No matter *how* tempted? No matter how difficult Q makes it?

RIKER
(beat; then firmly)
You have my word.

DATA'S COM VOICE
In orbit of Quadra Sigma III, sir. Ready to beam down rescue team to underground emergency area.

Picard and Riker get quickly to their feet, EXIT.

68–69 OMITTED

70 INTERIOR PLANET DISASTER AREA

The away reserve team MATERIALIZES. They are in a passageway which has been severely damaged by explosions. Water SPRAYS from the ceiling and is already ankle deep on the floor. Data scans the area with his tricorder.

DATA
This way.

They push ahead.

71 ANOTHER ANGLE—CORRIDOR

As they ARRIVE at a doorway. The door has been jammed by the explosion. Data steps over and—with his great strength—rips the door off his hinges and clears the opening.

The survivors are here. ABOUT A DOZEN of them, huddled together on the far side. Beverly and her teams wade through the water to them.

72 ANGLE ON BEVERLY AND SURVIVORS

As she kneels beside an injured WOMAN.

BEVERLY
You are going to be all right, now.

RIKER
Where are the others?

The woman shakes her head.

WOMAN
Gone. It's just us.

GEORDI
(urgent)
Commander!

Riker turns.

73 ANGLE ON GEORDI

CAMERA MOVES IN TO E.C.U. Geordi is staring at a pile of rubble.

GEORDI
There's someone there!

74–75 OMITTED

76 ANGLE ON DATA

With great strength he moves huge rocks with remarkable rapidity.

77 ANGLE ON GEORDI AND RIKER

They stand and look for a beat, then:

78 ANGLE ON DATA

As he lifts and carries the limp body of a child.

79 ANOTHER ANGLE

Beverly rushes over, and while Data holds the child, she quickly examines him.

80 ANGLE ON BEVERLY AND CHILD

From her expression it is clear the child is dead. All of her skill will not help.

BEVERLY
She's dead. If we'd only gotten here a little sooner . . . !

81 ANGLE ON RIKER

He steps closer. A dead child. A moment of truth.

DATA
Sir, if you indeed have Q's power . . .

82 OMITTED

83 ANGLE ON RIKER

He is fighting his emotions.

84 ANGLE INCLUDING BEVERLY

Puzzled.

BEVERLY
I don't understand. Can you bring her back to life?

RIKER
(long beat)
No!

84A EXTERIOR SPACE—*ENTERPRISE* (OPTICAL)

In orbit.

85–87 OMITTED

88 INTERIOR MAIN BRIDGE

Riker, followed by Data and Geordi, EXIT the turbolift. Riker CROSSES to Picard. Troi is watching Riker with such intensity she doesn't seem to be breathing.

RIKER

As soon as it's convenient, Captain, I insist on a meeting with you and your staff.

There is about Riker now a little of the force, the power, the arrogance of Q. Modified by the man himself—but he is definitely carrying himself with more presence.

89 ANGLE ON PICARD

It's as though he's been expecting this since the incident with Q.

90 ANOTHER ANGLE RIKER AND PICARD

The others are watching this exchange, curious about how Picard will respond.

PICARD

As soon as we are secure from the rescue operation, we'll meet in the conference room.

RIKER

Thank you.

Riker turns, stalks to the turbolift. Troi gives him a look of apprehension.

PICARD

Counselor?

TROI

Power—immense. Frightening. I can't read the intent—but there is terrible anger in him.

Off Picard's reaction:

FADE OUT.

ACT FIVE

FADE IN:

91 INTERIOR MAIN BRIDGE

Riker is already there, sits brooding. Picard ENTERS with Data, Troi, Geordi, Tasha and Worf. As Picard seats himself:

PICARD

We'll confer on the bridge here if no one . . .

Without looking in that direction, Riker gestures Picard to be silent and, surprised, Picard hesitates, during which Riker turns toward the others.

RIKER

The bridge is fine since I've called the entire staff . . .

PICARD

(interrupting)

Correction, Number One; knowing the decision you face, I've *permitted* you this gathering.

Riker seems genuinely amused by Picard's correction, as if yielding to a bright but headstrong child. Riker nods, uses a gentle tone.

RIKER

Of course, Jean-Luc.

Riker looks up startled to see Beverly and Wesley ENTER bridge from the turbolift.

RIKER

(continuing)

This meeting isn't for you, Wesley!

WESLEY

Why not, sir? You helped make me a bridge officer . . .

(corrects self)

. . . an *acting ensign*.

Looking from one to the other.

RIKER

All right, he stays. The first thing he'll hear is . . . because I've been given *unusual* powers, I'm not suddenly a monster. Except for those abilities, and I don't yet know *how* far they go . . . I'm the same William T. Riker you've always known.

There's a long silence, no one speaking up.

RIKER

(continuing)

Well? Everyone still looks uncomfortable.

PICARD

Perhaps we're all remembering the old saying . . . "power corrupts . . ."

RIKER

. . . "and absolute power corrupts absolutely." Do you believe I haven't thought of that, Jean-Luc?

PICARD

And have you noticed that you and I are now on a first-name basis?

A flicker of surprise on Riker's features indicates he really *hasn't.*

PICARD

(continuing)

Will, something has happened to you already. . . .

RIKER

In what way? Haven't you seen how much I've regretted not saving that child? *Captain,* using the Q power to save her might not have been wrong!

(to bridge crew)

No more than it was wrong to save the rest of you from those Animal Things.

PICARD

Let's keep in mind that particular danger was invented by Q.

TROI

What we represent to the Q, Will, are lowly animals, tormented into performing for their amusement . . .

RIKER

Actually, they think highly of us, Troi. We have a quality of . . . of growth which they admire . . .

GEORDI

Or fear?

PICARD

Number One, we've learned that the Q power does not admire us . . . Q has muddled your mind somehow.

RIKER

It's *your* mind that troubles me, Captain. Don't you understand his incredible gift to me?

Q (BROTHER) (offscreen)

Are these truly your ''friends,'' Brother?

92 ANOTHER ANGLE

All whirl toward the VOICE. It comes from a far corner of the bridge where a figure stands with its back to us. Q turns now, revealing himself draped in what is recognizable even in this century as the somber robes of something like the Franciscan Holy Order—and Q is playing it to the hilt with gentle voice, kindliness shining from his face, fingers pointed together as in prayer. He CROSSES IN to stand with Riker, head bowed in humility.

Q (BROTHER)

Let us pray for understanding, for compassion, for . . .

PICARD

(moving to Q)

Let us do no such damned thing!

(pulls at Q's robes)

What is this need of yours for costumes? Have you no identity of your own?

Q (BROTHER)

(softly; gently)

I come in search of truth.

The expression on Riker's face reveals that he is growing somewhat uncomfortable with this continuation of masquerade.

PICARD
You come in search of what humanity is!

Q has withdrawn a large cross symbol from his robes as if warding off Picard's words.

Q (BROTHER)
I forgive your blasphemy. . . .

PICARD
(indicates Q to Riker)
Can't you see it, Number One? He's nothing but a *flim-flam* man! That's what he's been since his first appearance at Farpoint!

WORF
(to Data)
Flim-flam?

Q (BROTHER)
(to Picard)
You offer Riker *jealousy!* What I offer him is clearly beyond your comprehension!
(turning to the others one by one)
How can you claim friendship for Riker while obstructing his way to the greatest adventure ever offered a human?!

PICARD
(alerted)
"Obstruct him"? Then it's *not* yet certain? He's *not* yet committed?

Q (BROTHER)
(quickly, loudly; *overlapping last line*)
The truly evil part of this is *your* jealousy, Captain.
(to Riker)
You love each one of your people! Demonstrate it! You have the power to leave each of them with a gift proving your affection.

Riker isn't sure of this. He looks to Picard inquiringly, but speaks a bit thickly at times.

RIKER

There'd be no . . . harm, would there, if I, if I gave them something I know they'd like?

Picard's next few expressions are a study in a change of decision. His first instinct is to recommend against it . . . and he almost voices it. But then, Picard begins to suspect that this may, in fact, give Riker a chance to understand the human effect of near-godlike power.

Q (BROTHER)

How touching. A plea to his former captain.

(watching Picard)

"May I please give some happiness to my friends, sir? Please, sir?"

PICARD

(beat)

In fact . . . I authorize and support that idea, Riker.

(to the crew)

And please cooperate with him, if you wish.

TROI

(troubled; cautioning)

Are you certain, sir? If . . .

PICARD

I'm quite certain, Counselor.

(to Riker)

By all means, demonstrate your gifts of affection.

Troi is clearly still nervous about this. Data too.

Q (BROTHER)

(eying Picard)

Remarkable! He rises now above jealousy.

93 ANGLE EMPHASIZING RIKER

Turning to his friends.

RIKER

Don't be frightened. There is *no* way I could harm any one of you. Shall I guess your dreams?

BEVERLY
(quickly)
Leave now, Wesley!

RIKER
No! Wesley, I may know best of all.
(smiles at Wesley)
Our friendship, our long talks . . .

BEVERLY
No, *please* . . . !

94 EMPHASIZING WESLEY AND RIKER (OPTICAL)

RIKER
(to Wesley)
Have your favorite wish, my young friend!

With a LIGHT FLASH, WESLEY becomes a handsome young Starfleet officer of about twenty-five years.

95 INTERCUT OTHERS

Their REACTIONS. Their surprise is complete. On a very intimate level that concerns themselves, this seems *godlike* power they are witnessing. Picard, on the other hand, seems to be analyzing, measuring, what is happening.

GEORDI
Hey, Wes, you've grown into a very good-looking guy!

Tasha gives a ''definitely'' to that sentiment. Troi is concerned about Beverly, who seems stunned as she walks nearer her son, scrutinizing him closely. Data gives Picard a puzzled ''what are you up to?'' look. Picard appears to be holding his breath as he anticipates further developments.

96 ANOTHER ANGLE (OPTICAL)

Riker is eyeing Data now.

RIKER
Data . . .

DATA
(forcefully shaking head)
No!

RIKER
It's what you've always wanted, Data, to become *human!*

Data almost says, "yes," but then:

DATA
Yes, sir, that is true. But I never wanted to compound one illusion with another. It might seem real to Q— even you, sir . . . but it would not be so to me. Was it not one of the captain's favorite authors who wrote, "This above all, to thine own self be true?"
(beat)
Sorry, Commander, I must decline.

Riker turns to Geordi. As he moves to him and removes the VISOR, unobtrusively handing it to Geordi:

RIKER
Well, my friend, I know what you want. Welcome to the wonderful world of vision.

Geordi looks around in awe. His eyes come to rest on Tasha.

GEORDI
You're as beautiful as I imagined, and more.

RIKER
Then we can throw the VISOR away?

Geordi slowly replaces the VISOR over his eyes.

GEORDI
I think not, sir. The price is a little high for me. I don't like who I would have to thank. I can still steer the ship with this.

97 ANGLE EMPHASIZING WESLEY AND BEVERLY

As Beverly appraises the new form of her son.

BEVERLY
If you accept this new *you,* Wesley, you'll lose wonderful times, so many important experiences . . .

98 EMPHASIZING WORF (OPTICAL)

As Riker moves to inspect him in turn.

RIKER
And Worf, who wants nothing . . .

WORF
Except honor and my duty fulfilled.

RIKER
(interrupting)
Proud warrior Worf, without a single tie to his own kind . . .

In a LIGHT FLASH, it's not Worf who changes but someone else who APPEARS at his feet—a Klingon warrioress. Her eyes flash as she looks up at her man Worf, an arm encircles him at the knees—her other arm holds a Klingon weapon—a *kligat*—as she looks around, sees nothing but aliens. Then moving with surprising speed, she comes to her feet and lashes out with her weapon at Troi, who is the person nearest. Worf moves quickly too, takes the blow intended for Troi, SLAMS the warrioress down. In Klingon tradition, she flattens herself to the floor and crawls, SNARLING, to embrace Worf's feet.

WORF
(whirling to Riker)
No! She is from a world now alien to me. I have no place in my life for this now!

99 ANGLE ON WESLEY

Moving to Riker. His voice is that of an adult male.

WESLEY
Mister Riker . . .
(shakes head)
. . . it's too soon for this . . .

RIKER
If it's because your mother objects . . .

WESLEY
No, I'd just like to get there on my own. Honest!

Picard is now looking very pleased . . . both with himself for estimating this correctly, and with his people for their common sense. Riker sees and understands.

RIKER
How did you know, sir? I feel like such . . . such an *idiot!*

PICARD
Quite right; you should!

RIKER
But it was . . . *such* a pleasure to have been able to do those things.

As Q PASSES, Picard blocks his path.

PICARD
It's all over, Q. You have no further business here.

Q (BROTHER)
Human, you have just destroyed yourself . . . !

PICARD
But only *after* you've paid off your wager, Q.

Q (BROTHER)
I recall no wager!

PICARD
I'm sure your fellow Q remember you agreed to never trouble our species again. Just as they're aware you've *failed* to tempt a human to join you. So Q, I strongly suspect you have some explaining of your own to do . . .

A sudden MAJOR FLASH OF BRILLIANT LIGHT . . . wiping out the entire SCENE for a moment. Then WE SEE REVEALED the bridge crew exactly as we saw them when this ACT began. Q is no longer there—Wesley is fifteen again—Worf is without his warrioress—Tasha is the familiar security chief. And all are at their duty positions, with Wesley assisting Data at ops, Beverly standing near Picard.

100 ANOTHER ANGLE EMPHASIZING PICARD

Everyone is speechless. Then, Picard breaks the silence.

PICARD
Extraordinary! Q sought to discover the distinguishing characteristic of humanity and never learned what Coleridge said: "It must be the possession of a soul within us that makes the difference."

GEORDI
Sir . . . we show the same "hole" in time again. Our instruments say we've just now beamed up from our rescue mission.

DATA
How can the Q handle time and space so well, and *us* so badly?

PICARD
Perhaps we'll discover some day that time and space are simpler than the human equation.
(toward Riker)
No coordinates laid in, Number One?

RIKER
Uh . . . yes, sir.
(toward Helm)
You have my coordinates, Mister La Forge.

Geordi gives Wesley a look, and a nod. Wesley calls it out eagerly.

WESLEY
Zero-zero-eight, Mark, three-three-nine, sir.

PICARD
(nods)
Engage!

101 EXTERIOR SPACE—*ENTERPRISE* (OPTICAL)

As it MOVES AWAY from us.

FADE OUT.

STAR TREK: THE NEXT GENERATION

Q Who?

#40272-142

Written by
Maurice Hurley

Directed by
Rob Bowman

STAR TREK: THE NEXT GENERATION

Q Who?

CAST

PICARD
RIKER
DATA
TROI
GEORDI
WORF
WESLEY
GUINAN
O'BRIEN
SONYA

Nonspeaking
CREW MEMBERS
SECURITY MAN

Q

Nonspeaking
BORG ONE
BORG TWO
BORG THREE

STAR TREK: THE NEXT GENERATION

Q Who?

SETS

INTERIORS

U.S.S. ENTERPRISE
CORRIDOR
MAIN BRIDGE
OBSERVATION LOUNGE
TURBOLIFT
MAIN ENGINEERING
TRANSPORTER ROOM
TEN-FORWARD
GUINAN'S OFFICE

SHUTTLECRAFT

BORG SHIP

EXTERIORS

U.S.S. ENTERPRISE

BORG SHIP

STAR TREK: THE NEXT GENERATION

Q Who?

TEASER

FADE IN:

1 EXTERIOR SPACE—THE *ENTERPRISE* (OPTICAL)

The *Enterprise* as it is traveling at impulse speed.

2 INTERIOR CORRIDOR OUTSIDE MAIN ENGINEERING (OPTICAL)

GEORDI is coming down the corridor. He sees a young—twenty-five to twenty-eight year old—Ensign who has newly arrived on the *Enterprise.* She is very energetic, and enthusiastic in an open and ingenuous way, which is both appealing and refreshing. Her name is SONYA. She is standing in front of a food dispenser panel.

SONYA

Hot chocolate, please.

The hot chocolate appears.

GEORDI

We don't ordinarily say "please" to food dispensers.

SONYA

(amused)

Since it's listed as "intelligent circuitry," why not? After all, working as much with artificial intelligence as we do can be dehumanizing—right? So maybe we can combat that tendency with a little simple courtesy.

She removes the cup of hot chocolate.

SONYA

(continuing)

Thank you.

They walk toward main engineering.

GEORDI

For someone who has just arrived, you certainly aren't shy with your opinions.

SONYA

Ooops—have I been talking too much?

GEORDI

No.

SONYA

(the words come out in a rush)

I do tend to be a motor mouth, especially when I get excited . . . and you don't know how exciting it is to get this assignment. Everyone in class . . . and I mean everyone—wants the *Enterprise.* I mean, it would have been all right to spend some time on Ranuos VI to do phase work with antimatter . . . that's my speciality.

GEORDI

I know—that's why you got this assignment.

SONYA

(off Geordi's smile)

Did it again. It's just that . . .

GEORDI

I know, you're excited, Sonya.

SONYA

Yes.

GEORDI

I don't think you want to bring that hot chocolate around these control stations.

SONYA

Sorry. I shouldn't even have this *in* engineering. We were talking and I just forgot I had it in my hand . . .

And as she turns to take it out of the room.

SONYA
(continuing)
I'll finish it over here.
(looks back, and seriously)
Lieutenant La Forge, it won't happen again.

Then as she turns around she crashes right into CAPTAIN PICARD.

2A PICARD

The cup full of chocolate hits him right in the chest.

2B SCENE

For a moment everyone freezes. Geordi starts forward.

GEORDI
Actually it's my fault, sir . . .

He looks down at Picard's soiled uniform.

PICARD
Yes, I'm aware of how often you order picnics to be held in here.

Sonya is about to die from embarrassment.

SONYA
Oh no. Oh, Captain . . . I'm sorry . . . oh . . .
(she tries to brush it off)
. . . I wasn't looking and . . .
(she pulls her hand away)
Oh . . . it's all over you.

PICARD
Yes, Ensign. It's all over me.

SONYA
At least let me . . .

In trying to brush it off, she just makes it worse. She looks up at Picard, who through it all is maintaining as much of his dignity as possible.

PICARD
Ensign . . . ah . . .

SONYA

(she straightens up to her best military posture)

Ensign Sonya Gomez.

GEORDI

Ensign Gomez is a recent academy graduate. She transferred on at Starbase one seventy-three.

Picard's attention is on the widening chocolate stain that Sonya is creating.

PICARD

Ensign . . .

(restraining her)

I think it would be simpler if you let me change my uniform?

GEORDI

Captain, I really have to accept responsibility for this.

Picard has been looking from one to the other, beginning to understand what is happening between Geordi and Sonya.

PICARD

Yes, Chief Engineer. I believe I do understand now.

SONYA

I'm very excited about this assignment, Captain, and I promise I'll . . .

(she looks at the chocolate stain on Picard's uniform)

. . . try very hard to serve you and this ship to the best of my ability.

PICARD

I'm sure you will. Carry on.

Picard then turns and strides off.

2C SONYA AND GEORDI

SONYA

First impressions, right! Isn't that what they say—first impressions are the most important?

GEORDI

I'll give you this . . . it's a meeting the captain won't soon forget.

SONYA

What a way to start my first assignment.

Off Geordi's reaction:

3 OMITTED

4 INTERIOR CORRIDOR

Picard walks past a crew member—who notices the stain on Picard's uniform, but quickly averts his eyes so as not to embarrass the captain. Picard turns and enters the turbolift.

4A INTERIOR TURBOLIFT

The doors close.

PICARD

Deck nine. Officers' quarters.

The turbolift moves off. Then stops. The doors open, and while still looking down at the stain on his uniform, Picard steps off.

4B INTERIOR SHUTTLE

Picard is not in a corridor of the *Enterprise*—he's on a shuttle! He turns around and the turbolift doors are gone.

4C SCENE

He looks up. There is a crew member at the controls.

PICARD

Crewman? What's going on?

The crew member turns.

4D CREW MEMBER

It's Q.

Q

There, there, my dear captain.

4E PICARD

Reacts.

PICARD

Q.

4F SCENE (OPTICAL)

Picard moves closer to Q.

Q

(re: the stain)

My, my—haven't we been careless?

Q passes his hand over the stain on Picard's uniform and the stain disappears.

Q

There—a little cleaning service I am more than happy to provide.

PICARD

We agreed you would never trouble my ship again!

Q

I always keep my arrangements, sir. We are nowhere near your vessel.

Picard looks out and sees a field of stars. Then back to Q.

FADE OUT.

ACT ONE

FADE IN:

5 EXTERIOR SPACE—THE *ENTERPRISE* (OPTICAL)

The *Enterprise* moving along at impulse speed.

5A INTERIOR CORRIDOR

Geordi and Sonya are walking to Ten-Forward. She is in a clean uniform.

GEORDI

I read your graduating thesis. I wouldn't have requested you if you weren't the best.

She's uncomfortable with the compliment and shrugs it off, changes the subject.

SONYA

Where are we going?

GEORDI

To Ten-Forward. We're going to forget about work. We are going to sit, talk, relax, look at the stars. You're going to learn to slow down.

SONYA

(very intense)

No, that's the one thing I can't do.

GEORDI

(gently)

You're awfully young to be so driven.

SONYA

Yes, I am. I *had* to be. I had to be the best because only the best get to be *here.* Out here on the edge.

(gripping his arm and giving it a shake)

Geordi, Geordi . . . uh . . .

(dropping the arm abruptly)

Lieutenant—

GEORDI
(grinning)
Geordi.

SONYA
Geordi. Whatever is out here we're going to be the *first* humans ever to see it. And is it here because we believe in it and have therefore created it, or has it created us?

GEORDI
The Grand Unified Theory and supersymmetry haven't been seriously discussed for years.

SONYA
They also haven't been disproved. I don't know if it's true or not, but I've got to try and find out.

GEORDI
You're more than a scientist; you're a philospher.

SONYA
No, no, I'm not. Oh, God, don't make me sound profound. There's just so much out there . . . here.

She is gesturing broadly as if somehow she can pull in and embrace the whole universe.

SONYA
(continuing)
I have to see it all. To understand it all. And we haven't got much time.

GEORDI
Sonya, it's going to be there for you. Believe me.
(a beat)
I promise, I won't let anything exciting slip past without letting you know.

6 INTERIOR TEN-FORWARD

GUINAN is behind the bar. There are a few N.D. crew members scattered around the room. The only one of our regulars in Ten-Forward is Geordi, who is sitting at a table by the window with Sonya—they are engaged in a very animated conversation.

6A GUINAN

Something gives her pause—like a whisper only she can hear. She is thoughtful for a beat . . .

6B SCENE

Guinan steps out from behind the bar and crosses to the center of the room.

6C ANOTHER ANGLE

She stands near Geordi's table for a beat gazing out at space. In the background Geordi continues his conversation with Sonya.

GEORDI (offscreen)
I understand that you're excited—so was I. This is your first assignment, everything is new, you are eager and that's great, but . . .

SONYA (offscreen)
I've always been an enthusiastic person, but . . .

He holds up his hand.

GEORDI (offscreen)
Do me a favor . . . for a minute, just listen.

SONYA (offscreen)
I always do that. Someone nice—and you are nice; I can tell—goes out of their way to give me some helpful advice . . . and I'm so busy talking . . .

In the background we see Geordi quiet her with a gesture.

SONYA (offscreen)
Not another word. Go ahead . . . talk.

6D GUINAN

Her brow knits—like she has just seen the first indications of a coming storm. She steps to a communications panel.

GUINAN
Bridge, this is Ten-Forward.

7 INTERIOR BRIDGE—EMPHASIZING RIKER

Who reacts to the unusual call.

RIKER

Guinan?! I don't believe you've ever called the bridge before.

GUINAN

I've never felt the need. Is everything all right?

RIKER

How do you mean?

GUINAN

Is there . . . anything . . . unusual happening?

RIKER

(looks around)

Anyone notice anything unusual?

(waits, then)

No—Guinan—nothing out of the ordinary. Why do you ask?

7A ANGLE IN TEN-FORWARD

A thoughtful Guinan responding.

GUINAN

I'm . . . I'm not certain. Just a feeling—something that happened once before. Probably nothing.

(beat)

Please forget I called. Ten-Forward out.

She turns and stares out into space.

8 OMITTED

9 INTERIOR SHUTTLECRAFT

Picard is in the shuttlecraft—with Q. Picard adjusts a control; Q smiles.

Q

The locator beacon won't help. They'll never look for you this far away.

Picard turns to the com controls.

PICARD

Enterprise—this is Picard.

There's no response.

PICARD

Stop this foolishness, Q. Return me to the *Enterprise.*

Q

I'd suggest you change your attitude. Petulance does not become you. We have business.

PICARD

Keeping me a prisoner out here will not force me to discuss anything with you.

Q

It will in time, my dear Captain.

10 INTERIOR TEN-FORWARD

Guinan steps up to near the table occupied by Geordi and Sonya and looks out at the stars.

SONYA

I appreciate your advice, Lieutenant. And I'll take it to heart.

Geordi notices Guinan's distraction.

GEORDI

Guinan?

She turns.

GUINAN

Can I get you something?

GEORDI

No—we're fine. Is everything all right?

She looks over at Geordi for a beat then:

GUINAN

I don't know.

But her expression belies the answer. Geordi nods, but something about her reaction causes him to:

GEORDI

(gets up)

I think I'll go check out engineering.

SONYA

I'll go with you.

Guinan watches them leave, then turns and once again looks out at the stars.

10A INTERIOR MAIN BRIDGE

The turbolift doors open, and TROI enters. There is a sense of foreboding in the timing of her arrival. Reaction from Riker. Troi crosses to her position.

TROI

Where's the captain?

RIKER

In his ready room.

Troi touches a com control.

TROI

Captain—this is Counselor Troi.

There is no response.

11 INTERIOR ANOTHER ANGLE

RIKER

Computer—locate Captain Picard.

COMPUTER

The captain is not on the ship.

Before they can react.

11A WORF

Runs a check on his security panel.

WORF
Commander, there is a shuttle missing from shuttle bay two.

RIKER
All stop.

WESLEY
Answering all stop.

12 EXTERIOR SPACE—THE *ENTERPRISE* (OPTICAL)

The *Enterprise* comes to a complete stop.

13 INTERIOR MAIN BRIDGE

For a beat everyone is silent . . . waiting.

WORF
I have hailed the shuttle on all frequencies—no response.

DATA
Sensors indicate no shuttle or other ships in this sector.

RIKER
We must assume the captain is aboard the shuttle.

WESLEY
But how could he get to the shuttle bay? How could he leave the *Enterprise* without us knowing? It's not possible.

RIKER
Take it easy, Wes. We'll find him. I want to begin a methodical search. Sensors on maximum scan. We'll use our present location as the center. Data, plot a search pattern from our present coordinates which will cover the most area in the shortest time.

Riker slowly moves back to his chair.

13A DATA

He makes some rapid calculations.

DATA
The search pattern has been input.

RIKER
Engage, Mister Crusher.

14 EXTERIOR SPACE—THE *ENTERPRISE* (OPTICAL)

The *Enterprise* pulls out of frame.

15 EXTERIOR SPACE—THE *ENTERPRISE* (OPTICAL)

Another angle as the *Enterprise* approaches from a long distance.

RIKER (voice-over)
First officer's log. Stardate (xx). We have not been able to determine why, or how, Captain Picard left the *Enterprise.* We can't even be certain he is in the missing shuttle, although that is the assumption on which we are proceeding. For the last six hours we have been searching without success.

16 INTERIOR MAIN BRIDGE

The situation has gone from tense to desperate.

DATA
We have covered the area in a spherical pattern which a vessel without warp drive could traverse in the time allotted.

RIKER
Widen the area . . .

16A DATA

He inputs the necessary information.

17 INTERIOR SHUTTLE

As before with Picard and Q. Picard attempts to power up the shuttle. All systems are inoperative.

Q

Do we stay out here years? Decades? Picard, I am ageless—you are not.

PICARD

Then the *Enterprise* will continue on with Riker as captain. Return me to my ship.

Q

You are an impossibly stubborn human.

(continuing)

If I return you to your ship, you will agree to give my request a full hearing?

Picard studies Q for a beat, then nods.

17A INTERIOR TEN-FORWARD

We pull back to reveal Picard and Q, now sitting in Ten-Forward.

Q

You're right, Picard. This is the proper venue for our discussion.

17B GUINAN

She reacts to the sudden appearance of Q and the captain.

18 INTERIOR MAIN BRIDGE—EMPHASIZING WORF

Who is studying his board.

WORF

Commander. My status board indicates that the shuttle is back in shuttlebay two.

Riker reacts.

RIKER

Computer—locate Captain Picard.

COMPUTER
Captain Picard is in Ten-Forward.

Off Riker's reactions we:

FADE OUT.

ACT TWO

FADE IN:

19 EXTERIOR SPACE—THE *ENTERPRISE* (OPTICAL)

The *Enterprise* is at a dead stop.

20 OMITTED

21 INTERIOR TEN-FORWARD

Picard and Q are seated by one of the front windows. Guinan comes over. Q immediately stands and backs off like a man about to be physically attacked.

Q

You!

GUINAN

None other.

Q

Picard, if you had half the sense you pretend to have, you would get her off your ship immediately—and if you like, I will be more than pleased to expedite her departure.

Picard looks to Guinan.

PICARD

You know him.

GUINAN

We had some dealings.

Q

Those dealings were two centuries ago. This creature is not what she appears to be. She's an imp—where she goes, trouble always follows.

PICARD

You're speaking of yourself, Q—not Guinan.

Q

Guinan? Is that your name now?

PICARD

Guinan's not the issue here—you are . . . . We had an agreement that you would stop meddling with us.

Q

And so I have.

PICARD

What do you want, Q? State your business and let's get on with it.

Q

I agree, Captain, enough about this creature—she's diverting us from the purpose of my being here.

RIKER (offscreen)

Which is?

Q looks up.

21A SCENE

Riker and Worf stride across Ten-Forward, to join them.

Q

Ahh, the redoubtable Commander Riker. And micro-brain.

(to Worf)

Growl for me—let me know you still care.

Worf reacts.

Q

(returning to the point)

My purpose? Why, to join you!

RIKER

To join us as what?

Q

A member of the crew. Willing and able—ready to serve.

Before Riker can react.

Q
(to Picard)
This ship is already home for the indigent, the unwanted, and the unworthy—so why not a homeless entity?

RIKER
Homeless?

Q
Yes.

RIKER
So, the other members of the Q Continuum kicked you out.

GUINAN
Not all of the Q are like this one. Some are almost respectable.

PICARD
Join us as what? To do what? Would you start as an ordinary crew member? What task is too menial for an entity?

Q
Do you mock me?

PICARD
Not at all. That is the last thing I would do. You, by definition, are part of our charter. Our mission is to go forth—to seek out new and different life-forms, and you certainly qualify as one of the most unusual life-forms I have ever encountered. To learn more about you is frankly quite provocative, but you are next of kin to Chaos.

Q
Captain, at least allow me to present my argument.

Q takes Picard's silence as permission to continue.

Q
(continuing)
After our last encounter,
(a look to Riker)
I was asked to leave the Q Continuum. Since then, I have been wandering vaguely—bored, really—my existence without purpose. Then, I remembered the good times I had with you . . .

RIKER
The good times!? The first time we met you put us on trial for the "crimes of humanity" . . .

Q
Of which you were exonerated.

RIKER
The next time we saw you, you asked me to join the Q Continuum.

Q
You made a large mistake in not accepting my offer.

PICARD
. . . and now you say you want to join us.

Q
Yes, more and more I realize that here—here is where I want to be. Think of the advantages. Now, I neither expect nor require any special treatment. If necessary, although I can't imagine why, I will renounce my powers and become as weak and incompetent as all of you.

PICARD
No.

Q
Oh, come on, Captain, in fairness . . . let me try. I deserve at least that much.

RIKER
Fairness?! You disrupt this ship—kidnap the captain!

Q

I add a little excitement, a little spice to your lives, and all you do is complain. Where's your adventurous spirit—your imagination? Think, Picard, of the possibilities.

PICARD

Simply stated—we don't trust you.

Q

Oh, you may not trust me, but you do need me. You're not prepared for what awaits you.

PICARD

I don't know that we are prepared, but I do know that we are ready to confront it.

Q

Really?

PICARD

Absolutely. That's why we are out here.

Q

Oh, the arrogance.

(to Guinan)

They don't have a clue about what's "out here."

GUINAN

They will learn—adapt. That's their great advantage.

Q

They are moving faster than expected—farther than they should.

PICARD

By whose calculation?

Q

You judge yourselves against the pitiful adversaries you have so far encountered—the Klingons, the Romulans, are nothing compared to what's waiting.

(continuing)

Picard, you are about to move into areas of the galaxy containing wonders more incredible than you can possibly imagine . . . and terrors to freeze your soul. I offer myself as guide—only to be rejected out-of-hand.

RIKER

I guess we'll just have to get along the best we can without you.

Q

What justifies this smugness?

PICARD

We're not smug—nor arrogant. We are resolute and we are willing. But more than that, we are determined. Your help is not required.

Q

Well, let's just see how ready you are.

GUINAN

Q—Don't do this!

He makes a move of his hand:

22 EXTERIOR SPACE—THE *ENTERPRISE* (OPTICAL)

The *Enterprise* is struck by a great surge of energy and streaks off.

23 INTERIOR TEN-FORWARD (OPTICAL)

Picard and the others react to the blur of stars streaking past. It's a velocity beyond the capabilities of the *Enterprise.*

24 INTERIOR MAIN BRIDGE

Data has command of the bridge. Everyone reacts to the sudden burst of speed.

25 EXTERIOR SPACE (OPTICAL)

The *Enterprise* comes out of the spin and stops.

26 INTERIOR TEN-FORWARD (OPTICAL)

The motion has stopped.

INTERCUT MAIN BRIDGE AS NEEDED

PICARD

Bridge, this is the captain—all stop.

WESLEY COM VOICE

Answering all stop.

PICARD

Status.

DATA COM VOICE

According to these coordinates we have traveled seven thousand light-years, and are located near system J-two-five.

RIKER

Estimate travel time to the closest starbase.

DATA COM VOICE

At maximum warp, in two years, seven months, three days, eighteen hours we would reach starbase one-eight-five.

Guinan looks out the window.

RIKER

Why?

Q

Why? Why, to give you a taste of your future. This is a preview of things to come, because if you continue at your present rate of exploration—very soon you will reach this part of the galaxy.

(to Picard)

Con permiso, Capitán. The hall has been rented—the orchestra engaged—it's time to see if you can dance.

With a flash, Q disappears.

PICARD

Guinan, have your people been in this part of the galaxy?

GUINAN

Yes.

RIKER

What can you tell us?

GUINAN

Only that if I were you, I'd start back right now.

Off their look . . .

27 EXTERIOR SPACE—THE *ENTERPRISE* (OPTICAL)

The *Enterprise* is moving through this new section of the galaxy.

PICARD (voice-over)

Captain's log supplemental. The entity Q has flung the *Enterprise* to a distant part of the galaxy, which we are going to take the opportunity to explore.

28 INTERIOR MAIN BRIDGE

Everyone is in their places.

WORF

Captain, the sixth planet in the system is class-M.

DATA

There is a system of roads on the planet, which indicates a highly industrialized civilization. But where there should be cities there are only great rips in the surface.

WORF

It is as though some great force just scooped all machine elements off the face of the planet.

DATA

It is identical to what happened to the outposts along the Neutral Zone.

WORF

We are being probed.

RIKER

What's the source of the probe?

Worf checks his console.

WORF

A ship. It is on an intercept course.

PICARD

On screen.

28A VIEWSCREEN (OPTICAL)

A strange ship approaches—it's unlike anything we have seen.

PICARD

Magnify.

The image on the screen enlarges. The shape of the ship is more apparent. It's boxlike, with none of the aerodynamic qualities associated with most spaceships, including the *Enterprise.* This is a case of form following function. We are about to have our first encounter with the BORG.

RIKER

Full scan. Go to Yellow Alert.

WORF

Going to Yellow Alert.

RIKER

Keep the shields down—we don't want to appear provocative.

Worf responds with a nod.

29 EXTERIOR SPACE—THE *ENTERPRISE* (OPTICAL)

As the great Borg ship approaches the *Enterprise.* Then stops.

30 INTERIOR TEN-FORWARD (OPTICAL)

Guinan is looking out at the Borg ship.

31 INTERIOR MAIN BRIDGE (OPTICAL)

As before—everyone watching the viewscreen.

PICARD

Data, what can you tell us?

DATA

The ship is strangely generalized in design. There is no specific bridge or central control area, no specific engineering section—I can identify no living quarters.

RIKER

Lifesigns?

DATA

There is no indication of specific life.

RIKER

Lieutenant Worf, what is its alert status?

WORF

I detect no shields, no weapons of any known design.

PICARD

Hailing frequencies.

WORF

Open.

PICARD

This is Captain Jean-Luc Picard of the *U.S.S. Enterprise.*

WORF

No response.

PICARD

Guinan.

32 INTERIOR GUINAN OFFICE (OPTICAL)

Guinan moves into her small office.

PICARD

Activate your viewscreen—I want you to monitor what's going on up here. I may need your input.

Guinan reaches out and activates her viewscreen. The image is the same as that on the the MAIN VIEWER.

GUINAN

I'm here. I can see the other ship.

PICARD

You are acquainted with this life-form?

GUINAN

Yes. My people encountered them a century ago. Our cities were destroyed—our people scattered across the galaxy. They are called the Borg—protect yourself or they will destroy you.

Picard looks at Riker.

RIKER

Shields up.

WORF

Yes, Sir.

33 INTERIOR MAIN ENGINEERING (OPTICAL)

SUDDENLY a strange creature appears—it's a BORG. It is a biped—a cyborg, part organic and part artificial. There is a metallike device implanted in its head. One arm is artificial, with a toollike contraption instead of a hand. The other arm is organic except for the hand. Its eyes are artificial. Its presence triggers RED ALERT.

GEORDI

Security to main engineering—we have an intruder.

34 INTERIOR MAIN BRIDGE

Off Picard's reaction as he and Worf exit.

FADE OUT.

ACT THREE

FADE IN:

35 EXTERIOR SPACE—THE *ENTERPRISE* (OPTICAL)

The *Enterprise* in this new section of the galaxy—with the Borg ship nearby.

36 INTERIOR MAIN ENGINEERING

Picard, Worf, and security team enter. The Borg is still making a visual survey of the room. It seems to look right through or pass the people as if they are of no consequence.

WORF
He came right through the shields!

Picard approaches. Q appears behind Picard—to offer sotto voce observations.

Q
Interesting, isn't it? Not a he—not a she. Not like anything you've ever seen. An enhanced humanoid.

PICARD
What do you want?

36A PICARD (OPTICAL)

He steps closer to the Borg. He holds up his open hand.

PICARD
We mean you no harm. Do you understand me?

The Borg strides toward one of the companels.

Q
Understand you? You are nothing to him. He has no interest in your life-form. He's just a scout—the first of many. He's here to analyze as much about you as he can—that's how they always start.

(continuing)
He may attempt to gain control of the ship. I wouldn't let him.

Q leaves.

36B SCENE

Picard tries to defuse this situation.

PICARD
Stop—we cannot allow you to interfere with the operation of this ship.

The Borg continues to move toward the companel.

PICARD
Lieutenant Worf.

Worf motions for one of his security team to intercept the Borg. The security man steps in front of the Borg. The Borg knocks the security man on his ass.

36C WORF (OPTICAL)

Worf pulls out his phaser. Worf fires—the stun setting means nothing.

36D SCENE (OPTICAL)

The phaser hit has no effect on the Borg. He, or it, steps to the companel and affixes the apparatus on his arm to the computer. SUDDENLY there is a drain on all systems. The lights dim.

PICARD
Worf—use whatever means to neutralize the intruder.

36E WORF (OPTICAL)

Worf adjusts his phaser and fires again.

36F SCENE (OPTICAL)

This phaser hit rips into the Borg, knocking him away. Before anyone can react—another Borg materializes. Worf and the others assume a defensive posture. The second Borg picks up where the first one left off.

36G WORF (OPTICAL)

fires his phaser.

36H SCENE (OPTICAL)

This Borg responds differently. The hit is absorbed. He is apparently surrounded with a force field of some kind. This Borg goes to the back panel. He accesses the computer—drains it.

Then he walks over to the first Borg and removes some parts from the first Borg's body and dematerializes. After a beat the dead Borg withers into a line of ash—which then disappears.

Off Picard reaction.

37 INTERIOR OBSERVATION LOUNGE (OPTICAL)

An abbreviated staff has been assembled; Riker, Data, Picard, and Troi.

PICARD

Because her people had contact with the Borg, I have requested that Guinan participate in this conference. You are aware of what just occurred in main engineering.

She nods.

PICARD

Tell, us exactly what happened between your people and the Borg.

GUINAN

I was not personally involved, but—from what I have been told they came through our system like a storm of Jaradan Aser beatles—and by the time they left, there wasn't much left of our society.

RIKER

Guinan, if they are that aggressive, then I wonder why neither Borg attacked. They could have—but they didn't.

GUINAN

They never do that as individuals. It's just not their way. When they decide to come, they will come in force. They do nothing piecemeal.

DATA

Then the initial encounter was solely for the purpose of gathering information.

GUINAN

Yes.

PICARD

How do we reason with them? Let them know that we are not a threat?

GUINAN

You don't. At least, to my knowledge nobody has so far.

WORF COM VOICE

Captain, we are being hailed.

PICARD

On screen.

37A SCENE—TO INCLUDE VIEWSCREEN (OPTICAL)

The image on the viewscreen is of the interior of the Borg ship. Not the bridge, because they don't have one. It is a great chamber with stacks and stacks of slots in which are individual Borg. We can see over a thousand of them, but the ship probably holds more. Some of them are making small controlled movements; otherwise they would appear to be at rest.

37B REACTIONS (OPTICAL)

Picard steps forward.

PICARD

This is Captain Jean-Luc Picard of the . . .

BORG

(interrupting)

We have analyzed your defensive capabilities as being unable to withstand us. If you defend yourselves, you will be punished.

Viewscreen repaints to exterior Borg ship.

PICARD

Counselor.

TROI

You are not dealing with an individual mind. They do not have a single leader. It is the collective minds of all of them.

PICARD

That would have some definite advantages.

TROI

Yes. A single leader can make errors. It is less likely for the combined whole.

Q (offscreen)

Picard.

Picard turns.

37B-A VIEWSCREEN (OPTICAL)

Q is now on the viewscreen.

Q

Are you certain you still don't want me as a member of your crew? This would be the time to ask, before everything goes too far beyond your control.

Before Picard can answer . . .

WORF (com voice)

Captain—They have locked onto us with some form of tractor beam.

PICARD

We're on our way.

Picard and the others exit.

37C EXTERIOR SPACE—THE *ENTERPRISE* (OPTICAL)

An energy beam from the Borg ship holds the *Enterprise.*

38 INTERIOR MAIN BRIDGE

Picard and the others take their positions.

DATA
Whatever this beam is, Captain, it is draining our shields.

RIKER
If they pull down our shields, we're helpless.

PICARD
On any heading—warp eight, engage.

38A WESLEY

As he inputs the information and attempts to take the *Enterprise* out of danger.

WESLEY
It's holding us here!

RIKER
Increase power!

WORF
The shields are weakening.

DATA
In eighteen seconds the shields will be down.

PICARD
Locate the exact source of the tractor beam—lock on phasers.

WORF
Phasers locked on target.

PICARD
Fire.

39 EXTERIOR SPACE—THE *ENTERPRISE* (OPTICAL)

The pinpoint phasers from the *Enterprise* hit into the Borg ship. But the force holding the *Enterprise* does not release.

40 INTERIOR MAIN BRIDGE

As before.

WORF

They still have us.

DATA

Shields are down.

41 EXTERIOR SPACE—THE *ENTERPRISE* (OPTICAL)

The *Enterprise* and the Borg ship. Another beam leaves the Borg ship and makes contact with the *Enterprise.*

41A EXTERIOR SPACE—THE *ENTERPRISE* (OPTICAL)

A CLOSER ANGLE as the Borg ship cores out a piece of the *Enterprise* hull.

42 OMITTED

43 INTERIOR MAIN BRIDGE

As before.

WORF

A type of laser beam is slicing into the Saucer Module.

RIKER

They are carving us up like a roast.

PICARD

With whatever force you need, terminate that beam.

44 EXTERIOR SPACE—THE *ENTERPRISE* (OPTICAL)

The beam has cut away a section of the *Enterprise* and is now taking it back to the Borg ship.

45 INTERIOR MAIN BRIDGE

As before.

PICARD

Fire!

Worf releases a series of blasts from the phaser bank.

46 EXTERIOR SPACE—THE *ENTERPRISE* (OPTICAL)

The phaser blasts rip again and again into the Borg ship—the beam holding the section of the *Enterprise* disappears into the Borg ship. Another volley from the *Enterprise* pounds the Borg ship.

47 INTERIOR MAIN BRIDGE (OPTICAL)

On the screen we see the battered image of the Borg ship. RED ALERT ends.

DATA
The tractor beam has released.

RIKER
Damage report.

WORF
Sections twenty-seven, twenty-eight, twenty-nine on decks four, five, and six destroyed.

PICARD
Casualties?

WORF
Eighteen were in those sections and are missing.

RIKER
They couldn't have survived it.

DATA
A force field is maintaining hull integrity.

PICARD
What is the condition of their ship?

WORF
They have sustained damage to twenty percent of their vessel. Life support minimal.

RIKER
(angry)
Why?!

For a beat everyone is in stunned silence.

PICARD

Conference.

RIKER

Worf—you had better remain at your station.

Worf watches them go.

48 INTERIOR OBSERVATION LOUNGE (OPTICAL)

Guinan is still there as they enter. Riker—Data—Picard—Troi.

GUINAN

I am so sorry, Captain.

Picard nods.

PICARD

Guinan—what else can you tell us about these creatures?

GUINAN

I know only bits and pieces.

PICARD

Anything would be helpful.

GUINAN

They are a mixture of organic and artificial life that has been developed over a thousand centuries.

Behind them Q is revealed (no Q flash).

47A INTERIOR MAIN ENGINEERING

The tension level is high. Sonya is a little dazed, but at her duties like any well-trained academy graduate. She and Geordi.

SONYA

(urgent)

I can't get the shields up.

GEORGI

Divert power from wherever you need it. Anywhere except life support.

SONYA

It wouldn't help. The circuits which control the shields have been fused.

GEORGI

If you can't reprogram them . . . reroute.

Her hands fly across the panels. Then stop.

SONYA

Eighteen people. Dead—just like that.

GEORGI

Push it out of your head.

SONYA

I can't. I keep seeing them.

GEORGI

Stop it. We'll grieve later. Right now . . . let's get those shields operative.

She shakes it off, and they both return to reprogramming the shield circuits.

Q

The Borg is the ultimate user, with the result that they are unlike any threat your Federation has ever faced. They have no interest in political conquest—or wealth or power as you know it. They simply want your ship—its technology. They have identified it as something they can consume and use.

RIKER

And you brought us here, exposed us to it, cost us the lives of shipmates . . .

Riker's calm breaks—he physically moves to assault Q.

Q

Stop—or you will surely die.

PICARD

Number One.

Riker stops; Picard turns to Q.

PICARD
(continuing)

Eighteen of our people have died. Please tell us that this is one of your illusions.

Q

Oh, no. This is as real as your so-called life gets.

A FLASH OF LIGHT and Q is gone.

GEORDI'S COM VOICE

This is Lieutenant La Forge, Captain. We have been able to restore power to the shields.

PICARD

Very good.

WORF'S COM VOICE

Captain, I have the casualty list coming on screen.

PICARD

Cancel—time for that later.

48A SCENE

They are quiet for a beat.

RIKER

If there's a chance we are going to have further dealings with the Borg—now or in the future—we had better find out as much about them as we can.

PICARD

Visit their ship?

RIKER

In my opinion, we have no choice, sir.

PICARD

(considers it; nods)

Agreed. Assemble a minimal away team and take a look at what's over there.

GUINAN

What?

RIKER

(to com)

Mister Worf. Report to transporter room three.

(to Data)

Data.

Riker and Data stand.

GUINAN

It's not my business, but I wouldn't go over there if I were you.

RIKER

Oh, I don't know, Guinan. They visited us . . . seems only fair that we return the courtesy.

Off Guinan as she watches them exit.

FADE OUT.

ACT FOUR

FADE IN:

49 EXTERIOR SPACE—THE *ENTERPRISE* (OPTICAL)

The *Enterprise*, still near the severely damaged Borg ship.

PICARD (voice-over)
Captain's log—supplemental. We have been attacked without provocation by a alien race which Guinan calls the Borg. Hopefully, we have neutralized their vessel. Commander Riker is leading an away team in an attempt to learn more about them.

50 INTERIOR TRANSPORTER ROOM—(OPTICAL)

Riker, Worf, and Data enter. All are wearing phasers.

WORF
There are no lifesign readings.

O'BRIEN
I have laid in coordinates which should set you down in the least damaged section of the Borg ship.

RIKER
Set phasers on stun, but let's be ready to increase the power if we need it.

They climb on the transporter pad.

RIKER
Energize.

The away team dematerializes.

51 INTERIOR BORG SHIP—(OPTICAL)

The away team materializes in the great open center of the Borg ship. All around there is some evidence of battle damage. The design of the interior is as functional as the exterior. There is no attempt at eye-pleasing colors.

Interspersed with the gray equipment racks are slots, which go from the floor to the ceiling and are occupied by individual Borg.

51A ANOTHER ANGLE

The away team looks around. The Borg closest to them are alive. The away team instantly assumes a defensive position—expecting the Borg to repel them. But the Borg do not move.

Data takes a tricorder scan of the area. They step closer to one of the Borg.

RIKER
I wonder why they don't react to us, and why the *Enterprise* did not read any lifesigns, especially when there are this many.

DATA
Perhaps because this ship was scanned for individual lifesigns. Apparently when they are in these slots, they become part of the whole and no longer read as separate life-forms.

RIKER
(touches his communicator)
Captain.

52 INTERIOR MAIN BRIDGE (INTERCUT AS NEEDED)

PICARD
Go ahead, Number One.

RIKER
Our readings were incorrect . . . the Borg crew survived, but they are in a kind of stasis.

PICARD
Explain.

RIKER
There are slots along the wall, kind of like compartments. There are two Borg in each.

DATA
Captain, I would theorize that the Borg are somehow

interconnected through these slots and are working collectively.

RIKER

We are going to look for some way to access their main computer.

52A ANOTHER ANGLE

As the away team moves down the corridor, they pass strange pieces of equipment, but nothing familiar.

52B DATA

Steps over to examine an empty Borg slot.

DATA

Each slot is designed for a specific Borg. Here is where the connection is made.

(he indicates a type of arm rest)

52C SCENE

Riker moves over to join Data—while Worf stands guard. They are very tense—at any moment the Borg could leave the slots.

RIKER

Like a juggernaut which could start moving at any moment.

DATA

The technology required to achieve this biological and artificial interface is far beyond our capabilities. There are many advantages.

RIKER

Speed being the obvious one. This ship literally *thinks* what it wants to do and it happens.

SUDDENLY a nearby Borg leaves its slot. The away team assumes a defensive posture, expecting an attack. Instead the Borg moves to a panel and executes a program, the purpose of which we do not know. Then, as the away team watches, the Borg returns to its slot.

DATA

Fascinating. Obviously they also function individually.

RIKER

And they either don't see us, or don't see us as a threat.

They move off down the corridor.

52D ANOTHER ANGLE (OPTICAL)

To show the relationship between the away team and the immense ship.

53 INTERIOR MAIN BRIDGE—*ENTERPRISE*

Picard is watching the Borg ship on the Main Viewer.

PICARD

Transporter room, this is the captain.

O'BRIEN

O'Brien here, Captain.

PICARD

If your lock on the away team wavers in the slightest—beam them back.

O'BRIEN

Count on it, Captain.

54 INTERIOR BORG SHIP

As the away team comes into another chamber. There are no walls, or doors as such. This ship lacks the compartmentalization which we are used to. The corridor will simply open onto a wider area.

Off to the side, part of the ship has been twisted in the phaser attack. Something about it catches Data's eye.

54A ANOTHER ANGLE

Riker moves to the other side of the room. Here are smaller horizontal slots which contain smaller—younger—Borg. The ''children'' are in various stages of ''assembly.''

RIKER

Captain—this is incredible. I have just entered what appears to be the nursery.

PICARD

Describe it.

RIKER

From the looks of it, the Borg are born as a biological life-form. Almost immediately after birth they begin getting artificial implants. They have apparently developed the technology to link artificial intelligence directly into a humanoid brain. Pretty astounding. Something else—I haven't seen any females.

DATA

Commander.

Riker turns from looking at the half-put-together child.

RIKER

What is it?

DATA

The ship appears to be regenerating.

54B SCENE

Riker and Worf quickly cross to Data. They look at a damaged portion of the ship.

DATA

Perhaps this explains why they have not taken notice of our presence. Their collective effort is directed at repairing their vessel.

RIKER

Captain, the Borg are using their combined power to repair the ship.

PICARD COM VOICE

Transporter chief, beam the away team directly to the Bridge.

55 INTERIOR MAIN BRIDGE (OPTICAL)

As the away team stacks up.

PICARD

Now, Mister Crusher—engage.

56 EXTERIOR SPACE—THE *ENTERPRISE* (OPTICAL)

The *Enterprise* streaks away—leaving the visibly battered Borg vessel in its wake.

56A INTERIOR MAIN BRIDGE

There is relief that they are putting some distance between themselves and the Borg.

56B OMITTED

57 INTERIOR MAIN BRIDGE

As before.

DATA

Captain—the Borg ship is in pursuit.

PICARD

On screen.

57A SCREEN (OPTICAL)

We can see the Borg ship coming toward us.

PICARD

Magnify.

The screen changes—the Borg ship fills more of the screen.

RIKER

Increase by ten to the third.

Now the Borg ship fills the screen—we can see the hull of the Borg ship change.

RIKER

It's continuing to regenerate itself.

PICARD

Let's see if we can outrun it.

(to com)

Lieutenant La Forge, I want maximum warp for as long as you can hold it.

58 INTERIOR MAIN ENGINEERING

Geordi is by the pool table. Sonya is in the background.

GEORDI

Yes, sir.

He's on the board—increasing the speed.

GEORDI

We are passing warp eight point five.

58A SCENE

The great engine is moving toward maximum output.

GEORDI

. . . warp nine.

He looks over and sees a very intense look on Sonya's face as she stares at the engine.

The Borg ship is gaining.

RIKER

Arm the photon torpedoes. Recommend we try to slow them down.

PICARD

Agreed.

WORF

Torpedoes armed.

PICARD

Fire.

GEORDI

What is it? Is there something the matter?

She turns toward him.

SONYA

No. You can study the theory—read the books—analyze schematics . . . but none of it prepares you for this. I have just never see or felt anything so awesome.

GEORDI

Well, let's see if we can't raise the level a few more notches.

Geordi moves to another position on the pool table. Sonya steps over across from him and watches with admiration as he fine-tunes the warp drive.

59 INTERIOR MAIN BRIDGE

As before.

60 EXTERIOR SPACE—THE PHOTONS (OPTICAL)

As the photon torpedoes leaves the *Enterprise*.

61 INTERIOR MAIN BRIDGE (OPTICAL)

All eyes are locked on the main viewer as the photon torpedoes head for the Borg vessel . . . and explode in a blinding flash of light.

WORF

They had no effect.

GEORDI (com voice)

Bridge, this is engineering. We are at warp nine point six five.

WORF

The Borg ship is still gaining.

The crew member at science one turns—it's Q.

Q

They will follow this ship until you exhaust your fuel. They will wear down your defenses. Then you will be theirs.

Picard looks from Q to the main viewscreen and the Borg ship which continues its relentless pursuit.

Q

(continuing)

You're out of your league, Picard. You should have stayed where you belonged.

Off Picard's reaction.

FADE OUT.

ACT FIVE

FADE IN:

62 EXTERIOR SPACE—THE *ENTERPRISE* (OPTICAL)

The *Enterprise* is moving at maximum warp, followed by the Borg ship.

PICARD (voice-over)
Captain's log supplemental. We are unable to maintain the gap between the *Enterprise* and the Borg ship.

63 INTERIOR MAIN ENGINEERING

Engine is pounding. Geordi moves from the pool table. Sonya is beside him—now under pressure, she is very calm.

SONYA
We are at the design limit.

GEORDI
Agreed. Bridge, this is engineering.

PICARD (com voice)
Go ahead.

GEORDI
You've got all we can give you.

64 INTERIOR MAIN BRIDGE

Picard, Riker, Data, Troi, and off to the side is Q.

PICARD
I understand, Lieutenant La Forge.

WORF
Captain—the enemy vessel is firing on us.

The ship goes to RED ALERT.

65 EXTERIOR SPACE—THE *ENTERPRISE* (OPTICAL)

The *Enterprise* at maximum warp. The missile arrives—but instead of striking the ship, it forms a kind of umbrella which engulfs the *Enterprise.*

66 INTERIOR MAIN BRIDGE

As before.

WORF
There are no reports of any damage to the *Enterprise.*

DATA
The target was not the ship. The weapon was designed to drain the shields.

WORF
Shield effectiveness was been reduced twelve percent.

WES
The Borg ship is closing.

WORF
They are firing again.

67 EXTERIOR SPACE—THE *ENTERPRISE* (OPTICAL)

A similar missile leaves the Borg ship and streaks toward the *Enterprise.*

68 INTERIOR MAIN BRIDGE

As before.

WORF
Shields have been reduced by forty-one percent. Another hit and we will be defenseless.

Q
They are wearing you down. Soon you will be helpless.

RIKER
Arm the photon torpedoes.

WORF
Torpedoes armed.

PICARD

Fire the photons.

69 EXTERIOR SPACE—THE PHOTONS (OPTICAL)

As the photons leave the *Enterprise* en route to the Borg ship. The torpedoes explode, but the Borg ship is undamaged.

70 INTERIOR BRIDGE

As before.

WORF

The Borg ship was not damaged.

Q

You can't outrun them. You can't destroy them. If you damage them, the essence of what they are remains—they regenerate and keep coming . . . eventually you will weaken—your reserves will be gone . . . . They are relentless.

WORF

The Borg ship is firing.

71 EXTERIOR SPACE—THE *ENTERPRISE* (OPTICAL)

As the missile from the Borg ship hits the *Enterprise.*

72 INTERIOR MAIN BRIDGE

This time the ship is rocked.

WORF

We have lost the shields again.

73 EXTERIOR SPACE—THE *ENTERPRISE* (OPTICAL)

The Borg ship closes on the *Enterprise.* It fires a beam at the *Enterprise.* Which hits in the area of the nacelles. The *Enterprise* comes out of warp, as does the Borg ship.

74 INTERIOR MAIN ENGINEERING

Geordi is at the pool table.

GEORDI
Bridge—we have lost the warp engines.

74A OMITTED

75 INTERIOR MAIN BRIDGE

As before.

Q
Now where's your smugness—your arrogance? Do you still profess to be prepared for what awaits you?

WORF
The Borg ship is reestablishing its tractor beam.

RIKER
Lock on photon torpedoes.

WORF
Yes, sir.

DATA
Without our shields—at this range there is a high degree of probability that a photon detonation could destroy the *Enterprise.*

Riker and Picard exchange looks.

RIKER
Prepare to fire.

Q
I'll be leaving now. You thought you could handle it—so handle it.

PICARD
Q. End this.

Q
What makes you think I am either inclined to terminate or capable of terminating this encounter?

PICARD

If we all die, here and now—you will never be able to gloat. You wanted to frighten us—we're frightened. You wanted to show that we are inadequate—for the moment I will grant that. You want me to say that I need you. Right now—I need you.

We would expect Q to smirk, but he doesn't. He gives Picard a steady look.

And with a little motion.

76 EXTERIOR SPACE—THE *ENTERPRISE* (OPTICAL)

With the same explosion of speed which got us here, the *Enterprise* is flung back to where it started.

76A INTERIOR MAIN BRIDGE (OPTICAL)

Picard and the others react to the streaking stars on the viewscreen as they spin.

76B EXTERIOR SPACE—THE *ENTERPRISE* (OPTICAL)

Comes to a stop.

77 INTERIOR MAIN BRIDGE (OPTICAL)

RED ALERT ends.

RIKER

Position.

WESLEY

Zero—seven—six Mark two—two—five. Back where we started.

Q

That was a difficult admission. Another man would be humiliated to say those words. Another man would die before asking for help.

Picard gives Q a steady look.

PICARD

I understand what you have done here, Q, but the lesson could have been learned without the loss of eighteen members of my crew.

Q

If you can't take a little bloody nose—maybe you had better go back home and crawl under your bed. It's not safe out here. It's wondrous—with treasures to satiate desires both subtle and gross—but it is not for the timid.

Q leaves in a Q flash.

PICARD

Set a course for the closest Starbase.

WESLEY

Course set for Starbase eight three.

78 EXTERIOR SPACE—THE *ENTERPRISE* (OPTICAL)

As the *Enterprise* moves off to the Starbase.

79 INTERIOR TEN-FORWARD

Picard is there with Guinan.

GUINAN

Q has set a series of events in motion. Your contact with the Borg came long before it should. When you're ready, it might be possible to establish a relationship with them, but now—now, you are only raw material to them. And since they are aware of your existence . . .

PICARD

They will be coming.

GUINAN

You can depend on it.

PICARD

Q might have done the right thing for the wrong reason.

GUINAN

Meaning . . .

PICARD

Perhaps we needed a good kick in our complacency to get us ready for what's ahead.

Picard leaves Ten-Forward.

Off Guinan reaction:

FADE OUT.

STAR TREK: THE NEXT GENERATION

Deja Q

#40273-161

Written by
Richard Danus

Directed by
Les Landau

STAR TREK: THE NEXT GENERATION

Deja Q

CAST

PICARD
RIKER
DATA
BEVERLY
TROI
GEORDI
WORF

GUINAN
ENGINEER'S VOICE

Nonspeaking

SECURITY GUARDS
SUPERNUMERARIES

Q
Q2
DOCTOR GARIN
SCIENTIST

Nonspeaking

TECHNICIANS

STAR TREK: THE NEXT GENERATION

Deja Q

SETS

INTERIORS

U.S.S. ENTERPRISE
MAIN BRIDGE
ENGINEERING
CORRIDOR
DETENTION CELL
CAPTAIN'S READY ROOM
TEN-FORWARD
TURBOLIFT

SHUTTLECRAFT

EXTERIORS

U.S.S. ENTERPRISE

SHUTTLECRAFT

STAR TREK: THE NEXT GENERATION

Deja Q

PRONUNCIATION GUIDE

BRE'EL	bree-EL
CALAMARAIN	kal-ah-mah-REIGN
DELTIVED	DEL-tih-ved

STAR TREK: THE NEXT GENERATION

Deja Q

TEASER

FADE IN:

1 EXTERIOR SPACE—THE *ENTERPRISE* (OPTICAL)

The ship orbits Bre'el, a small, verdant planet orbited by a single moon, irregularly shaped.

PICARD (voice-over)
Captain's log, Stardate 43539.1. We have moved into orbit around Bre'el to investigate a potentially catastrophic threat to the population from a descending asteroidal moon . . .

2 INTERIOR MAIN BRIDGE (OPTICAL)

To include MAIN VIEWER. PICARD, TROI, and RIKER in the command chairs. DATA and WORF at their stations. SUPERNUMERARY at conn. On the main viewer is DOCTOR GARIN, a middle-aged man. He is obviously very troubled. Another SCIENTIST is at his side. In the background various TECHNICIANS check monitors. It has the look of controlled chaos that fills a hurricane center during a big storm.

DATA
The satellite's trajectory continues to deteriorate, Captain. . . . This orbit will bring it to within five hundred kilometers of the planet's surface.

GARIN
We're predicting the atmospheric drag will bring it down on the next orbit.

SCIENTIST
Have you been able to find any explanation for this?

DATA
No, Doctor . . . it is a most unusual phenomenon.

PICARD
Won't the moon disintegrate prior to impact?

SCIENTIST
No, it has a ferrous crystalline structure and will be able to withstand tidal forces, Captain . . . .

RIKER
Couldn't we just blow it into harmless chunks?

DATA
The total mass of the moon would remain the same, Commander. And the impact of thousands of fragments would spread destruction over an even wider area.

PICARD
How long before impact . . . ?

DATA
Twenty-nine hours . . . projected somewhere on the western continent. It would destroy an area eight hundred kilometers in radius.

SCIENTIST
That damage would be insignificant, Captain, compared to the seismic repercussions . . . massive landquakes, and tsunami . . .

GARIN
The force would raise a cloud of dust around the planet, leading to a significant temperature reduction. We could be looking at our own ice age.

PICARD
(keying insignia)
Commander La Forge, is there any way the *Enterprise* might be able to coax this satellite back where it belongs . . . ?

INTERCUT:

3 INTERIOR ENGINEERING

GEORDI at a console. SUPERNUMERARIES at various positions. The matter/antimatter blender bubbling with power.

GEORDI

We'd need to apply a delta-vee of at least four kilometers per second. Even with warp power to the tractor beam, it would mean exceeding recommended impulse engine output by at least forty-seven percent. It'd be like an ant pushing a tricycle . . . a slim chance at best . . .

RIKER

(to Picard)

Given a choice between slim and none, I'll take slim any day . . . .

PICARD

Make it so.

RIKER

Lieutenant Worf, signal all ships in this sector to rendezvous and join us in relief efforts.

WORF

Aye, sir.

PICARD

(to main viewer)

We'll keep you informed of our progress. Picard out.

4–8 OMITTED

9 EXTERIOR SPACE—THE *ENTERPRISE* (OPTICAL)

The tractor beam flares out of the ship and grabs onto the small moon. The warp engines flare brighter as we apply power. The ship is trying to "plow" the moon into a higher orbit.

10 INTERIOR BRIDGE (OPTICAL)

As before. Picard and Riker looking at the viewer. The tractor beam holds the small moon. The moon does not move.

Picard gets up and walks closer to the viewer.

RIKER
Can you give us any more, Geordi . . . ?

GEORDI (com voice)
Not without burning out the tractor beam emitter . . . the circuits are already beyond their thermal limit.

DATA
Delta-vee is ninety-two meters per second. The mass is too great. We are having an effect, but it is negligible.

In the background, a strange noise . . . . It begins low . . . more like a million voices than a million machines . . . .

RIKER
What is that . . . ?

DATA
Unable to identify source . . .

It gets louder . . .

GEORDI (com voice)
Impulse engines passing saftey limits. We're seconds from automatic shutdown.

PICARD
Reduce engines . . . tractor beam off . . .

The sound continues to grow . . . and seems to surround the ship . . . they react . . . almost deafening now . . .

RIKER
Worf, what the hell do the sensors show . . . ?

WORF
The sound is not registering, Commander . . .

The sound swirling inside and all around . . . ends with a slight POP. Q APPEARS, naked, suspended above everyone, as though a puppet held by invisible strings.

Q

Red Alert.

PICARD

Q.

And Q promptly crashes to the floor. On reactions . . .

11–16 OMITTED

FADE OUT.

ACT ONE

FADE IN:

17 EXTERIOR SPACE—THE *ENTERPRISE* (OPTICAL)

As it orbits Bre'el, maintaining its distance to the moon, Klyo.

PICARD (voice-over)
Captain's log, supplemental. We are no closer to finding a solution to the deteriorating orbit of the Bre'el moon . . . but with the arrival of Q, we now have a good idea of the cause.

18 INTERIOR BRIDGE

Starting with Q putting on his jumpsuit . . .

GEORDI (offcamera)
We couldn't drive the tractor emitters hard enough, Captain . . . .

Panning to find Picard is getting a debriefing on the failed moon attempt from Geordi . . .

GEORDI
The beam was flexing, and it was impossible to transfer enough kinetic energy to the moon . . .

PICARD
Our options?

GEORDI
We did everything by the book and a little extra . . . we need more time or more power, and we're short on both. I'll take a look and see if there are any rules I haven't broken.

PICARD
Keep me advised.

Geordi EXITS. Picard turns toward Q with loathing in his eyes . . .

RIKER

We know you're behind this, Q . . . .

Q

(re: the jumpsuit)

It's not at all my best color . . . behind what . . . what are you blathering about, Riker . . . ?

Picard moves to confront him . . .

PICARD

What kind of twisted pleasure does it give you to bring terror into their lives . . . ?

Q

What? Whose lives?

PICARD

The millions of people down there who are watching as their moon falls out of the sky . . .

Q

I haven't the vaguest idea what you're talking about . . . and I have a much more serious problem . . . I am no longer a member of the Continuum. My superiors have decided to punish me.

Picard frowns . . . refusing to participate with this game of Q's . . .

PICARD

And punish us as well, it seems . . .

He ignores Q, moves away . . .

Q

They said I've spread too much chaos through the universe, and they have stripped me of all my powers.

They look at him with disbelieving eyes. Off their reaction—

Q

You do not believe me . . . ? Would I humiliate myself like this?

RIKER

If it served your purposes, yes.

Q

It is the truth. I stand before you, defrocked. I'm condemned to be a member of this lowest of species. A normal, imperfect, lumpen human being.

TROI

Turning you into a human was part of their punishment . . . ?

Q

No, it was my request. I could have chosen to exist as a Markoffian sea lizard or a Belzoidian flea, anything I wished—so long as it was mortal—but I only had a fraction of a second to mull and I chose . . . "this" . . . and asked them to bring me here . . .

TROI

Why?

Q

(moving to Picard)

Because in all the universe you are the closest thing I have to a friend, Jean-Luc.

Q smiles to Picard . . . Picard's look says it all. Data aims a Tricorder at Q.

DATA

He is reading as fully human.

Q

(looks around the Bridge)

Is there an echo in here?

TROI

I'm even sensing an emotional presence in him. I would normally describe it as being terrified.

Q

How rude.

Enough of this . . . Picard rises, moves back into the fray.

PICARD

Q, what is it you want . . .

Q

Your compassion . . .

(a beat, off Picard's look)

All right . . . Sanctuary on your ship . . . dreary as that may sound to both of us . . .

PICARD

Return the moon to its orbit.

Q

I have no powers. Q the ordinary.

PICARD

Q, the liar. Q, the misanthrope.

Q

Q, the miserable. Q, the desperate. What must I do to convince you people . . . ?

WORF

Die.

Q

Very clever, Worf. Eat any good books lately?

PICARD

Fine. You wish to be treated as a human?

Q

Absolutely.

PICARD

Mister Worf, throw him in the brig.

WORF

Delighted, Captain.

Q

Jean-Luc . . . you can't do this . . . .

Worf moves to him . . .

WORF

You will walk or I will carry you.

Q

Given the options—I'll walk.

As they EXIT . . .

Q

(to Picard)

You've disappointed me, Jean-Luc . . . I'm very disa . . .

And Worf closes the turbolift doors . . . . Riker and Picard exchange a glance.

18A INTERIOR TURBOLIFT (FORMERLY SCENE 19)

Worf leads him along the corridor . . . .

Q

It was a mistake . . . I never should have picked human . . . I knew it the minute I said it. To think of the future in this shell . . . forced to cover myself with fabric because of outdated human morality, to say nothing of being too hot or too cold, growing feeble as the years pass, losing my hair, catching a disease, being ticklish, sneezing, having an itch, a pimple, bad breath, having to bathe . . .

WORF

(acknowledges)

Too bad.

19 INTERIOR CORRIDOR (FORMERLY SCENE 20)

Q and Worf exit the turbolift and walk down the corridor.

Q

''Klingon'' . . . I should have said ''Klingon.'' In my heart, I *am* a Klingon, Worf . . . . So you understand I could never survive in confinement . . .

The universe has been my back yard . . . . This is cruel and unusual punishment. As a fellow Klingon, if you would speak to the captain on my behalf, I would be eternally grateful . . . which doesn't mean as much as it used to, I admit.

19A INTERIOR DETENTION CELL (OPTICAL)

WORF
Be quiet or disappear back where you came from.

Worf ushers him in.

Q
I can't disappear any more than you can win a beauty contest. If I ask a very simple question, do you think you can grasp it without troubling your intellect too much . . . ? Ready? If I still had powers, would I permit you to lock me away?

WORF
You have fooled us too often, Q.

Q
Perspicacity incarnate. Please don't feel compelled to tell me the story of "the boy who cried *Worf*"?

WORF
Computer, activate force field.

The room is now divided by a rim of lights. Q tests the force field. We see the EFFECT. Worf leaves. A security guard holds position . . .

Q
(yelling at Worf)
I demand to be let out of here, do you hear me? You will deactivate this cell immediately.
(no answer)
"Romulan." I should have said "Romulan," you Klingon goat!

And he sits down in frustration.

20 OMITTED

21 INTERIOR READY ROOM

Picard and Riker seated at the desk.

PICARD
The question is—what sort of jaded game is he playing this time?

RIKER
Maybe he just wants a big laugh. He'll take Bre'el IV to the edge of disaster, then pull the moon back.

PICARD
(thoughtful)
Or he may have nothing to do with it at all.

RIKER
Do you honestly believe Q is telling the truth?

PICARD
Oh, I agree that is highly unlikely. But we have to proceed with our current dilemma as though Q is powerless to prevent it, don't we?

RIKER
As he sits, and watches us struggle . . .

PICARD
I don't see much choice.
(speaking to com)
Mister Worf, hail the Bre'el IV science station . . .

WORF (com voice)
They're standing by, Captain . . .

Picard turns on his monitor to reveal Garin and the Scientist.

PICARD
I'm sorry to report that our first attempt to restore the moon to its proper orbit has failed.

GARIN

We have less than twenty-five hours before impact . . . .

RIKER

Our chief engineer is working on ways to reinforce our tractor beam.

PICARD

There is hope . . . but if you have an evacuation plan . . .

GARIN

We have already started moving people from the coastal areas of the Western Continent. . . .

PICARD

(acknowledges)

We will make another attempt shortly. . . . Picard out.

He turns off the monitor . . .

RIKER

I gotta tell you Geordi is not optimistic . . .

Suddenly, the room begins to glow . . . . Picard and Riker exchange glances and head for the door.

PICARD

What the devil . . . ?

As they exit . . .

22 INTERIOR MAIN BRIDGE

The EFFECT continues. Picard and Riker ENTER from the ready room . . . Data and supernumeraries are reacting.

RIKER

Data . . . ?

DATA

Sensors are showing broadband emissions . . . including berthold rays . . . .

RIKER

Lethal?

DATA

No, Commander. Overall exposure is under seventy-five rems. Very low intensity. More like a soft medical scan. . . . I would speculate that we are being probed. . . .

PICARD

By whom?

DATA

The sensors cannot identify point of origin. It seems to be coming from all around us. . . .

Off their reactions . . .

22A INTERIOR ENGINEERING

Geordi reacts as the EFFECT rolls by. . . .

22B INTERIOR DETENTION (OPTICAL)

Q is asleep with a rather pleasant expression on his face as the EFFECT zips right through the force fields holding him prisoner. . . . As the probe penetrates the field there is an additional EFFECT. The probe finds him and lingers on his face . . . and as it suddenly zips away. . . .

FADE OUT.

ACT TWO

FADE IN:

22C EXTERIOR SPACE—THE *ENTERPRISE* (OPTICAL)

In orbit.

23 INTERIOR DETENTION (OPTICAL)

Picard ENTERS. . . . Q, lying on his bunk, opens an eye. . . .

Q

Ah, you've come to apologize . . . how nice . . . no offense taken . . . all is forgiven . . .

He rises.

PICARD

Enough. I want to know exactly what is going on, Q. . . .

Q

But, Jean-Luc, how can I know what is going on? I have been in this dungeon of yours, helpless and alone . . . bored to tears . . .

PICARD

We have a moon that is inexplicably falling out of orbit . . . and now the ship has been probed with berthold radiation. . . .

Q

(covering up some concern)

When? I wasn't aware of it.

(off Picard's look)

Truthfully, Jean-Luc. I have been entirely preoccupied by a most frightening experience of my own. A couple of hours ago, I started realizing this body was no longer functioning properly . . . I felt weak, the life oozing out of me. . . . I could no longer stand . . . and then I lost *consciousness* . . .

PICARD

You fell asleep. . . .

Q

It's terrifying . . . how can you stand it day after day . . . ?

PICARD

One gets used to it. . . .

Q

What other dangers are in store for me . . . ? I am totally unprepared for this. . . . I need guidance. . . .

Picard frowns, getting nowhere.

PICARD

I am unwilling to play along, Q. If you must keep up the charade, you will do it alone. . . .

As he starts to leave . . .

Q

Jean-Luc . . . wait . . .

He walks into the FORCE FIELD . . . bounces back . . .

Q

This is getting on my nerves . . . now that I have nerves. . . .

Picard pauses at the door . . .

Q

You have a moon with a deteriorating orbit. . . . I've known moons across the universe . . . big ones, small ones. . . . I'm an expert. . . . I can help you with this one . . . if you let me out of here.

Picard reacts.

PICARD

Q, we're dealing with millions of lives . . . if you have the power to . . .

Q

I have no power. . . . But I still have the knowledge . . . locked in this puny brain. You cannot afford to dismiss that advantage, can you?

Picard must hold himself back . . . finally keys his insignia . . .

PICARD

Mister Data, please report to detention cell three. Computer, remove the force field.

(to Q)

If this is what I must do to save those lives, I will.

The field is removed. Q tentatively crosses past the barrier. . . .

PICARD

(continuing)

You will not be left alone for one moment while you are on this ship, Q. If you are human, which I seriously doubt, I suggest you work hard to earn our welcome.

Q

Oh, I'll earn your welcome. You only dislike me. There are others in the cosmos that truly despise me.

Data ENTERS.

PICARD

You are hereby assigned to Q for the remainder of his stay. . . . escort him to Mister La Forge in engineering . . .

Q

Can I have a Starfleet uniform . . . ?

That does not require an answer. . . . Picard EXITS. . . . Data studies Q.

Q

What are you looking at?

DATA

I was considering the possibility that you are telling the truth . . . and really are human.

Q

It's the ghastly truth, *Mister* Data . . . I can now stub my toe with the best of them.

DATA

(recognizing)

An irony.

(off Q's reaction)

It would mean you have achieved in disgrace what I have always aspired to be.

A beat on Data, then . . .

23A INTERIOR CORRIDOR

Q accompanying Data to engineering.

Q

Humans are such commonplace little creatures. They roam the galaxy looking for something, and they don't even know what it is.

DATA

The human race has an enduring desire for knowledge, and for new opportunities to improve itself. . . .

Q

There is certainly room for improvement. The truth is, Data, they are a minor species in the grand scheme. Not worth your envy . . .

DATA

Oh, I do not feel envy.

Q

Good.

DATA

I feel nothing at all. That is part of my dilemma. I have the curiosity of the human . . . but there are some questions I will never be able to answer. . . . What is it like to laugh or to cry or to experience any human emotion . . . ?

Q

Believe me, life's a lot simpler without feelings . . . a *lot* simpler. . . .

And as they proceed down the hall . . .

24 INTERIOR ENGINEERING (OPTICAL)

Q is with Data and Geordi, *bending over,* studying data, photographs at the pool table. . . .

GEORDI

The moon will hit its perigee in ten hours . . . we match its trajectory . . . increase emitter coolant rate so we can apply continuous warp-equivalent power nine to the tractor beam. We can keep pushing it for nearly seven hours, and I think that might do it . . . but there's a problem. . . .

DATA

The *Enterprise* will be dangerously close to the atmosphere.

GEORDI

That's the problem.

Q

This is incredible.

GEORDI

You see something here, Q?

Q

I think I just hurt my back. I'm feeling pain. I don't think I like it. What's the right thing to say . . . "ow"?

GEORDI

(frustrated)

Yeah . . .

Q

Ow. I don't think I can straighten up. . . .

DATA
(keying insignia)
Medical assistance to engineering . . .

GEORDI
Q, I've got a few people down on Bre'el IV who are gonna be hurt if we don't . . .

Q
(interrupting)
Yes, with your marvelous plan, you will not only tear the moon to pieces . . . but your precious ship as well.

GEORDI
You have a better idea . . . ?

Q
I would certainly begin by examining the cause and not the symptom.

GEORDI
We've done that, Q . . . and there's no way to determine . . .

Q
This is obviously the result of a large celestial object passing through at near right angles to the plane of the star system . . . probably a black hole . . .

DATA
Can you recommend a way to counter the effect?

Q
Simple. Change the gravitational constant of the universe.

GEORDI
(reacts)
What . . . ?

Q
Change the gravitational constant of the universe. And thereby alter the mass of the asteroid . . .

GEORDI

Redefine gravity. How am I supposed to do that?

Q

You just do it. Where is that doctor anyway . . . ?

DATA

Geordi is trying to say that changing the gravitational constant of the universe is beyond our capabilities.

Q

Oh. In that case, never mind.

Beverly ENTERS from the engineering turbolift.

Q

Ah, Doctor Crusher, Starfleet shipped you back into exile, I see . . .

DATA

Q says he has hurt his back . . .

BEVERLY

(disbelieving)

Uh huh.

Geordi's mind is working now . . . as Beverly examines Q's back, he goes to the computer, starts working on something . . .

BEVERLY

Well, I wouldn't believe it if I didn't see it with my own eyes, . . . and I still don't believe it . . . according to this, you have classic back trauma, muscle spasms . . .

Q

I've been under a lot of stress. Family problems . . .

BEVERLY

You won't get any sympathy from me. You've been a pain in our backside often enough . . .

Q

Your bedside manner is admirable, Doctor. I'm sure your patients recover quickly just to get away from you.

She gives him a hypospray and he immediately feels better . . . at the computer—

GEORDI

You know, it might work . . . .

Data moves to Geordi . . .

GEORDI

We can't change the gravitational constant of the *universe*,, but if we wrap a low-level warp field around that moon, we could reduce *its* gravitational constant . . . make it lighter so we *can* push it.

Q

Glad I could help.

(reacts)

Ow . . . I think.

BEVERLY

Now what?

Q

Something's wrong with my stomach . . . .

BEVERLY

It hurts?

Q

It's making noise.

BEVERLY

Maybe you're hungry.

25–28 OMITTED

29 INTERIOR TEN-FORWARD

Q and Data ENTER . . .

Q

What do I ask for? I've never eaten before.

DATA

The choice of meal is determined by individual tastes.

Q

What do you like?

DATA

Although I do not require sustenance, I occasionally ingest a semiorganic nutrient suspension in a silicon-based liquid medium.

They sit at the bar.

Q

Is it good?

DATA

It would be more accurate to say it is "good *for* me" as it lubricates my bio-functions.

Q

It doesn't sound too appealing. What else is there?

DATA

A wide variety of items . . . the replicator can make anything you desire.

Q

How am I supposed to know what I desire?

DATA

I have observed that many food selections are influenced by the mood of the person ordering . . .

Q

I'm in a dreadful mood. . . . Get me something appropriate. . . .

DATA

(considers)

When Counselor Troi is in an unhappy mood, she often has something chocolate . . .

Q

Chocolate . . .

DATA

For example, a hot fudge sundae. I cannot speak from personal experience, but I have seen it often has a profound psychological impact.

A waiter comes over.

Q

I'll have ten hot fudge sundaes.

The waiter reacts.

DATA

I have never seen anyone eat ten.

Q

I'm in a really bad mood. And since I've never eaten before, I should be very hungry.

The waiter shrugs and moves off. Q reacts as he sees—

29A ANGLE—GUINAN

Down the bar, coming out from the back. . . . She sees him, reacts . . . Q frowns . . .

Q

(sotto, to Data)

This . . . is not a moment I've been looking forward to.

She slowly comes over . . . with a controlled grin, a long beat as they look each other. Finally . . .

GUINAN

I heard you were drummed out of the Continuum.

Q

I prefer to look at it as a significant career change.

GUINAN

Just one of the boys, huh?

Q

One of the boys with an IQ of two-thousand and five.

DATA

The captain and much of the crew are not yet convinced that he is truly human.

GUINAN

Is that right?

Guinan never takes her eyes off Q as she casually picks up a fork from behind the counter . . . and sharply stabs Q's hand . . .

Q

AAAH . . .

GUINAN

He's human.

Q

(to Data)

This is a dangerous creature. You have no idea . . . How could Picard allow her to join the crew and not me . . . ?

GUINAN

It must be frightening . . . totally defenseless . . . after being omnipotent all those centuries . . .

Q

(intimidated)

I'm warning you . . . I still have friends in high places . . .

GUINAN

. . . terrorizing one race after another . . . teasing them like helpless animals . . . delighting at the fear of your victims . . .

Q

(sarcastic)

From now on, I'll do missionary work . . .

DATA

That would be a very noble cause, Q.

GUINAN
(re: Data)
You could learn a few things from this one.

Q
Sure, the robot who teaches the course in humanities.

DATA
I am an android, not a robot.

Q
I *beg* your pardon.

GUINAN
Get used to it, Q.

Q
What?

GUINAN
Begging. You're a pitiful excuse for a human, and the only way you're going to survive is by the charity of others.

She moves down the bar.

Two waiters bring Q's ten hot fudge sundaes. . . . He's depressed, turns to Data, sighs—

Q
I'm not hungry.

On Data's reaction . . .

30 INTERIOR MAIN BRIDGE

Picard, Riker, Worf, supernumeraries.

WORF
Captain, sensors are picking up a cloud of energetic plasma . . . bearing three-four-one Mark two-zero . . . range twelve kilometers and closing . . .

PICARD
On screen.

30A ANGLE—INCLUDE MAIN VIEWER (OPTICAL)

An amorphous mass, shapeless and changing.

WORF
Energy patterns are reading as highly organized . . .

RIKER
(to Picard)
A life-form?

PICARD
Mister Worf, attempt to make contact . . .

WORF
Receiving a signal, sir . . . on speaker . . .

Worf puts it on speaker. It sounds like a series of computer modem signals . . . hurts the ears . . .

RIKER
Computer, analysis of signal . . .

COMPUTER
Signal patterns indicate intelligence. Unable to derive necessary referents to establish translation matrix.

30B INTERIOR TEN-FORWARD (OPTICAL)

As people react to the cloud in view out the windows. Guinan reacts more than the others . . .

GUINAN
Calamarain . . .

. . . And as she glances at Q, who hasn't seen it yet . . . there is a shot of light from the cloud which shoots through the window . . . and immediately isolates Q . . . he yells . . . avoids them briefly . . . but they move after him . . . as Data reacts . . .

30C INTERIOR MAIN BRIDGE

As before.

WORF
We are being hit by a field of energetic tachyons . . . penetrating the hull . . . location . . . deck ten . . . forward . . .

PICARD
Red Alert.

RIKER
Increase power to shields . . .

GEORDI (com voice)
Increasing power by twenty percent . . .

WORF
No effect . . .

GEORDI (com voice)
Increasing to forty percent . . .

WORF
Still no effect . . .

30D INTERIOR TEN-FORWARD (OPTICAL)

The light EFFECT has wrapped up Q's legs as he scrambles helplessly to escape. Data tries to assist, but the light EFFECT effectively blocks him off . . .

30E INTERIOR ENGINEERING

Geordi working feverishly . . .

GEORDI
Adjusting shield harmonics. . . . Diverting power to the forward grids.

30EA INTERIOR MAIN BRIDGE

As before.

WORF
The added harmonics are blocking the tachyon field.

30F INTERIOR TEN-FORWARD (OPTICAL)

The light EFFECT is cut off . . . Q is freed . . . still terrified . . . rolling on the ground . . .

Q

HELP ME. SOMEBODY HELP ME . . . !

On Guinan's reaction . . .

GUINAN

How the mighty have fallen.

FADE OUT.

ACT THREE

FADE IN:

31 EXTERIOR SPACE—THE *ENTERPRISE* (OPTICAL)

Orbiting Bre'el. The plasma cloud is still ominously present.

PICARD (voice-over)
Captain's log, supplemental. We have sustained light damage from an attack by an alien species known as the Calamarain. They apparently have a grievance with Q . . . no doubt one of many life-forms that do.

32 INTERIOR BRIDGE

Picard, Riker, Data, Worf, Troi are on the bridge. Q paces nervously. His rhetoric remains, but there is an underlying fear that we've never seen from him.

Q
The Calamarain are not very hospitable creatures. They exist as swirls of ionized gas.

PICARD
What did you do to them to motivate such a vengeance?

Q
Nothing bizarre. Nothing grotesque.

RIKER
You tormented them—

Q
A subjective term, Riker. One creature's torment is another creature's delight. They simply have no sense of humor . . . a character flaw with which you can personally identify.

RIKER
I say we turn him over to them.

Q

Oh, my mistake . . . you do have a sense of humor . . . a dreadful one.

RIKER

I'm serious.

Picard is adding things up . . . realizing . . .

PICARD

Of course. You knew this would happen, didn't you?

Q

I assure you one cannot anticipate the Calamarain, Picard. . . . They're intelligent, yes . . . but undependable . . . very flighty . . .

PICARD

But you have so many enemies, Q, of various shapes and sizes. . . . Certainly you must have been concerned that once you became mortal . . . some of them might try to look you up . . .

Q

It occurred to me.

PICARD

With all your chatter about "friendship," the real reason you're here is for protection, isn't it?

Q

You're so bright, Jean-Luc. Yes, of course, you're correct. I know human beings. You are all sopping over with compassion and forgiveness. The human race can't wait to absolve almost any offense. It's an inherent weakness in the breed.

PICARD

What you call weakness, some of us would call strength.

Q

Call it what you want, Picard. I know you'll protect me even though I've tortured you now and again . . .

RIKER

Fighting off every species you've insulted would be a full-time mission. And it's not the one I signed up for.

PICARD

Indeed. Human or not, I want no part of you. We will deposit you at the first starbase. Let them deal with you. . . .

Q

But I can be a valuable member of your team, Picard . . .

PICARD

As though you have the faintest notion about team*work* or cooperation . . .

Q

I can learn. I'm human.

PICARD

Then I suggest you apply to Starfleet Academy . . .

RIKER

Don't use me as a reference.

DATA

He *has* provided important theoretical guidance for Geordi's analysis of the Bre'el satellite, Captain.

Reactions. Surprise at Data speaking up on his behalf.

TROI

It seems you have an advocate, Q.

DATA

I am only stating a fact, Counselor.

Picard reluctantly acknowledges that fact . . . keys his insignia . . .

PICARD

Mister La Forge, your status?

33–34 OMITTED

INTERCUT:

35 INTERIOR ENGINEERING

At the console . . .

GEORDI
I've been putting together a program to extend the forward lobe of our warp field. The field coils are not designed to envelop such a large volume. But I'm attempting to modify their alignment parameters.

DATA
Maintaining field integrity will be difficult, Geordi.

GEORDI
I think we can do it manually. The moon's reaching its perigee in fourteen minutes . . .

36 INTERIOR MAIN BRIDGE

PICARD
Mister Data, escort Q to engineering . . .
(to Q)
You will assist Mister La Forge.

Data and Q EXIT.

PICARD
Mister Worf, hail the Bre'el IV science station.

36A INTERIOR TURBOLIFT

Data and Q . . . Q fuming . . .

Q
Picard really thinks I can't cut it on his starship . . . I can do anything his little trained minions can do.

DATA
I do not perceive that your skills are doubted, Q. I believe the captain is more concerned with your ability to interact successfully with . . . his "little trained minions."

The turbolift opens . . . they EXIT.

36B INTERIOR CORRIDOR—CONTINUOUS

Leading to engineering.

DATA

Human interpersonal relationships are most complex. . . . Your experiences may not have adequately prepared you.

Q

I don't want human interpersonal relationships. I just want to prove to Picard that I'm indispensable.

DATA

To function aboard a starship, or in any human activity, you will have to form relationships.

Q

Why does this have to be so hard . . . ?

DATA

Of more immediate importance is your ability to work within groups . . .

Q

I've never been any good in groups . . . it's difficult working in a group when you're omnipotent . . .

Moving down the corridor toward engineering . . .

37–38 OMITTED

39 INTERIOR MAIN BRIDGE (OPTICAL)

Doctor Garin and the scientist are on the main viewer. . . . Troi has left the bridge.

GARIN

The tides reached ten meters on the last orbit. They are already beginning to swell again. We have a lot of frightened people down here, Captain. . . .

PICARD

Your moon has begun moving toward its perigee, Doctor. . . . We are prepared to make our attempt . . .

SCIENTIST

(acknowledges)

Our population has already taken shelter . . . but I'm afraid no shelter will be adequate if you fail . . . especially for the people on the Western Continent.

GARIN

Whatever the results, we know you've done your best, Picard. It's appreciated.

PICARD

I'll keep you advised, Doctor. Picard out.

WORF

Captain, sensors are reading increased energy output from the Calamarain . . .

39A PICARD

Reacts . . .

GEORDI (com voice)

La Forge to bridge. The moon has reached its minimum orbital distance. . . . It's time, Captain . . .

RIKER

We'll have to lower shields . . .

PICARD

(knowing the risks)

Proceed.

(beat)

Mister Worf, keep a close eye on Q's friends out there . . .

WORF

Understood.

40 INTERIOR ENGINEERING

Geordi and supernumeraries are working the controls as Data and Q ENTER . . . Q, the "camp director" . . .

Q

Okay, everyone, here's what we're going to do . . .

Geordi reacts . . .

GEORDI

Q, everybody already knows what they're going to do, except for you. . . . Now here's what I need . . .

Q

La Forge, obviously my knowledge and experience exceed yours . . . by about a billion times . . . so if you'll just step aside gracefully . . .

GEORDI

(impatient)

Your experience will be most valuable to *me* if you can manually control the field integrity . . .

Q

(reacts)

Don't be foolish. That's a waste of my talents . . .

GEORDI

Get to the controls or get the hell out of here . . .

And he moves off to serious business . . .

GEORDI

Data, you're my liason to the bridge. . . . I'll need you with me. . . .

Q

(to Data)

Who does he think he is to give *me* orders . . . ?

DATA

Geordi thinks he is in command here . . . and he is correct.

Q swallows hard . . . moves to the controls . . . as Data moves to Geordi . . .

40A INTERIOR MAIN BRIDGE

RIKER
Engineering, holding at station keeping, range six hundred and forty meters.

DATA (com voice)
Containment fields to flight tolerance.

40B INTERIOR ENGINEERING

Q running the controls . . . moving to find Data monitoring sensors with Geordi . . .

DATA
Warp core to ninety percent.

GEORDI
Engage field coils. Tractor beam to standby. Field output . . . ? *Field output* . . . ?

Q
(reacts, bored)
Two-seventeen . . .

GEORDI
Impulse engines to full. Ready to engage tractor beam.

RIKER'S COM VOICE
Lowering shields. Engage tractor beam.

41 OMITTED

42 EXTERIOR SPACE—THE *ENTERPRISE* (OPTICAL)

As in the tease, the tractor beam locks onto the moon.

42A INTERIOR ENGINEERING

GEORDI
Extending warp field forward.

42B ANGLE—MONITOR (OPTICAL)

A computer graphic shows the field extending from the ship and embracing the moon . . . only it doesn't quite get it all . . .

PICARD (com voice)
Engineering, is that the forward limit?

DATA
Yes, Captain . . . we are unable to encompass the entire moon . . .

PICARD'S COM VOICE
Do you recommend we proceed . . . ?

A beat as they look to Geordi . . .

Q
(shakes his head)
The two parts of the moon will have different inertial densities . . .

42C ANGLE—MOVING WITH GEORDI

GEORDI
I can adjust the field symmetry to compensate . . .

Q
I doubt it.

GEORDI
You don't know what this ship can do, Mister . . .
(keying insignia)
Yes, Captain . . . I think it still might work . . . increasing power to tractor beam and warp field . . .

Q
(to La Forge)
And if you're wrong, the moon will crumble due to subspace stress. . . . Don't say I didn't warn . . .

GEORDI
Shut up, Q.

Leaving his post . . .

Q

I will not be spoken to in this manner. . . .

GEORDI

(do something about him)

Data . . .

DATA

Q, I strongly advise that you return to your post.

Q reacts, listens to Data, hangs his head, returns to his post. . . .

DATA

(checking readings)

Inertial mass of the moon has decreased to approximately two-point-five million metric tons . . .

GEORDI

It's working. We can move it. Firing impulse engines . . .

42D EXTERIOR SPACE—THE *ENTERPRISE* (OPTICAL)

As the impulse engines provide thrust . . .

43 INTERIOR MAIN BRIDGE (OPTICAL)

As before. The computer graphic is on the main viewer.

DATA (com voice)

The moon's trajectory has moved point-three percent . . . point-four percent . . .

Worf reacts to something he sees on sensors . . .

WORF

Emergency . . . shields up . . .

RIKER

Disengage tractor beam . . .

WORF

Calamarain attacking . . .

He's interrupted as the *Enterprise* suffers a massive impact . . .

WORF
Shields holding . . . tachyon field repelled . . .

GEORDI (com voice)
Captain, the impact of the blast is pushing us into the upper atmosphere. . . .

44–45A OMITTED

45B EXTERIOR SPACE—THE *ENTERPRISE* (OPTICAL)

Glows as it hits the atmosphere. . . .

45C INTERIOR ENGINEERING

DATA
Hull temperature rising . . . two thousand degrees . . . two thousand five hundred degrees.

GEORDI
Moving to full impulse power . . . we've gotta get out of here. . . .

45D INTERIOR MAIN BRIDGE

WORF
Calamarain are resuming attack . . .

Suddenly, the ship is shaken again . . . and now the light EFFECT invades the bridge . . .

WORF
They've overpowered the shields . . . hull penetration . . . deck thirty-six . . . engineering . . .

RIKER
Geordi, can you direct any more power to the shields . . . ?

45E INTERIOR ENGINEERING

GEORDI
We need all the power we have to get out of the atmosphere, Commander.

The LIGHT EFFECT reaches and grabs Q, who yells. . . . Data is on his feet on his way to help Q . . . who is being wrapped up in the EFFECT like a caterpillar in a cocoon . . . being raised up in the air . . .

Geordi gets an idea to repel the attack. . . .

GEORDI
(to a supernumerary)
Try activating the structural integrity field.

As Q is lifted, Data grabs him in a tug of war . . . when suddenly Data is enveloped by the EFFECT . . . Geordi reacts . . .

GEORDI
(yelling orders)
It's not working. Structural field harmonics on manual.

He moves to the console, begins making manual adjustments . . .

RIKER'S COM VOICE
Hull temperature falling, Geordi . . . we're in the clear. . . .

GEORDI
Diverting power to forward section. *Now.*

The light disappears. . . . Data and Q fall to the ground. . . . Geordi rushes to Data, who isn't moving. . . . Others join him. . . .

GEORDI
Data . . . Data . . . ?

Q, not getting any attention . . .

Q
What about me?

FADE OUT.

ACT FOUR

FADE IN:

46 OMITTED

46A EXTERIOR SPACE—THE *ENTERPRISE* (OPTICAL)

In orbit.

46B OMITTED

46C INTERIOR SICKBAY (FORMERLY SCENE 46B)

Data is unconscious. Geordi and Beverly are both working on him . . . Picard, Riker and Q watching. Q seems confused, unsure of how to act or what to do.

GEORDI

The charge nearly knocked out his positronic net.

RIKER

What can you do for him?

GEORDI

We'll try to discharge and reset the motor pathways, recouple autonomic nodes . . .

BEVERLY

There's overpressure in his fluidic systems, thermal shock . . . If he was mortal, he'd be dead.

Q

(with a subtext of guilt)

Let us not overstate matters here, Doctor . . . I *am* mortal and I survived . . .

They stare at him. . . .

Q

(off their reaction)

The cheers are overwhelming.

PICARD
(quietly seething)
You exceed your own standards of selfish preoccupation. Have you no concern for the officer who very probably saved your life?

Q does, but this is hard for him to admit. . . .

Q
(more hope than conviction)
He's strong, he'll survive.

GEORDI
Osmotic pressure still negative. Maybe if we bypassed the flow regulator . . .

BEVERLY
It would be helpful if everybody just got out of here now. . . .

GEORDI
We'll let you know as soon as there's anything to tell you.

Picard and Q EXIT . . . Riker lingers for business . . .

RIKER
Geordi, the moon's trajectory . . . ?

GEORDI
All we did was buy ourselves another orbit at most. . . . We can try again when it comes back to the perigee. . . .

RIKER
And when we drop our shields, the Calamarains go after Q again. . . .

GEORDI
(bitter about Data)
He's not worth it, Commander.

Riker acknowledges . . . EXITS.

47 INTERIOR READY ROOM

Picard sits at his desk, doing some busywork . . . sipping tea . . . a chime at the door . . .

PICARD

Come . . .

Q ENTERS . . . they take a beat to look at each other . . . and Q is in an unusually somber mood. . . .

Q

You're right, of course. I am extraordinarily selfish. It's served me so well in the past. . . .

PICARD

It will not serve you here.

Q

Don't be so hard on me, Jean-Luc. You've been mortal all your life. You know all about dying. I've never given it a second thought. Or a first thought for that matter.

(beat)

I could have been killed. If not for Data . . . that one, brief delay he created, I would have been gone. No more me. And nobody would have missed me, would they?

Picard looks across at Q for a long, long beat . . . no compassion from our captain here . . .

Q

And yet Data may have sacrificed himself for me. Why? Why would he risk his own life for mine?

PICARD

That is his special nature. *He* has learned the lessons of humanity well. . . .

Q

I ask myself if I would have done the same for him. And I am forced to realize the answer is no. And I feel . . . I feel *ashamed.*

PICARD

I am not your father confessor. You will not receive absolution from me, Q. You have brought nothing but pain and suffering to my crew. And to this very moment, I am not entirely convinced that this is still not your latest attempt at a bad joke.

Q

It is a bad joke. On me. I am the joke of the universe. The king who would be man.

(beat)

As I learn more and more about what it is to be human, I am more and more convinced that I will never make a good one. I just don't have what it takes, Jean-Luc. Without my powers, I'm frightened of everything. I'm a coward. I'm miserable.

(beat)

And I don't think I can go on this way.

And he is clearly broken. . . . He EXITS . . . on Picard's reaction . . .

47A–48A OMITTED

49 INTERIOR SICKBAY

Geordi and Beverly are still working on Data, who is conscious, but has not regained full use of his program . . .

Q ENTERS . . .

BEVERLY

He's going to be all right.

GEORDI

We're recalibrating his language circuits . . . he can't talk to us yet.

Q goes to Data's side. Data looks up at him.

Q

There are creatures in the universe who consider you the ultimate achievement, android. No feelings, no emotions—no pain. And yet you covet those qualities of humanity. Believe me, you are not missing anything.

(beat)
But if it means anything to you, Data . . . you are a better human than I.

He goes out and the doors close on him. Data looks at Beverly and Geordi. . . .

49A INTERIOR TURBOLIFT

Q ENTERS, morose . . .

Q
Where's the main shuttlebay?

COMPUTER VOICE
Main shuttlebay is located on Deck Four.

Q
Take me there . . .

50–55 OMITTED

56 INTERIOR BRIDGE

Picard, Riker, and Worf.

WORF
An unscheduled shuttlecraft has just been launched.

PICARD
On main viewer.

56A ANGLE—VIEWER (OPTICAL)

The shuttlecraft moves away from the ship.

PICARD
Opening hailing frequency.

WORF
Frequency open.

PICARD
Shuttle occupant. Identify yourself.

The screen changes to reveal Q in the shuttle cabin.

Q
Don't try to talk me out of it, Jean-Luc.

PICARD
Q? Return to the ship at once.

Q
I just can't get used to following orders.

WORF
Captain, the plasma cloud is moving toward the shuttle.

Q
It's easier this way. They won't bother you after I'm gone.

RIKER
Engineering, prepare to extend shields . . .

Q
Please, do not fall back on your tired cliché of charging to the rescue in the nick of time. . . . I do not wish to be rescued. . . . My life as a human being is a dismal failure. Maybe my death can have a little dignity.

PICARD
There is no dignity in suicide. . . .

Q
Yes, I suppose you're quite right. The death of a coward. So be it.
(beat)
Anyway, as a human, I'd die of boredom.

He pushes a button, goes off-line and the starfield with shuttlecraft returns . . . on reactions . . .

57–59 OMITTED

60 EXTERIOR SPACE (OPTICAL)

The Calamarain in the distance . . . closing on the shuttlecraft.

61–67 OMITTED

FADE OUT.

ACT FIVE

FADE IN:

68 EXTERIOR SPACE (OPTICAL)

As before, the Calamarain move toward the shuttlecraft.

69 INTERIOR MAIN BRIDGE

Picard frowns . . .

PICARD

This goes against all my better judgment . . .
(keys insignia)
Transporter room three, lock on to Shuttle One . . . beam it back to its bay.

ENGINEER'S VOICE

Aye, Captain . . .

PICARD

Well, it's a perfectly good shuttlecraft . . .

ENGINEER'S VOICE

Captain, unable to transport . . . . For some reason, I can't lock on . . .

RIKER

Worf, are you sensing any sort of interference from the Calamarain?

WORF

No, Commander, but they are continuing to move toward the shuttle.

RIKER

Geordi, extend shields around Shuttle One . . .

69A INTERIOR ENGINEERING

Geordi moving to action . . .

GEORDI
Extending shields . . .
(reacts)
Commander . . . the shields are frozen . . .

RIKER (com voice)
Cause . . .

GEORDI
Unknown.

69B INTERIOR MAIN BRIDGE

RIKER
Lock on tractor beam . . .

GEORDI (com voice)
Tractor beam is not functioning either . . .

RIKER
What the hell is going on?

70 INTERIOR SHUTTLECRAFT (OPTICAL)

Q, at the controls. Suddenly beside him, APPEARS a man dressed in the same clothes as Q's. Q reacts.

Q2
Not bad, Q. Not great. But not bad.

Q
(surprised)
Q . . .

Q2
Sacrificing yourself for these humans . . . ? Do I detect a selfless act . . . ?

Q
You flatter me. I'm only trying to put a quick end to a miserable existence.

Q2
(re: the suit)
What a dreadful color.

Q

What are you doing here?

Q2

I've been keeping track of you.

Q reacts, pleasantly surprised . . .

Q

Really? I always felt you were in my corner . . .

Q2

Actually, I was the one who got you kicked out . . .

(off Q's look)

You're incorrigible, Q, a lost cause. I can't go to a single solar system without apologizing for you . . . and I'm tired of it. . . .

Q

I wasn't the one who misplaced the entire Deltived asteroid belt . . .

Q2

This is not about me.

(beat)

I have better places to be. But somebody had to keep an eye on you in case you still found a way to cause trouble . . . even as a member of this limited species. . . .

Q2

(sarcastic)

I hope I've kept you amused.

Q2

Barely. But these humans are rather interesting . . . . I'm beginning to understand what you see in them. After all the things you've done, they're still intent on keeping you safe.

Q

A genetic weakness of the race.

Q2

And they're still at it. They just tried to beam you back or whatever they call it. . . . I stopped them. . . .

Q

(gallows humor)

Well then, if the Calamarain will just hurry up and finish this, we'll get you on your way. . . .

Q2

No, I put them on hold too. There's still this matter of the selfless act . . .

Q reacts . . .

Q2

You and I both know that the Calamarain would have eventually destroyed the *Enterprise* to get to you . . . and that's really why you left. . . .

Q

(sensing hope)

It was . . . a tiny bit selfless . . . wasn't it . . . ?

Q2

And there's my problem. I get back to the Continuum and tell them you committed a selfless act just before the end. . . . I'm gonna be tied up with questions and explanations for centuries. . . .

Q

Q, I've learned my lesson. . . .

Q2

(bullshit)

Remember who you're talking to here . . . all-knowing, all-seeing . . .

(sighs)

Fine. You have your powers back. Try to stay out of trouble . . .

He DISAPPEARS. Q smiles, rises . . . tries on his powers by snapping his fingers, immediately CHANGING his jump suit into a Starfleet uniform . . .

Q

And they wanted to destroy me, did they?

He holds out the palm of his hand.

71–79 OMITTED

80 EXTERIOR SPACE (OPTICAL)

The Calamarain disappear.

81 INTERIOR SHUTTLE (OPTICAL)

Q holding out the palm of his hand. There is now a glow on it.

Q

If you think I tormented you in the past, my little friends—wait until you see what I do with you now.

Q2's head comes down through the hull . . .

Q2 (voice-over)
(a warning)

Q—?

He stops.

Q

I was just seeing if you were still watching.

He blows on the palm of his hand. The glow is blown away. Q2 reacts, nods okay.

82 INTERIOR BRIDGE (OPTICAL)

Picard, Riker, Troi, Worf, Data, Geordi on the bridge.

DATA

Sir, the aliens have disappeared.
(beat)
And so has the shuttle.

RIKER

Scan the sector . . .

DATA

I have, sir.

PICARD

(reacts)

Well, I guess that's the end of Q.

A cue for the APPEARANCE of a Mexican mariachi band . . . Q as the lead trumpet . . .

Q

Au contraire, Mon Capitaine . . . heee's back . . .

And as they blare into a song . . . Q waves his arms and confetti is falling out of nowhere . . . and the crew finds fat cigars in their mouths . . . which they promptly discard. . . .

Q

I have been forgiven, embraced by my brothers and sisters of the Continuum . . . . I am immortal again, omnipotent again. . . .

RIKER

Swell.

Q

Don't fret, Riker . . . my good fortune is your good fortune.

Two beautiful babes APPEAR in bikinis with their arms around Riker. . . .

RIKER

I don't need your fantasy women, Q . . .

Q

You've become so stolid, Commander. . . . You weren't like this before the beard . . .

(off Riker's look)

Very well . . .

He snaps his fingers and the girls are now caressing Worf . . . who reacts . . .

PICARD

Q . . .

Q

But I feel like celebrating . . .

PICARD

I don't.

Q frowns, snaps his fingers . . . and the girls DISAPPEAR. . . .

PICARD

All of it.

Q snaps his fingers and the band DISAPPEARS, and Q is dressed again in the Starfleet uniform.

PICARD

Now, at the risk of being rude . . .

Q

Yes, I have once again overstayed my welcome. As a human, I was ill-equipped to thank you, Picard. But as myself, you have my everlasting gratitude.

(beat)

Until next time, of course. But before I go, there is a debt I must repay . . .

And he moves to Data . . .

Q

. . . to my professor of the humanities . . . I have decided, my dear Data, to give you something very, very special . . .

DATA

(reacts)

If your intention is to make me human, Q . . .

Q

No no no no no . . . don't be foolish . . . I would never curse you by making you human. . . . Let's just call it a going-away present.

Data reacts and Q grins at him and suddenly Q disappears and Data bursts into a belly laugh . . . reactions . . .

GEORDI
Uh, Data . . . Data? Why are you laughing?

Data collects himself.

DATA
I do not know. But it was a wonderful . . . *feeling.*

WORF
Bre'el IV hailing us, Captain.

PICARD
On screen, Lieutenant.

82A–89 OMITTED

90 ANGLE—INCLUDE MAIN VIEWER (OPTICAL)

Garin and the scientist are all smiles. . . .

GARIN
Captain Picard . . . you've done it . . .

PICARD
I'm sorry . . . ?

SCIENTIST
The moon is back in its normal orbit. How did you manage it?

PICARD
(reacts)
I didn't. Stand by, Bre'el IV . . .

RIKER
Let's see it, Worf . . .

The viewscreen changes to the moon in orbit around the planet . . .

PICARD
Mister Data, your analysis . . .

DATA
The moon's altitude is fifty-five thousand kilometers;

projected orbit is nearly circular. There is no further danger to the planet.

Picard and Riker exchange a look. Picard acknowledges, relieved . . .

PICARD

Good. Ensign, set a course for Station Nigala IV.

(sitting)

Perhaps there's a little humanity left in Q after all.

As he raises his hand to "engage," a cigar appears in it . . .

Q (voice-over)

(whispered so only he can hear it)

Don't bet on it, Picard.

91 OMITTED

92 EXTERIOR SPACE—THE *ENTERPRISE* (OPTICAL)

It warps away to continue its journey.

FADE OUT.

STAR TREK: THE NEXT GENERATION

QPid

(f.k.a. Q Love)

#40274-194

Teleplay by
Ira Steven Behr

Story by
Randee Russell
and
Ira Steven Behr

Directed by
Cliff Bole

STAR TREK: THE NEXT GENERATION

QPid

CAST

PICARD
RIKER
DATA
BEVERLY
TROI
GEORDI
WORF

COMPUTER VOICE

Non-Speaking

SUPERNUMERARIES

Q
VASH
SIR GUY OF GISBOURNE
ELDERLY SERVANT

Non-Speaking

VARIOUS ARCHEOLOGY
COUNCIL MEMBERS
A VULCAN COUNCIL MEMBER
TROOP OF MEN-AT-ARMS
EXECUTIONER
CASTLE GUARDS
SERVANTS
MEMBERS OF THE COURT

STAR TREK: THE NEXT GENERATION

QPid

SETS

INTERIORS

U.S.S. ENTERPRISE
MAIN BRIDGE
CAPTAIN'S READY ROOM
TEN-FORWARD
CORRIDOR
PICARD'S QUARTERS
VASH'S QUARTERS
MEETING ROOM

SHERWOOD FOREST
A GLADE

NOTTINGHAM CASTLE
MAID MARIAN'S CHAMBERS

EXTERIORS

U.S.S. ENTERPRISE
SHERWOOD FOREST
NOTTINGHAM CASTLE

STAR TREK: THE NEXT GENERATION

QPid

PRONUNCIATION GUIDE

clavicular	klaw-VICK-you-lahr

STAR TREK: THE NEXT GENERATION

QPid

TEASER

FADE IN:

1 EXTERIOR SPACE—THE *ENTERPRISE* (OPTICAL)

The ship orbits a small, orange-hued planet.

PICARD (voice-over)

Captain's log, stardate 44741.9. We have arrived at Tagus III, where the *Enterprise* is to serve as host of the Federation Archeology Council's annual symposium.

2 INTERIOR READY ROOM

PICARD, intensely studying his monitor screen.

PICARD (voice-over)

I look forward to giving tomorrow's keynote address with great anticipation.

The DOOR CHIME SOUNDS.

PICARD

Come.

TROI ENTERS. Picard barely glances up from the monitor. Troi smiles at Picard's preoccupation.

TROI

I thought you'd want to know, Captain, the council members have all been beamed aboard and assigned quarters.

PICARD

Excellent.

TROI
(a hint)
It really is quite late, Captain.

Picard motions her over to the monitor.

PICARD
Tell me, Counselor, in regard to my lecture, which do you suppose would provide greater clarity? A chronological structure, or a division of each excavation's findings into various sociological, religious, and environmental subgroupings?

TROI
I thought you had already decided on a chronological structure.

PICARD
(nodding; but not quite convinced)
Still, there is something to be said for a more scientific approach.

TROI
Captain, may I make a suggestion?

PICARD
By all means.

Troi finally has the captain's complete attention.

TROI
Relax! You've written a brilliant speech.

PICARD
It needs to be. Tomorrow I'll be addressing some of the greatest scientific minds in the Federation. Switzer, Klarc-Tarn-Droth, McFarland. Giants in the field of archeology. Next to them I'm nothing but an enthusiastic amateur.

TROI
I doubt they think of you as an amateur . . . not when it comes to the ruins of Tagus III.

PICARD
(modestly)
Well, I *have* done my homework . . . . I've examined the findings of every archaeological expedition conducted on the planet's surface . . .

TROI
It's unfortunate the Taguans no longer allow outsiders to visit the ruins.

PICARD
(wistful)
Indeed. Especially since we still know so little about their origin . . .

He gestures toward the monitor.

PICARD
Hopefully, I've been able to construct some intriguing theories of my own.

TROI
I'm sure the council members will agree that you have.

PICARD
(smiling)
Your support is appreciated, Deanna.

Picard stands.

PICARD
Screen off.

Close-up of screen as it goes blank.

3 INTERIOR PICARD'S QUARTERS

The door OPENS. Picard ENTERS looking somewhat fatigued.

The first thing he notices—is a *Horga'hn* sitting on his desk. Picard looks at it, curious . . . Where the hell did this thing come from? Then . . .

VASH (O.S.)
Bring back any memories?

Picard turns to see VASH stepping out of the shadows near the door. For a moment he's taken completely off-guard.

PICARD

Vash? How did you get in here?

She smiles . . . and moves closer.

VASH

I came in through the window.

Picard barely has the chance to regain his aplomb when she snakes an arm around him and they kiss. It's going to last awhile.

FADE OUT.

ACT ONE

FADE IN:

4 INTERIOR PICARD'S QUARTERS—MORNING

Vash, wearing the same outfit from the night before, and Picard, in his dress uniform, sit at a table eating a breakfast of rolls and jam. Though there is still a warm afterglow from the evening's activities, Picard is slightly ill at ease about playing host to Vash aboard the *Enterprise.*

PICARD

I had no idea you were a member of the archaeology council.

Vash only smiles.

PICARD

You are a member?

(a beat)

Aren't you?

VASH

(smiling)

More or less.

PICARD

Why have you come to Tagus III?

VASH

To see you, of course.

PICARD

Is that the only reason?

VASH

Isn't it enough?

She's moves closer to him. It's an intimate moment.

PICARD

(smiling)

I wish I could believe you.

VASH
(smiling right back)
I'd be disappointed if you did.
(a beat)
I really have missed you, Jean-Luc.

But before they can act on a mutual impulse, the DOOR CHIMES. Picard waits until Vash steps away before answering.

PICARD
Come.

BEVERLY strides in.

BEVERLY
I'm sorry I'm late . . .
(noticing Vash)
Oh, excuse me. I didn't know you had company.

PICARD
That's quite all right, Doctor. Beverly Crusher, allow me to introduce Vash. A friend of mine with the archeology council.

The two women exchange greetings.

BEVERLY
(to Vash)
I didn't mean to interrupt. The captain and I often share morning tea.

VASH
Yes, Jean-Luc has told me all about you.

BEVERLY
Really? When was that?

VASH
On Risa. Where we met.

Beverly is finding this all very interesting.

BEVERLY
I see.

(to Picard)

That must have been during your vacation last year.

PICARD

(giving nothing away)

So it was.

BEVERLY

(to Vash)

I'm surprised he never mentioned you.

VASH

So am I.

She shoots Picard a look, but no explanation is forthcoming.

VASH

Are you busy, Doctor?

BEVERLY

Not at the moment.

VASH

I was wondering—I would love to see some more of this marvelous ship . . .

BEVERLY

I'd be delighted to show it to you. If that's all right with you, Jean-Luc.

PICARD

Of course.

But he doesn't seem thrilled at the prospect. As Vash passes him on the way out . . .

VASH

(sotto voce)

Don't worry, I promise to behave myself.

Picard does not look reassured.

5 INTERIOR TEN-FORWARD

The lounge is only lightly populated at the moment.

Riker is seated alone having a drink.

Beverly and Vash ENTER.

BEVERLY

And this is Ten-Forward, where the council's welcoming reception is to be held this afternoon.

VASH

(liking what she sees)

I couldn't think of a better location.

(a beat)

Tell me, does Jean-Luc come here often?

BEVERLY

No, not often.

VASH

I didn't think so.

BEVERLY

The captain is a very private man.

VASH

He certainly acted that way when we first met.

(smiling)

But I managed to loosen him up.

Beverly would definitely like to learn more about this woman.

BEVERLY

Would you like something to drink?

VASH

Please.

Beverly walks over to the bar. Vash checks out the view from the window as Riker APPROACHES.

RIKER

Eternity never looked so lovely.

VASH

Excuse me?

RIKER

I was referring to the view. Eternity never looked so lovely.

Vash gives him a shrewd appraisal.

VASH

You must be Commander Riker.

RIKER

(surprised)

I'm afraid you have me at a disadvantage.

VASH

I didn't mean to interrupt. I believe you were about to tell me that my eyes are as mysterious as the stars.

Riker is intrigued. How the hell did she know?

RIKER

(thinks he's figured it out)

You're a Betazoid.

VASH

Not at all. It's just that Jean-Luc does quite a good imitation of you.

RIKER

He does?

Beverly comes back with the drinks.

BEVERLY

I see you two have met.

RIKER

Not exactly.

BEVERLY

Vash is a member of the archeology council. And a friend of the captain.

RIKER

So I've gathered.

BEVERLY
They met during his visit to Risa.

RIKER
On Risa?
(amused)
That must have been a better vacation than he let on.

VASH
You mean he never mentioned me to you either?

RIKER
Believe me, if he had, I would have remembered.

VASH
(a bit frustrated)
You'd think he'd have told someone about me.

COMPUTER VOICE
Doctor Crusher, please report to sickbay.

BEVERLY
On my way.
(to Vash)
I'm afraid I won't be able to finish up our tour.
(a beat)
Perhaps Commander Riker could fill in for me.

RIKER
It would be my pleasure.

Beverly leaves. Riker and Vash head for the door.

VASH
So you're the one who asked Jean-Luc to buy the *Horga'hn.*

RIKER
That was me.

VASH
Tell me, Commander, do you collect sexual fertility symbols?

RIKER

I wouldn't call it a very large collection.

And they're out the door.

6 INTERIOR BRIDGE

DATA and GEORDI at the science station, WORF at tactical. N.D.'s elsewhere.

Riker and Vash EXIT the aft turbolift.

RIKER

And that brings us to the main bridge, the command center of the *Enterprise,* and the end of our tour.

He brings her over to the science station.

RIKER

Vash, I'd like you to meet Commander La Forge and Commander Data . . .

An exchange of greetings. Riker gestures over to Worf, who looks on with disapproval.

RIKER

And this is Lieutenant Worf.
(noticing Worf's scowl)
Something wrong, Lieutenant?

WORF

Sir, I was not informed that council members had been granted bridge clearance.

RIKER

I think we can make an exception in this case, Mister Worf. Vash is the captain's guest.

Interested glances all around. Worf is somewhat at a loss for what to say.

WORF
(finally)

Welcome aboard.

Riker leads Vash over to the command area.

VASH

Is this where Jean-Luc sits?

RIKER

(pointing it out)

That's the big chair.

To everyone's surprise, she sits down in it. It provides a definite sense of power.

VASH

I can see where being a starship captain does have its rewards.

PICARD (voice-over)

I'm glad you approve.

All eyes turn to Picard who has just exited the ready room. Vash stands.

VASH

Jean-Luc. Commander Riker was just showing me the bridge.

Picard looks at Riker.

RIKER

Doctor Crusher was called to sickbay.

Picard nods. An awkward beat of silence.

PICARD

So, did you enjoy your tour?

VASH

Very much.

PICARD

Good.

Another awkward moment.

VASH

I guess I'll head back to my room now and get ready for the reception.

PICARD

By all means.

(a beat)

Well, I suppose I'll see you then.

VASH

I look forward to it.

She turns and makes the long walk back up the ramp to the turbolift.

RIKER

(watching her go)

Fascinating woman.

No comment from Picard.

7 ANGLE ON

Data and Geordi. Geordi has also watched Vash EXIT the bridge.

As the turbolift doors close, he breaks into a grin.

DATA

You find something humorous, Geordi?

GEORDI

Didn't you notice how ill at ease the captain seemed around Vash?

DATA

Yes. However, I see nothing amusing in his hostility toward her.

GEORDI

That wasn't hostility, Data.

(off Data's look)

He likes her.

(a beat)

A lot.

Still smiling, Geordi turns back to the science monitor. A puzzled Data is left pondering the intricacies of human relationships.

8 EXTERIOR SPACE—THE *ENTERPRISE* (OPTICAL)

The ship maintains standard orbit.

9 INTERIOR TEN-FORWARD

The reception. COUNCIL MEMBERS mingle with the crew. A rather informal time is being had by all.

10 NEW ANGLE

Vash has cornered TROI over by a buffet table.

VASH
I don't understand; I thought being ship's counselor meant the captain confided in you.

TROI
He does. When he feels it's necessary.

VASH
And he never spoke to you about me?

TROI
Not that I can recall.

VASH
Not even a hint?

TROI
You must understand, the captain is a very . . .

TROI & VASH
(together)
Private man.

VASH
I know . . .

She spots Picard, who is deep in discussion with a Vulcan council member.

VASH
Will you excuse me?

TROI
Certainly.

Vash walks off.

11 NEW ANGLE

Vash passes by Worf, Geordi, Beverly, and Data.

WORF
(still watching Vash)
Nice legs.
(off Geordi's look)
For a human.

12 NEW ANGLE

Picard and the Vulcan.

PICARD
I agree, the Vulcan excavations on Tagus III were extensive. Unfortunately, they were confined to the northeastern part of the city.

Vash appears at his elbow.

VASH
Jean-Luc, we need to talk.

One look and Picard knows she means it.

PICARD
(to the Vulcan)
Pardon me.

He and Vash move to a private spot.

PICARD
The reception seems to be a success.

VASH
Forget the reception for a moment. How come you've never mentioned me to your friends?

PICARD
What would you have had me tell them?

VASH

Maybe that we met, for one thing. That we had an adventure together. Some fun . . .

PICARD

I'm afraid that wasn't possible.

VASH

Why not?

PICARD

It would have been . . . inappropriate.

VASH

I wasn't expecting you to go into any intimate details.

PICARD

A captain does not share his personal feelings with his crew.

VASH

Is that a Starfleet regulation? Or did you make that one up yourself?

PICARD

I'm sorry if you're upset.

VASH

And I'm sorry if my being here embarrasses you.

And with that she turns and walks away.

HOLD ON a perplexed Captain Picard.

13 INTERIOR MAIN BRIDGE

Riker at command. N.D.'s at conn and ops.

Picard ENTERS from the forward turbolift.

RIKER

How was the reception?

PICARD
(brusque)

Splendid.

He EXITS into the ready room.

14 INTERIOR READY ROOM

Picard ENTERS and stops as he SEES—

15 Q

Seated at the captain's desk, dressed in a Starfleet uniform.

Q

Jean-Luc! How wonderful to see you again.

ON PICARD'S REACTION . . .

FADE OUT.

ACT TWO

FADE IN:

16 INTERIOR READY ROOM—CONTINUOUS (OPTICAL)

As before.

Q

Well, don't just stand there, say something.

Picard advances into the room.

PICARD

Get out of my chair.

Q

I was hoping for something more along the lines of "Welcome back, Q. It's a pleasure to see you again, old friend."

PICARD

We are not friends.

Q

You wound me, mon Capitaine.

Q snaps his fingers, and now it's Picard who sits at his desk and Q who stands before him.

Q

There, perhaps now your manners will show some improvement.

PICARD

What brings you here, Q? Have you been banished from the Continuum once again?

Q

Hardly. They're still apologizing to me for the last time.

PICARD

Then what is it you want?

Q

Must I always have a reason to stop by? I was in the sector and . . .

(Picard doesn't buy it)

All right. You force a confession from me. The truth is I have a debt to settle.

PICARD

A debt?

Q

To you, Picard. And it gnaws at me. It interferes with each day.

PICARD

I have no idea what you're talking about . . .

Q

Without your assistance at our last encounter, I never would have survived. I would have taken my own life but for you, Jean-Luc.

PICARD

We all make mistakes.

Q

Your good deed made possible my reinstatement into the Continuum. And I resent owing you anything . . . so I'm here to pay up. . . . What shall it be? Tell me and I'll be gone . . .

PICARD

Just be gone. That will suffice nicely.

Q

No, it must be something . . . something . . .

(searching)

. . . *constructive.* My new word for the day.

PICARD

Some other time, all right? Right now I have several things to attend to.

Q

Yes, your speech. I've read it. I found it dull and pedantic. Much like yourself.

(an idea)

I could help you with it.

PICARD

No.

Q

You've never actually been to the ruins in Tagus III, have you?

PICARD

They've been sealed off for over a century.

Q

How can you write about what you haven't seen?

16A ANGLE (OPTICAL)

Q is suddenly wearing a safari suit . . .

Q

(brightening)

I'll take you there!

PICARD

Impossible. That would mean breaking Taguan law.

Q

Must you always be so ethical?

(thinking)

I suppose we could travel back in time. You could see what Tagus III was like two billion years ago. They really knew how to have fun in those days.

PICARD

I'm afraid my answer is still no. My lecture will have to stand on its own. Now, will you please leave my ship?

Q

Then you refuse my help?

PICARD

Completely.

A beat as Q broods. Then finally . . .

Q

(mildly)

You're simply impossible to find a gift for, Picard.

And he's gone.

PICARD

(to conn)

Commander Riker, report to my ready room.

Riker ENTERS.

RIKER

Yes, Captain?

PICARD

I've just been paid a visit by Q.

RIKER

Q?

(concerned)

Any idea what he's up to?

PICARD

He wants to do something nice for me.

Riker REACTS. That definitely sounds like trouble.

RIKER

I'll alert the crew.

OFF Picard's look of approval:

17 INTERIOR CORRIDOR—MINUTES LATER

Picard EXITS the turbolift. He heads down the corridor on the way to meet with one of the council officials. At the hall he hesitates, turns left instead of right.

18 NEW ANGLE

Picard HALTS at a doorway. RINGS the bell.

VASH (voice-over)

Who's there?

PICARD

It's me.

VASH (voice-over)

Who?

PICARD

Jean-Luc.

The door slides open. Vash stands in the entrance.

VASH

Yes.

PICARD

May I come in?

VASH

What for?

PICARD

To talk.

VASH

I'm listening.

PICARD

If it's all the same to you, I'd rather this discussion not take place in a public corridor.

He slips past her.

19 INTERIOR VASH'S QUARTERS

The first thing Picard notices are various digging tools piled in a corner. He looks over at Vash.

VASH

I thought these were "private" quarters.

Picard picks up a padd off the table.

20 INSERT PADD

A map of the ruins of Tagus III.

21 BACK TO SCENE

Picard places the padd back on the table.

PICARD

And I thought I was the only reason you came to Tagus.

VASH

I never fooled you for a second.

She moves closer to Picard.

VASH

Still, you are the most important reason.

PICARD

Am I?

Vash steps away.

VASH

That's the trouble with being such a well-known liar. Even when I tell the truth, no one believes me.

Picard refuses to be swayed.

PICARD

I'm afraid all this equipment will have to be confiscated.

VASH

Is that necessary?

PICARD

I could have you placed in the brig.

VASH

Why don't you?

PICARD

If the Taguans were to catch you down there . . .

VASH

You gave me the same warning about Sarthong V.

PICARD

I remember.

VASH

Well, it didn't stop me from going there. I brought back some very impressive artifacts, too.

PICARD

Which you no doubt sold for a nice profit.

VASH

(angry)

It's what I do!

PICARD

Not while you're on board my ship. I will not allow it.

VASH

Let's get one thing straight, Picard. I cannot change who I am for you or anyone else.

PICARD

Nor can I change who I am.

VASH

(calmly)

Then we have nothing more to say to each other.

PICARD

So it would seem.

Picard leaves. Vash sits at the table. She's depressed and upset.

22 NEW ANGLE (OPTICAL)

Q's head APPEARS from the bulkhead behind her. He's obviously overheard their discussion and found it fascinating.

23 INTERIOR CORRIDOR

As Troi, Geordi, and Data walk down it . . .

GEORDI

What do you think it is?

DATA

What do I think what is?

GEORDI

About her. That, you know, *gets* to the captain.

DATA

Perhaps it is their common interest in archaeology.

TROI

I don't think so.

DATA

But, Counselor, as an archaeologist, her company would certainly be intellectually stimulating to the captain.

GEORDI

She's not just stimulating his intellect, Data . . .

TROI

It's really none of our business.

They turn a corner and come face to face with . . .

23A Q (OPTICAL)

Leaning against a wall. Wearing a Starfleet uniform again.

Q

You want to know about Picard and that woman? I'll tell you . . .

We HEAR the SOUND of BIRDS CHIRPING in the air.

Q

(sneering)

It's love.

He DISAPPEARS.

24 INTERIOR PICARD'S QUARTERS (OPTICAL)

Picard ENTERS, disgruntled. He goes into his bedroom, which is dark. As he enters, he sees a figure under the covers in his bed. A slight smile creeps to his lips. He moves to the bed, pulls back the covers to reveal Q.

Q

Sleeping alone, Picard?

PICARD

I'm in no mood for your foolishness, Q.

Q

I thought there was something different about you. You seemed tense, preoccupied. Somewhat . . . smaller.

(a beat)

At first I thought it was that horrible lecture of yours. But I was mistaken.

PICARD

Whatever game you want to play will have to wait until tomorrow.

Picard gets into bed, but Q refuses to be ignored.

Q

I had such hopes for you, Jean-Luc. I thought you were a bit more evolved than the rest of your species. But now I realize you're as weak as all the others.

(a beat)

Still, it pains me to see the great Picard brought down by a woman.

Picard tries to feign lack of interest.

PICARD

What woman?

Q

Don't play coy with me, Captain. I witnessed your little spat with Vash. Nor will I soon forget that look of misery on your face. The pain. The anguish. If I didn't know better, I would have thought you were already married.

PICARD

You really must be bored, Q. You're letting your imagination run away with you.

Q

This human emotion of love is a dangerous thing, Picard. You are obviously ill equipped to handle it. She's found a vulnerability in you . . . a vulnerability that I've wanted to find for years. If I had known this sooner, I would have arrived as a female. Mark my words, Jean-Luc, this is your Achilles heel. . . .

PICARD

Believe what you wish.

Q

You deny you care for this woman?

Picard doesn't answer.

Q

Believe me, Picard, I'd be doing you a big favor if I simply turned her into a klabnian eel.

PICARD

(very seriously)

Stay away from her, Q.

Q

I only want to help . . . my debt to you . . .

PICARD

(interrupting)

. . . is hereby nullified. I don't want your help . . . your advice . . . your favors . . . or for that matter—you. Can you understand that once and for all?

Q

You would have me stand idly by while she leads you to your destruction?

PICARD

Yes!

Q

As you wish.

And once again, he's gone.

A concerned Picard is left wondering what Q meant by that last remark.

25 INTERIOR MEETING ROOM—NEXT MORNING

As Picard and Riker ENTER . . .

RIKER

Knock 'em dead, Captain.

Picard nods and moves toward the podium; Riker, toward the audience.

26 ANOTHER ANGLE

All seats are filled in anticipation of Picard's lecture. Vash sits among the council members. Our regular crew members are present as well.

26A ANGLE—PICARD

As he steps up to the podium. He's waited for this moment a long time.

PICARD

Ladies and gentlemen, members of the archeology council. Welcome. It is the mystery of Tagus III that brings us together today . . . a mystery that has invited more argument and deduction than the best Sherlock Holmes or Dixon Hill tale. Well, if you'll excuse the conceit, you're about to hear my own detective story.

26B–26C OMITTED

26D ANGLE—TROI AND BEVERLY (OPTICAL)

Suddenly, a hunting cap, with feather, appears on Beverly's head. As Troi attempts to point this phenomenon out to Beverly, a similar cap appears on her own head. They stare at each other in disbelief.

PICARD (voice-over)

For several years, I have been trying to unravel the

secrets of Tagus III. Needless to say, I have not succeeded.

26E ANGLE—PICARD

Still unaware that anything is amiss.

PICARD

However, I have, I believe, turned up some new information, that if nothing else, raises a whole new set of mysteries that I hope we can discuss during our time together.

26F ANGLE—RIKER AND GEORDI (OPTICAL)

Riker reacts to the quarterstaff that appears in his hand; Geordi to the mandolin that appears in his.

PICARD (voice-over)

There have been nine hundred and forty-seven known archaeological excavations conducted on the planet's surface.

26G ANGLE—DATA (OPTICAL)

Who finds himself wearing a cowl . . . and holding a leg of lamb.

PICARD (voice-over)

Out of that number, some seventy-four are generally considered to have revealed findings of major importance.

26HA ANGLE—WORF

Astounded by the chaperon that has appeared on his shoulders.

PICARD (voice-over)

The earliest took place some twenty-two thousand years ago.

26H ANGLE-PICARD (OPTICAL)

Who, along with the rest of the theater audience, is beginning to realize that something peculiar is going on.

PICARD

The last was completed within the last four hundred years.

Suddenly he's dressed in a jerkin and cap of familiar Lincoln green. The audience REACTS. So does Picard. Then, as a yeoman's bow appears in his hand . . .

PICARD

What the hell . . . ?

He VANISHES.

27 EXTERIOR FOREST—DAY (OPTICAL)

Picard, Riker, Geordi, Data, Worf, Beverly, and Troi all APPEAR at the same time . . . all dressed in period costume. Beverly and Troi wear men's clothing. Beverly also carries a sword; Troi, a longbow and arrows. Data is bald except for a soupbowl fringe plastered to his forehead. Riker wears a yellow jerkin and carries his quarterstaff. Worf is dressed like a dandy, and Geordi still holds his madolin.

As they all react . . .

PICARD

(raging)

Q!

FADE OUT.

ACT THREE

FADE IN:

28 EXTERIOR FOREST—DAY

As our heroes survey the scenery around them . . .

TROI

Is this Tagus III?

PICARD

I doubt there are many oak trees on Tagus. No, my guess is this is supposed to be Earth.

(off reactions)

Sometime around the twelfth century. And this is England, Sherwood Forest to be precise. Or at least Q's re-creation of it.

RIKER

That explains these costumes.

PICARD

Exactly, Number One.

(a beat)

Or should I say, Little John.

Riker studies Picard to see if he's serious.

BEVERLY

If he's Little John, that would make you . . .

PICARD

I know. Robin Hood.

A beat as this sinks in.

WORF

Sir, I protest. I am not a merry man.

DATA

On the contrary, Lieutenant Worf, your clothing identifies you with the character of Will Scarlett. Just as Geordi's mandolin suggests he is Alan-A-Dale.

RIKER

And you, Mister Data, bear a striking resemblance to one Friar Tuck.

Data examines his stomach.

WORF

I will not play the fool for Q's amusement.

He takes off his cap, looks at it in disgust, and slams it on the ground.

PICARD

You're quite right, Worf.

(loudly)

Do you hear that, Q? You may as well return us to our ship immediately.

They react to a horse's shrill whinny and turn to see . . .

29–30 OMITTED

30A SIR GUY OF GISBOURNE

Mounted on a sleek charger, sword drawn.

SIR GUY

I have you at last, Robin Hood.

As he charges at Picard . . .

30B NEW ANGLE

Worf draws his own sword to defend his captain . . .

30C ANOTHER ANGLE

Sir Guy rides past Worf, cutting him across the shoulder with his sword. Worf is ready to fight on, but . . . Suddenly an arrow slams into a tree next to Picard . . .

30D ANGLE—SEVEN MEN AT ARMS

Coming over a nearby hill. Longbows at the ready.

30E RESUME ANGLE—PICARD AND WORF

Three more arrows strike trees around them. Picard sees there's only one hope to escape.

PICARD

Quick. Into the forest.

31-31B OMITTED

31C ANGLE—WORF

Prepares to cover their retreat.

31D ANGLE—PICARD

Hanging back, as the others disappear into the trees.

PICARD

Mister Worf. That's an order.

Worf follows Picard into the forest.

31E OMITTED

31F NEW ANGLE

A furious Sir Guy turns to his men, who search the underbrush.

SIR GUY

Enough, you fools. We'll never find them in the greenwood.

32 INTERIOR FOREST—A GLADE—DAY

Picard and his crew are resting. He approaches Worf, who is being tended to by Beverly (sans tricorder).

BEVERLY

(applying a makeshift bandage)

I've managed to stop the bleeding.

33 NEW ANGLE (OPTICAL)

Q appears on horseback. He's garbed in the cloak and livery of the High Sheriff of Nottingham.

An angry Picard approaches Q.

PICARD
It's about time you showed up, Q.

Q
I'd prefer it if you addressed me as your Honor, the High Sheriff of Nottingham.

PICARD
We will not share in this pointless fantasy of yours.

Q dismounts.

Q
Fine. Wait here and do nothing. By midday tomorrow, you'll all be safely back on board your ship. But you will have to accept the consequences of your inaction.

PICARD
What consequences?

Q
What's the one thing Robin Hood is famous for?

A beat. Nobody answers. Then . . .

GEORDI
Robbing from the rich to give to the poor?

Q
Besides that.

DATA
Are you referring to his rescue of Maid Marian from Nottingham Castle?

Q
Right you are, Data.

Q looks over at Picard with glee.

Q
And it just so happens that Sir Guy of Gisbourne has

decreed that Marian's head comes off tomorrow at noon.

PICARD
(grimly)
Vash.

Q smiles. He's enjoying himself thoroughly.

Q
The choice is yours, my dear Robin. You can either take your ease here within the sylvan glade or risk your life to save a woman you care nothing about.

PICARD
My feelings toward Vash are irrelevant. I'd attempt to save any innocent life, as you well know.

Q
But what of your merry men? Are you willing to put them in jeopardy as well? Is Vash's life worth losing hers or his or even *his . . . ?*
(the last being Worf)
Though I admit he would make a perfect throw rug at Nottingham Castle.

PICARD
Q, I ask you to end this now, before anyone else gets hurt.

Q swings up onto the horse.

Q
Impossible. You see, I've given this fantasy, as you call it, a life of its own. I don't know how things will turn out anymore than you do.
(a beat)
But of one thing I am certain. If you dare set foot in Nottingham Castle, blood will be spilled.

He and the horse vanish.

34 EXTERIOR NOTTINGHAM CASTLE—DAY (OPTICAL)

Establishing.

35 INTERIOR MAID MARIAN'S CHAMBERS—DAY

A small, stark room in the tower; minimal furniture to include a wooden bench. Vash, dressed in Marian's virginal white, paces the floor. She's watched by an ELDERLY SERVANT.

SERVANT
You'll wear yourself out with all that pacing, M'lady.

VASH
I told you to stop calling me that. My name's Vash.

SERVANT
My poor lamb, it's a brain sickness you've got for sure. Can't I get you something to ease your suffering?

VASH
I could use a drink.

SERVANT
It wasn't spirits I was thinking of, M'lady.

She picks up a wooden box.

SERVANT
I have here some nice fresh leeches to drain the fever.

Vash points to the door.

VASH
Out. Get out.

The servant rushes to the door, but before she can get there it opens and Sir Guy ENTERS.

SERVANT
Oh, her mind's in an awful turmoil, Sir Guy.

Sir Guy stares at Vash with undisguised desire.

VASH

Who the hell are you?

SERVANT

M'Lady, everyone in Nottingham knows Sir Guy of Gisbourne.

VASH

Sir Guy of what?

Her servant rolls her eyes towards heaven and, shaking her head, hurries out of the room.

Sir Guy closes the door behind her.

SIR GUY

Do not mock me, Lady Marian. I'm prepared to offer you one final chance to change your mind.

He grabs hold of her.

SIR GUY

Will you marry me?

Vash pulls away and slaps him across the face.

SIR GUY

(coldly)

I see. Then the execution will proceed as scheduled.

Sir Guy turns to leave.

VASH

What execution?

SIR GUY

(turning back)

I warn you, Marian, this pathetic attempt at feigning madness will not save your life.

VASH

(shocked)

You mean I'm the one getting executed?

Though Vash is at a loss to explain how she came to be in this current predicament, a lifetime of adventure has honed her survival instincts to a razor's edge.

VASH

Sir Guy, wait—Can't we talk this over?

(a beat)

I admit, I haven't been myself lately.

(flashing her best smile)

Perhaps we've both been a bit hasty.

She sits down on the bench. Pats the space next to her.

VASH

Please.

Sir Guy smiles. Delighted.

36 EXTERIOR SHERWOOD FOREST—DAY

We hear bad mandolin playing in the background as Troi pulls back on a bow and lets fly an arrow. We HEAR the THWACK of impact. CAMERA PANS OVER to the tree that was her intended target. There's no sign of the arrow.

PAN OVER a few feet to the right. Data is standing with an arrow in his chest.

Troi hurries over.

TROI

Data, are you alright?

A beat, as Data checks his systems.

DATA

The arrow impacted just above my sixth intercostal support, penetrating my secondary subprocessor.

Data moves his arm up and down and in and out.

DATA

(continuing)

Fortunately, none of my biofunctions seem impaired.

Data pulls the arrow out of his body. He offers it to Troi, who is much relieved.

DATA

Do not get discouraged. I believe your aim is improving.

36A NEW ANGLE

Beverly is checking Worf's wound in the background as Geordi sits on a log strumming the mandolin . . . it sounds like fingernails on a blackboard.

Worf gets up, crosses to Geordi, and takes the mandolin out of his hands. He walks over and smashes it against a tree. Hands the neck back to Geordi.

WORF

Sorry.

37 NEW ANGLE

A relieved grin from Riker as he watches Picard buckle on his sword.

RIKER

It's about time we got out of here, sir.

PICARD

Not *we,* Commander. You and the others are to wait here until I return.

RIKER

You're not planning to go after her alone, are you?

The others gather around.

PICARD

This is not a mission. It's personal, between Q and myself. I don't want any of you involved.

RIKER

But, Captain . . .

PICARD

You have your orders, Commander. I expect you to follow them.

With a final glance at his crew, Picard heads off towards Nottingham.

On Riker's worried look we . . .

FADE OUT.

ACT FOUR

FADE IN:

38 EXTERIOR COURTYARD INSIDE WALLS OF CASTLE—NIGHT

Cold, imposing, and lit by flickering torches. We see a limited section of the yard . . . Heraldic banners hang from the walls. A circular staircase rises to the tower.

Only a few servants are visible as a haughty Q (still dressed as the High Sheriff) surveys his domain with smug satisfaction.

Nearby is an EXECUTIONER. Off to the side, a TINKER, with his back to us, repairs the chains on a pair of shackles. The massively built executioner is busy sharpening the blade of his broad axe against a foot-powered grindstone. He pauses to inspect his work. Q, passing by, barely taps the edge of the blade with his index finger.

Q

A touch sharper, shall we?

The executioner starts up the grindstone.

Q suddenly halts in confusion as he discovers a surprising sight before him.

39 NEW ANGLE

Vash and Sir Guy, looking surprisingly chummy as they approach from another part of the courtyard. She carries a bouquet of fresh-picked flowers. Sir Guy holds up a pomegranate. Vash smiles and demurely nibbles it.

A suspicious Q approaches them.

Q

Such benevolence, Sir Guy, allowing the condemned prisoner fresh air.

SIR GUY

You're mistaken, Sheriff. Maid Marian has consented to be my wife.

Q looks at Vash in disbelief.

Q

But that's impossible!

Vash motions to a servant, who approaches with a tray and two goblets of wine.

VASH

(innocently)

Not at all. Though I admit a maiden seldom has the opportunity to win herself such a noble husband.

She takes a goblet from the tray and hands it to Sir Guy. . . .

SIR GUY

A toast to the most beautiful bride-to-be in all of England.

He goes to drink.

Q

Hold there, Sir Guy.

He knocks the goblet to the ground.

SIR GUY

Have you taken leave of your senses?

Q

It could be poisoned. Some foul scheme of Robin Hood. She's in league with him still, I'll warrant.

VASH

Robin Hood?

A beat as Vash absorbs this rather bizarre accusation. She has no choice but to bluff her way through it.

VASH

Oh, Robin Hood . . . that was over long ago.

Q

Why, all of Nottingham knows you're in love with him.

VASH

That's a lie.

(to Sir Guy)

He . . . bewitched me. Put me under some evil spell.

Sir Guy gives her hand an encouraging pat.

SIR GUY

Just as I suspected.

(to Q)

You can add sorcery to the list of charges against that rogue.

Q

But, Sir Guy, if anyone has been bewitched it's you.

Sir Guy stands. His hand is placed firmly on the hilt of his sword.

SIR GUY

Silence. Any further impudence and it'll be your head on the chopping block.

(a beat)

Guards, escort the Lady Marian to her chamber.

VASH

(standing)

But I'd much rather stay with you.

SIR GUY

Of course you would, my child. But I have important business to discuss with the sheriff.

(a beat; then dripping with implication)

And you must prepare for your wedding.

VASH

I count the hours.

She kisses him. She allows herself to be led away, but not before her eyes flash him the promise of future delights.

Sir Guy and Q watch her depart.

SIR GUY

Lovely creature.

Q

(with grudging admiration)

She is intriguing.

Q is determined not to allow his well-laid scheme to go astray.

Q

Sir Guy, perhaps it would be wise to keep this wedding a secret for now.

SIR GUY

What are you babbling about?

Q

You still hope to capture Robin Hood, don't you?

SIR GUY

I live for the moment.

Q

(thinking of Picard)

Well, if he were to hear that Marian's life is no longer in danger, there would be no need for him to come to Nottingham to rescue her.

Sir Guy slaps Q on the back.

SIR GUY

By heavens, you're right. No word of my wedding shall leave these walls.

(a beat)

What better way to celebrate a marriage than with an execution?

Sir Guy and Q share a chuckle, then go their separate ways.

Q

(musing)

This could be fun.

40 NEW ANGLE

Q crosses by the tinker hammering at a chain. The tinker looks up once Q has passed him by, REVEALING himself to be Picard in disguise.

41 INTERIOR MAID MARIAN'S CHAMBER—NIGHT

Vash paces around the room. Suddenly she stops, listening to what could be a faint rustling. The noise ceases. Vash continues to pace. The rustling resumes, louder now. Again, Vash stops pacing. The sound, and now it's clearly the rustling of vines, is coming from outside her open window. She moves towards the embrasure, when SUDDENLY a hand APPEARS on the ledge. With a final GRUNT, Picard lifts himself through the window. Vash throws herself at him.

VASH

Jean-Luc. Am I glad to see you!

She throws herself into his arms and kisses him.

VASH

You would not believe what I've been through. One minute I'm on the *Enterprise* . . . the next thing I know I'm here in Nottingham. First, they're going to chop my head off . . . and now I'm supposed to marry someone named Sir Guy . . . and everyone insists on calling me Marian . . .

PICARD

Yes, I know.

VASH

You do? But how . . .

For the first time she notices his outfit.

VASH

You're *Robin Hood*?

PICARD

My staff and I were brought here by an old adversary of mine named Q. I'll tell you the rest once we're safe.

He leads her towards the window.

PICARD

Come, we don't have much time.

VASH
Are the others outside?

PICARD
They're waiting for us back in Sherwood.

That brings Vash to a quick stop.

VASH
You mean you came alone?

PICARD
Yes, now let's . . .

VASH
What kind of plan is that?

PICARD
An excellent one if you'd only hurry up.

But Vash refuses to budge.

VASH
You do realize our lives are at stake here.

PICARD
Only too well.

VASH
And this is the best strategy you could come up with?
One man against an entire castle.

PICARD
I suppose you know of a better one.

VASH
How about this? You go. I'll stay here.

She walks away from the window.

PICARD
And do what?

VASH
Marry Sir Guy if I have to.

PICARD
(ironic)
That is brilliant.

VASH
If there's a way to escape, I'll find it, eventually. With my head still attached.

PICARD
You don't really expect me to leave you here?

He reaches for her. She pulls away.

VASH
I can take care of myself.

PICARD
Must you be so stubborn?

Suddenly the door is flying OPEN and Sir Guy enters backed by a retinue of SOLDIERS.

SIR GUY
There'll be no escape for you this time, Robin Hood.

PICARD
(to Vash)
Behind me.

He steps in front of her and reaches for his sword. But Vash is quicker. She pulls the blade out of his scabbard and points it at his chest.

VASH
You should have left while you had the chance.

Sir Guy advances on them, smiling.

SIR GUY
Well done, my dear.

VASH
(sweetly)
Consider it my wedding present to you.

The Guards lead Picard away.

42 EXTERIOR COURTYARD—NIGHT

Picard and the guards come down the stairs. He barely glances at a beaming Q as he's hurried away. Sir Guy follows behind.

Q

Congratulations, Gisbourne. I see you've snared the jackal.

SIR GUY

It's Marian who deserves the credit. Took him with his own sword.

On Q's astonished REACTION . . .

43 INTERIOR MAID MARIAN'S CHAMBER—NIGHT

Vash is seated at a table, writing feverishly. Her SERVANT ENTERS and scuttles across the room to her.

SERVANT

You sent for me, M'Lady?

VASH

You must take this letter to Robin's men.

SERVANT

You want *me* to go to Sherwood Forest? At this time of night?

VASH

You'll leave immediately.

SERVANT

(glancing out the window)

But it's dark. I'll get lost.

Vash continues to write.

SERVANT

Besides, it's not safe. What with all them hedge robbers and worse lurking about.

VASH

Please, this is urgent.

SERVANT

You ask me, you'd be better off staying with Sir Guy. He's got a future. Why, you'll be living in London before you know it.

VASH

But you must go. Otherwise, they're going to kill him.

She's about to offer the folded letter to the servant, when the door SWINGS open. Vash leaps up, dropping the letter on the table as Q ENTERS.

VASH

How dare you come barging in here this way!

Q

I come to offer apologies for my harsh words earlier. I had no idea you were so ruthless. The cold-blooded way you betrayed Robin was most impressive.

Q is now standing right by the table. Vash forces herself not to glance down at the letter.

VASH

That's most gracious of you.

Q

I admit I was surprised . . .

(a beat)

Though perhaps not as surprised as Jean-Luc.

Now it's Vash's turn to be surprised.

VASH

You're Q.

Q

(bowing)

And you are a very interesting woman.

He notices the letter.

Q

What's this?

She tries to snatch it away.

VASH

Give me that.

But it's too late.

Q

A letter to Riker?

(reading)

Quick . . . Come to Castle . . . Must save captain . . .

(cheerfully)

Why this is wonderful. Such marvelous duplicity. You certainly fooled Sir Guy. And me as well.

(a shrewd glance at Vash)

I do believe you're worth further study.

VASH

(turning on the charm)

Am I?

Q

Unfortunately, we won't have the time.

(shouting)

Guards!

They enter.

Q

Take this traitor away.

(to Vash)

It appears there's going to be a double execution.

Vash is marched from the room.

And as Q gloats over this latest turn of events:

FADE OUT.

ACT FIVE

FADE IN:

44 EXTERIOR COURTYARD—THE NEXT DAY

A CROWD has gathered to SEE the show. Sir Guy and Q sit together at a dais at one end of the courtyard.

45 NEW ANGLE

The stairs leading to the tower. We HEAR VOICES coming down offcamera, drawing close.

PICARD (voice-over)

My fault?

VASH (voice-over)

Yes, your fault.

PICARD (voice-over)

We'd have been safe in Sherwood if you hadn't grabbed my sword.

Picard and Vash, both wearing shackles, come into VIEW as they walk toward CAMERA . . .

VASH

I grabbed it to prevent you from being killed.

PICARD

You should never have interfered.

VASH

You were the one interfering.

PICARD

I was trying to rescue you.

VASH

Next time don't bother.

PICARD

I won't.

They come to a halt in front of the executioner's block. Q steps forward to meet them.

Q

Don't you two ever stop arguing?

No response.

Q

Tell me, Picard, as you stand here facing the termination of your insect existence, do you see what has led you to this end?

(beat, no reply)

Was she worth it?

PICARD

Can we just get this over with?

VASH

(hurt)

Are you implying I'm not worth it?

But Picard keeps his eyes fixed on Q.

PICARD

Your game was for my benefit, Q. She is innocent in all this.

Q

She is many things, none of them innocent.

PICARD

Let her go.

VASH

Jean-Luc, you do care.

Q

A gallant gesture, Picard. But a futile one.

(a beat)

Farewell. I hope you'll both be happy together.

He moves aside as Sir Guy rises to his feet.

SIR GUY
(to Picard & Vash)
You have been found guilty of outlawry and high treason. Do you have anything to say before sentencing is carried out?

Impassive stares from the prisoners.

SIR GUY
Ready them for the block.

The guards remove the chains.

45AA NEW ANGLE

A group of hooded monks have entered the courtyard. Beneath the hoods are Riker, Worf, Geordi, Data, Beverly, and Troi.

45A ANGLE—PICARD AND VASH

Already kneeling at the block.

45B ANGLE—THE MONKS (OPTICAL)

Taking in the scene in front of them. Worf reaches for the sword beneath his robe. Geordi lays a restraining hand on Worf's arm.

GEORDI
Too many of them. We'd never get to the captain . . .

RIKER
Data, we need a diversion. Now.

Data opens his left arm, revealing the circuitry and blinking lights within. He pulls out three small components and fastens them together.

DATA
(to Riker)
Please stand back, Commander. Microfusion cells can be somewhat dangerous under high temperatures . . .

Riker stands back. Data tosses the components into the tinker's fire. The fire FLARES briefly, then there is a small explosion and a dramatic pyrotechnic discharge that startles the executioner and the onlookers.

Amidst the confusion that follows, Picard leaps to his feet and rams his elbow into the executioner's stomach, knocking him to the ground. Picard then grabs hold of one of his guards, and pulls his sword free of its scabbard.

45C OMITTED

45D NEW ANGLE

Riker, Worf, Geordi, Troi, Beverly, and Data (who has closed the panel on his arm) throw off their monks' robes.

VOICES
It's the outlaws. Robin's band.

Sir Guy unsheathes his sword.

SIR GUY
Guards. Take Marian to the tower.

Vash whirls and punches one of her captors, but two others drag her up the stairs.

Picard SEES Vash being taken away and tries to follow. A guard tries to block him and is cut down.

46 NEW ANGLE

As our crew beats back the attacking soldiers.

46A DATA

Holds out his arm and ''clotheslines'' one soldier as he charges by. Then Data looks up at . . .

46B ANOTHER SOLDIER

Who lunges toward him with a sword. The man stops in midthrust, shocked, as . . .

Data catches the tip of the blade between his thumb and forefinger . . . and slowly CURLS it back.

47 NEW ANGLE

Q watches the battle that rages around him, with delight.

48 NEW ANGLE

Picard comes face to face with Sir Guy.

SIR GUY

I'll have you know I'm the greatest swordsman in all of Nottingham.

A quick flurry of cuts and parries as they test each other's skill.

PICARD

That's very impressive.

They engage again.

PICARD

But there's something you should know.

A furious series of strikes ending with their swords crossed at the hilt, their faces inches apart.

SIR GUY

And what would that be?

PICARD

I'm not from Nottingham.

He pushes Sir Guy away.

49 NEW ANGLE

Gradually Picard forces Sir Guy up the stairs leading to Marian's room. Sir Guy, panic building, takes a vicious cut at Picard's head. Picard ducks, thrusts upward, and stabs Sir Guy through the body.

Sir Guy tumbles off the staircase.

50 INTERIOR MARIAN'S CHAMBER (OPTICAL)

Vash listens to the SOUNDS of battle.

Suddenly, the door SWINGS and Picard races in.

VASH

Jean-Luc.

She runs into his arms. Picard is fed up with all this, tosses the sword to the floor.

PICARD
(shouting)
It's over, Q. Now get us out of here.

Q APPEARS in the room.

Q
(applauding)
My compliments, Captain. I doubt Robin Hood himself could have done better.

PICARD
If any of my people are hurt . . .

Q
Sadly, they're all fine . . . but the point is they could have been killed, and you might have been too . . . all for the "Love Of A Maid." My debt to you is paid, Picard, if you have learned how weak and vulnerable you really are . . . if you can finally see how "Love" brought out the worst in you . . .

VASH
Nonsense. You're absolutely wrong. It brought out the best in him.
(to him, intimately)
His nobility, courage, self-sacrifice. His tenderness.

Q
(to Vash)
You're good. Very good.

PICARD
(end of his patience)
Enough of this.

Q
Indeed.

He snaps his finger and Picard DISAPPEARS.

51 OMITTED

52 INTERIOR MEETING ROOM (OPTICAL)

The room is empty. Picard, in uniform, suddenly APPEARS at the podium. Riker and the others APPEAR back in the audience, exactly where they were sitting before. All of them are back in their Starfleet uniforms. They look around in confusion.

RIKER

Everybody here?

TROI

Where's Vash?

Picard scans the room. No sign of her.

PICARD

Computer, locate Council Member Vash.

COMPUTER VOICE

Council Member Vash is not aboard the *Enterprise*.

Off his look of concern . . .

52A EXTERIOR SPACE—THE *ENTERPRISE* (OPTICAL)

Still in orbit.

53 INTERIOR READY ROOM (OPTICAL)

Picard ENTERS. As the doors CLOSE behind him, Vash MATERIALIZES.

VASH

Hello, Jean-Luc.

PICARD

(smiling)

Well, this is a relief. I was afraid that Q . . .

VASH

There were a few things he wanted to discuss with me.

PICARD

I'm surprised he wasn't too busy gloating over his victory.

VASH
(beat)
He *was* right about one thing, Jean-Luc. As ridiculous as it was, his game did prove how much you care.

PICARD
I may not share my feelings with my crew, but I do have them.

A warm moment passes between them.

VASH
I'm going to miss you, Picard.

PICARD
I wouldn't be surprised if our paths cross again.

VASH
I'll see to it.

They kiss.

PICARD
So, where are you off to now?

VASH
I haven't made up my mind.

VASH
Remind you of someone you know?

PICARD
(amused in spite of himself)
As a matter of fact . . . yes.

Q
(to Vash)
We are going to have fun. I'll take you places no human could ever hope to see.

VASH
(to Picard)
Who can resist an offer like that?

Picard sees there's no way to change her mind. He advances on Q.

PICARD

As payment in full for your debt to me, you will guarantee her safety . . .

Q

She will not be harmed, Jean-Luc. I promise you that.

Picard looks over at Vash. A silent farewell.

Q

Well, aren't you going to kiss her good-bye?

Picard and Vash stare at him until he gets the hint.

Q

Oh, all right.

He VANISHES.

Vash smiles at Picard.

VASH

Well, aren't you?

A final kiss. Then Vash steps back.

VASH

Goodbye, Jean-Luc.

She VANISHES.

55 CLOSE-UP OF PICARD

A beat. Then a trace of a smile appears on his face.

56 EXTERIOR SPACE—THE *ENTERPRISE* (OPTICAL)

Turning towards the unknown.

FADE OUT.

STAR TREK: THE NEXT GENERATION

True-Q

#40276-232

Written by
Rene Echevarria

Directed by
Robert Scheerer

STAR TREK: THE NEXT GENERATION

True-Q

CAST

PICARD
RIKER
DATA
BEVERLY
TROI
WORF
GEORDI
NURSE ALYSSA OGAWA
NURSE'S COM VOICE

Q
AMANDA ROGERS
ORN LOTE

Non-Speaking

SUPERNUMERARIES

Non-Speaking

AMANDA'S PARENTS

STAR TREK: THE NEXT GENERATION

True-Q

SETS

INTERIORS

U.S.S. ENTERPRISE
MAIN BRIDGE
ENGINEERING
TEN-FORWARD
READY ROOM
SHUTTLEBAY TWO
OBSERVATION LOUNGE
MEDICAL LAB
CORRIDOR

GAZEBO
AMANDA'S QUARTERS
TAGRAN CONTROL ROOM

EXTERIORS

U.S.S. ENTERPRISE
TAGRA IV

STAR TREK: THE NEXT GENERATION

True-Q

TEASER

FADE IN:

1 EXTERIOR SPACE—THE *ENTERPRISE* (OPTICAL)

Holding position near a starbase.

PICARD (voice-over)
Captain's log, stardate 46192.3. We have arrived at Starbase one-one-two and are loading relief supplies destined for Tagra IV, an ecologically devastated planet in the Argolis Cluster. We have also taken on a rather unusual passenger.

2 INTERIOR READY ROOM—CLOSE—PICARD

PICARD
Welcome to the *Enterprise*. We're delighted to have you aboard.

3 WIDEN

To include BEVERLY and eighteen-year-old AMANDA ROGERS.

AMANDA
Thank you, sir.

Amanda is excited and a bit nervous; she can hardly believe she's being welcomed to the *Enterprise* by its captain.

PICARD
Congratulations. I understand you were selected from among hundreds of applicants for this internship.

AMANDA
Yes, sir. I still can't believe they chose me. . . . There were lots of people with better records. . . .

BEVERLY

Your transcript is very impressive. . . .

(to Picard)

She's done honors work in neurobiology, plasma dynamics, and eco-regeneration. I'd call that pretty well rounded.

AMANDA

That's a nice way of saying I haven't made up my mind about what I want to do with my life.

BEVERLY

I've arranged to have you work in all the major departments while you're here. I'm willing to bet that by the time it's over, you'll have a pretty good idea what field you're interested in.

PICARD

(smiles)

Or at least what fields you're *not* interested in.

Amanda smiles; they're making her feel welcome aboard this strange new ship. The door chime SOUNDS.

PICARD

Come.

RIKER ENTERS.

RIKER

We're bringing up the last of the cargo, sir. We should be ready to leave within the hour.

Picard nods his acknowledgement.

PICARD

Commander, would you escort Ms. Rogers to her quarters? I have to discuss the Tagrans' medical needs with Doctor Crusher.

Riker nods; Amanda stands.

PICARD

You've won yourself a rare opportunity. Avail yourself of it.

AMANDA

I will, sir.

Picard smiles; she crosses toward the door.

4 INTERIOR CORRIDOR

As Riker and Amanda make their way down it. She walks with downcast eyes, stricken with shyness in front of the dashing first officer. Riker smiles to himself, decides to try and put her at ease.

RIKER

It'll take a few days before you know your way around. If you ever need help, just use one of the companels. . . .

He gestures to a companel as they pass it.

AMANDA

We're on Deck Seven, section . . .

(unsure)

Four?

RIKER

(surprised)

That's right.

AMANDA

(smiles)

I practically memorized the specs on the way here.

RIKER

You're a quick study.

They've arrived at the door to her quarters.

RIKER

This is it.

5 INTERIOR AMANDA'S QUARTERS

As she and Riker ENTER. Her bags are already there, having been brought directly from the transporter room.

Amanda looks around, seems a little surprised.

AMANDA
Is this for me?

RIKER
All yours.

AMANDA
It's so . . . big.

RIKER
(smiles)
For honor students, only the best.

She looks around.

AMANDA
I could've brought "the zoo."

RIKER
The zoo?

AMANDA
That's what my parents call it. Three dogs isn't so many, is it?

RIKER
(smiles)
Depends on how they get along.

AMANDA
I'd have a dozen, but my mother said enough is enough.

They share a smile.

AMANDA
I'm sure going to miss them.

RIKER
We'll try and keep you so busy you won't have time to.
(he smiles)
I'd better be going; I have to get back to the cargo bay.

AMANDA
Thanks for walking me down.

Amanda watches Riker EXIT; her eyes linger on the door as it shuts behind him. She turns and suddenly her eyes widen in shock.

6 NEW ANGLE (OPTICAL)

Amanda's room is suddenly full of PUPPIES . . . a dozen of them, yapping and wagging their tails. Amanda's hand flies to cover her mouth in dismay.

AMANDA
Oh, no . . . I didn't mean it. . . .

She kneels as the puppies rush to her feet.

AMANDA
You can't be here. . . . Go away.

A handful of the puppies DISAPPEAR.

AMANDA
All of you.

The rest of the puppies in front of her DISAPPEAR as well, leaving two behind her. She can't help but pet them for a moment before saying:

AMANDA
You too.

They VANISH also. Amanda flops herself down so she's sitting on the floor. She looks scared . . . like someone keeping a terrible secret. . . . Off her reaction we . . .

FADE OUT.

ACT ONE

FADE IN:

7 INTERIOR MEDICAL LAB (OR STORAGE AREA)

Beverly is showing Amanda the readout dials on a medical TRICORDER.

BEVERLY

See these readouts? This is your heart rate, your blood pressure . . . all your vital signs.

Amanda looks at the dials with interest.

BEVERLY

You're in good shape.

(wry)

You might just live to be my age.

Amanda smiles. Beverly indicates the storage shelf from which she took the device.

BEVERLY

All these tricorders have to be tested before they get put in the supply containers we're taking to Tagra IV.

She indicates the small carrying cases stacked on a nearby table.

AMANDA

So I scan myself with each one to make sure all the readouts are working?

BEVERLY

(nods)

If they're not, put that unit aside and we'll run a diagnostic on it.

Beverly puts the tricorder she's been holding in a container.

Amanda takes another tricorder off the shelf and starts scanning herself.

BEVERLY

So I understand you were accepted to the academy. . . . I have a son there.

AMANDA

Being posted on the *Enterprise,* I guess you don't get to see him very often . . . ?

BEVERLY

(smiles)

Not as often as I'd like.

AMANDA

Do you have any other children?

BEVERLY

My husband died a number of years ago. Wes was our only child.

Amanda is quiet for a moment.

AMANDA

Was he old enough to know his father?

BEVERLY

Jack died when he was five.

AMANDA

My parents died when I was a baby. I don't remember anything about them. . . . Sometimes I wonder what they were like.

Beverly can appreciate how she might want to know about them.

BEVERLY

I understand your adopted parents are in Starfleet.

AMANDA

(nods)

They're marine biologists. . . . They were just posted to the Bilaren system.

Beverly is called on the com.

NURSE (com voice)

Sickbay to Doctor Crusher . . . you wanted to be told when the cultures were ready.

BEVERLY

On my way.

(to Amanda)

I have to go. When you've finished with the tricorders, Nurse Ogawa can help you take them down to the shuttlebay for loading.

AMANDA

Okay.

They share a warm smile, and Beverly leaves her to her task.

8 EXTERIOR SPACE—THE *ENTERPRISE* (OPTICAL)

At impulse.

9 INTERIOR SHUTTLEBAY TWO

The place is buzzing with activity. N.D.'s bustle around, packing crates and loading them into the SHUTTLECRAFT.

Amanda has just delivered the tricorders she's been checking to GEORDI; he holds a padd and has his hands full coordinating everything.

GEORDI

Thanks for your help. We need every spare hand we can get; this is one of the biggest relief efforts we've ever mounted.

AMANDA

Why are you taking everything down in shuttlecraft?

GEORDI

We can't use the transporters because of all the ionization in the Tagran atmosphere.

AMANDA

From the baristatic filters?

GEORDI

(a little surprised)

How'd you know that?

AMANDA

I did a paper on eco-regeneration.

Geordi smiles and motions for Amanda to follow him over to a shuttlecraft.

GEORDI

Then you know that a thousand baristatic filters put out a lot of ionization. . . .

AMANDA

(that many?)

A thousand . . . ?

GEORDI

They've managed to pollute their atmosphere pretty badly.

AMANDA

It's amazing . . . that they go to such lengths to clean the air . . . instead of regulating the emissions that cause the problem.

GEORDI

(simply)

You're right.

Geordi and Amanda share a rueful look; it all seems so shortsighted to them.

Riker ENTERS and we see him in the background talking to an N.D. Amanda's attention is diverted.

Geordi is half way inside a console by now so he doesn't notice.

GEORDI'S VOICE

All the filters can do is keep things from getting worse. They shoot negative ions into the planet's stratosphere—

Amanda watches Riker as he takes a padd from an N.D. and begins checking it over. The N.D. moves away, leaving Riker standing alone near the overhand that contains the control booth.

GEORDI'S VOICE

(continuing)

—where they come into contact with airborne pollutants and transfer their charge. The filters have positively charged intake vents that the pollutants become attracted to; that sets up a kind of ionic current in the atmosphere.

Amanda isn't even hearing his techno-ramble; her attention is now completely on the handsome figure cut by the first officer.

9A CLOSE ON A TOOL CASE

On the railing of the overhang. It suddenly moves forward, as though of its own volition, and teeters on the edge of the stack.

9B ANGLE ON AMANDA

As her eye is caught by the movement. Then, the case shifts forward again and begins FALLING right toward Riker. There isn't even time to shout a warning. . . .

Amanda reaches out instinctively and suddenly the *case's fall is diverted*—as if some unseen force lanced out from her outstretched arm—and it crashes to the ground just a few feet away from him.

Everyone in the room reacts with a start. It looks for all the world to have been a near miss.

GEORDI
(calling from across the room)
Commander, are you all right?

Riker's a little shaken. Geordi crosses toward him.

RIKER
Yeah . . . I didn't even see it coming. . . .

No one except Amanda knows what really happened. And from the look on her face, we can see that she is disturbed and frightened by the strange event.

10 INTERIOR AMANDA'S QUARTERS

Amanda is alone in her quarters, mulling over the strange events of the past few days. If only there were someone she could talk to about it all. But what if they thought she was a freak? They used to burn witches!

A SOUND at the door. Amanda leaps off the bed and stares at it. Maybe they've found her out?

AMANDA
(hesitantly)

Come in.

The door opens to reveal TROI standing there holding a puppy.

TROI

Commander Riker told me you liked dogs. . . .

Amanda is delighted. She moves forward to take the puppy.

AMANDA
(to puppy)

What's your name?

TROI

This is Henry.

AMANDA
(smiles)

Henry?

TROI
(shrugging)

Don't ask me.

AMANDA

Where'd he come from?

TROI

Ensign Janklow is going to the Gantol excavations for three weeks. He's been trying to find someone to take care of Henry.

AMANDA
(instantly)

I'll do it.

TROI
(smiles)

Okay. But be warned—he has an appetite for boots.

Amanda laughs and puts Henry down to explore the room.

AMANDA

By the time Ensign Janklow gets back I'll have Henry shaking hands.

She and Troi move to chairs and sit.

TROI

Doctor Crusher tells me you're considering a career in zoology.

AMANDA

I was . . . but this morning I decided to become a Starfleet doctor . . . then by this afternoon I realized I was really meant to be a chief engineer.

They share a smile.

AMANDA

What does a ship's counselor do? Maybe that's what I'll want to be by tomorrow.

Troi smiles at the young woman's enthusiasm.

AMANDA

There are just so many things I'm interested in. . . . Sometimes I worry that I'll never focus on just one thing. . . .

TROI

There's nothing wrong with keeping your options open.

AMANDA

I'm just afraid I won't have enough time for everything I want to do. I mean—

(ticking them off)

—there's school, and then graduate study, and a career . . . and of course I want to get married and have children—lots of children—and more animals. . . .

(beat, reflecting)

Maybe I should study agriculture . . . have a big farm somewhere. . . .

Troi laughs at her boundless eagerness and energy.

TROI

Amanda . . . whatever you choose, I'm sure you'll be good at it.

AMANDA

I know one thing. . . . I wouldn't mind coming back to the *Enterprise* when I graduate.

TROI

Who knows? Maybe you will.

Off Amanda's reaction . . .

11 EXTERIOR SPACE—THE *ENTERPRISE* (OPTICAL)

As it cruises at impulse.

12 INTERIOR ENGINEERING

As Geordi and Amanda cross away from the warp core toward the pool table, where DATA is working.

GEORDI

—this is the main control area. We can access just about any primary circuit from these panels.

(indicating)

That's a Jefferies tube over there—

AMANDA

Where most of the major systems conduits are routed.

GEORDI

(smiles)

You've done your homework.

She looks back toward the warp core . . . it is humming strongly, blue lights rippling.

AMANDA

It's hard to imagine how much energy is being harnessed in there. . . .

Data overhears this.

DATA

Imagination is not necessary; the scale is readily quantifiable.

(glancing at console)

We are presently generating twelve point seven-five billion gigawatts per second.

Amanda smiles at him—then, suddenly an ALARM sounds. Geordi hurries to a console near Data.

DATA

The temperature in the reaction chamber has increased by forty-seven percent.

GEORDI

(working)

The injector couplings are frozen—I can't slow the reaction. . . .

DATA

Temperature increase is at one hundred six percent . . . and rising.

GEORDI

(to com)

La Forge to bridge!

PICARD (com voice)

Picard, here.

GEORDI

We're heading for a core breach! We're going to have to try and vent the plasma!

DATA

(working)

Plasma inductors are not responding.

GEORDI

We're going to lose containment. . . .

13 NEW ANGLE (OPTICAL)

Favoring Amanda, with the pulsing reactor behind her.

GEORDI
(to Data)

Bring down the isolation door—we have to eject the warp core.

Data works the control.

GEORDI
(to others)

Everybody out! Move it!

Suddenly a blinding white FLASH obscures the warp core (the explosion is so powerful that we don't see pieces of metal flying toward us, just the OPTICAL EFFECT).

Amanda's hands fly up in an instinctive gesture. . . . The roiling EFFECT surges toward her—and stops expanding just before it touches her hands.

Everyone turns and looks at her in amazement. Slowly, as if she's exerting some great effort, she forces the explosion back . . . back . . . until it is once again contained in the reaction chamber.

Only when she's finished and everyone is safe does she allow herself to react to the enormity of what she's done. . . .

Suddenly she's a scared young girl again. . . .

DATA

Temperature in the reaction chamber is back to normal.

Data, of course, is unflappable. But the impossibility of what they've just witnessed has left everyone else in the room stunned silent.

FADE OUT.

ACT TWO

FADE IN:

14 INTERIOR OBSERVATION LOUNGE (OPTICAL)

Picard, Riker, Geordi, and Troi look up as Beverly ENTERS.

BEVERLY
She's a little shaken up, but she'll be all right.

Everyone's relieved to hear this—despite the mystery posed by the incident in engineering, they've all grown quite fond of Amanda.

RIKER
You said she was adopted. . . . Could she be an alien?

BEVERLY
She's human . . . and there's nothing unusual about her, not that my instruments can detect.

PICARD
(to Geordi)
Commander, have you been able to determine the cause of the warp breach?

GEORDI
No, sir. Everything was normal and then . . . it's like the laws of physics suddenly went out the window.

Suddenly Q APPEARS in one of the seats. He's wearing a Starfleet uniform.

Q
And why not? They're terribly inconvenient.

PICARD
(dismayed)
Q . . .

Q
Mon Capitaine.

PICARD
Are you responsible for the incident in engineering?

Q

Of course. I needed to find out if what I suspected about the girl was true.

PICARD

That being?

Q

That she's Q.

This notion, dropped lightly by Q, falls like a bombshell on the others.

TROI

Amanda . . . is a *Q . . . ?*

BEVERLY

How is that possible? Her parents . . . her biological parents . . . were human.

Q

Not exactly.

They regard him curiously.

Q

They had assumed human form . . . in order to visit Earth. For an amusement, I suppose . . . but in vulgar human fashion they proceeded to conceive a child.

He shrugs, not comprehending this strange behavior.

Q

Then, like mawkish humans, they became attached to it. What *is* it about those squirming little infants that you find so appealing?

BEVERLY

I'm sure that's beyond your comprehension, Q.

Q

I desperately hope so.

TROI

What happened to Amanda's parents?

Q

They died in an accident. None of us knew whether the child would inherit the capacities of a Q . . . but recently, they began to emerge. As an expert on humanity—I was sent to investigate.

RIKER

(sarcastic)

You, an expert on humanity . . . ?

Q

(likewise)

Not a very challenging field of study, I'll grant you. . . .

GEORDI

Are you saying you caused the core breach—just to test her?

TROI

What if she hadn't been able to stop it?

Q

(it's obvious)

Then I would've known she wasn't Q.

There are reactions to this cavalier attitude.

BEVERLY

Now that you know, what do you intend to do?

Q

Instruct her, of course. If that child doesn't learn how to control her power . . . she could accidentally destroy herself. Or all of you. Perhaps your entire galaxy.

PICARD

Somehow I find it hard to believe that you'd come here to do us a favor. . . .

Q

You're quite right—I wouldn't. But there are those in the Continuum who have an exaggerated sense of responsibility . . . and think we should take precautions to keep the little dear from running amok.

BEVERLY

And once you've taught her . . . you'll go away?

Q

And leave her *here* . . . when she's Q? Of course not . . . she'll come to the Continuum, where she belongs.

BEVERLY

(irate)

Wait a minute . . . you can't just come in here and take her away from everything she's known. . . .

Q

I assure you, I can—

BEVERLY

She has plans for herself. . . . She wants a career, a family—

Q

I can rescue her from that miserable existence.

BEVERLY

That "miserable existence" is all she's known for eighteen years. You have no right to take it away from her.

Q

Mon Capitaine . . . I really think we need to speak privately.

He lifts his hand—there's a FLASH . . . and the two of them are suddenly in—

14A OMITTED

15 INTERIOR READY ROOM

Q

There. Isn't that better? Doctor Crusher gets more shrill with each passing year. . . .

PICARD

What is it you really want, Q? Why bring Amanda here . . . to the *Enterprise?*

Q

(expansively)

Where better than here, among my dear friends? After all . . . you know so much about the Q . . . you're the perfect people to introduce me to the child. Let her know she can trust me.

This brings an outright laugh from Picard.

PICARD

Trust you—!

Q

Jean-Luc . . . you wound me. . . .

PICARD

I don't trust you, and I certainly wouldn't expect Amanda to.

Q

She'd better—because I'm all she's got. She needs me to prepare her . . . for her future with the Q.

PICARD

She may not want that future. The decision is hers.

Q

Yes, yes—fine.

(amused by the thought)

But do you really think she'll want to remain a feeble mortal?

Picard ignores his mocking tone, thinks for a moment . . . not liking what he comes up with.

PICARD

If Amanda is a Q . . . she'll need to understand what that means.

(firm)

I'll introduce you, but we cannot continue to fight like

this in front of Amanda. For her sake, we'll have to appear to be . . .

Q

Pals?

PICARD

Civil.

Q shrugs his assent.

PICARD

We need time to explain this to her.

Q

I knew I could count on you, Jean-Luc.

Q DISAPPEARS. Picard EXITS the ready room.

15A INTERIOR BRIDGE

As Picard crosses to Data.

PICARD

Mister Data . . . I want you to access any available records on Amanda Rogers.

DATA

Yes, Captain.

PICARD

I want to know more about her biological parents . . . about their death. I find it odd that any Q could die in an accident.

DATA

It does not seem consistent with what we know of them.

PICARD

I'm convinced Q isn't telling us everything. See what you can find out.

DATA

Aye, sir.

16 INTERIOR AMANDA'S QUARTERS (OPTICAL)

Beverly and Amanda are sitting together on the couch. Though she is still grappling with the enormous implications of what she's been told, the news does explain certain things that have been happening.

AMANDA

It started happening about six months ago . . . things I wished for suddenly appearing . . . objects moving on their own. . . . I thought I was going crazy. . . .

(beat)

In a funny way, finding this out is kind of a relief.

BEVERLY

I can understand that.

(beat)

The person I mentioned . . . from the Q Continuum . . . would like to meet you. If you want to . . .

Amanda takes a breath. Things are moving awfully fast, but she might as well start facing what's coming.

AMANDA

I'm ready.

Beverly starts toward the door . . . but before she reaches it, Q WALKS THROUGH IT, heading right for Amanda, who looks startled.

Q

There's my girl!

Beverly gives him a look.

The door OPENS, revealing Picard, who ENTERS and moves toward Amanda, trying to make this a comfortable introduction. He finds himself in the odd position of having to put Q in the best possible light.

PICARD

Amanda, this is Q.

(beat)

He is . . .

(searching)

. . . an acquaintance of ours. We've known him for years.

Q is circling Amanda, sizing her up as though she's a racehorse. It makes her quite uncomfortable.

Q

Very impressive the way you contained that explosion. What else have you done?

His brusque tone isn't helping to put Amanda at ease.

AMANDA

I . . . don't understand.

Q

Telekinesis, teleportation, spontaneous combustion of someone you didn't like—that sort of thing.

Amanda looks baffled, and Picard steps in to help.

PICARD

I think what Q means to ask is . . . have you deliberately used your abilities . . . ?

AMANDA

Not until I came here. The first time was when the container almost fell on Commander Riker.

Q

You did so well with that I decided to give you a real challenge . . . the warp core breach.

He takes her face in his hands, turning it this way and that.

Q

She clearly has potential. I see no reason why she can't come back to the Continuum right now.

AMANDA

What?

PICARD

(warning)

Q—

AMANDA

I don't want to go anywhere. . . .

Q

Don't worry. With time you'll be able to overcome the disadvantages you suffered as a child. No one will hold it against you that you were human.

Amanda turns to Picard in distress.

AMANDA

Captain Picard—?

Q advances on Amanda.

Q

Let's go, Amanda.

PICARD

(stepping forward)

She doesn't want to—

But as Q reaches Amanda she reacts, lifting her arm . . . and suddenly Q goes flying across the room, crashing into a wall.

AMANDA

Leave me alone! I'm not going anywhere with you!

A shaken Q looks at her with new respect . . . and the awareness that this isn't going to be as easy as he thought.

17 INTERIOR READY ROOM

Picard is with Q; he's irate at Q's behavior. Q is vaguely listening; he fussily brushes and tugs at his uniform, as if it had been mussed in his fall.

PICARD

You agreed she has the right to decide her own future . . . yet the first chance you get, you try to abduct her.

Q

You overreact as usual, Jean-Luc. I assure you—I was merely testing her power. She's quite a little spitfire, isn't she?

PICARD

What's going on, Q? What's your real purpose in being here?

Q

I've made that quite clear. The Continuum has a vested interest in this young woman. . . .

PICARD

If you intend to protect that investment, I suggest you approach her differently.

Q

She's just a little skittish. She'll have to start behaving like a Q.

PICARD

If I'm not mistaken, she just did.

Q flashes him an irritated look, not appreciating the reminder.

17A INTERIOR AMANDA'S QUARTERS

Beverly is with Amanda, still upset after the incident with Q.

AMANDA

I don't want anything to do with that Q person. I don't *care* about having powers. . . .

She looks at Beverly, pleading her case for denial.

AMANDA

You understand, don't you? I have things I want to do. . . . I'm going to the academy. . . . I want a career; I want to join Starfleet. . . .

BEVERLY

You can still do those things. . . .

AMANDA

But now it's so—complicated. This power I have . . . it's just going to get in the way. I don't want to have to deal with it. . . .

Beverly regards her sympathetically . . . understanding the feelings, but knowing the truth.

BEVERLY

But you have to.

Amanda looks at her.

BEVERLY

I know how you feel. It would be so much easier if none of this had happened . . . if it would just go away.

(beat)

But it's not going to go away.

Amanda is silent, hearing the cold wash of reality.

BEVERLY

You need someone to help you. And the person who can help you—is Q.

AMANDA

But he's horrible.

BEVERLY

But he's the only one who can help you understand who you are. There are hard choices you're going to have to make about your future . . . and you can't make them by ignoring the truth.

Amanda stares at her . . . and accepts, for now, her plight.

AMANDA

You're right.

(beat)

But I don't want any of this to disrupt my time here. I want to do everything I'm expected to do . . . and I don't want you to treat me any differently.

(beat)

Please?

Beverly smiles, recognizing the young woman's need for normality.

BEVERLY

You've got a deal. The first free hour you have, report

to me in the medical lab. I have an experiment I need help with.

Amanda grins; the familiarity of the routine is comforting to her.

AMANDA

Yes, ma'am.

Beverly EXITS.

17B INTERIOR CORRIDOR

Q walks along the corridor on his way to Amanda's quarters. No one is around. Suddenly a DARK SHADOW appears on the wall ahead of him. Q stops, annoyed. We HEAR the voice of the shadow . . . it is futzed and sepulchral.

Q SHADOW

Your progress, Q?

Q

As anticipated, there have been some problems . . . but the humans are cooperating. I need more time.

(matter-of-fact)

There is a possibility we won't have to terminate her.

The businesslike tone of Q's report makes it that much more chilling. . . .

FADE OUT.

ACT THREE

FADE IN:

0A INTERIOR CORRIDOR

As Q walks toward Amanda's quarters. He stops outside the door, takes a breath, and starts to walk through the door. Then he checks himself and, with a grimace, makes himself push the control.

18 INTERIOR AMANDA'S QUARTERS (OPTICAL)

As she hears the chime.

AMANDA

Come in.

The door opens and Q ENTERS. Amanda stays seated and composed.

Q

(ingratiating)

Hello, my dear . . .

But Amanda stares stonily at him, not responding at all. Q takes a breath . . . realizes he's going to have to eat some crow. It doesn't come easily.

Q

I've been told that I behaved badly. I . . .

(almost choking)

. . . a-pol-ogize. . . .

Amanda nods a cool acknowledgment.

Q

Apparently you had every right to chastise me . . .

(he's had enough of groveling)

. . . but what's done is done. Right?

Amanda eyes him, steely.

AMANDA

I'd like to ask you some questions.

He recognizes the edge in her voice, which is challenging and not to be intimidated.

Q

Anything . . .

AMANDA

What, exactly, are the Q?

Q

It would be so much easier to show you than to tell you. If you'd just agree to take a short visit to the Continuum—

But Amanda's having none of that.

AMANDA

No. Just tell me.

Q

To put it simply . . . we are omnipotent. There is nothing—nothing—we can't do.

AMANDA

And what do you do with this power?

Q

Whatever we want.

AMANDA

Do you use it to help others?

Q

I think you've missed the point. You've obviously spent far too much time among humans.

He moves closer to her, trying to spin a web of enticement.

Q

As a Q, you can have your heart's desire instantly . . . whatever it might be. Would you like precious jewels? Works of art? Would you like to visit the rings of Tautine?

AMANDA

I don't care about any of those things.

Q

Of course not. You're a Q. But surely there is something you want . . . something you never dreamed would be possible . . .

Amanda is silent. . . . Q senses that there is something she longs for. There is a long beat.

Q

What is it, Amanda? Just tell me . . .

She looks up at him, wrestling with this. . . . She doesn't exactly trust him, but if she's going to find out about these strange new abilities of hers . . .

AMANDA

I've always wanted to see what my parents looked like . . . my real parents.

Q

How quaint.

(beat)

So do it.

AMANDA

What do you mean?

Q

Summon the image.

AMANDA

But . . . I don't know how.

Q reacts with a little exasperation.

Q

Think about them . . . evoke the memory. . . .

AMANDA

But—

Q

Amanda. You can do this. Trust me.

He kneels near where she's seated.

Q

Close your eyes . . . concentrate. . . .

Amanda wants this so badly that she puts aside her skepticism and does as he asks.

Q

In your mind, return to the time when you were an infant. . . . Think about your parents. . . . Try and remember them. . . . Now, open your eyes.

An IMAGE begins flickering on the couch . . . finally MATERIALIZES completely . . . a young man and woman, she holding a swaddled baby. They are playing with the baby, tickling it under the chin, etc., and smiling with what could only be described as unadorned love.

Amanda opens her eyes . . . sees the image . . . is transfixed. She rises, walks toward the couple, staring at them.

AMANDA

They look so happy. . . .

(realizing)

They loved me. . . .

Amanda stares at the group on the couch . . . raw emotion swelling in her. Q smiles. . . . He knows he's gotten to her.

Amanda turns around to him . . . but when she does . . . he's gone. She's left with a lot to think about.

19 EXTERIOR SPACE—THE *ENTERPRISE* (OPTICAL)

As it cruises at impulse.

20 INTERIOR MEDICAL LAB (OPTICAL)

Beverly is walking Amanda through the various steps involved in the neural tissue experiment she's been working on.

Amanda uses a DROPPER to add a tiny amount of liquid to a BEAKER of solution.

She then takes a TRICORDER and scans the beaker.

AMANDA

Ten percent benasopil.

Beverly gives her a nod of encouragement. Amanda seems distracted, unable to concentrate.

AMANDA

So I add thirty milliliters to each of the cultures . . .

BEVERLY

Twenty milliliters . . .

AMANDA

Right, twenty . . . I wait for it to be metabolized . . . add—another twenty?

(off Beverly's nod)

. . . wait for *it* to be metabolized . . . over and over until the bacilli can't absorb any more.

BEVERLY

That's it.

(hands her a padd)

Just be sure and record the rate of mitosis in each dish.

AMANDA

Mitosis . . . right.

Beverly regards her, aware that her concentration is fuzzy.

BEVERLY

You seem a little distracted.

AMANDA

Well . . . I just saw my parents. My real parents.

Beverly stares at her, amazed.

AMANDA

Q showed me how . . .

She looks up at Beverly.

AMANDA

Can you imagine how that felt . . . ?

Captain Picard and his crew are placed on trial by Q to answer for all of humanity's foibles.

Q asks the age-old question—does absolute power corrupt absolutely?—when he gives Commander Riker the power of the Q.

The *Enterprise* crew get their first glimpse of what will become their greatest adversaries: the Borg.

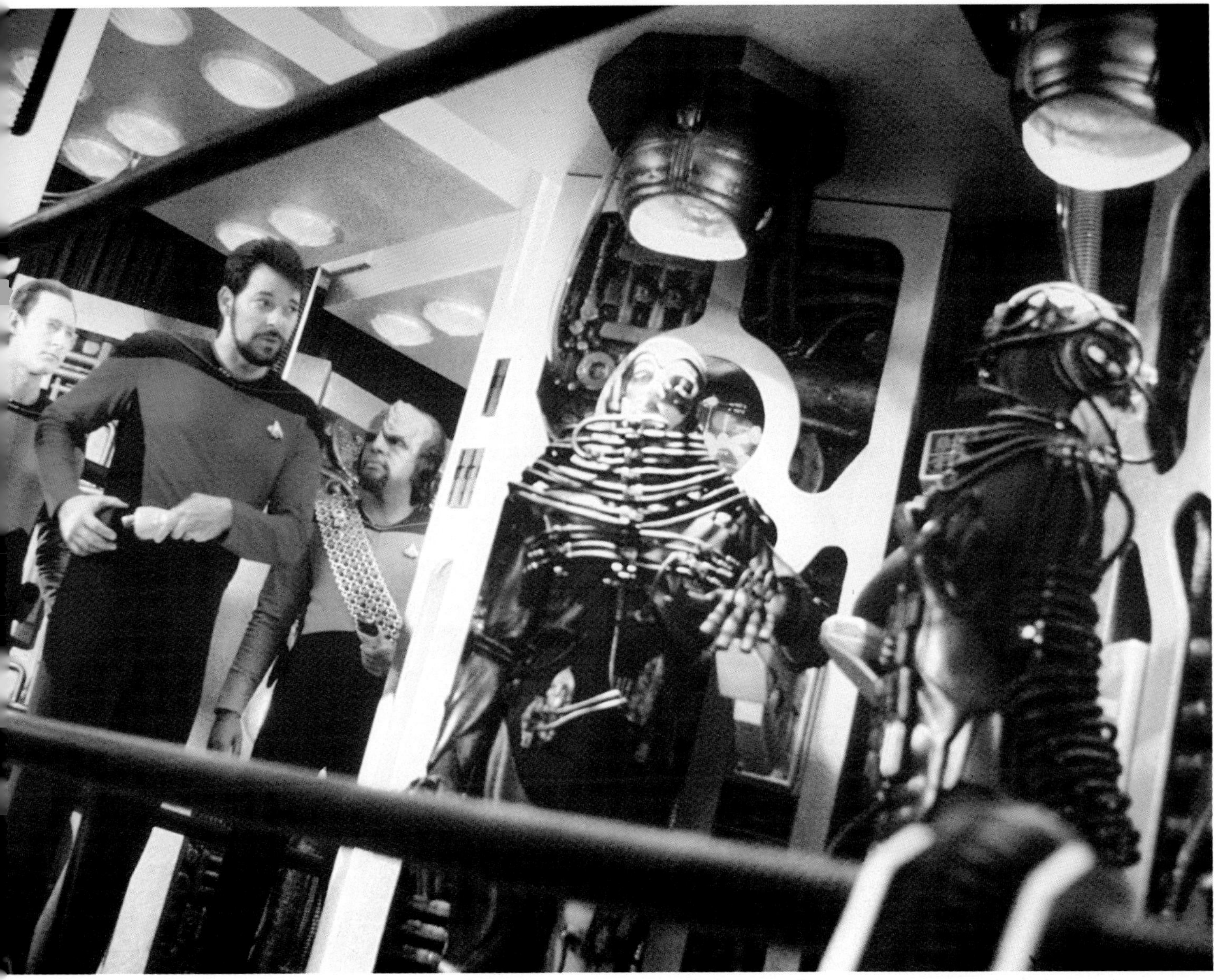

Riker leads a landing party into the heart of darkness, a Borg ship.

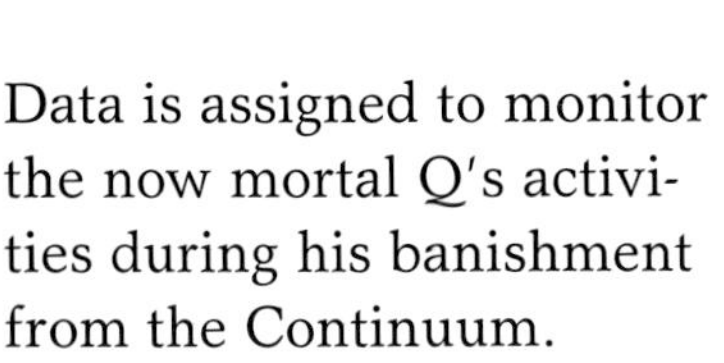

Data is assigned to monitor the now mortal Q's activities during his banishment from the Continuum.

Donning the guise of the Sheriff of Nottingham, Q decides to repay a favor by sending Picard to Sherwood Forest. *(Michael Paris)*

Captain Picard and the rest of the *Enterprise*'s senior staff are transformed into Robin Hood and his Merry Men as part of an elaborate scheme by Q. *(Michael Paris)*

Q informs Amanda Rogers that her deceased parents were not human, but were once members of the Q Continuum.

Vash's quest to sell ancient artifacts from the Gamma Quadrant hits a snag when she encounters an old acquaintance aboard Deep Space 9.

Picard is offered a chance to change his past, and is suddenly reliving his days at the Bonestell Recreational Facility with his Starfleet Academy friends, Cortin Zweller and Marta Batanides. *(Robbie Robinson)*

Q is chastened by Quinn, who remindes Q that he was once banished from the Continuum for his actions. *(Robbie Robinson)*

Q adds a few touches to *Voyager*'s Polynesian holodeck program. *(Robbie Robinson)*

Captain Janeway experiences a real war in the Q Continuum as images from the American Civil War; unfortunately, the firing squad that Captain Janeway and Q are facing could kill them. *(Robbie Robinson)*

In an anti-time future, Picard confronts Q, certain that the crisis facing all reality is somehow Q's fault. *(Robbie Robinson)*

All-powerful, near-omniscient, Q sits in judgment of the human race. *(Robbie Robinson)*

BEVERLY

No . . . I don't think I can.

AMANDA

You were right. . . . I can't ignore what's happened to me. . . .

(a beat as she fights choking up)

. . . but . . . I don't know if I can cope with it.

Beverly's heart aches for this overburdened child.

BEVERLY

You're stronger than you think, Amanda. . . .

There is a beat as Amanda struggles with her feelings.

AMANDA

When I looked at my parents . . . right there, in front of me . . . I realized—I caused this to happen. I wanted to see them . . . and I did.

(beat)

If it were you . . . if suddenly you could have anything you wanted . . . what do you think you'd do?

BEVERLY

(slight laugh)

I have no idea—

AMANDA

No, think about it. Really *think.* Suddenly you have the power to do anything. What would it be?

Forced into looking at it from this perspective, Beverly is a bit overwhelmed.

BEVERLY

I . . . I'm not sure. I'd probably want to cure people . . . people who were hopelessly ill.

AMANDA

Would you bring your husband back?

Beverly stares at her. She is overwhelmed by the question. . . .

BEVERLY

Oh, Amanda, I don't know. . . . I don't think I could decide about something like that until I was faced with it. . . .

AMANDA

(simply)

I am faced with it.

Beverly regards her . . . understanding more than ever the heavy weight that Amanda bears. She returns to the commonplace—

BEVERLY

Go on with your work. I'll be back to check on you later.

Beverly EXITS. Amanda turns and begins working. After a moment, Q APPEARS.

Q

I thought she'd never leave.

AMANDA

(startled)

I don't think I'll ever get used to that. . . .

Q

It's time for another lesson.

AMANDA

I have to do this experiment first.

Q peers at the work, unable to fathom that it could hold any interest.

Q

What is it you're doing?

AMANDA

We're delivering live vaccine bacilli to Tagra. I'm supposed to find the best nutrient solution for keeping them alive while they're in stasis.

Q

(sarcastic)

How fascinating . . .

(suddenly animated)
I have a splendid idea. We'll combine your work . . . with our lesson. I'll show you how to finish this in no time.

AMANDA
(hesitant)
I think I'd better do it the way Doctor Crusher showed me.

Q
Why? I'm sure the doctor would be delighted if you could speed things along. Think what it would mean . . . you could handle double . . . triple the work load.

This sounds reasonable.

AMANDA
Well . . . I guess so.

Q motions that she look at the culture dishes.

Q
All right. As you look at the tissue samples . . . form an image of them in your mind. . . .

Amanda's curiosity is mounting. She stares at the culture dishes . . . concentrating on the image. . . .

21 INTERIOR MAIN BRIDGE (OPTICAL)

Data is working at an aft science station. Picard ENTERS from the ready room and approaches Riker, who is in his chair.

PICARD
Number One . . . Doctor Crusher has some live vaccine bacilli for delivery to Tagra. . . . They'll need to be shipped in a stasis field. Will you make the arrangements?

RIKER
I'll get right on it.

He heads up the ramp to the turbolift.

DATA
Captain, there is a message from Tagra IV.

PICARD
On screen.

An alien humanoid named ORN LOTE appears on the viewscreen; he is in a small room which is a control station for one of the planet's baristatic filters.

ORN LOTE
Enterprise, I am Orn Lote, engineer. We are having difficulties with the reactor that powers our baristatic filters on the Southern Continent. We may have to shut it down for repairs.

PICARD
Perhaps my chief engineer could assist you . . . ?

ORN LOTE
I hope so. If we are forced to disable the reactor, it would take months to reestablish the ionic currents the filters have formed in the atmosphere.

PICARD
Send us your design specifications—I'm sure we can do something.

ORN LOTE
Thank you, Captain.

Lote's face disappears and is replaced by a starfield.

DATA
Captain . . . may I see you for a moment?

Picard starts up the ramp.

PICARD
What is it, Mister Data?

DATA
I have some information regarding Amanda Rogers's parents.

Picard reaches the aft science station.

DATA

Records indicate that they died in Topeka, Kansas. Their home was destroyed during a tornado.

PICARD

A tornado? Why wasn't it dissipated by the weather modification net?

DATA

Unknown, sir. The bodies were found in the rubble after the storm had passed.

PICARD

(a beat as he ponders)

See if you can find out any details. I'd like to know more about that storm.

DATA

Yes, Captain.

22 INTERIOR MEDICAL LAB (OPTICAL)

Riker ENTERS and stops when he sees Q and Amanda. Q is standing in front of her. . . . Her eyes are closed, as though concentrating on something. The minute Q sees Riker—

Q

If it isn't Number Two . . .

RIKER

(ignoring him; to Amanda)

I'm looking for Doctor Crusher. I don't know what nutrients she wants to ship with the bacilli.

AMANDA

I'm not sure. . . . I'll tell her to contact you.

RIKER

Thanks.

He smiles and turns to go. She doesn't want him to leave and blurts out the first thing that comes to mind.

AMANDA
You could wait for her here . . . ?

She realizes how this sounds, tries to be more casual.

AMANDA
If you wanted to . . .

RIKER
(smiles)
Just tell her I'll be in shuttlebay two.

He EXITS, and Q eyes her, recognizing that she has feelings for Riker.

Q
You're attracted—to *him*?

Embarrassed, she turns away from him.

AMANDA
Of course not . . .

Q
I think you are. How repulsive . . . how can you stand that hair all over his face?

But Amanda is saved from further inquiry by Beverly's entrance.

AMANDA
Doctor . . . Commander Riker was looking for you. . . . He said he'd be in shuttlebay two.

BEVERLY
Thank you.

She notices the apparatus of Amanda's experiment.

BEVERLY
(surprised)
You've finished already?

Amanda smiles; she feels a sense of satisfaction.

BEVERLY
How did you do it so quickly?

Beverly picks up the padd and looks it over.

AMANDA
(proudly)
Q helped me. . . . We did it in less than half the time it would've normally taken.

BEVERLY
That explains this data.
(puts the padd down, addresses Q)
I needed to know the rates of mitosis. By artificially accelerating them you made the experiment useless. Now I'll have to do it over again.

AMANDA
(crestfallen)
I'm sorry, Doctor . . .

Q
Don't be sorry. If she wants to do things the hard way, that's her business.

BEVERLY
(firm)
Why did you interfere with what she was doing?

Q
She's Q. . . . Making her plod through human chores is an insult to her.

BEVERLY
She has asked not to be treated differently.

Q
That doesn't mean you have to bore her to death.

BEVERLY
I don't interfere with what you're trying to teach Amanda—

Q
You wouldn't be *capable* of interfering—

BEVERLY

(right over him)

I don't think it's too much to ask for you to do the same—

Q waves his hand and suddenly Beverly is TRANSFORMED into a YAPPING IRISH SETTER for a few beats. Q is amused by this, but Amanda is horrified. She waves her hand and TRANSFORMS Beverly back. Beverly continues with what she was saying, unaware of what happened.

BEVERLY

—and you stay out of mine.

Q nods in mock seriousness.

Q

Now that you put it like that, I think you're absolutely right.

He smiles winningly at Beverly. Amanda is aghast, but mostly relieved that Beverly didn't seem to notice what happened.

FADE OUT.

ACT FOUR

FADE IN:

23 INTERIOR BRIDGE

Data is once more at the aft science station.

DATA

Captain . . .

PICARD

Yes, Mister Data?

DATA

I have more information regarding the tornado that killed Amanda Rogers's parents.

Picard crosses immediately to him.

PICARD

What is it?

Data indicates the screen of the monitor (which we do NOT see), and Picard leans in to it.

DATA

It was unusually compact, yet extremely powerful—its recorded wind velocity was characteristic of a funnel three times its size.

A beat as Picard registers the implications of what he's just heard.

PICARD

Download the files to my ready room. I'll study them in there.

DATA

Yes, sir.

He begins working as Picard heads for the ready room.

24 INTERIOR AMANDA'S QUARTERS (OPTICAL)

Amanda with Q.

AMANDA

Doctor Crusher was only trying to help me. . . . You shouldn't have turned her into a dog. . . .

Q regards her with a twinkle in his eye. He knows she is feeling more receptive to him.

Q

Now, be truthful, Amanda. Wasn't it amusing?

(beat)

Just a little?

AMANDA

(acknowledging, a little smile)

Well . . .

Q

There, you see? My dear, what's the point of having these abilities if you can't enjoy them?

(briskly)

Now—have you been practicing your teleportation?

AMANDA

Yes. But it's kind of hard. I keep ending up somewhere I don't want to be.

Q

You're going to have to start honing your abilities. It won't do to be sloppy . . . let's see . . . perhaps a little game?

He smiles warmly at her.

Q

I'm going to hide somewhere on the ship. . . . You try to find me.

AMANDA

But how do I know—

But he DISAPPEARS before she can finish. Amanda isn't sure what to do.

Q'S VOICE
(from all around)
Don't worry, Amanda. You can do it. . . .

She closes her eyes and concentrates, as if she's trying to sense where he's gone. She seems to make a decision and DISAPPEARS.

CUT TO:
25 INTERIOR SHUTTLEBAY TWO (OPTICAL)

As Amanda REAPPEARS amidst the bustle of activity in the room. A few people notice her, but she ignores them as she looks around for Q.

She turns around, perplexed, not seeing him. Then, she spots a STORAGE CONTAINER in a corner. She concentrates, and it DISAPPEARS, revealing Q inside.

Q
Not bad. Not bad at all.

He DISAPPEARS again. Amanda once more concentrates to locate him and then DISAPPEARS herself.

CUT TO:
26 INTERIOR ENGINEERING (OPTICAL)

As Amanda APPEARS in the area between the pool table and the warp core.

Geordi and Data are there, but they don't see her because they're looking at a monitor and talking. Amanda looks around for Q as they work.

GEORDI
The trick is to come up with a field modulator that doesn't require shutting down their reactor. . . .

DATA
If we use a field modulator, we can devise a mechanism that integrates into the existing system while it is in operation.

In the background Amanda has failed to find Q. She is about to wave her hand and look for him elsewhere when he *sticks his head out of the pulsating chamber that is the heart of the warp core.*

Q
You're still thinking like a human. . . .

Geordi and Data turn at the sound of his voice in time to see Q's head DISAPPEAR back into the reaction chamber and Amanda DISAPPEAR altogether a moment later.

Off their reactions . . .

CUT TO:

27 EXTERIOR SPACE—THE *ENTERPRISE* (OPTICAL)

As Amanda APPEARS and is stunned to find herself *standing on the ship's hull*—she has materialized outside, in space, atop the Saucer Module.

Q stands nearby, smiling. Behind them we see the rear of the ship with its warp nacelles. There is no wind . . . no sound. . . . A small but dramatic field of asteroids sweeps by them. . . .

It is a breathtaking moment . . . and Q lets the impact sink in.

Amanda looks around, awestruck. . . . After a moment she smiles a smile so bright it almost shames the passing stars.

Q is pleased. This is exactly the reaction he had hoped for. He waves a hand and they both DISAPPEAR.

28 OMITTED

29 INTERIOR AMANDA'S QUARTERS (OPTICAL)

As Q and Amanda APPEAR. She is still breathless with the wonder of what she has experienced. Q gazes at her, well aware of the impact of his little game.

Q

Now do you understand? What do humans have to offer that even begins to compare with that?

She is still reeling. . . .

Q

Your future contains wonders you can't even imagine. . . . The universe could be your playground. . . .

The sudden intrusion of door CHIMES invades Q's rhapsodic vision. He eyes her.

AMANDA

Doctor Crusher and Counselor Troi . . . they're taking me to dinner.

He shakes his head, annoyed.

Q

You don't *have* to eat, you know. It's just a nasty human habit you could easily do without.

He DISAPPEARS. Amanda crosses to the door and opens it; Beverly and Troi are there.

BEVERLY

Hello, Amanda. Are you ready?

AMANDA

Yes . . .

But Amanda's attitude is one of reluctance, not anticipation.

30 INTERIOR TEN-FORWARD (OPTICAL)

Where Amanda, Beverly, and Troi are having dinner. Amanda hasn't touched her food.

TROI

Is there something else you'd like to order, Amanda?

AMANDA

No, thank you. I'm just . . . not hungry.

(beat)

Actually, I don't even have to eat. It's a human trait.

TROI

I see.

(beat)

How are you feeling about all this now? It must be overwhelming.

AMANDA

It was at first. But now . . . I'm actually enjoying myself.

RIKER'S VOICE

Hello, ladies . . .

They look up to see Riker has approached the table.

TROI

Hello, Wil . . .

Beverly nods her greeting . . . and Amanda breaks out in an eager, pleased smile.

AMANDA

Commander Riker . . . why don't you join us?

RIKER

Thanks, but I'm meeting someone.

He smiles and moves off; Amanda's face falls and she gazes after him.

BEVERLY

(to Amanda)

How are the lessons going? Is Q being patient with you?

But Amanda isn't really listening. She's watching Riker, who joins an attractive WOMAN at another table. Troi and Beverly exchange glances.

Amanda watches Riker . . . laughing with the woman at some shared joke. Amanda's eyes narrow . . . and suddenly Amanda waves her hand and both she and Riker DISAPPEAR. Troi and Beverly are astonished.

31 EXTERIOR GAZEBO—NIGHT (OPTICAL)

In the woods, as Amanda and Riker APPEAR under its roof. Amanda wears an elegant evening dress; Riker is formally attired.

The gazebo's white slatted joints are intertwined with vines. It is night, and the few leafy branches that are visible are enough to suggest that the gazebo is deep in an enchanted forest.

Riker realizes that the very elaborateness of what she's now doing demonstrates the depth of her infatuation with him, and he knows he needs to be careful with her feelings.

RIKER
(evenly)
What's this all about?

AMANDA
I thought it might be nice for us to spend some time alone together.

She smiles radiantly at him. . . .

RIKER
I think you should take us back to Ten-Forward.

She moves toward him . . . wanting to be seductive . . . needing to be taken seriously as a woman.

AMANDA
Are you sure? Wouldn't you like to be here with me for a while?

She gestures.

AMANDA
The moonlight is beautiful. . . . Isn't it nicer here than in Ten-Forward?

RIKER
It's very pleasant. But that's not the point. . . .

AMANDA
Oh . . . ?

She twines her arms around his neck.

AMANDA
I think it is. . . .

He takes her wrists and pulls them off him.

RIKER
No . . .
(beat)
You can't just snatch people away and put them in your fantasies . . . and expect them to respond.

AMANDA
Don't you like me . . . even a little?

RIKER
I think you're a lovely young woman. But—none of this is real.

Amanda stares at him. . . . She had expected that he would be swept off his feet by her grand fantasy.

AMANDA
My feelings are real. . . .

RIKER
I know that . . . but—you can't make someone . . . love you.

Amanda's eyes narrow again.

AMANDA
Can't I?

She concentrates . . . and Riker's expression suddenly changes. He looks at her with devotion. . . .

RIKER
Amanda . . .

He moves toward her, takes her in his arms in a passionate embrace.

RIKER
You're so beautiful. . . .

He kisses her fully, Amanda enjoying the exquisiteness of the moment. . . . They break apart and he buries his head in her neck.

AMANDA
Do you love me?

RIKER
Yes . . . more than anything . . .

She stands for a moment as he kisses her neck and shoulder. . . . A sad expression steals over her. She steps back from him . . . and his expression changes back to normal Riker. He blinks, not sure of what's happened.

AMANDA
(softly)
You're right . . . none of this is real. . . .

She turns her back on him, embarrassed now at the whole situation.

AMANDA
I thought it would be romantic . . . but it's empty. . . .

RIKER
(solicitous)
Amanda . . .

But she's humiliated, near tears . . . moves away from him.

AMANDA
Just go back to Ten-Forward. . . .

Riker DISAPPEARS. Then she bursts into tears, a young woman in a lovely gown . . . standing in the gazebo deep within the enchanted forest . . . alone in her fantasy.

32 EXTERIOR SPACE—THE *ENTERPRISE* (OPTICAL)

As it cruises at impulse.

33 OMITTED

33A INTERIOR READY ROOM (OPTICAL)

Q APPEARS before Picard.

Q
Bon jour, mon Capitaine. You wanted to talk to me?

PICARD
Yes. I want to ask you about Amanda's biological parents. When they decided to remain on Earth, what was the reaction in the Continuum?

Q
We found it incomprehensible.

PICARD
Were they pressured to come back? Were they threatened with punishment if they didn't?

Q
What are you getting at, Picard?

PICARD
The circumstance of their death was a bit odd . . . a tornado that escaped the weather modification net . . . and then touched down in only one spot—Amanda's home.

Q
(shrugs)
You never can predict the weather. . . .

PICARD
Tornadoes develop from existing storm fronts . . . and there *were* no storm fronts in Kansas that day. Witnesses reported that the funnel materialized spontaneously . . . directly over Amanda's home . . . destroyed it . . . and then disappeared.

Q
If you say so. I wasn't there.

PICARD
Were Amanda's parents executed . . . by the Q Continuum?

Q hesitates before answering.

Q
And what if they were?

PICARD
Then I think Amanda has the right to know that before she makes a choice about her future.

Q
Don't be foolish, Picard. She has no choice. She never did.

Picard starts to retort, but Q rides over him.

Q

If she is truly Q, she must come where she belongs, to the Continuum. . . .

Q pauses, looks levelly at Picard.

Q

But if she is some kind of hybrid . . . neither human nor Q . . . then I'm afraid she'll have to be . . .

Q's gesture is clear; they will kill her.

PICARD

Are you that despicable, Q?

Q

Don't be naive. You have no idea what it means to be Q. With unlimited power comes the need for responsibility. Do you think we can allow an omnipotent being to roam free in the universe?

PICARD

And . . . what have you concluded? Does she live . . . or does she die?

Q

I haven't decided yet.

And on that impasse . . .

FADE OUT.

ACT FIVE

FADE IN:

34 EXTERIOR SPACE—THE *ENTERPRISE* (OPTICAL)

Now in orbit around Tagra IV. The planet's atmosphere is noticeably brownish from heavy smog.

PICARD (voice-over)
Captain's log, stardate 46193.8. We have arrived at Tagra IV and have begun delivering supplies. In the meantime, I am faced with a crisis of a different nature.

35 INTERIOR OBSERVATION LOUNGE

Picard with Beverly and Troi.

PICARD
I have no reason to believe Q is lying. He has orders from the Continuum. . . . If Amanda doesn't prove herself to be fully Q . . . he must kill her.

TROI
We have to tell her. . . .

BEVERLY
I'm not sure we should. . . . It seems almost cruel.

TROI
Maybe she can protect herself. . . . After all, she has a great deal of power.

BEVERLY
So did her parents, and it didn't save them.

There is a silence as Picard reflects on the arguments. Then—

PICARD
I'm inclined to agree that Amanda deserves to know the truth of the situation. We don't have the right to withhold such crucial information.

(beat)

But it won't be easy telling her. . . .

The others are sympathetic to his plight.

36 INTERIOR SHUTTLEBAY TWO

Riker and Orn Lote in conversation.

RIKER

What's your impression of the field modulator, Mister Lote?

LOTE

Quite ingenious, quite ingenious, indeed . . .

(coughs)

I'm amazed at the way it can be incorporated into the existing system.

Geordi approaches.

GEORDI

We're all loaded. We can head for the surface whenever you're ready.

LOTE

I'm eager to see the field modulator in place, Commander.

He suddenly degenerates into a cough. . . . He fumbles for a small oxygen-type mask that hangs from his belt, puts it over his nose and mouth, and draws few quick breaths to calm his inflamed bronchi.

RIKER

Why don't we get going . . . ?

36A–36E OMITTED

37 EXTERIOR SPACE—THE *ENTERPRISE* (OPTICAL)

In orbit of Tagra IV.

38–38A OMITTED

39 INTERIOR READY ROOM (OPTICAL)

Amanda is with Picard, who has told her of Q's true purpose. She is pale but composed.

AMANDA

Kill me? Why?

PICARD

They're not convinced you're fully Q.

She stares at him, incredulous.

PICARD

They were responsible for the death of your parents. . . .

AMANDA

(stunned)

My parents—?

There is a beat as she absorbs this dreadful information . . . and then begins to get angry.

AMANDA

What *right* do they have?

She looks around the room, challenging Q to come forward.

AMANDA

Answer that, Q. Or are you afraid to face me?

Q APPEARS.

Q

You're such a plucky little thing. I do enjoy you, you know.

PICARD

Amanda's question deserves an answer, Q. You've made yourself judge, jury, and—if necessary—executioner. By what right do you appoint yourself to this position?

Q

Superior morality . . .

PICARD

I recall how you used your superior morality when

we first encountered you. You put us on trial for the crimes of humanity.

Q

The jury is still out, Picard. Make no mistake.

PICARD

Your arrogant pretense to being the moral guardians of the universe strikes me as a bit pale today. You have shown no evidence that you are guided by a superior moral code—by any code whatsoever. You may be nearly omnipotent—I won't deny your parlor tricks are impressive—but morality? No, I don't see it. I don't acknowledge it. I would put human morality against the Q's any day.

Q looks at him sharply.

PICARD

Perhaps that's the fascination we humans hold for you . . . ? That by our puny example we give you a glimmer of the one thing that eludes your omnipotence—a moral center.

Q refuses to react in any way.

PICARD

If so, I can think of no crueler irony than for you to destroy a young woman whose only crime . . . is being too human.

Q has perhaps been struck by the truth of Picard's words . . . but of course can't acknowledge that. He applauds.

Q

Jean-Luc, Jean-Luc . . . sometimes I think the only reason I come here is to listen to these wonderful speeches of yours. But in this case your concerns are unwarranted. We've decided not to harm her. We're prepared to offer her a choice.

AMANDA

(wary)

What kind of choice?

Q

You can come with me to the Continuum—

AMANDA

Or . . . ?

Q eyes her.

Q

The other choice is more difficult.

(beat)

You have within yourself the ability to refrain from using the power of Q. If you can do that—you can stay here.

AMANDA

Then I'm staying here.

Q

Think carefully. . . . It won't be easy. Your parents were offered the same choice . . . and they were unable to resist using their power.

AMANDA

All I've wanted . . . since this whole thing began . . . was to be a normal human being again. I know I can resist.

Before Q can respond—

WORF (com voice)

Worf to Picard—there is an emergency message from Commander Riker.

PICARD

On my way.

He goes immediately for the bridge, followed by Amanda and Q.

40 INTERIOR BRIDGE (OPTICAL)

As they emerge from the ready room. Riker is on the viewscreen from the reactor control room. Geordi and Lote are in background.

RIKER

Captain, the damage to the reactor was greater than the Tagrans led us to believe. The field modulator is installed and operational, but it's not going to be enough. . . . The reactor's gone into overload. . . .

PICARD

Can you correct the problem?

RIKER

La Forge is trying to stabilize the unit now. We'll stay as long as possible. . . . There are thousands of people in the area, and if that reactor goes . . .

LOTE

(on viewscreen, to Riker)

Commander—over here, quickly!

Riker moves off toward Lote and Geordi in the background. Picard turns stonily to Q.

PICARD

Is this your doing, Q—?

Q spreads his hands in genuine innocence.

Q

Not this time, Picard.

And he DISAPPEARS.

PICARD

Mister Worf, see if there's anything we can do to cut through the interference and beam them out of there.

WORF

Aye, sir.

Riker moves back toward the front of the viewscreen.

RIKER

Captain, La Forge is trying a neutrino infusion. There's a chance it'll smother the reaction. . . .

WORF
Sir, there is too much ionization in the atmosphere; transporters are useless.

41 ANGLE ON AMANDA

Through all this, she has been staring at the viewscreen, stricken with the possibility of what might happen.

GEORDI (com voice)
It didn't work, sir. Meltdown is imminent.

Amanda narrows her eyes. . . .

42 ANGLE FAVORING VIEWSCREEN (OPTICAL)

As Riker and Geordi stand there, helpless . . . then, from the back of the control room . . .

LOTE
Commander . . . look at this. . . .

They turn and inspect a console.

GEORDI
This is impossible. . . .

He turns back to the viewscreen.

GEORDI
I don't know what's happening, sir—but the reaction is stabilizing on its own.

Picard turns . . . looks at Amanda . . . but she's concentrating on the viewscreen.

DATA
Sir . . . I am reading a massive energy fluctuation in the planet's atmosphere.

PICARD
On screen.

The control room disappears from the viewscreen and is replaced by a view of the planet itself, smog-shrouded.

43 AMANDA

Stares at it . . . concentrating . . .

44 ON THE VIEWSCREEN (OPTICAL)

The brown veil over the planet is dissipating . . . and Tagra IV is transformed into a lush, blue-green world. . . .

45 THE CREW

Stares at the phenomenal transformation.

DATA
Atmospheric contaminants have dropped to less than one part per trillion.
(glancing at Picard)
The ecosystem has been restored to its natural state.

PICARD
Amanda . . . ?

She turns and looks at him . . . and then Q APPEARS.

Q
You see? It's harder to resist than you thought. . . .

AMANDA
I couldn't let all those people die. . . .

She looks around the bridge . . . at Picard . . . at Q. . . .

AMANDA
Ever since I got here, I've been fighting this. Denying the truth. Denying what I *am.*

She regards them all, a little sad, but knowing she's right.

AMANDA
I am Q.

A look of concentration crosses her features and—Beverly APPEARS . . . looking a bit startled. Q is tapping his foot impatiently.

AMANDA

Doctor Crusher . . . I've decided . . . I can't stay . . .

(beat)

I can't stay here.

Q

Now that you've come to your senses, can we be off?

AMANDA

No. First I'm going to visit my parents. And it might take a while to explain all this, so you'll have to be patient.

Amanda turns to Beverly. . . . Beverly opens her arms and hugs her.

AMANDA

I hope I can come visit you sometime. . . .

BEVERLY

(smiling)

You're a Q. . . . You can do anything you want.

Amanda smiles, pulls away. She regards them . . . bittersweet tears in her eyes. . . . She and Q DISAPPEAR.

Our people are left alone, with their memories of a very special young woman. . . .

46–48 OMITTED

FADE OUT.

STAR TREK: THE NEXT GENERATION

Tapestry

#40276-241

Written by
Ronald D. Moore

Directed by
Les Landau

STAR TREK: THE NEXT GENERATION

Tapestry

CAST

PICARD
RIKER
DATA
BEVERLY
TROI
WORF
GEORDI

COMPUTER VOICE

Q
MARTA BATANIDES
MAURICE PICARD
NAUSICAAN #1
MALE VOICE
PENNY MUROC
COREY ZWELLER

Non-Speaking

TWO NAUSICAANS

STAR TREK: THE NEXT GENERATION

Tapestry

SETS

INTERIORS

U.S.S. ENTERPRISE
MAIN BRIDGE
SICKBAY
TEN-FORWARD
TURBOLIFT
BEVERLY'S OFFICE
TROI'S OFFICE
OBSERVATION LOUNGE

STARBASE
PICARD'S QUARTERS
MARTA'S QUARTERS
BONESTELL RECREATION FACILITY
GAMBLING CENTER
BAR

EXTERIORS

U.S.S. ENTERPRISE

STAR TREK: THE NEXT GENERATION

Tapestry

PRONUNCIATION GUIDE

BATANIDES	buh-TAN-ih-deez
BONESTELL	BON-es-tell
NAUSICAAN	NAW-si-can
SCOBEE	SKO-bee

STAR TREK: THE NEXT GENERATION

Tapestry

TEASER

FADE IN

1 INTERIOR SICKBAY (OPTICAL)

The room is in a state of frenetic activity. N.D. NURSES and DOCTORS are rushing about, grabbing equipment and moving consoles in preparation for some imminent emergency. BEVERLY grabs her medical tricorder as she directs people to action.

BEVERLY
(to nurse)
Get the stasis units in here and bring them on-line.
(to another nurse)
Tell Doctor Selar to use ward three for the ambulatory cases, I'll take the—

COM VOICE
Transporter room four to sickbay. They're coming in now.

BEVERLY
Acknowledged.
(to everyone)
Back everyone.

They all clear out the center of the room as RIKER, PICARD, WORF, and THREE N.D. CREW MEMBERS MATERIALIZE. Worf is carrying Picard over one shoulder. Riker has a nasty-looking head wound and is pointing his phaser as if defending them. One N.D. is also injured and lying on the floor, while the other two are standing up with phasers drawn.

Once the beam-in has finished, Beverly and the nurses rush to aid the wounded. Beverly moves to Picard as Worf puts him down on the operating table. We can now see that there is a large SCORCH mark on Picard's chest. Beverly immediately begins scanning him with her tricorder.

BEVERLY
What happened?

RIKER

The Lenarians attacked us outside the conference room.

BEVERLY

(off tricorder)

He's in cardiac arrest.

(to Nurse)

Get the pulmonary support unit.

The CLAMSHELL is moved into place over Picard's chest. Worf and Riker move away to give them room and look on with concern. Beverly continues to read the tricorder.

BEVERLY

Internal hemorrhaging . . . the bio-regulator in his artificial heart's been fused . . . damage to the spleen and liver . . . what kind of weapon did this?

WORF

A compressed tetryon beam.

BEVERLY

(to Nurse)

Forty cc's inaprovaline . . .

An ALARM SOUNDS from the clamshell.

BEVERLY

Activity in the isocortex is falling. Cortical stimulator.

A nurse hands her a device, which Beverly places on his forehead. A monitor in the room begins to show a flatline and ALARMS are continuous now.

BEVERLY

Now.

Picard's body JERKS . . . then nothing.

BEVERLY

Again.

His body JERKS again . . . nothing.

2 NEW ANGLE

We are now looking DOWN at the scene in sickbay from directly overhead . . . as we begin to PUSH DOWN onto Picard's face, Beverly and the others can be seen working frantically on him, but there is NO SOUND except for a slowly building RUSHING NOISE, similar to the sound of the ocean. As Picard's face fills the frame, the rushing sound builds to a ROAR and suddenly the scene . . .

FADES TO WHITE.

FADE IN:

3 LIMBO

SILENCE. Picard is standing in a blindingly WHITE LIMBO without walls or ceiling. He is dazed and confused . . . unsure where he is or what's happening to him. He struggles to look around, but he cannot discern anything in this uniformly bright place. Suddenly an even more INTENSE LIGHT fills part of the scene. Picard holds up a hand to shield his eyes from this painfully intense light, but he does not retreat. He struggles to look into the light.

3A P.O.V. PICARD (OPTICAL)

The glowing luminescence has a form . . . it is the shape of a FIGURE standing in the light.

3B PICARD

Determined to find out who this is, moves toward the silhouetted figure. He finally stops in front of it. He can barely look into the light at all.

4 THE FIGURE (OPTICAL)

Reaches out for him with one hand.

5 PICARD

Reaches out toward the hand . . . they clasp hands and suddenly . . .

6 NEW ANGLE

Revealing Q standing with Picard, holding his hand. Q is wearing white flowing ethereal robes.

Q

Welcome to the afterlife, Jean-Luc.

(beat)

You're dead.

OFF Picard's shocked reaction . . .

FADE OUT.

ACT ONE

FADE IN:

7 LIMBO—CONTINUOUS

Picard angrily drops Q's hand.

PICARD

What's going on, Q?

Q

I told you. You're dead. This is the afterlife. And I'm God.

PICARD

You are *not* God.

Q

Blasphemy! You're lucky I don't cast you out, or smite you or something.

Picard is unamused.

PICARD

I don't know what game it is you're playing, but I am not going to participate.

Q

What an ego.

(sarcastic)

Did you think the great Jean-Luc Picard would never die?

PICARD

Q, whatever you've done to—

Q

I haven't *done* anything.

(beat)

Check your heart rate. Go ahead.

Picard hesitates . . . then puts a hand to his throat. . . . He reacts with shock as he finds nothing.

Q

No pulse? What a surprise.

Try as he might to deny it, Picard is coming to the realization that Q is on the level. But he still fights against a facile acceptance of Q's word.

PICARD

How do I know this isn't another one of your tricks?

Q

Think, Jean-Luc. Why would I go to all the trouble of faking your death when I could simply kill you whenever I felt like it?

PICARD

Is that what happened?

Q

I wouldn't want to steal the credit. . . . It was a rather disgruntled Lenarian actually.

This strikes a chord with Picard. He begins to remember what happened. . . .

PICARD

The conference . . .

Q

(impatient)

Yes, yes. The conference, the unexpected attack, the compressed tetryon beam . . . the bottom line is, your life ended about five minutes ago under the inept ministrations of Doctor Beverly Crusher.

Picard takes a moment to think about this. He pushes away the idea that Q might be telling the truth.

PICARD

No. I am *not* dead. I refuse to believe there is an afterlife which is run by you.

(beat)

The universe is not that badly designed.

Q gives a bored and frustrated sigh.

Q

Very well. If you really require more evidence of your postmortem status, I'll just have to provide some . . .

Suddenly, Picard hears a deep VOICE coming from behind him.

MAURICE'S VOICE

Jean-Luc . . .

Picard freezes in place at the all-too familiar voice.

8 NEW ANGLE

Picard slowly turns around and sees his father, MAURICE PICARD, standing behind him. Maurice is in his eighties, but seems healthy and vital.

PICARD
(shocked)

Father . . .

Maurice is clearly disapproving.

MAURICE

I told you not to go running off to that academy. I told you that Starfleet would bring you to a bad end. But you wouldn't listen. Now look at you . . . dead before your time.

Picard's words are meant for Q, but he can't take his eyes off of his father's face.

PICARD

All right, Q . . . enough.

Q
(innocent)

Enough what?

MAURICE

Why couldn't you listen? Didn't you understand that I was only looking out for your best interests?

Picard turns to Q in rage.

PICARD
(hard)
Q, stop this.

MAURICE
Even now, after all these years . . . you still manage to disappoint me, Jean-Luc.

9 ON PICARD

The words knife through Picard. He turns back around . . . but Maurice is GONE. Picard stares out into the white emptiness for a moment.

PICARD
I hope you're enjoying this, Q.

Q
This isn't for me. This is for *you,* Jean-Luc . . . I wanted to give you an opportunity to make peace with your sordid past.

Picard turns back to Q after a beat, determined not to let Q call the tune.

PICARD
I find it hard to believe that you're doing this for the benefit of my soul.

Q
Now that you've finally shuffled off the mortal coil, we're free to spend some time together. I simply want you to be at peace with yourself.

PICARD
"Some time together". . . . How much time?

Q
Eternity.

Beat.

PICARD
So I'm in Hell.

Q

That's the spirit, Jean-Luc. Don't let a little thing like death slow down that rapier wit.

Q

(beat)

Now you're sure you don't have any regrets or feelings of guilt about your former life? I can't have you whining and complaining through eternity.

PICARD

If I'm truly dead, then my only regret is dying . . . and finding you here.

Q

(mock)

You wound me, mon Capitaine. After all, I wasn't the cause of your death . . .

He holds up a hand and a DEVICE APPEARS in it. It's about the size of a softball, and part of it is burnt and fused.

Q

(re: device)

. . . *this* was.

Picard recognizes the form, but it's still a shock.

PICARD

Is that . . . ?

Q

Your artificial heart.

He tosses the device to Picard, who catches it. Picard looks down at it with a sort of horrific wonder. There is something very strange about holding one's own heart. He examines it closely.

Q

You might have lived if you'd had a real heart instead of this unreliable piece of technology.

(beat)

How did you manage to lose yours anyway?

Picard pauses . . . looks at the device for a long moment.

PICARD
(quiet)
It was a . . . mistake.

Q immediately senses that he's onto something here. He presses Picard further.

Q
Something you regret?

PICARD
(finally admitting)
I regret a great many things from those days . . .

Q
Really?

Q looks off to one side.

9A OMITTED

10 NEW ANGLE

In the direction Q is looking, there are now four people standing in the dark: NAUSICAAN #1, #2, #3, and a YOUNG PICARD. The Nausicaans are large, burly aliens with hideous features. The young Picard is about twenty-one years old and is wearing an old-style Starfleet uniform.

The following happens very quickly:

Young Picard has Nausicaan #1 on the ground and is holding him in some type of wrestling lock. Nausicaan #2 pulls a nasty-looking weapon with a long serrated blade from his belt as Nausicaan #3 grabs young Picard's arms. Nausicaan #2 then DRIVES his weapon THROUGH young Picard's back. The young Picard LAUGHS just before he falls to the ground.

11 ON PICARD AND Q

Who have just seen the above action play out.

Q
It wasn't very smart of you to take on three Nausicaans like that.

Picard walks over and stands above the still form of his younger self, which is lying on the ground. (The Nausicaans are gone.)

PICARD

No, it wasn't.

Q

And did I hear you laugh? It's so unlike you to have a sense of humor . . . especially about getting stabbed through the back.

Picard still can't take his eyes off the image of his younger self.

PICARD

I was . . . a different person in those days . . . an arrogant, undisciplined young man with far too much ego and far too little wisdom.

(beat)

I was more like you.

Q

I'm sure you were far more interesting in those days. A pity you had to change.

PICARD

The only pity is that I had to be impaled through the back before I learned my lesson.

(beat)

I started that fight with the Nausicaans. . . . I started it because I was young and cocky. . . .

He looks down at the artificial heart he is still holding.

PICARD

If I had been more responsible at that age . . . I wouldn't have needed this heart . . . and I wouldn't have died from a random energy surge thirty years later.

Q

So if you had it to do all over again . . . ?

12 ON PICARD

He looks thoughtful as he recalls the events of his youth.

PICARD
(quiet)
Things would be different . . .

We MOVE IN CLOSE on Picard's face and suddenly a WOMAN'S HAND SLAPS him across the face.

CUT TO:

13. INTERIOR STARBASE—PICARD'S QUARTERS

Picard is wearing an old-style ensign's uniform, and he is standing in a standard set of quarters on a Starbase. An angry WOMAN is standing in front of him. OFF Picard's shocked expression.

FADE OUT.

ACT TWO

FADE IN:

14 INTERIOR STARBASE—PICARD'S QUARTERS (CONTINUOUS)

Picard is still shocked. The angry woman turns on her heel and EXITS in a huff. Suddenly there is APPLAUSE and LAUGHTER from offcamera. Picard turns to see . . .

15 COREY AND MARTA (OPTICAL)

Who are standing in the room. COREY ZWELLER is a tall, lanky, twenty-one-year-old, with long hair that probably barely passes regulations. MARTA BATANIDES is a short, pretty woman, and is also roughly twenty-one. They are both wearing old-style Starfleet ensign uniforms, and the jackets are unbuttoned, suggesting a casual gathering.

Picard immediately recognizes them both, but he's still trying to adjust to where he is. Corey and Marta are both laughing and applauding Picard—neither knows that the man standing before them is not twenty-one.

MARTA
(applauding)
Bravo! Bravo!

COREY
(applauding)
Nicely done.

PICARD
Cortan? Cortan Zweller?

COREY
(surprised)
Of course it's me. . . . Boy, she must've hit you pretty hard.

Marta moves to him and jokingly pats his cheek where the woman slapped him.

MARTA
You're slowing down, Johnny. You should've seen that one coming.

Picard looks at her with real warmth.

PICARD

Marta . . .

Marta frowns at him. . . . She's starting to become genuinely concerned.

MARTA

Are you okay?

PICARD

I'm . . . just a little disoriented . . .

COREY

Oh, please. Now he's just playing for sympathy.

Corey begins to button up his jacket.

COREY

I want to get something to eat and head over to the casino at Bonestell. Who's coming?

PICARD

I'll . . . catch up with you later.

Marta is still concerned about Picard.

MARTA

Are you sure you're all right?

PICARD

No, no. I'm fine Marta—Marty, really.

Marta still isn't quite convinced, but Corey only rolls his eyes.

COREY

Come on, Marty. I bet he has another date anyway.

Marta gives Picard a wry look.

MARTA

That's it, isn't it?

(pokes him in chest)

You are incorrigible.

Marta begins buttoning her jacket too as she and Corey head for the door.

COREY
(to Picard)
Try not to end up in the hospital.

They EXIT. Picard looks after them for a beat, trying to ground himself in what's going on. He looks down at his own uniform and notes the insignia. Q suddenly APPEARS, wearing a normal captain's uniform and holding a swagger stick.

Q
(barks)
Attention on deck, Ensign Picard!

Picard almost stands at attention out of reflex before catching himself.

PICARD
(irritated)
Q . . .

Q
That's Captain Q to you, young man.

PICARD
What's the point of creating this . . . fantasy?

Q
It's no fantasy. This is all very real, I assure you. You're twenty-one years old again . . . a brash young man, fresh out of the academy.

Picard looks down at his hands and then looks at himself in a mirror.

PICARD
I don't look it.

Q
To everyone else, you do.

Picard tries to punch holes in Q's story.

PICARD
I thought you said I was dead. . . . Now you tell me I'm alive?

Q

You mortals can be so obtuse. Why do you persist in believing that life and death are such static and rigid concepts?

(beat)

I can take your life and then give it back to you with the snap of a finger.

PICARD

Let's say for the moment that it's true . . . what purpose does it serve to bring me here?

Q

You said you regretted a great many things from this time in your life. Well, now you have a chance to change some of them.

Picard takes a moment to assess all this. . . . It's a great deal to assimilate.

PICARD

Change. You mean change the past. Q, even if you have brought me back in time somehow . . . surely you must realize that any alteration in this timeline could have a profound impact on the future—

Q

Spare me your egotistical musings on your pivotal role in history. Nothing you do here will cause the Federation to collapse or the galaxy to explode. To be blunt . . . you're not that important.

PICARD

I won't do it. I won't alter history.

The look on Picard's face tells Q that he's not getting anywhere.

Q

Oh, very well . . . if you attach so much importance to the continuity of time . . . I can personally guarantee that nothing you do here will end up hurting *anyone,* or have an adverse effect on what you know as history. The only thing at stake here is your life and your peace of mind.

(beat)

You have my word.

Picard laughs in his face.

Q

It's bad form to laugh at one's god. Whether you believe me or not, you're *here* and you have a second chance. . . . What you do with it is entirely up to you.

(beat)

Do you know where you are?

Picard looks around for a beat and thinks back.

PICARD

Starbase Earhart . . . we came here just after graduation . . . to wait for our first deep space assignments.

Q makes himself comfortable on a couch.

Q

That's right. It's two days before your unfortunate encounter with a Nausicaan sword . . . you have that long to make whatever changes you wish. If you can avoid getting stabbed through the heart this time—which I doubt—I'll take you back to what you think of as the present and you can go on with your life . . . with a real heart.

PICARD

So then I won't die?

Q

Of course you'll die. It'll just be at a later time.

PICARD

What if I don't avoid the fight . . . ? What if I don't make any changes?

Q

Then you die on the table and we spend eternity together.

PICARD

Wonderful.

Q

I'm glad you think so.

(beat)

I am curious about one thing. . . . *Johnny,* why did that rather attractive woman slap you just now? Something you said?

Picard thinks back, trying to remember.

PICARD

That woman's name was . . . Corlina. I was supposed to take her to dinner . . . on this night . . .

(beat)

But then she found out that . . .

(embarrassed)

I'd made a second date with another woman . . . named Penny. Corlina was . . . somewhat upset.

Q

I'm impressed. I had no idea you could be such a cad.

Picard suddenly remembers something.

PICARD

Computer, what time is it?

COMPUTER VOICE

Sixteen eleven hours.

Picard's expression sags a little, and Q picks up on it immediately.

PICARD

In fact, Penny should be . . . waiting for me . . . right now.

OFF his expression.

CUT TO:

16 INTERIOR BONESTELL FACILITY—BAR

The bar is a dilapidated, run-down hole in the wall with mismatched furnishings, dirty walls, and indifferent service. The clientele consists mostly of passed-out bodies and disreputable figures conducting illegal deals in the shadows.

In short, it is exactly the kind of place to attract young Starfleet officers fresh from the academy and looking for a little adventure. (NOTE: *No* Ferengi should be seen in this episode. They had not been ''discovered'' during this time period.)

There is a DOORWAY off to one side which leads to a connecting room.

Picard is sitting at the bar on a stool with one leg too short, talking to a woman named PENNY. She is an attractive woman, well into her forties and beginning to show it. Penny has a world-weary look of experience, and she sees Picard only as a twenty-one-year-old. Picard is very uncomfortable and there is a long silence.

PENNY

You're awfully quiet today. What happened to the dashing young ensign from last night . . . the one with the winning smile and the smooth talk about my eyes?

PICARD

Nothing. I'm just a little more . . . contemplative.

PENNY

And what are you contemplating?

She crosses one leg over the over, exposing a good deal of skin in the process. Picard can't help but notice.

PICARD

Penny, perhaps we could just . . . talk for a while. I don't know anything about you . . . where you come from . . . what your interests are . . . your last name . . .

PENNY

(matter of fact)

I come from Rigel, my last name is Muroc, and I like men in uniform.

She leans over and begins running her hand over his thigh. Her look is openly seductive.

Penny

I think that's enough talk.

At this moment, Corey and Marta walk through the bar area. They both give Picard knowing smiles and looks before EXITING through the opposite DOORWAY.

PICARD
Penny . . . I don't think it would be fair . . . to you to pretend that I'm really interested in a . . . relationship right now. . . .

PENNY
Who said anything about a relationship?

She kisses him full on the mouth . . . then pulls away at his lack of response. Penny considers him for a moment . . . her expression hardens and an edge creeps into her voice.

PENNY
What's wrong . . . ? Don't I look as attractive as I did last night?

PICARD
What? No, not at all. You're a very . . . handsome woman.

PENNY
Handsome . . . that's something you say to old ladies.

She moves to leave, but Picard reaches out and stops her.

PICARD
Penny. To me you are definitely not an old lady.

Penny grabs her drink and throws it in his face.

PENNY
I wasn't after your pity.

She EXITS. Picard begins to wipe the drink off his face with a hand. . . . Suddenly someone hands him a TOWEL from behind the bar.

Q'S VOICE
Penny for your thoughts?

17 NEW ANGLE

Picard turns and discovers Q standing behind the bar dressed as a bartender. Picard takes the towel in irritation and dries his face.

Q
You never told me you were such a lady's man.

PICARD
I was a puerile adolescent who let himself be ruled by his hormones instead of his head.

There is suddenly the NOISE of a CROWD YELLING APPROVAL coming from offcamera. Picard and Q turn toward the DOORWAY.

Q
It seems your friends know how to have a good time. Maybe you should go take some lessons.

Suddenly a pushy VOICE is heard coming from the other end of the bar.

MALE VOICE
Hey, you! Get over here with those drinks before I tear your head off!

Q looks over toward where the voice came from.

Q
(to Picard)
Excuse me.
(to offcamera customer)
Are you addressing me . . . ?

Another CHEER can be HEARD coming from the doorway. Picard moves toward it in curiosity.

18 INTERIOR BONESTELL FACILITY—GAMBLING CENTER

If the bar was decrepit, the gambling center is disgusting, with even more decay and filth. There are various gaming devices and tables scattered around the room, but the center is dominated by a large DOM-JOT TABLE. Dom-jot is a cross between billiards and craps. People place bets on various multicolored images on the table as players take turns hitting balls with cue sticks. There are many bumpers and pockets, and lights come on according to the state of play.

Picard ENTERS and sees that the CROWD gathered around the dom-jot table is cheering on Corey, who is wielding his cue stick with professional confidence. Corey's opponent is an ALIEN who holds his cue stick in misery. Picard moves to stand next to Marta.

MARTA
(re: Corey)
He's winning.

PICARD
Of course.

MARTA
I thought you had a date.

PICARD
(beat)
She . . . decided to leave.

MARTA
(ironic)
You're getting old, Johnny.

Corey hits a final ball and a LIGHT goes on. The crowd goes wild. The alien opponent puts down his stick in disgust and throws a few gold ingots on the table. Corey triumphantly collects his winnings as the crowd disperses to other tables.

COREY
Thank you . . . thank you all . . .

Picard and Marta move over to him.

MARTA
Very nice . . . forget about Starfleet and just play dom-jot for a living.

COREY
(cocky)
This is nothing . . . it's just a little trigonometry, and some minor wrist action. Barokie—now *there's* a game.

Suddenly there is VOICE from offcamera.

NAUSICAAN #1'S VOICE
(loud)

Human!

19 NEW ANGLE

Revealing that Nausicaan #1 has just entered the gaming area. The three officers turn to look at him.

NAUSICAAN #1
(to Corey)

Play dom-jot . . . human?

He smiles a predatory smile. Picard reacts with dread . . . he recognizes the Nausicaan and knows the events that are about to unfold. OFF Picard's reaction . . .

FADE OUT.

ACT THREE

FADE IN:

20 INTERIOR BONESTELL FACILITY—GAMBLING CENTER

Continuous action from Act Two. Corey sizes up the Nausicaan . . . thinks he sees an easy mark.

COREY
(smiles)
I think I could be persuaded to play one more game.

Picard moves quickly to Corey.

PICARD
(quiet, urgent)
No, don't play him.

COREY
Why?

PICARD
It'll cause trouble.

Corey looks at him quizzically. Picard needs to think of something quickly.

PICARD
He's a Nausicaan . . . they can be very ill-tempered when they lose.

COREY
(flip)
So can I.

Corey turns to play, but Picard grabs his arm.

PICARD
(forcefully)
Corey, listen to me. This is a bad idea. Don't play him.

Corey pulls away from Picard's grip. He looks at Picard with a trace of irritation.

COREY

What's gotten into you?

(to Nausicaan)

Let's go.

Corey and the Nausicaan set up the table as Picard looks on with frustration. Marta throws him a quizzical glance, but shrugs it off and then moves to get a good look at the game as a CROWD begins to gather around the table again.

21 NEW ANGLE

As Q (still dressed as the bartender) ENTERS and moves to stand with Picard. The game between Corey and the Nausicaan begins in the background as Q and Picard talk.

Q

I see you've found your Nausicaan friend.

Q pointedly looks at Picard's back and chest.

Q

(continuing)

You seem unimpaled so far.

PICARD

Sorry to disappoint you.

Corey scores a point on the table and exchanges a pleased look with Marta. The Nausicaan is unmoved and Picard looks grim.

Q

Ensign Zweller seems to be doing well.

PICARD

He's going to lose. The Nausicaan is cheating.

Q

Really? I'm beginning to like these Nausicaans.

PICARD

If history repeats itself, Corey will figure it out later tonight, and then he'll want revenge.

Q

And will you help your best friend avenge this injustice?

The tables have turned in the game, and the Nausicaan is starting to pile up a series of points, one after the other.

PICARD

I did the first time. I found a way to rig the table so that Corey could win in a rematch.

Q

You? Cheated? Picard, I'm impressed.

PICARD

It was a foolish mistake. The Nausicaan and his two friends didn't take the loss very well. They were outraged . . . they wanted a fight . . .

(beat)

And I gave them one.

Q

A beautiful story . . .

(puts fist to his chest)

Gets you right here, doesn't it?

The Nausicaan is now running the table on Corey, racking up point after point. Corey is watching him carefully, with anger and suspicion mixing on his face. The Nausicaan scores the final point and the crowd CHEERS.

NAUSICAAN #1

Dom-jot!

(as if the idea were a joke)

Human play dom-jot!

The Nausicaan laughs heartily and throws his stick at Corey, who has little choice but to catch it. The Nausicaan scoops up his winnings and EXITS. Corey's face hardens in cold fury.

CUT TO:

22 INTERIOR STARBASE—PICARD'S QUARTERS

Corey, Marta and Picard are gathered here. Corey is very upset.

COREY

I've played a lot of dom-jot, in a lot of places, and I've *never* seen the balls roll that well for anyone. Did you see the way he rolled the terik into straight nines? That's a one-in-a-million shot and he did it twice.

MARTA

So he was cheating. . . .

PICARD

It may have simply been extraordinary luck.

COREY

I was watching the way he held the cue. Every time he needed to make a tough shot, he held the cue close to his waist. I think he had some kind of magnetic device in his belt. It must've been controlling the balls.

MARTA
(angry)

That's terrible.

COREY

We have to get even.

MARTA

What do you have in mind?

COREY

We could do the same thing to him that he did to us. Cheat. We'll rig the table so his device will backfire on him.

Picard puts his foot down before this goes any farther.

PICARD

That won't solve anything.

COREY

It'll teach him that he can't go around cheating Starfleet officers.

PICARD

What it will do is provoke him. And provoking a Nausicaan is not a good idea.

COREY
(cocky)
I can handle him.

PICARD
What if he's not alone . . . ? What if he brings some friends along next time?

COREY
Well . . . then I guess I'll have to depend on *my* friends to help me out.

PICARD
Corey . . . there must be a better way to handle this. . . .

Corey looks at him in astonishment.

COREY
When did you start backing away from a good fight?

PICARD
We're not cadets anymore . . . we're officers. We have to start . . . setting a higher standard for ourselves.

Corey still can't believe he's hearing this from Picard, but Marta has begun to agree with Picard.

MARTA
Maybe he's right. . . . Maybe this isn't such a good idea.

COREY
(pleading)
Look, we've only got one more day before we all have to report to our ships. Let's have one last adventure together. . . . We may not see each other again for a long time.

Marta is on the fence, but Picard holds firm.

PICARD
No. I'm sorry, Corey, but I won't do it.

That swings Marta's vote.

MARTA

It was a good idea, Corey . . . but let's just forget about it . . .

Corey looks at them both with amazement and disappointment. He almost says something . . . then finally just shakes his head in disgust and EXITS without a word. There is a long beat before Marta turns to Picard.

MARTA

He'll get over it.

PICARD

I hope so.

Marta smiles at him in a strangely amused sort of way. She is seeing him a little differently now . . . starting to see something very attractive about this new attitude from Picard. He notices her look.

PICARD

What?

MARTA

Nothing . . . it's just that usually you'd be the one plotting revenge.

PICARD

(dry)

That would be more in character, wouldn't it?

MARTA

Much.

(with humor)

But I always suspected you had a hidden streak of responsibility somewhere.

PICARD

(ironic)

Maybe I'm just getting . . . a little older.

Marta touches the rank insignia on Picard's uniform.

MARTA

(re: insignia)

Maybe these bars are starting to feel a little heavy, *Ensign.*

(beat)

Ensign Picard and *Ensign* Batanides . . . sounds weird, doesn't it?

PICARD

(ironic)

It's going to take some getting used to.

Marta gives him a very direct look.

MARTA

It's too bad we can't get used to it together.

Picard looks at her, a little surprised. Marta realizes that she's given voice to more than she meant to—she's definitely attracted to Picard as more than just a friend. She quickly amends her statement so it doesn't sound so intimate.

MARTA

(quickly)

The—the three of us, I mean.

But Picard has picked up on the subtext and is not fooled by her hasty retreat.

PICARD

Of course.

They look at each other for a long moment . . . the sexual tension in the room fairly crackles. But before things progress any farther, the door CHIMES and the moment is broken.

PICARD

Come.

Q ENTERS, dressed as a delivery boy and carrying a large arrangement of flowers.

Q

Is there a John-Luck Pickard here?

Marta gives Picard a resigned look.

MARTA
(with humor)
From one of your conquests, no doubt. I guess some things *aren't* going to change.

She smiles and EXITS. Once she's gone, Q turns to Picard.

Q
Did I interrupt something sordid, I hope?

PICARD
No, you did not.

Q
Pity. She's quite attractive.

PICARD
We were friends, nothing more.

Q
Is that *another* regret I hear?

Q has touched a nerve here, and Picard can't deny it.

Q
My, my . . . we're simply riddled with regrets about our youth, aren't we?

PICARD
My friendship with Marta is not something I regret.

Q
But you do wish you'd been more than just . . . friends, don't you?
(beat)
Well . . . here's your chance to change all that.

Picard faces Q squarely, determined not to let Q get to him.

PICARD
(irritably)
What do you want, Q?

Q

I thought you might like to know that Mister Zweller has decided to ignore your advice.

Picard is shocked.

Q

(continuing)

He's in the Bonestell Facility right now . . . rigging the table to beat the Nausicaan. I guess you weren't that persuasive.

Picard thinks for a beat, then EXITS with a determined look on his face. Q smiles and smells the flowers with a satisfied look on his face.

CUT TO:

23 INTERIOR BONESTELL FACILITY—GAMBLING CENTER—NIGHT

The gambling center is closed for the evening and the lights are off. Corey is underneath the dom-jot table, working with a couple of tools, when Picard quietly ENTERS. Picard looks around quickly, but they're clearly alone. He moves silently over to the table.

PICARD

(softly)

Corey . . .

Corey smacks his head into the table in surprise.

COREY

Ow!

Corey sees Picard and breathes a sigh of relief.

COREY

Johnny . . . don't sneak up on me like that. I thought you were the gambling foreman.

PICARD

Sorry.

COREY

It's all right. I'm glad you're here.

(points to tool)

Hand me the magnaspanner.

He leans back under the table.

PICARD

I'm not here to help you; I'm here to stop you from making a serious mistake.

Corey looks at him in disbelief . . . he still isn't taking him seriously.

COREY

(sarcastic)

You sound like my mother.

PICARD

Cheating the Nausicaan could have serious consequences for all of us. It's a risk we can't afford to take.

COREY

You *are* my mother.

(mocking)

Well, Mom . . . gee, I guess I'll have to go tell the Nausicaans I don't mind if they cheat me—

PICARD

(hard)

This isn't a joke, Corey.

The humor fades from Corey's face.

COREY

It better be.

A tense beat between the two of them. Corey finally breaks the silence . . . he keeps his voice low and very even.

COREY

Now, I'm going to finish my work here. If you want to help me—fine. If you don't, then I'll see you back at the starbase.

Corey turns back to the table, but Picard takes him gently but firmly by the arm.

PICARD

I said you're not doing this.

Picard's expression is unyielding. Corey looks from Picard's face down to the hand on his arm.

COREY
(quiet)
Are you going to hit me, Johnny?

Picard considers him for a beat . . . realizes that he won't cross that line with his friend. Picard drops his hand after a beat.

PICARD
No.
(beat)
But I will tell the gambling foreman that someone's been tampering with his dom-jot table.

Corey can't even put his sense of betrayal and anger into words. He stares at Picard for a long beat . . . then drops the tool in his hand.

COREY
(cold)
All right, have it your way . . .
(with contempt)
. . . *Ensign* Picard.

With a pained and angry look, Corey EXITS, leaving Picard alone in the deserted center.

CUT TO:

24 INTERIOR STARBASE—MARTA'S QUARTERS—NIGHT

A re-dress of Picard's quarters. Marta has taken her jacket off and is sitting on the edge of the bed, listening to Picard, who is upset about the prior scene.

PICARD
I just couldn't make him understand.

MARTA
At least he did finally give it up. . . .

PICARD
Yes, but . . . he didn't take it very well.

MARTA

Oh, you know Corey. . . . He'll forget all about it by tomorrow.

PICARD

I hope so. We were friends for many years after this.

(off her look)

Or at least . . . I hope we will be.

Marta looks at him for a moment . . . a smile keeps playing about her lips as if she is about to burst out laughing.

PICARD

(puzzled)

You keep smiling at me.

MARTA

(light)

I've just never seen you like this before. You're so . . . *serious.*

PICARD

Do I really seem that different?

MARTA

(smiles)

I don't know . . . maybe I'm just not used to seeing you in an officer's uniform . . .

(beat, then more thoughtful)

No . . . it's more than that . . . you *do* seem different. . . .

(beat)

I mean, I'm not complaining. . . . I think it suits you.

Marta gives him a very direct look . . . and that spark of sexual tension can be felt in the room again.

PICARD

Really?

MARTA

Yes. I think it's very . . .

(she hesitates)

. . . attractive.

There is another silent moment as they search each other's expressions. The tension between them begins to build. Picard struggles with the feelings, begins to turn away in order to break the moment . . . but Marta stops him.

MARTA

Johnny . . . have you ever thought about us . . . getting together?

PICARD

Actually . . . I have. For a long time.

There is a charged silence. Picard is trying to resist, uncomfortable with the fact that, for him, many years have passed.

MARTA

Why didn't you ever say so?

PICARD

I . . . don't know.

(beat)

At the moment . . . I can't imagine why I didn't. . . .

MARTA

Well . . . you've said it now.

They hold each other's eyes for a moment . . . then Marta takes a step toward him . . . she lifts a hand and brushes her fingertips across his lips . . . then carefully moves closer . . . their lips touch briefly in a tentative kiss. They part slightly and look at each other again . . . then they kiss in a deep and passionate embrace.

FADE OUT.

ACT FOUR

FADE IN:

25 INTERIOR STARBASE—MARTA'S QUARTERS—DAY (OPTICAL)

CLOSE ON Picard, who is sleeping in the bed alone. It's the next morning. A HAND reaches out and strokes his face gently. . . . Picard smiles and slowly rolls over . . . he opens his eyes and finds Q lying on top of the covers next to him.

Q

Good morning, darling.

Picard jerks back in shock. Q smiles as Picard grabs his uniform and begins to dress.

Q

A little jumpy this morning, are we? Feeling guilty perhaps?

PICARD

I don't have anything to feel guilty about, Q.

Q

No?

(mocking)

"We were friends, Q. Nothing more."

PICARD

You're the one who gave me the opportunity to change things. . . .

Q

So what happens next?

Picard thinks for a beat.

PICARD

I don't know. But I do know that things will be different.

Q looks at him for a beat.

Q

I'm sure.

Q VANISHES.

CUT TO:

26 INTERIOR BONESTELL FACILITY—BAR—DAY

It's still pretty early in the day for there to be many customers at the bar. Picard ENTERS and looks around for a beat before seeing Marta sitting at a far table with her back toward him. Picard smiles and moves to her. He puts a hand on her shoulder and gently kisses her head.

PICARD

Morning.

Marta stiffens in her seat.

MARTA

Johnny.

Picard moves around and suddenly sees the expression on her face—she looks miserable and has probably been crying recently. Picard sits down with concern.

PICARD

What's wrong?

A long beat as Marta tries to put words together. She toys with a mug of coffee in front of her and has a great deal of difficulty meeting Picard's eyes. She tries to smile.

MARTA

Well . . . this is the morning after, huh?

Picard is suddenly in uncharted waters. He wasn't expecting this reaction from her, and he's not sure how to deal with it.

PICARD

I suppose so.

An awkward beat.

MARTA

I . . . don't quite know where to begin . . .

He takes her hand gently.

PICARD

Marta . . . I don't regret what happened last night . . . and I hope you don't, either.

She looks into his eyes, but her emotions are in turmoil.

MARTA

I don't know . . . we've been friends for a long time . . . and now . . .

PICARD

I hope last night has only brought us closer.

A long beat as Marta looks down into her coffee.

MARTA

Do you remember the first day we reported to the academy?

PICARD

(smiles)

Very well.

MARTA

They marched us into Scobee Hall in our stiff new uniforms . . . and then Admiral Silona gave us the old welcome aboard speech.

(beat)

He said, I want you all to look to the left of you and then look to the right of you . . .

PICARD

(remembering)

. . . One of you isn't going to make it through the next four years.

MARTA

I remember thinking . . . that's me. *I'm* not going to make it. Then I looked to my right . . . and there you were with this cocky look on your face . . . and you said, "We'll see about that." From that moment, I knew I wanted you as a friend.

She looks into his eyes . . . her face fills with pain.

MARTA
And now . . . I'm afraid we've ruined that friendship.

Picard realizes what a profound mistake this has been. He thinks for a long beat . . . then tries to reach out to her and make things better.

PICARD
Perhaps we should just . . . pretend that this never happened and try to . . .

He trails off as she shakes her head.

MARTA
I wish I could. It would make it easier to say good-bye tomorrow.
(takes deep breath)
We're all supposed to get together later . . . the last big night on the town before we ship out. . . . Now I'm not sure it's such a good idea. . . .

PICARD
I don't want you to do anything that'll be uncomfortable . . .

She regards him sadly, then—

MARTA
I'll be there. We planned this. . . . I don't want to disappoint Corey.

She stands and quickly EXITS. Picard sits alone at the table for a long beat.

27 NEW ANGLE

Revealing Q standing near Picard.

Q
Let's see . . . in the past twenty-four hours, you've managed to get slapped by one woman, have a drink thrown in your face by another, and alienate your two best friends. I'd say you're doing quite nicely so far.

Picard doesn't respond. . . . His thoughts are still on the scene with Marta.

Q

Just one more thing to do . . . avoid getting stabbed through the heart tonight.

Picard nods to himself . . . he's ready for this to end.

CUT TO:

28 INTERIOR BONESTELL FACILITY—GAMBLING CENTER—NIGHT

The gambling center is bustling with activity again. Picard, Corey, and Marta are sitting at a table in one of the corners. There is an awkward tension among the three of them, and the drinks before them go largely untouched. A few beats of silence go by; then Picard tries to get the conversation going.

PICARD

(to Corey)

I think you'll like serving aboard the *Ajax* . . . I understand Captain Narth is an excellent officer.

COREY

(not really responsive)

So I hear.

Another awkward silence. Marta glances at Picard, then looks away. The tension is heavy. Picard tries one last time to break the ice.

PICARD

(lifts a glass)

Well . . . here's to the class of 'twenty-seven.

Corey and Marta try to smile as they all clink glasses and drink. As Corey drinks, he notices something at the far end of the room.

29 NEW ANGLE

Which shows Nausicaans #1, #2, and #3 all ENTER the gambling center. Corey puts down his drink at the sight of the three burly aliens. Picard and Marta follow his gaze just as Nausicaan #1 sees Corey at the table. Corey tries to ignore the Nausicaans and forces himself to look down at his drink. But Nausicaan #1 moves over to the table and his two companions follow him.

NAUSICAAN #1

(taunting)

Play dom-jot, human? Give you a better chance.

(no response)
Give you a bigger stick maybe.

The Nausicaans laugh. Corey slowly looks up at them and Picard stands up to intercede.

PICARD
I don't think we're interested.

NAUSICAAN #1
(to others)
They are *undari.*
(to Corey)
Cowards.

Corey and Marta stand up.

COREY
What did you say?

Picard gets between them.

NAUSICAAN #1
(to Corey)
Coward. Like all Starfleet. You talk and you talk . . . but you have no *guramba.*

Corey takes a step toward him.

COREY
Why don't we find out—

Picard puts a hand to his chest and keeps them apart. Picard notices as Nausicaan #2 puts a hand on the hilt of his sword.

PICARD
(to Corey)
Don't be a fool.
(to Nausicaan)
There are plenty of other people to play dom-jot. Go on about your business.

The Nausicaan ignores him and looks from Corey to Marta.

NAUSICAAN #1
(to Marta)
Maybe I play with you . . . give you a good time.

That tears it for Corey. The following happens *very* quickly:

Picard sees Nausicaan #2 begin to draw his weapon as Corey cocks back his arm to throw a punch. Picard throws an elbow into Corey's chest, knocking him backward and preventing him from starting a fight. Corey is caught completely by surprise, and he tumbles hard over the table and chair. There is a beat of shocked silence from everyone.

Suddenly the Nausicaans begin to laugh at the spectacle of the quarreling officers. The tension is broken as they go off to another area of the gambling center.

NAUSICAAN #1
(to others)
Orcho lok resnik, Starfleet. . . .

As they move away, Picard turns around to see Marta helping Corey up. Picard holds out a hand, but Marta's eyes flash at him.

MARTA
You've done enough.

PICARD
Corey, I'm sorry. He was drawing a weapon . . .

He trails off as Corey gets to his feet and takes a step toward him. The anger and pain in Corey's eyes is obvious. For a moment, it looks as if Corey might actually hit Picard. But in the end he just speaks softly and firmly.

COREY
I don't know who you are anymore . . . but you're not my friend.

The words wound Picard just as surely as if Corey had hit him. Corey walks away. Marta holds Picard's eyes for a moment.

MARTA
Good-bye, Johnny.

Marta EXITS. Picard is left standing alone in the gambling center, as his two best friends in the world walk out of his life. Q moves into view and stands next to Picard.

Q
(quietly)
Congratulations, mon Capitaine. You did it.

Picard doesn't respond to Q. Suddenly we HEAR Worf from offcamera.

WORF'S VOICE
Can I help you?

Picard turns around and we . . .
CUT TO:

30 OMITTED

31 INTERIOR ENTERPRISE—MAIN BRIDGE

Picard is standing near the aft science station, and Worf is standing next to him. Picard is wearing a *blue* uniform with the rank of lieutenant, and he is holding a padd. DATA is sitting at the aft station. Worf impatiently repeats his question.

WORF
Can I help you, Mister Picard?

PICARD
Worf . . .

Picard is confused by the transition, and he takes a moment to get his bearings. Worf finally takes the padd out of his hand. Data turns around in curiosity.

WORF
(off padd)
This is not for me. You should take it to Commander La Forge in engineering.

Worf gives the padd to Picard and turns back to his console. Picard looks down at his uniform in surprise.

PICARD
(to himself)
What's happened . . . ?

WORF
Is something wrong?

PICARD

I'm not sure . . .

(beat, then to Worf)

Mister Worf, what's my rank and position?

Worf and Data exchange concerned looks.

WORF

(puzzled)

You are a lieutenant junior grade . . . the assistant astrophysics officer.

Picard puts a hand to his head as if he were dizzy.

DATA

Are you feeling all right?

Picard doesn't answer.

PICARD

Who's the captain of this ship?

Worf and Data are genuinely concerned now.

DATA

Captain Thomas Halloway.

(beat)

Perhaps I should escort you to sickbay.

PICARD

(quickly)

No. I think I can find my way. Thank you, Commander.

Picard EXITS to a turbolift.

CUT TO:

32 OMITTED

33 INTERIOR BEVERLY'S OFFICE (OPTICAL)

Picard ENTERS the office. Someone is sitting in Beverly's chair, which is turned away from the doorway.

PICARD
Beverly, something's happened to me. I'm not sure—

He stops as Q turns around in the chair, wearing a white lab coat and a reflective mirror on his head.

Q
(German accent)
What seems to be de trouble, Lieutenant Picard?

PICARD
Q, what have you done?

Q
I've done exactly what I promised, Jean-Luc. I've returned you to the present.

PICARD
This is not the present I remember. You said nothing would change.

Q
And nothing has changed . . . except for you. But then, that's what you wanted, wasn't it? To change the man you were in your youth? Well, you did it—and this is the man you are today.
(beat)
You should be happy . . . you have a real heart beating in your chest, and you get to live out the rest of your life in safety . . . running tests . . . making analyses . . . and carrying reports to your superiors.

Q VANISHES. OFF Picard's reaction . . .

FADE OUT.

ACT FIVE

FADE IN:

34 INTERIOR ENGINEERING

GEORDI and an N.D. ENGINEER are working near the pool table as Picard (still in blue uniform) ENTERS, still carrying his padd. Everything and everyone is exactly as it should be except for Picard. He looks around the familiar scene . . . unsure how to respond to all this.

GEORDI
(to engineer)
. . . so tell Duffy that we'll need to adjust the main deflector later this afternoon. Oh, and have him look into that inducer problem.

The engineer nods and walks away. Geordi finally notices Picard. There is a change in how Geordi and everyone else knows and thinks about Picard: to them he's no longer the mighty captain; to them he's a mild-mannered, slightly nerdy guy . . . similar to the way they view Barclay.

GEORDI
(moving to pool table)
Hi, Jean-Luc. What's new in astrophysics?
(beat)
Do you need something?

PICARD
(remembering padd)
I have the . . . spectral analysis for you.

He hands Geordi the padd. Geordi glances at it briefly, then sets it down. He's in the middle of something and the padd isn't that important.

GEORDI
Thanks.
(to engineer)
Lynch, try shunting the power through the lateral conduit.

The woman nods and works. Geordi moves to his office. Picard can't help but follow to see what's going on . . . he's used to knowing everything that's happening aboard this ship. Geordi sits at his panel and frowns at the display.

GEORDI

(frustrated, to himself)

So where's the problem . . . ?

PICARD

What's going on?

GEORDI

(distracted)

Oh, something's causing a power spike in the starboard warp coil. If I don't track it down soon, the captain's going to have my head on a platter.

PICARD

Have you tried flushing the transfer conduits with trioxina?

GEORDI

(dismissive)

No.

Geordi stands and moves to another console and begins to work. Picard continues to try helping.

PICARD

The conduits sometimes get blocked by neutrino emissions when the plasma—

Geordi smiles, puts his arm around Picard, and gives him a polite brush-off.

GEORDI

Hey . . . I know you're trying to make full lieutenant this year . . . but I think we can handle this from here.

Geordi moves away, leaving Picard standing alone and feeling totally out of place. After a beat, he EXITS.

CUT TO:

34A INTERIOR TEN-FORWARD

Picard ENTERS and looks around. After a beat, he sees Riker and TROI seated at a table near the window. He goes over to them.

PICARD

Am I interrupting?

They look up. They, like Geordi, are not intimate friends with this man and are a little surprised to be approached by him. They exchange glances.

RIKER

Not at all. Have a seat.

Picard sits down.

PICARD

(to Riker)

I wonder if I could talk with you for a moment . . . about my future on the *Enterprise.*

RIKER

Of course, Lieutenant. Jean-Luc, isn't it?

TROI

Maybe I should go.

PICARD

No, please, Counselor . . . I would very much like to hear your thoughts . . .

They sit back and look at him expectantly.

PICARD

First of all . . . I'd like you to be straightforward with me. How do you evaluate me as an officer?

They exchange glances again.

TROI

Your performance reports have always been good. You're thorough . . . dedicated . . .

RIKER

Reliable, steady . . .
(beat, then, unable to come up with anything else)
. . . punctual.

Picard understand that they're damning him with faint praise.

PICARD

I see.

(beat)

What would you say if I told you I thought I was capable of being more than that . . . ?

RIKER

Maybe we should discuss this at your next evaluation. . . .

PICARD

I'd very much appreciate it if we could discuss it now.

Another beat. They acquiesce.

PICARD

I would like to try . . . to move beyond astrophysics . . . into engineering or security perhaps. Something which might even lead to a command.

Riker and Troi exchange a glance.

RIKER

Frankly, Lieutenant . . . I don't think that's realistic . . .

PICARD

Why?

A waiter appears to clear their table.

TROI

I really don't think this is the place to be discussing—

PICARD

Please. This is important to me. I know I can do more.

She gives another glance to Riker, then leans in to Picard.

TROI

Hasn't this been the problem all along? Throughout your career . . . you've had lofty goals . . . but you've never been willing to do what's necessary to attain them.

Picard turns to Riker.

PICARD

Would that be your evaluation as well, Commander?

RIKER

(uncomfortable)

I'd have to agree with the counselor. You talk about wanting more . . . but when it comes to doing something about it, you hang back. If you want to get ahead, you have to take chances . . . stand out from the crowd . . . get noticed.

PICARD

I see.

RIKER

(trying to salve the wound)

We don't want to lose you. . . . You're a good officer.

PICARD

Just not—one who stands out.

RIKER

Look . . . why don't I talk to Commander La Forge . . . maybe there's something in engineering.

(beat)

PICARD

But . . . command?

RIKER

Well . . . we'll see.

This is clearly a crumb thrown to make him feel better. It doesn't.

DATA (com voice)

Senior officers please report to the captain's ready room.

RIKER

(to com)

Acknowledged.

TROI
(to Picard)
I think we should talk about this later.

Riker and Troi EXIT, leaving Picard sitting alone at the table. He looks around for a moment.

PICARD
(quietly)
All right, Q. Enough of this. You've made your point.

But there is no answer.

PICARD
Q . . .?

Picard comes to the awful realization that Q isn't going to just wipe it away this time . . . that he may have to live out his life like this.

GEORDI (com voice)
La Forge to Lieutenant Picard. I'm still waiting for your final sensor usage log.

PICARD
(to com, resigned)
I'm on my way, sir.

Picard gets up to leave.

CUT TO:

34B INTERIOR CORRIDOR/TURBOLIFT

Picard ENTERS the turbolift.

PICARD
(to com)
Main engineering.

The lift starts MOVING. The expression on Picard's face is as depressed as we've ever seen him.

PICARD
Are you having a good laugh now, Q? Does it amuse you to think of me living out the rest of my life as a dreary man in a tedious job?

The turbolift finally STOPS and Picard EXITS TO:

35 LIMBO—CONTINUOUS

The whiteness as seen before. Picard turns around and finds Q standing before him.

Q

I gave you something most mortals never experience . . . a second chance at life. And now all you can do is complain?

PICARD

I can't live out my days as that person. That man is bereft of passion and imagination. That's not who I am.

Q

Au contraire. He's the person you wanted to be . . . one who was less arrogant and undisciplined as a youth.

(beat)

One who was less like me.

A beat as Picard realizes that Q is right. Q takes the opportunity to rub it in.

Q

The Jean-Luc Picard you wanted to be, the one who did *not* fight the Nausicaan, had quite a different career from the one you remember.

That Picard never had a brush with death . . . never came face to face with his own mortality . . . never realized how fragile life is . . . how important each moment can be . . . so his life never came into focus. He drifted through much of his career, with no plan or agenda . . . going from one assignment to the next, never seizing the opportunities that presented themselves. . . .

(beat)

He didn't lead the away team on Milika III to save that ambassador . . . he didn't take charge of the *Stargazer*'s bridge when its captain was killed . . . and no one ever offered him a command.

(beat)

He learned to play it safe. And he never, ever got noticed by anyone.

A beat as Picard is forced to admit that Q was right all along.

PICARD

You're right. You gave me the chance to change, and I took that opportunity. But I freely admit now that it was a mistake.

Q's eyes sparkle for a moment.

Q

Are *you* asking *me* for something, Jean-Luc?

Picard swallows his pride.

PICARD

Yes.

(beat)

Give me a chance to put things back to the way they were before.

Q

Before, you died in sickbay. Is that what you want?

Picard thinks for a moment, but he's determined.

PICARD

I would rather die as the man I was . . . than live the life I just saw.

They look at each other for a long beat. Q seems to be waiting for something. Finally Picard breaks the silence.

PICARD

Please.

Q smiles a self-satisfied smile as we suddenly . . .

CUT TO:

36 INTERIOR BONESTELL FACILITY—GAMBLING CENTER

Picard is standing between Corey and Nausicaan #1. He has been put back into the scene from Act Four during the confrontation.

NAUSICAAN #1
(to Corey)
Coward. Like all Starfleet. You talk and you talk . . . but you have no *guramba.*

This time, before Corey can respond, Picard looks up into the eyes of the Nausicaan.

PICARD
What did you say?

Nausicaan #1 looks down at him in surprise. . . . This human had been pretty conciliatory until now.

NAUSICAAN #1
I said you are a coward.

PICARD
That's what I thought you said.

Without a word Picard HITS the Nausicaan right in the face. The Nausicaan fairly explodes with rage. With a throaty ROAR, he swings at Picard, who manages to duck out of the way and deliver a swift blow to the Nausicaan's midsection. Marta and Corey quickly join in and a brief mêlée ensues as the six of them knock each other about and destroy half the furniture in the place.

37 PICARD

Manages to hold his own for a while . . . taking on one, then another of the giant warriors in turn. There is a sense in his actions and bearing that he is enjoying this fight . . . enjoying it as he did when it originally happened many years ago.

Then (repeating the action seen in Act One) Picard gets Nausicaan #1 on the ground in a wrestling lock. Nausicaan #2 pulls a nasty-looking weapon with a long serrated blade from his belt as Nausicaan #3 grabs Picard's arms. Nausicaan #2 then DRIVES his weapon THROUGH Picard's back.

38 ON PICARD'S FACE

As the serrated metal blade comes out of his chest. Picard drops to his knees and lets out a LAUGH of pure joy before falling to the ground. . . .

MATCH CUT TO:

39 INTERIOR SICKBAY—ON PICARD'S FACE

He is laughing, still on the operating table as seen in the Teaser.

40 WIDER

Revealing Beverly, Worf, and Riker looking on in puzzlement. Only a few minutes have passed since the events seen in the Teaser. Beverly is leaning over him with a medical DEVICE.

BEVERLY
(off monitor)
His vital signs are stabilizing. . . .
(beat)
Captain . . . ? Jean-Luc . . . ?

Picard's eyes open at last, and he looks up at Beverly, still smiling.

BEVERLY
You've been injured . . . but I think it's going to be all right.

Picard's surprised at being here at all. With a final chuckle, he closes his eyes. The others all exchange glances.

CUT TO:

41 EXTERIOR SPACE—THE *ENTERPRISE* (OPTICAL)

The ship at impulse power.

42 INTERIOR OBSERVATION LOUNGE

Picard is finishing a long talk with Riker.

PICARD
. . . I still don't know what to make of it all. Was it a dream? Or one of Q's elaborate tricks?

RIKER
A lot of people who've been near death have talked about strange experiences . . . but they're not usually so detailed.

PICARD

Part of me cannot accept the idea that Q would have given me a second chance . . . that he would demonstrate that much . . . compassion.

(beat)

But if it was Q . . . I owe him a debt of gratitude.

RIKER

In what sense? It sounds like he put you through hell.

PICARD

There were many things in my youth that I'm not proud of. . . . They were loose threads . . . untidy parts of myself that I wanted to remove.

(beat)

But when I pulled on one of those threads . . . I unraveled the tapestry of my life.

Riker smiles at some inner joke.

RIKER

(off Picard's look)

I was just trying to imagine you as a hell-bent-for-leather young officer insulting a Nausicaan twice your size. I wish I'd gotten a chance to meet that Jean-Luc Picard.

Picard smiles and leans back in his chair. He's more at ease discussing this part of his life than he ever has been before . . . a small demon has been put to rest and he can talk about his youth with a new joy and pride.

PICARD

Well, to tell the truth . . . that wasn't the first time I'd had a run-in with a couple of surly Nausicaans. . . .

RIKER

Really?

PICARD

Oh, yes . . .

(beat)

During my sophomore year I was assigned to do some training on Morikin VII. Well, there was a Nausicaan outpost on one of the outlying asteroids . . .

43 EXTERIOR SPACE—ON OBSERVATION LOUNGE (OPTICAL)

Picard and Riker are sitting in the observation lounge together. As Picard continues to tell Riker a tall tale from his youth, we PULL BACK and watch as the ship flies away into the star-filled void of space.

FADE OUT.

STAR TREK: DEEP SPACE NINE

Q-Less

#40511-407

Teleplay by
Robert Hewitt Wolfe

Story by
Hannah Louise Shearer

Directed by
Paul Lynch

STAR TREK: DEEP SPACE NINE

Q-Less

CAST

SISKO
O'BRIEN
BASHIR
DAX
KIRA
ODO
QUARK

Q
VASH
KOLOS
BAJORAN CLERK
BAJORAN WOMAN

Non-Speaking

STOL
N.D. FERENGI
N.D. BAJORANS
HUMAN WOMAN

Q

STAR TREK: DEEP SPACE NINE

Q-Less

SETS

INTERIORS

DEEP SPACE 9
- CORRIDOR
- IMFIRMARY
- COMMANDER'S OFFICE
- AIRLOCK
- ASSAY OFFICE
- PROMENADE
- VASH'S GUEST QUARTERS
- HABITAT RING
- REPLIMAT
- QUARK'S
- UNDER THE STAIRS

RUNABOUT
- SERVICE BAY

EXTERIORS

DEEP SPACE 9
RUNABOUT

STAR TREK: DEEP SPACE NINE

Q-Less

PRONUNCIATION GUIDE

Betazed	BAY-tuh-zed
Braxite	BRAX-ite
Cardassian	car-DASS-ee-en
Erabus	AIR-uh-bus
Errikang	ERR-i-kang
Gamzian	GAM-zee-on
Hoek	HOE-ick
Kolos	KOH-los
Lantar	LAN-tar
Mulzirak	MULL-zir-ak
Mundahla	mun-DAHL-uh
Nurzin	NER-zin
oo-mox	OO-mox
postganglionic	post GANG-glee-uhn-ick
preganglionic	pre GANG-glee-uhn-ick
Promethean	pro-MEE-thee-uhn
Risa	RYE-suh
Rohain	ROE-hane
Rul	RULE

Rytsan	WRITE-zan
Sampalo	sam-PAH-low
sarium	sar-EE-um
Surax	sewer-AX
Tanesh	tuh-NESH
Tartaras	tar-TAR-uhs
Teleris	TELL-her-iss
Vadris	vah-DRIS
Viterian	VIE-ter-ee-an

STAR TREK: DEEP SPACE NINE

Q-less

TEASER

FADE IN:

1 INTERIOR REPLIMAT

BASHIR in midconversation with a beautiful BAJORAN WOMAN (a civilian). She gazes at him dreamily as he tells his tale.

BASHIR
. . . So there I was, fighting the toughest battle of my life. I looked around hoping to spot a friendly face . . . only to discover my colleagues were gone. . . .
(a beat for dramatic effect)
I was . . . alone.

The Bajoran beauty, hanging on his every word, nods sympathetically.

2 NEW ANGLE

To include O'BRIEN, seated at a nearby table. He can't decide what annoys him more, Bashir's "performance," or the woman's moonstruck response.

BASHIR
I admit, for a moment there, I considered giving up. I could feel the seconds ticking away . . . panic building up inside me. I knew my only chance was to trust my instincts. I closed my eyes . . .
(he reenacts the moment)
. . . took a deep breath . . . and just like that, it came to me. The answer I was waiting for . . . *a pericardial membrane.*
(his eyes pop open)
I looked down and wrote it into my computer terminal, just as the buzzer sounded, ending the exam.
(modestly)
And that, I suppose, is the stuff of which salutatorians are made.

BAJORAN WOMAN
(only *second?*)
*Salut*atorian?

BASHIR
(minor setback)
I mistook a preganglionic fiber for a postganglionic nerve during the orals or I would have been *vale*dictorian.
(shrugs)
It was a trick question.

His companion is duly impressed.

BAJORAN WOMAN
Fascinating.

BASHIR
(smoothly)
Not nearly as fascinating as . . .

SISKO'S COMBADGE
Doctor Bashir . . . Chief O'Brien . . . report to landing pad five immediately.

BASHIR
(to woman)
Bad timing.

BAJORAN WOMAN
(very encouraging)
There'll be another time.

Bashir smiles, rises . . . so does O'Brien. They make their way toward the turbolift.

BASHIR
(to O'Brien)
Starfleet medical finals . . . gets them every time.

O'Brien's deadpan stare says it all.

3 INTERIOR LANDING PAD FIVE AIRLOCK

The *Ganges* is docked at the airlock. SISKO and KIRA are using handheld suction-like clamps to pull open the runabout's hatch. They've gotten the clamps from a portable service module, which has been left near a half-repaired open panel. They're unable to open the hatch.

KIRA

It's no use.

O'Brien and Bashir ENTER the airlock, both wondering what's going on.

SISKO

Chief, we've got to get this hatch open. Lieutenant Dax and Ensign Pauley are trapped in there.

O'Brien pops open a panel beside the hatch.

KIRA

The runabout barely made it back through the wormhole. By the time they docked, power levels were near zero.

O'BRIEN

(checking panel)

There's not even enough juice left in the ship to release the servos.

Bashir consults his medical tricorder.

BASHIR

(to Sisko)

Life support's down, and oxygen levels have dropped dangerously low.

Kira whips out her phaser and points it at the hatch.

KIRA

We'll have to burn through.

SISKO

Forget it, Major. That hatch is made of duranium composite. It would take you an hour to get through.

BASHIR

(re: tricorder)

We don't have that much time.

(a beat)

That's odd.

(to Sisko)

How many passengers did you say were on the *Ganges*?

SISKO

Two.

BASHIR

I'm reading three.

As Sisko reacts to the news . . .

O'BRIEN

We need to get power to the hatch servos.

(pointing to the service module)

Major, hand me that EPI capacitor.

Kira looks at the module, not quite sure what O'Brien means.

O'BRIEN

(continuing)

Top shelf, all the way to the left.

Kira finds the capacitor and hands it to him.

O'BRIEN

(continuing)

Stand clear.

O'Brien reaches into the runabout panel and jury-rigs a connection.

O'BRIEN

(continuing)

Give her a go.

Kira hits the door panel. The door slides partway open. There is a whoosh as air rushes in. Sisko and Kira force it wide enough so that Bashir and O'Brien can ENTER.

4 INTERIOR RUNABOUT

They find DAX, Pauley, and a woman passenger (lying facedown on a console) slowly regaining consciousness. Bashir goes to Dax, who waves him off.

DAX

I'm fine; check the others.

While Bashir examines Ensign Pauley, O'Brien helps the woman to her feet. As she turns to O'Brien, he gives a look of startled recognition.

O'BRIEN

Miles O'Brien . . . From the *Enterprise.*

Vash, in weakened condition, makes a show of remembering.

VASH

Yes, of course.

O'BRIEN

What are you doing on the *Ganges?*

Vash weakly tries to pick up a twenty-fourth–century equivalent of a duffel bag . . . O'Brien moves to assist her, takes the bag for her.

DAX

We found her in the Gamma Quadrant. She's been there for over *two years.*

O'BRIEN

(reacts, glances at Sisko)

Two years . . .?

Bashir supports a groggy Ensign Pauley.

SISKO

Doctor, we better get these people over to the infirmary.

Bashir nods and leads them out of the ship. O'Brien assists Vash.

BASHIR

Right this way.

5 INTERIOR LANDING PAD FIVE AIRLOCK

Out of the ship, they walk toward the exit, by a Starfleet engineer (*Enterprise*-style uniform) who's got his head inside the panel beside the door, obviously attempting repairs. . . .

O'BRIEN

(to Vash)

How did you get to the Gamma Quadrant two years ago?

VASH

(a weak smile)

A friend dropped me off.

O'Brien reacts curiously. So does Sisko. And as they EXIT . . .

6 NEW ANGLE—ON THE STARFLEET ENGINEER

Who now looks out of the panel back toward the departed passengers . . . and it is Q. . . .

FADE OUT.

ACT ONE

FADE IN:

7 INTERIOR INFIRMARY

Bashir scans Vash with a tricorder and consults the readout.

VASH

Will I live?

BASHIR

You're fine. In fact, you're in remarkable shape.

VASH

Thank you, Doctor. I try.

BASHIR

(embarrassed)

I'd say you've managed quite well for someone who's been out of contact with civilization for over two years.

VASH

I'd hardly call the Gamma Quadrant uncivilized. Some of the cultures I've encountered have histories dating back millions of years.

BASHIR

(fascinated)

Really . . . ? I'd love to hear about them. We have no idea what's beyond the wormhole. . . .

VASH

(playful)

Perhaps I'll write a book . . .

BASHIR

It's certain to be a best seller around here . . .

(completing the exam)

Well, no sign of disease or malnutrition, no parasitic infections . . .

VASH

You sound disappointed.

BASHIR

I am. Now I don't have any reason to keep you here.

Bashir puts away his medical tricorder.

VASH

(smiles)

You almost make me wish I wasn't feeling well.

Bashir smiles back.

8 INTERIOR COMMANDER'S OFFICE

Dax is making her report to Sisko.

SISKO

(confirming)

. . . and she claims she knew nothing about the wormhole . . . ?

DAX

She was very surprised when I told her about it. I don't think she ever expected to see this part of the galaxy again.

SISKO

How could she get there in the first place if she didn't go through the wormhole?

DAX

She didn't want to talk about it. Said it was a personal matter.

SISKO

This doesn't make sense. A human alone in the Gamma Quadrant for two years. Let's check her background. See what we can find out about her.

DAX

She claims to be an archaeologist.

SISKO

That's a good place to start.

As he turns to access his desk monitor . . .

9 EXTERIOR SPACE DEEP SPACE 9 (OPTICAL)

10 INTERIOR PROMENADE—THE ASSAY OFFICE

Establishing.

11 INTERIOR ASSAY OFFICE

Vash, her duffel bag on the counter, is speaking with a BAJORAN CLERK.

VASH

You're sure this place is safe?

BAJORAN CLERK

The assay office is the most secure area on the station.

The clerk opens one of the storage chambers.

BAJORAN CLERK

(continuing)

The chambers are surrounded on all sides by individual force fields.

VASH

How are the locks controlled?

BAJORAN CLERK

Once you secure a chamber, it can't be opened except with your personal authorization code, combined with a verified retinal print.

VASH

(probing)

Cardassian MK-seven scanner?

The clerk looks offended at the mere suggestion. MK-seven indeed.

BAJORAN CLERK

MK-twelve with an L-ninety enhanced resolution filter.

Vash thinks about it.

VASH

I suppose it'll have to do.

Vash unzips the bag. Vash takes a variety of artifacts out of her duffel and hands them one at a time to the clerk, who looks over each object, then gives them to his assistant, who puts them in the cubicle.

BAJORAN CLERK

Computer, begin inventory for cubicle nineteen. One statue, stone, thirty-odd centimeters tall, approximately twenty kilograms . . . assorted gems . . . gold necklace . . . one dagger, bronze and gold, about twenty-five centimeters.

12 NEW ANGEL (OPTICAL)

The assistant puts away the dagger, and Vash places a metal box on the counter. Vash opens the container to REVEAL a beautiful GEODE glowing with a pulsing internal light.

BAJORAN CLERK

(continuing)

Beautiful. I've never seen anything quite like it. Some kind of Promethean quartz?

VASH

That's what I thought at first, but it's molecular density and refraction index are much higher.

BAJORAN CLERK

(to Vash, admiring the geode)

Remarkable.

Vash closes the box and hands it to the clerk, who puts it away and closes the cubicle.

BAJORAN CLERK

(continuing, to computer)

End inventory.

He gives her a data clip. The assistant leaves.

BAJORAN CLERK
(to Vash)
Please enter an access code.

She taps a combination into the clip. The clerk indicates a small eyepiece attached to the counter. Vash places her eye against the scanner. There's a slight hum as her retinal print is filed.

VASH
(once she's done)
I'll be back to pick everything up tomorrow. I've booked passage on the Mulzirak transport.

13 NEW ANGLE

To include Sisko standing in the doorway.

SISKO
You're not leaving us so soon, are you?

VASH
I'm afraid so.

Sisko falls into step beside her as she EXITS the assay office.

14 INTERIOR PROMENADE—CONTINUOUS

As they walk along the street.

SISKO
The Daystrom Institute will be very disappointed.

VASH
(taken aback)
The Daystrom Institute?

SISKO
Their scientists are anxious to hear about life in the Gamma Quadrant.
(continuing)
Every place you've been, everything you've seen, no matter how insignificant, could prove important.
(fishing)
Including how you got there.

VASH

I'm sorry, Commander, but that's a . . .

SISKO AND VASH

(simultaneously)

Personal matter.

They pass by Quark's, where we see QUARK and the assay office assistant in animated conversation. We don't hear what they're saying, but the assistant's surreptitious nod towards Vash lets us know the gist of their conversation.

VASH

(thoughtful)

So now the Daystrom Institute is interested in me. That's ironic.

SISKO

Professor Woo seemed especially eager to speak to you again.

VASH

Did he really? I suppose he told you that he suspended my membership from the institute's archaeological council.

SISKO

On two occasions. Something about the illegal sale of artifacts . . .

VASH

Let's just say when it comes to choosing between science and profit . . . I'll choose profit every time.

SISKO

I think the professor is hoping in this case you'll make an exception.

VASH

(considering)

You know, I haven't been back to Earth in . . . it must be twelve years.

SISKO

Here's your chance. I could arrange passage . . .

VASH
(smiling)

I think I'd like that.

Sisko nods. It's a done deal.

15 INTERIOR THE *GANGES*

O'Brien finishes closing up some open panels as Sisko ENTERS. O'Brien looks up.

O'BRIEN

I don't understand it, Commander. I can't find anything wrong with her. This ship's completely functional.

SISKO

It didn't look that way this morning.

O'BRIEN

Oh, don't get me wrong. The power reserves are empty, the inertial damping fields are barely operating, and the warp drive containment field is on the verge of collapse.

SISKO

But . . .

O'BRIEN

But there's nothing wrong with any of them. Once we put power back into the *Ganges,* she should be fully operational.

SISKO

Did you check the central power linkages?

O'BRIEN

Yes, sir. I ran a level-one diagnostic. Everything checks out. I can't explain it. It's like something tapped into the ship's systems and drained them dry.

He picks up his tools. Sisko follows him out of the runabout.

16 INTERIOR AIRLOCK

Sisko and O'Brien in motion.

SISKO

Tell me, Chief, how well do you know this Vash woman?

O'BRIEN

Hardly at all. Only met her that one time she was aboard the *Enterprise.*

SISKO

What was she doing there?

O'Brien is hesitant, choosing his words carefully in an attempt to be discrete.

O'BRIEN

Well Sir, Vash and Captain Picard were friends . . . close friends . . . if you follow my meaning. Seems they met on Risa a few years back.

17 INTERIOR CORRIDOR

As they come out of the airlock.

O'BRIEN

(continuing, to Sisko)

I figure she must be a special woman . . . to be friends with the captain and all.

SISKO

Somehow she doesn't seem to be his type.

O'BRIEN

The captain likes a good challenge, sir.

Before Sisko can respond, the corridor lights dim, and there's a low-pitched WHINE. Then as quickly as they faded, the lights flicker and come up again, and the noise ceases. As Sisko and O'Brien react. . . .

18 INTERIOR OPS

Kira and Dax at their stations. Sisko and O'Brien ENTER from the turbolift.

SISKO

Status report?

O'Brien hurries to his station.

DAX

We suffered a broad-spectrum power drain.

KIRA

The power transfer is completely inoperative. The energy was drawn out faster than it could handle.

O'BRIEN

I'll have to replace the entire unit.

DAX

(to O'Brien)

Chief, are you reading any graviton flux around the transfer systems.?

O'BRIEN

(runs a diagnostic)

I am detecting a low-level graviton disturbance. . . . How did you know?

DAX

That's exactly what happened when we lost power on the *Ganges.*

On reactions . . .

FADE OUT.

ACT TWO

FADE IN:

19 INTERIOR CORRIDOR—HABITAT RING

O'Brien and Vash walk along a passageway.

O'BRIEN
These were originally Cardassian living quarters. The bed may take some getting use to.

VASH
As an archaeologist, I've spent half my life sleeping in tents. To me any bed is a luxury.

O'BRIEN
(smiling)
You've obviously never slept on a Cardassian mattress.

They arrive at a door to one of the guest quarters.

O'BRIEN
If you need anything, just ask the computer.

VASH
Thanks, Chief.
(beat)
By the way, how's Jean-Luc?

O'BRIEN
The captain? Last time I saw him he was fine.

VASH
(enigmatic smile)
Well, now that I'm back, I'll have to look him up.

They nod good-bye and Vash ENTERS . . .

20 INTERIOR GUEST QUARTERS

Vash looks around with mild disapproval. She's not exactly in love with the decor. She crosses over to the bed and checks the mattress. Sure enough, it's a monstrosity.

She tosses her duffel bag on the bed and turns around, only to bump smack into . . . Q, still wearing his *Enterprise*-style uniform.

Q

Really, Vash, I can't believe you're still pining for Jean-Luc, that self-righteous do-gooder.

VASH

I should have listened to him when he warned me about you . . .

Q

You're hurt, so you lash out. I understand. But be of good cheer. I bring wonderful news.

(a beat)

I'm back. I can see now it was cruel of me to leave you.

VASH

That's very touching. But you didn't leave me, I left you.

Q

You left me, I left you. . . . Details, mere details. The important thing is we're back together again . . . a team . . . joined at the hip . . .

VASH

Not a chance.

Q

Come now, you know you missed me.

VASH

Don't flatter yourself.

21 NEW ANGLE (OPTICAL)

Vash starts to turn away and is startled as her duffel bag appears on her shoulder, courtesy of Q.

Q

I thought first we'd visit the Teleris Cluster . . . look in on the cloud dancers of Mundahla. Or maybe head over to the Lantar Nebula to view the Sampalo relics on Hoek IV.

VASH

Not interested.

She throws the bag down, only to have it instantly reappear on her shoulder.

Q

I know. Vadris III. Charming little world. The natives think they're the only intelligent life in the galaxy. . . .

VASH

(more forcefully)

No.

Q

Oh, very well. You choose this time.

VASH

I choose never to go anywhere with you again, Q . . .

Q

You don't know what you'll be missing. When we started this little partnership, I promised to take you places no human had ever seen. . . .

VASH

And you have. Thank you . . . and good-bye.

She opens the door . . . waits for him to exit. A beat, then seemingly resigned to his fate, he slowly walks toward it, but instead of leaving he turns to confront her.

Q

Two years in the Gamma Quadrant hardly qualifies as a grand tour of the universe. There's still the Delta Quadrant to explore, not to mention all the other galaxies.

VASH

It's over, Q. I want you out of my life. You're arrogant and overbearing, and you think you know everything.

Q

But I do know everything.

VASH

That makes it even worse.

Q

Okay . . . fine . . . I understand . . . I hear you. What is it you *really* want?

She looks at him, shakes her head. . . . He cannot fathom that she'd really be serious about leaving him.

VASH

I want . . . the life I had before I met you.

Q

(sarcastic)

Ah yes, a stellar life indeed. The eminent Vash. Barred from the Royal Museum of Epsilon Hydra IV, persona non grata on Betazed. Wanted dead on Myrmidon for stealing the Crown of the First Mother.

VASH

Dead or alive.

Q

Preferably dead. It's a wonder you haven't offended every sentient race in the galaxy.

VASH

You're the one who almost got me killed on Errikang VII. And they weren't exactly thrilled to see you on Brax either. What did they call you there? "The God of Lies?"

Q

They meant it affectionately.

The Door CHIMES.

VASH

Come in.

22 ANGLE ON THE DOOR (OPTICAL)

QUARK ENTERS the room, but before he can say a word . . .

Q
(to Quark)

Go away.

Quark DISAPPEARS.

VASH

Q, bring him back.

Q

What business could you possibly have with that repulsive little troll?

VASH

I don't know. You didn't give him time to tell me. Now bring him back this instant.

Q

Oh, very well.

Quark REAPPEARS. Vash looks around, and Q is gone. (Lose one Q FLASH.)

23 ANGLE ON QUARK

A picture of confusion.

VASH

Can I help you?

Quark looks Vash up and down. Likes what he sees. He turns on some of that old Ferengi charm.

QUARK

My name is Quark. It's come to my attention that you have access to certain items. Items that could perhaps turn a tidy profit.

VASH

I'm listening.

Quark leans closer as if sharing an intimate secret.

QUARK

For a percentage, I might be able to arrange a buyer for your trinkets. Perhaps an auction.

Vash thinks it over for a beat.

VASH

I'll only accept payment in gold-pressed latinum.

QUARK

I'll shower you in it.

(a beat, re: their split)

Fifty-fifty?

VASH

Mister Quark, I believe you're trying to take advantage of me.

She begins to massage Quark's ear. The Ferengi shivers with joy.

QUARK

Mmmm. You have a talent for *oo-mox.*

VASH

So I've been told.

Quark forces himself to pull away.

QUARK

I will not be distracted by your feminine wiles. I demand forty percent.

She reaches out and resumes *oo-mox*ing him. Quark practically purring like a kitten.

QUARK

All right, thirty.

VASH

(re: Quark's ears)

What magnificent cartilage.

QUARK

Twenty-two and don't stop.

VASH

You've got a deal.

Vash removes her hand from Quark's ear. It's like dumping cold water on the Ferengi.

VASH

(all business)

I expect you to make all the necessary arrangements.

QUARK

(admiring her business acumen)

Oh, you're good. You're very, very good.

And gently touching his throbbing ear, Quark EXITS.

24 NEW ANGLE

As Vash turns around and finds Q sitting on her couch.

Q

How perfectly vile. If that's the kind of company you kept before you met me, it's no wonder you ended up with Picard.

VASH

(emphatic)

Go away.

The door CHIMES again.

VASH

Enter.

Q

My, aren't we the hub of activity?

Bashir ENTERS the room. Bashir notices that Vash looks upset.

BASHIR

I'm sorry. Am I interrupting anything?

Vash glances back at the couch. Q is gone.

VASH

Not at all, Doctor. Come in.

BASHIR

Thank you, and please, call me Julian.

VASH

(smiles)

Julian. Is this a medical visit?

BASHIR

To tell the truth, I was going to try to come up with some official reason for dropping by, but your excellent health has robbed me of any excuses.

VASH

Well, that didn't seem to stop you.

BASHIR

I thought I should contribute to your good health by buying you dinner. Quark's makes a lovely couscous. And the company, I hope, might be mildly entertaining.

Vash sizes up Bashir. She likes what she sees.

VASH

Sounds like fun.

25 ANGLE ON Q (OPTICAL)

As he REAPPEARS behind Bashir. Vash sees him.

VASH

(continuing)

But first I need to freshen up. Can I meet you in say, twenty minutes?

Q frowns and DISAPPEARS.

BASHIR
(victory)
Those twenty minutes will feel like an eternity.

Bashir EXITS and Vash turns to find Q standing before her. (Lose Q FLASH.)

Q
These mating rituals you humans indulge in really are quite disgusting.

VASH
Get out.

Q
You know you don't mean that.

VASH
Out.

Q
You're making a terrible mistake. You'd be lost without me.

VASH
I can take care of myself.

Q
Can you really? We'll see about that.

Q disappears.

26 INTERIOR REPLIMAT—FIVE MINUTES LATER

Bashir sits at a table. A waiter approaches. It's Q in Bajoran clothes and nose.

BASHIR
Just a cup of mint tea.

Q
You're making a terrible mistake.

BASHIR
Why? Have the replicators malfunctioned again?

Q

I'm talking about Vash. Stay away from her.

BASHIR

My god, you're an impertinent waiter.

Q

I'm a friend . . . with some friendly advice. Vash is nothing but trouble.

BASHIR

Really, I don't think it's any of your business. In fact, I'm meeting her for dinner now. . . .

Bashir gets up to leave.

Q

Are you sure you're feeling up to it?

(beat)

You look tired.

BASHIR

I feel fine.

Q

You look tired. Very, very tired.

Bashir yawns.

BASHIR

Funny, I am feeling a bit spent. Maybe I should go lie down for a few minutes.

A dazed Bashir wanders off. . . .

Q

(an aside)

Hopefully by yourself, for a change.

Bashir passes . . .

27 O'BRIEN

Who's too busy staring at Q to notice the doctor.

O'BRIEN

Bloody hell.

O'Brien turns and hurries away.

28 INTERIOR OPS

Kira, Dax at their stations, Sisko conferring with Kira at the operations table.

KIRA

Sir, the Klingon scoutship has departed docking bay eleven.

SISKO

Good. I'll tell Odo he can relax now.

O'Brien ENTERS from the turbolift.

O'BRIEN

Sir, we've got a problem. I just saw Q on the Promenade.

SISKO

Q? Here?

Off Sisko's look of concern . . .

KIRA

What's Q?

SISKO

A powerful and extremely unpredictable entity. I was at a Starfleet briefing on him, two years ago.

O'BRIEN

He's a blasted menace, is what he is.

DAX

What does he want with us?

SISKO

Whatever it is, you can be sure we won't like it.

O'BRIEN
(a realization)
You might ask Vash.

DAX
Why Vash?

O'BRIEN
They know each other.

SISKO
From the *Enterprise?*

O'BRIEN
I believe they actually met in Sherwood Forest.
(off Sisko's puzzled look)
One of the little jokes Q played on the *Enterprise* crew.

29 NEW ANGLE

As the lights fade and the air is filled with a high pitched whine. This time it takes considerably longer before the lights come back up and the sound stops.

Kira consults the operations table.

KIRA
Main power grid has dropped eighty percent.

DAX
Sensors are reading a massive graviton buildup.

SISKO
How long to get us back up to full power?

DAX
It's already beginning to normalize.

KIRA
If we have one of these outages during a docking procedure, we could lose an entire pylon.

O'BRIEN

I've double-checked every system. For the first time in a month, there's nothing wrong with any of them . . . it's got to be Q. Another one of his stupid jokes.

SISKO

I'm not laughing.

30 INTERIOR QUARK'S (OPTICAL)

Quark and Vash sit at the end of the bar. Vash watches Quark's face, looking for his reaction as he gazes intently into the box at the geode.

VASH

I figure we'd auction this off last.

Quark closes the box with a snap.

QUARK

(dismissive)

Interesting . . . but hardly of any intrinsic value.

VASH

(coolly)

Really? I thought it was the best piece in the collection.

QUARK

Obviously my associates have more sophisticated tastes than you're used to.

(beat)

But just so it's not a total loss, *I'll* take it off your hands for say . . . seven bars of gold-pressed latinum.

VASH

(amused)

It's worth fifty times as much.

QUARK

Ridiculous . . . All right, eighteen bars, but you must swear never to tell a soul about my foolish generosity.

VASH
(takes the box from Quark)
If you want it you're going to have to be a lot more foolish than that.

QUARK
All right. Thirty.
(he reaches for the box)
Now give it to me.

Vash slides the box out of reach.

VASH
Bidding will start at two hundred bars of latinum.

Quark can barely control his frustration. He takes a gulp of his wine.

QUARK
I can't decide which is more intoxicating, this Gamzian wine or your negotiating skills.

Vash acknowledges the compliment—just as Sisko steps up to the bar.

SISKO
(to Vash)
We need to talk.

QUARK
The lady and I are having a private conversation.

SISKO
It can wait.

Quark backs off. He EXITS offscreen as Sisko sits down at the bar.

VASH
Commander, have you seen that doctor of yours? He was supposed to meet me here half an hour ago . . .

SISKO
(interrupting, purposeful)
Tell me about Q.

31 ANGLE ON Q

Who turns in his seat from the table behind them.

Q

I'll tell you anything you want to know, Commander. Just answer one question. . . . Is Starfleet penalizing you, or did you actually request such a dismal command?

On Sisko's reaction we . . .

FADE OUT.

ACT THREE

32 FADE IN:

INTERIOR QUARK'S—(OPTICAL)

As before.

SISKO

I want you off this station.

Q

Let's not be hasty, my happy-go-lucky friend; this dreary little gulag could use a little color, a little excitement. And who better to provide it than . . . moi?

(eying Sisko's uniform)

Though I must say I approve of your new tailor.

And in the blink of an eye, Q changes outfits to match Sisko's, except that Q's has captain's rank insignia.

SISKO

I'm not impressed by your parlor tricks. These power outages are going to stop . . . right now.

Q

Why tell me?

(hurt realization)

Oh, I see. Go ahead, blame Q if it makes you feel any better. I suppose it's my fate to be the galaxy's whipping boy.

(a sigh)

Heavy is the burden of being me.

SISKO

If you're looking for sympathy, you've come to the wrong place.

Q

Actually, what I had in mind was some witty repartee, but I see I'm not going to get any of that either.

(to Vash)

At least, your beloved Jean-Luc knows how to turn a phrase. . . .

VASH

Take the hint, Q . . . *No* one wants you around.

Q

(mood darkening)

Really, Vash, this playing hard to get is growing tedious.

And Q gets quite expansive and public as he continues . . . heads turn to his voice as he says . . .

Q

(continuing)

You might keep in mind that I am the Q and you are the lowly human. I will decide when this partnership ends.

(to both Vash and Sisko)

Do you understand?

SISKO

(to Q, as the room reacts)

Why don't you and I continue this discussion in private?

Q

(brightening)

An excellent idea.

And in the blink of an eye, Vash and everyone else in the bar DISAPPEARS. Q and Sisko are now completely alone.

33 NEW ANGLE

As Q props his feet up on the table, right where Vash was sitting.

Q

You're right. This is much better.

Sisko hits his combadge.

SISKO

Sisko to ops.

Q

All gone.

Sisko grabs Q by the collar.

SISKO

Bring them back, Q. Now.

Q is delighted by this show of aggression.

Q

Or what? You'll thrash me?

(mischievous grin)

Shall we settle this mano a mano?

And suddenly . . .

34 INTERIOR QUARK'S—MAIN FLOOR (OPTICAL)

The patrons of the bar are back, surprised to find themselves standing in a square, forming a human boxing ring, around . . .

35 Q AND SISKO

Who are now dressed as boxers, circa 1900. Q, sporting a handlebar mustache, assumes an old-fashioned boxing pose.

Q

Marquis of Queensberry rules?

SISKO

What?

Q bounces around like Gentleman Jim Corbett.

Q

Fisticuffs, pugilism, the manly art of self-defense. Isn't it wonderfully barbaric? Go on. Take a poke at me. That is what you want to do, isn't it?

SISKO

Don't tempt me.

36 CLOSE ON QUARK AND VASH

Who are among the onlookers.

QUARK
(to Vash)
I'll wager five bars of latinum on Sisko.

VASH
(poker face)
You're on.

37 BACK TO THE ACTION

Sisko turns away from Q, but Q smacks him lightly on the back of the head. Sisko tries to ignore Q, but Q keeps punching him.

Q
Come on, fight back. This is supposed to be brutal.

Q punches Sisko again. Sisko turns around and faces Q. Q pops Sisko in the face, rocking Sisko's head back. Sisko smashes Q with a right hook to the head. Q goes flying into the crowd. As he crashes to the ground . . .

38 NEW ANGLE (OPTICAL)

The crowd is dispersed to their regular places around the bar.

QUARK
(to Vash, smug)
You can pay me out of your profits from the auction.

Q struggles to his feet.

Q
(shocked)
You hit me . . . . Picard never hit me.

SISKO
I'm not Picard.

Q
Indeed not. You're much easier to provoke.
(grinning)
How fortunate for me.

Q disappears. Sisko finds himself back in his Deep Space 9 uniform.

VASH
(quiet despair)
He's never going to let me go.
(a beat)
Unless you can help. . . .

SISKO
I wouldn't get my hopes up.
(off her look)
It was a lucky punch.

39 EXTERIOR SPACE—DEEP SPACE NINE—STOCK (OPTICAL)

40 INTERIOR THE PROMENADE (DAY TWO)

An Andorian (KOLOS) emerges from the airlock near Quark's. He is followed closely by a jewel-bedecked Ferengi. The Ferengi gazes warily at his surroundings. He spots Kolos. The two aliens exchange hostile glances as they walk the Promenade.

Nearby three mysterious cloaked and hooded humanoids surreptitiously watch the Ferengi and the Andorian, then follow them to Quark's. We never see their faces.

41 ANGLE ON THE SECURITY OFFICE

Close on ODO as he checks out the new arrivals with a suspicious eye.

Without warning, the Promenade lights go out and the whine returns (as before, but with an increase in intensity). Odo looks up into the darkness.

ODO
Not again.

42 INTERIOR OPS

As the lights come back up, we see Sisko, Kira, Dax, and O'Brien at their stations.

O'BRIEN
(exasperated)
Damn it, Q. Enough is enough.

Just then . . . a blast of air explodes through OPS, knocking everyone about. Alarm klaxons sound.

DAX
(over the roar of the wind)
We're losing atmosphere.

SISKO
Decompression protocol—raise the confinement shields.

O'Brien engages the necessary controls.

O'BRIEN
Shields up.

The wind ceases abruptly. The ops staff regain their balance.

SISKO
(to Kira)
Damage report.

KIRA
(consulting console)
We've got a minor hull breach in one of the upper bulkheads.

O'BRIEN
I'm getting reports of hull fractures throughout the station.
(checking monitors)
Emergency systems appear to be functioning. Repair crews are responding.

43 INTERIOR CORRIDOR (OPTICAL)

Dax uses a tricorder to examine a jagged hole in a bulkhead. Sisko watches with interest.

DAX
(concerned)
The breach was caused by some kind of focused graviton pulse.

SISKO

Every time we've had a power drain, it's been followed by an increase in the graviton field. If this continues, we could wind up with a breach in one of our reactor cores. We'd lose half the station.

DAX

Maybe it's time to open negotiations with Q?

A beat. Sisko's thoughtful. Something about all this doesn't seem right.

SISKO

I'm not convinced that Q's behind this.

Off Dax's reaction.

SISKO

(continuing)

Playing with the lights and punching holes in the hull doesn't strike me as his style.

44 INTERIOR SECURITY OFFICE

Quark ENTERS Odo's office.

QUARK

You wanted to see me? Make it quick. I've got important business.

ODO

Yes, I know. You're auctioning off some artifacts from the Gamma Quadrant.

QUARK

(realization)

You were eavesdropping on my conversation with Vash.

(a beat)

What were you this time? The table? One of the chairs? The wine bottle?

ODO

(superior)

When are you going to realize that you have no secrets from me?

QUARK

I have nothing to hide. I'm selling quality merchandise to a select clientele.

ODO

What makes them so select?

QUARK

They're all ridiculously wealthy . . . and not too bright.

ODO

(shakes his head)

I'll never understand this obsession with accumulating material wealth. You spend your entire life plotting and scheming to acquire more and more possessions, until your living areas are bursting with useless junk. Then you die and your relatives sell everything and start the cycle all over again.

QUARK

(looking for an edge)

Isn't there anything you desire?

ODO

I have my work. What more do I need?

QUARK

(eyes light up at the thought)

A suit of the finest Andorian silk? A ring of pure Surax? A complete set of Tanesh pottery?

(on Odo's lack of response)

How about a latinum-plated bucket to sleep in?

Odo considers it, but just doesn't see the point.

45 INTERIOR PROMENADE (OPTICAL)

Vash EXITS the assay office, on her way to Quark's, duffel bag filled with artifacts. But before she gets very far, she bumps into a waiting Q. (Lose Q FLASH.)

Q

Ah, I'm so glad you're packed. I hope you said good-bye to all your new friends.

VASH

I don't have time for this now.

Vash tries to get around Q, who steps in her way.

Q

You've led a charmed life these past two years . . . under my benevolent protection.

VASH

I can take care of myself.

Q

Can you really? Remember that bug bite you got on Erabus Prime? If I hadn't been there . . .

Q waves his hand, and in a FLASH Vash loses her hair except for a few sloppy strands. Vash touches her head. For a moment, she's terrified, but she refuses to let Q best her.

VASH

(defiant)

I am not going with you.

Q

The galaxy can be a dangerous place when you're on your own.

Another FLASH and Vash's face and arms are covered by horrible oozing boils. The people on the Promenade recoil from her in abject horror. Q is enjoying himself immensely.

VASH

(not giving up)

It's over, Q.

A third FLASH. Vash falls to her knees. She is wracked with palsy and her skin is a deathly gray.

Q

(to Vash, as if nothing has happened)

I'll leave you now to reconsider my offer of friendship.

Q vanishes in a flash, and at the same time Vash returns to normal. As one of the bystanders moves to help her . . . on her reaction . . .

FADE OUT.

46–47 OMITTED

ACT FOUR

FADE IN:

47A EXTERIOR DEEP SPACE 9—STOCK (OPTICAL)

SISKO
(voice-over)
Station log, stardate 46531.2. The station's power is continuing to be drained and converted into gravitons. At this rate, our life support systems will fail in fourteen hours.

48 INTERIOR OPS (OPTICAL)

O'Brien, Dax, Sisko, and Kira at the operations table.

O'BRIEN
Sir, we'll never find the source of the power drain using these bloody Cardassian internal sensors. They're just not sensitive enough.

SISKO
Is there any way to recalibrate them?

O'BRIEN
It would take days. We just don't have the time.

DAX
What if we make the power drain easier to detect?
(on reactions)
If we flood the station with ionized tritium gas, we should be able to trace the particle flow to the source.

O'BRIEN
Tritium? Isn't that pretty toxic?

DAX
Only when it's highly concentrated. We would use a very small amount.

SISKO
Do it. If we can't get this under control in the next eight hours, we'll begin evacuation procedures.

Q APPEARS, an arm wrapped around Sisko's shoulders.

Q
(with false intimacy)
Still chasing your own tail? Picard and his lackeys would have solved all this technobabble hours ago.
(a beat)
No wonder you're not commanding a starship.

Sisko physically disengages himself from Q's embrace as . . . Kira hits her combadge.

KIRA
Security to ops.

Q
(to Kira)
My, aren't we the feisty little go-getter.
(to Sisko)
I'd keep my eye on this one. Chances are, she's after your job.

O'BRIEN
Why don't you do something constructive for a change? Like torment the Cardassians.

Q gives O'Brien a blank stare.

Q
Do I know you?

O'BRIEN
O'Brien . . .
(on Q's lack of recognition)
From the *Enterprise.*

Q
The *Enterprise.*
(it dawns)
Ah yes. Weren't you one of the little people?

O'Brien shoots Q a dirty look and goes about his business.

Q

(to Sisko)

Quite a motley crew you've assembled here, Benji. My advice is to evacuate now and save all this pointless guesswork.

SISKO

Q, either tell us what's going on or get the hell out of the way.

Q

I'll tell you what's going on. While you're conducting futile experiments, Vash is down below engaging in base commerce and setting Federation ethics back two hundred years.

(one of the boys)

Believe me, she's far more dangerous to you than I am.

Q VANISHES and on the reactions, we cut to:

49 INTERIOR QUARK'S

The dabo table has been replaced by an auctioneer's podium. The bidders—Kolos, the three cloaked figures, and the jewel-bedecked Ferengi—are joined by two others—a second Ferengi and another N.D. alien.

The bidders are scattered about the room, some standing, some sitting, some just lounging against the bar. The two Ferengi stare daggers at each other from a distance.

50 ANGLE ON THE BAR

As Kolos makes his way over to Quark and Vash.

QUARK

Kolos, my friend. I don't know which pleases me more, your smiling face or your overflowing purse.

KOLOS

(not smiling)

Quark, you obsequious toad, your so-called Gamma Quadrant merchandise had better be legitimate or I'll toss you out the nearest airlock.

QUARK
No cause for alarm; each piece comes complete with a statement of authenticity from Vash herself, the Federation's foremost expert on the Gamma Quadrant.

KOLOS
In that case, stop sniveling and give me a synthale.

Quark hands Kolos a drink, and the bidder rejoins his competitors.

VASH
(sarcastic)
Are they all that pleasant?

QUARK
I don't care about their manners. The important thing is they're honest collectors in antiquities, every one.

VASH
How honest?

QUARK
As honest as you and I.

VASH
(dryly)
We better keep a close eye on them.

Quark leans closer to Vash.

QUARK
My dear, I've been thinking, what would you say to a permanent partnership? With your knowledge of the Gamma Quadrant and my business connections, we could make a fortune.

VASH
Sorry, Quark, I've slept in my last tent. I'm looking forward to a nice quiet life back on Earth.

QUARK
(laughs)
You won't last a month. You're like me. You live for excitement, adventure, profit.

VASH

Not anymore.

QUARK

Would you care to make a wager on that?

Before Vash can take Quark up on it, the station shakes violently . . . everyone struggles to stay on their feet. . . .

51 INTERIOR OPS

Close on Dax and Sisko at the science station as they react to the shake . . .

DAX

(consulting her console)

The graviton field has increased by sixty percent.

SISKO

How soon can we begin the sensor sweep . . . ?

DAX

Not until we've increased tritium levels to one part per million. . . . It should only be another seven, eight minutes . . .

KIRA

(reacts to sensors)

Commander . . . we're being pulled out of our normal position.

SISKO

Coult it have something to do with this graviton field?

He looks at O'Brien for answers, but he is mystified as he studies monitors . . .

O'BRIEN

I don't understand it. . . .

SISKO

(to Kira)

Use the control thrusters to stabilize our position.

KIRA

Firing thrusters . . .

51A EXTERIOR DEEP SPACE 9 (OPTICAL)

The station moves through space. The control thrusters fire in an attempt to brake the station, but it continues to move off course.

51B INTERIOR OPS

As before.

KIRA

(refers to readout)

We're still moving.

A tense beat. Then . . .

O'BRIEN

If the graviton field is feeding off the station's power, maybe we can cut its supply by shutting down the reactors.

SISKO

(decisive)

Put life support on emergency backup. Take everything else off-line.

O'Brien activates the necessary controls. The lights go down, then come back up dimmer than usual. (The lighting will remain low until power levels change again in Act Five.)

KIRA

(shakes her head)

We're still being pulled out of position. . . .

SISKO

What's our heading?

DAX

Bearing one-five-seven, Mark one-three.

KIRA
(reacts)
Straight into the wormhole.

On their stunned reactions we . . .

52 EXTERIOR DEEP SPACE 9 (OPTICAL)

The station hurtling through space.

FADE OUT.

ACT FIVE

FADE IN:

53 EXTERIOR DEEP SPACE 9 (OPTICAL)

The station continues to drift into space. . . .

54 INTERIOR QUARK'S

The lights are dimmer than usual. The bidders are looking around, sensing trouble. Quark stands at the podium, attempting to calm them. The lure of profit has overcome his usual cowardice.

KOLOS
(speaking for all)
I tell you, something's wrong.

QUARK
(thinking on his feet)
Calm down, Kolos. This is a normal power-recalibration procedure. Nothing to worry about.

VASH
(sotto voce)
Doesn't seem normal to me . . .

QUARK
Shhh.
(to the crowd)
Now, as you know, payments must be in gold-pressed latinum, and all transactions are final.
(a beat)
Remember, bid high and bid often.

Vash takes the podium. Holds up an intricately carved stone statue.

VASH
Ladies and gentlemen, our first item is a statue from the Gamma Quadrant's Verath system. First I suppose I should talk a little bit about the Verathan civilization, which reached its height some thirty thousand years ago . . .

Quark can't believe this. He interrupts Vash and pulls her aside.

QUARK

What are you doing?

VASH

Placing the statue in its historical context.

QUARK

Here, give me that.

(takes the statue)

This isn't the Daystrom Institute. Watch closely.

Quark walks back to the podium.

QUARK

(continuing)

Friends, have you ever purchased a one-of-a-kind artifact, only to discover some other collector has six more just like it?

The two Ferengi bidders exchange hateful looks.

QUARK

(continuing)

Well, now you can avoid that kind of embarrassment.

(holds up statue)

It's rare . . . it's beautiful . . . it's a Gamma Quadrant original, and it can be yours, for the right price.

(a beat)

Bidding will start at ten bars of gold-pressed latinum.

(responding to hand signals)

I see ten. Fifteen. Sixteen. Who'll say seventeen and be the first to own a piece of the Gamma Quadrant?

The bidding continues.

55 OMITTED

56 INTERIOR OPS (OPTICAL)

Close on a graphic displaying a complete station diagram. A wave of color moves across the diagram until the entire interior has changed color.

56A NEW ANGLE

As O'Brien consults his console . . .

O'BRIEN
Tritium levels throughout the station have reached one part per million.

Sisko nods to Dax.

DAX
Initiating sensor sweep . . .

She works the panels and STUDIES HER MONITOR as O'Brien does the same at his station. . . . As they watch, the color drains out of the docking ring.

O'BRIEN
We can rule out the docking ring. . . .

DAX
(nods)
The tritium gas seems to be draining toward the central core. . . .

SISKO
Where in the central core?

O'BRIEN
Let me see if I can get a more precise reading. . . .

Everyone waits anxiously as O'Brien manipulates his console.

O'BRIEN
(disappointed)
It's not clear enough. I can't pinpoint the exact location.

Kira moves to a station near Sisko.

KIRA
Based on our current trajectory, we'll hit the wormhole in eighteen minutes. . . .

SISKO

(sighs, frustrated)

What the hell could be pulling us into the wormhole . . . ?

(beat, to O'Brien)

Do we have time to transfer auxiliary power to the deflectors, Chief?

O'BRIEN

Sir, there's not enough power left to make any difference . . . if we get sucked into that wormhole, we'll be in a billion pieces by the time we reach the Gamma Quadrant.

Off reactions . . .

57–59 OMITTED

60 INTERIOR QUARK'S

As Quark bangs his fist on the podium.

QUARK

Sold to Kolos for thirty-six bars of gold-pressed latinum.

Quark brings up the next item. A knife.

QUARK

Next we have a . . . a dagger, studded with some very interesting looking gems. Think of it as both a weapon *and* an investment. Bidding will start at forty.

The bidders start signaling to Quark.

QUARK

Forty. Forty-two, forty-five. Don't hold back, you know you want it, give me fifty . . .

(getting into it)

Fifty. We have fifty.

61 NEW ANGLE

to include Q seated at the bar. (Lose Q FLASH.)

Q
(to all)
I hate to interrupt such a thrilling display of naked avarice, but I feel it's only fair to warn you that the station is hurtling toward its doom. It's very unlikely any of you will survive to enjoy your purchases.

That stops the bidding cold.

Q
(continuing)
Just thought I'd mention it.

QUARK
Ladies and gentlemen, I assure you, everything is under control.

Quark shouts to his help.

QUARK
(continuing)
Drinks for everyone.

The bidders are still uneasy. Vash moves toward Q.

QUARK
(continuing)
And free use of the holosuites at the conclusion of the auction.

This mollifies the crowd. Vash reaches Q. In the background, Quark continues taking bids. (Note: Quark's dialogue runs simultaneously to Q and Vash's conversation.)

VASH
I don't think I realized until this moment how evil you really are. . . . You would kill all these people to get even with me.

Q
I must admit, the thought had occurred to me. But the fact

QUARK
(speaking in the background)
Now, if I'm not mistaken, bidding was halted at . . . sixty bars of gold pressed latinum. Do I hear sixty-five? Seventy . . . ? Come on, a piece of the Gamma Quadrant to bury in the heart of your most hated rival. Eighty, that's

is, this station is in enough trouble without me. I will, however, gladly save you. All you have to do is ask.

VASH

I'll take my chances with the others.

Q

As you wish. Now, if you don't mind, I'll just sit here and watch. I've never seen a space station torn apart by a wormhole before.

the spirit. Eighty-five . . . Think of it, Kolos, wouldn't this make a perfect companion piece to that statue you purchased . . . ? Ninety . . . Ninety-five . . . Can we break a hundred . . . ? A hundred . . . You make me proud. A hundred and five . . . Do I hear any other bids . . . ? Final call . . . Sold to my cousin Stol for one hundred and five bars of gold-pressed latinum.

62 INTERIOR OPS

Everyone at their stations, still searching for a solution.

KIRA

What if we pumped more tritium gas into the central core? The sensors might be more accurate with a greater concentration.

O'BRIEN

It might work. But in four years, we'd all be dead from tritium poisoning.

DAX

(inspired)

Wait a minute . . . of course . . .

(to O'Brien)

Bring the reactors back on-line . . .

O'BRIEN

The reactors? But they'll just feed more energy to the graviton field.

DAX

(certain)

If we generate enough energy, it should create a power drain big enough to trace.

KIRA

It might also push us faster into the wormhole . . . a *lot* faster . . .

SISKO

It's a chance we've gotta take.

(a beat)

Bring us to full power, Mister O'Brien. Everything you've got.

O'BRIEN

(not totally convinced)

Aye, sir.

O'Brien makes the adjustments to his console. The lights come up, and the station shakes as it gathers speed. Sisko and Dax remain focused on the monitor, hoping to find the answer in time.

63 OMITTED

64 INTERIOR QUARK'S (OPTICAL)

Lighting normal. Quark holds up a lovely multicolored alien necklace.

QUARK

Sold to Rul the Obscure for a hundred and fifty-one latinum bars.

(a beat)

And now, our final item. And I think you'll agree with me it was well worth the wait.

Vash opens the metal box and shows the geode to an appreciative crowd.

QUARK

(continuing, confident)

Bidding will start at two hundred bars of gold-pressed latinum.

One of the cloaked figures nods.

QUARK

(continuing)

Two hundred. Can I get two fifty? Two fifty. Three hundred anyone?

Kolos raises three fingers.

QUARK
(continuing)
Three hundred bars.

The bidding continues at a rapid-fire pace.

QUARK
(continuing, in ecstasy)
Three hundred and fifty? Four hundred? Four hundred . . . Five . . . Five hundred and twenty . . .

Finally Kolos raises six fingers (all on the same hand). Quark can't believe it.

QUARK
(continuing)
Six hundred bars of gold-pressed latinum.

65 INTERIOR OPS (OPTICAL)

Close on Dax's monitor the station schematic with the central core lit.

DAX
It's not in any of the crossover bridges . . . or the Habitat Ring. . . . It's in the upper core.

KIRA
(reading monitors)
Three minutes, fourteen seconds . . . to the wormhole . . . we're picking up speed.

Dax's monitor now shows a distinct bright area in one section of the core.

DAX
I've got it.
(moving)
The power drain's coming from the Promenade.

Sisko and Kira follow Dax . . .

SISKO
You have ops, Chief . . .

They EXIT to the turbolift . . .

66 INTERIOR QUARK'S

The bidding on the geode continues hot and heavy.

KOLOS

Twenty-five hundred.

Q

Twenty-five hundred . . . and one.

67 INTERIOR PROMENADE

Sisko, Kira, and Dax EXIT the turbolift. They fan out, consulting the tricorders.

DAX

(off a tricorder)

This way.

They head toward . . .

68 INTERIOR QUARK'S

Kolos reacts to Q's bid.

KOLOS

(impatient)

Three thousand bars of latinum. My final offer.

QUARK

(dizzy with greed)

Three thousand bars.

Q

A million.

Quark can die happy now.

QUARK

A million bars of gold-pressed latinum.

Sisko, Kira, and Dax ENTER the bar.

DAX

Over here.

Quark sees them and gets a worried look.

QUARK
(trying to wrap things up)
A million . . . Going once . . .

KIRA
(consulting tricorder)
It's by that podium.

QUARK
(seeing Sisko getting closer)
A million going twice.

Sisko, Kira, and Dax reach the podium. Dax points the tricorder at the box.

DAX
That's it.

QUARK
Three times . . .

SISKO
This auction is over. . . .

QUARK
(desperate)
Sold.

Quark points to Q.

SISKO
(hits combadge)
Chief, shut down the reactors. We found it.

Q
And about time, too.

68A NEW ANGLE (OPTICAL)

As Dax opens the box to reveal the geode, now glowing brighter than ever.

QUARK
(closes the box)

Sorry, all transactions are final. This item now belongs to that gentleman over there.

Quark indicates Q, who disappears, much to Quark's consternation. Dax studies the geode with her tricorder. . . .

DAX

(ignoring Quark)

I'm reading a massive graviton buildup inside this container . . . it's increasing exponentially. We've got to get it off the station *now* . . .

Sisko removes his combadge . . . hits it . . .

SISKO

Chief, lock on to my combadge and prepare to transport it five hundred meters off the docking ring. . . .

Sisko tosses the combadge into the geode container. . . .

SISKO

Energize.

A transporter beam DEMATERIALIZES the box.

68B EXTERIOR SPACE

The box materializes away from the station . . . suddenly it explodes into light. . . .

68C INTERIOR PROMENADE—SECOND LEVEL (OPTICAL)

Sisko, Dax, Kira and Vash come over the footbridge to the observation windows. Through the windows, the bright flash spreads wider . . . and reactions as their faces reflect the light. . . .

69 OMITTED

70 EXTERIOR SPACE (OPTICAL)

The brilliant flash of light becomes a WINGED ENERGY CREATURE. The creature unfurls its wings and soars away. It grows more and more distant until it disappears just as the wormhole IGNITES.

70A INTERIOR PROMENADE—SECOND LEVEL

All eyes on the observation windows as Sisko, Dax, Kira, and Vash contemplate the wonders of the universe.

71–73 OMITTED

74 EXTERIOR DEEP SPACE 9—STOCK (OPTICAL)

Everything back to normal.

SISKO
(voice-over)
Station log, stardate xxxxx.x. With the embryonic life-form off the station, graviton levels have returned to normal. We've used the control thrusters to return the station to its original position.

75 INTERIOR QUARK'S (OPTICAL)

Quark slides a drink across the bar to Vash. In the back, we can see Dax, sitting and drinking coffee.

QUARK
So . . . you're off to the Daystrom Institute. I bet you can hardly wait. . . . Long boring lectures . . . endless conferences . . . whining students dogging your every step . . . sounds delightful.
(a beat)
Of course . . .
(stops himself)
No, you wouldn't be interested.

VASH
In what?

QUARK
(leans close, whispers)
I hear they've uncovered the ruins of a Rohai provincial capital on Tartaras IV. If you could obtain some Rohai artifacts . . .

VASH
Forget it, Quark. I'm going back to Earth.

Quark goes to attend to other customers.

Q (O.C.)

An abysmal place.

Vash glances to one side. Sure enough, Q has made an appearance.

VASH

Tartaras V?

Q

Earth. Don't get me wrong. A thousand years ago it had character . . .

(continuing)

The crusades, the Spanish Inquisition, Watergate. But now . . . it's mind-numbingly dull.

VASH

Please, by all means, don't come with me.

Q

Trust me, you'd be a lot happier poking around the ruins on Tartaras V.

VASH

I don't remember asking for your advice.

A beat.

Q

You know, I still feel I owe you a million bars of gold-pressed latinum.

VASH

Keep it. Just give me back my life.

Q

You'll regret it if I do.

VASH

I'm willing to take that chance.

Q smiles, but there's a hint of melancholy we've never seen in him before.

Q
(finally giving up)
All right. If you insist. But things won't be the same without you. When I look at a gas nebula, all I see is a cloud of dust, but seeing the universe through your eyes allowed me to experience . . . wonder.
(grumpy)
I'm going to miss that.

VASH
I guess, in some ways, I'm going to miss you too.

A beat as they exchange a silent good-bye.

Q
Well, maybe I'll drop in on you sometime.

VASH
(a friendly smile)
God, I hope not.

A beat. Q smiles in understanding and DISAPPEARS. Quark rejoins her.

VASH
So Quark, what's the quickest way to Tartaras V?

Vash and Quark exchange a knowing grin and walk off together, speaking inaudibly as they plot strategy. This is the beginning of a beautiful friendship.

75A ANGLE ON DAX

Who watches Vash and Quark EXIT. Dax shakes her head with a bemused expression. She finishes her coffee and gets up to go, almost running into . . .

75B BASHIR

Who has just entered the bar.

BASHIR
(yawning)
I feel like I've slept for days.
(a beat)
Did I miss something?

And on Dax's smile . . .

75C EXTERIOR SPACE—DEEP SPACE 9

And . . .
FADE OUT.

STAR TREK: VOYAGER

Death Wish

(fka: Untitled Q)

Teleplay by
Michael Piller

Story by
Shawn Piller

Directed by
James L. Conway

STAR TREK: VOYAGER

Death Wish

CAST

JANEWAY
KIM
PARIS
CHAKOTAY
TUVOK
TORRES
DOCTOR
KES
NEELIX
COMPUTER VOICE
Q1
Q2
RIKER
NEWTON, ISAAC
GINSBERG, MAURY

Non-Speaking
N.D. SUPERNUMERARIES

STAR TREK: VOYAGER

Death Wish

SETS

INTERIORS

U.S.S. VOYAGER
BRIDGE
JANEWAY'S QUARTERS
BRIEFING ROOM/HEARING ROOM
KIM'S QUARTERS
MESS HALL
READY ROOM
SICKBAY
TRANSPORTER ROOM
TUVOK'S OFFICE

Q CONFINEMENT

EXTERIORS

U.S.S. VOYAGER

DESERT ROAD

ROAD STOP

STAR TREK: VOYAGER

Death Wish

PRONUNCIATION GUIDE

BARYON	bare-ee-ON
GOROKIAN	guh-RO-kee-uhn
KERKIRA	kehr-KIH-ruh
KYLERIAN	kih-LAYR-ee-uhn
MAGNETODYNAMIC	mahg-NET-oh-di-NAHM-ik
NOGATCH	NOH-gach
RAREBIT	REHR-buht
VALKYRIES	VAL-kih-reez

STAR TREK: VOYAGER

Death Wish

TEASER

FADE IN:

1 INTERIOR KIM'S QUARTERS

KIM is practicing his clarinet . . . playing something classical as he looks at his sheet music. PARIS is sitting with his feet up, reading a padd. After a particularly difficult and high-pitched phrase, Kim repeats it once and then again . . . and somebody starts pounding on the wall next door. . . . Kim stops, looks over, frowns . . .

KIM
(yelling)
Sorry!

Sighs, puts his clarinet down. . . .

PARIS
Obviously, Ensign Baytart doesn't appreciate music. . . .

KIM
It's the darn fluid conduits running through the walls. . . . They conduct sound. . . . You'd think when they designed this thing they would've . . .

PARIS
(interrupting)
The ship was built for combat performance, Harry, not for musical performance. Nobody figured we'd be taking any long trips. . . .

KIM
Where am I supposed to practice?

PARIS
How 'bout the cargo bay?

KIM

Bad acoustics.

PARIS

(joking, deadpan)

We could get Baytart transferred to the night shift. . . .

KIM

We couldn't do that.

(beat)

Could we . . . ?

Paris gives him a dry look.

PARIS

So you have an excuse to give your mother why you didn't practice when you were gone.

KIM

I'm trying to prepare for an important performance!

PARIS

Really? Are we scheduled to rendezvous with the Delta Quadrant Symphony Orchestra . . . ?

KIM

Susan Nicoletti and I have been working on a new orchestral program for the holodeck. . . .

PARIS

Lieutenant Nicoletti? The one I've been chasing for six months? Cold hands? Cold heart?

KIM

(with a personal grin)

Not when she plays the oboe.

Paris considers this revelation. . . .

CHAKOTAY (com voice)

Chakotay to all senior officers. Please report to the bridge.

As they react and EXIT . . .

PARIS

You know, Harry, I've always wanted to learn to play the drums. . . .

2 INTERIOR BRIDGE

TUVOK, CHAKOTAY, TORRES are already in place. JANEWAY ENTERS from her ready room . . . looks to Chakotay for a report. . . . Paris and Kim ENTER, go to their stations during the following—

CHAKOTAY
(to Janeway)

We've been surveying an unusual comet for the last twenty minutes. . . . I thought you'd want to take a look. . . .

JANEWAY
(reacts, curious)

On screen.

3 ANGLE—INCLUDE THE VIEWSCREEN (OPTICAL)

And see the comet.

JANEWAY
(continuing)

What's so unusual about it, Commander?

CHAKOTAY

Its trajectory is erratic . . . and our sensors aren't detecting any stellar or planetary gravitational fields that could account for its motion.

She checks readouts on a monitor.

JANEWAY

Then, you're saying it *isn't* a comet. . . .

CHAKOTAY
(acknowledging)

And yet it looks, feels, and tastes just like a comet.

JANEWAY
(off readings)

Well, there's a slight chance that there are

magnetodynamic forces acting on the comet that are too subtle for our sensors to detect.

(beat, looks up with a scientific enthusiasm)

Or it might be something we've never encountered before.

She smiles. . . .

JANEWAY

B'Elanna, go down to transporter room two. . . . Let's beam aboard a sample for examination. . . .

TORRES

Aye, Captain . . .

She EXITS. . . .

JANEWAY

Harry, see if you can lock on to a core fragment. . . .

KIM

(working)

Having no trouble penetrating the crust, Captain.

JANEWAY

Good.

4 INTERIOR TRANSPORTER ROOM

Torres ENTERS . . . moves to the command post. . . . The supernumerary moves away. . . .

JANEWAY (com voice)

Janeway to Torres. We're ready when you are, Lieutenant.

Working—

TORRES

Setting up a class-three containment field, Captain . . .

(beat)

Field in place.

JANEWAY (com voice)

Commence transport.

TORRES

Energizing.

5 ANGLE (OPTICAL)

On the transporter pad . . . as the MATERIALIZATION EFFECT produces not a core fragment, but a male humanoid, about forty, in a Starfleet red uniform. Torres reacts. . . . The man smiles at her, steps through the containment field which appears briefly . . . and down off the platform . . .

Q2

Hello, my name is Q.

And as Torres reacts . . .

FADE OUT.

ACT ONE

FADE IN:

6 INTERIOR TRANSPORTER ROOM—CONTINUOUS

Torres hits her combadge.

TORRES

Torres to Janeway. You better get down here, Captain.

INTERCUT:

7 INTERIOR BRIDGE

JANEWAY

Problem, Lieutenant?

TORRES

Yes, ma'am. That transport from the comet . . . it brought a man aboard. . . . He says his name is Q. . . .

JANEWAY

(knows Q by reputation, reacts with concern, to Chakotay)

Red Alert.

(to com)

I'll be right down. . . .

As she starts to EXIT . . .

Q2 (com voice)

Oh no, please don't bother, Captain. . . .

8 INTERIOR TRANSPORTER ROOM

Q2 talking into Torres's combadge . . .

Q2

(continuing)

Let me take you to lunch, instead. . . .

9 INTERIOR MESS HALL (OPTICAL)

Q2 and Janeway APPEAR simultaneously. . . . NEELIX and KES and other supernumeraries there react. . . .

Q2
(to Janeway, shaking her hand)
What a pleasure it is to meet you.
(re: shaking)
Am I doing this right? It's been such a long time since I've had the opportunity to greet anyone. Oh, please, have a seat . . . here—

10 ANGLE (OPTICAL)

The table he's pointing to suddenly changes: now it is set with fancy tablecloth and candelabra and fine china and comfortable chairs . . . and a hot meal. . . .

JANEWAY
(takes a deep breath)
My name is Kathryn Janeway, captain of . . .

Q2
(overlapping)
. . . the Federation Starship *Voyager,* yes, yes, I know all that . . .
(leading her to sit)
Look, Welsh rarebit just like your grandfather used to make. . . .

Janeway looks at it with curiosity. . . . So does . . .

11 NEELIX

From his vantage point with Kes a few yards away. . . .

NEELIX
"Rarebit." She never told me she likes Rarebits. What *is* a Rarebit anyway? Is this some new chef she's interviewing?

Kes doesn't know.

12 RESUME

Urging her on—

Q2

Please, eat—it's the least I can do to express my appreciation.

JANEWAY

Appreciation . . . for what?

Q2

Letting me out of my captivity.

JANEWAY

(cautious, not sure if she should believe him)

You were being held against your will . . . inside the comet?

Q2 is looking around at this new environment, breathing it all in . . . seeing all the other people, smiling and nodding hello to the stares. . . .

Q2

Hmm, oh, in a manner of speaking. . . . You, all of you . . . are . . . *mortals*, aren't you?

He says the word with awe. . . . He moves around the room. . . .

JANEWAY

Who was holding you prisoner, Q?

Q2 ignores the question, caught up in the wonder of the moment . . . moves to Kes. . . .

Q2

And you, you only live seven years. . . .

KES

(curious)

That's right.

Q2

How I envy you.

KES

Why is that?

Q2

Because the one thing I want in life . . . more than any other . . . is . . . to die.

Reactions . . . Janeway has had enough. . . .

JANEWAY
Look, I don't know what you want here, but I know who you are. . . . Every captain in Starfleet has been briefed about your appearances on the *Enterprise*, and I warn you. . . .

Q2
(overlapping)
My appearances? Oh, no, I never . . . You've mistaken me for . . . Well, no matter, I really must get on with my "business" before the others realize I'm here. . . .
(a speech)
. . . When someone asks you about me, and they will, would you tell them I said . . .
(interrupting himself)
I've had three hundred years to think of appropriate last words. . . . I wanted something memorable, quotable, you know . . . ?
(the speech again)
"I die not for myself but for you."
(normal)
I know. I know. Enigmatic. Provocative. But they'll understand. Well, good-bye to you all. Many thanks. Here's the end of me. . . .

13 ANGLE (OPTICAL)

And he waves an arm and there's a flash, but when it clears he's still there . . . but all the men in the room have disappeared.

Q2
Oh, dear. That's wasn't right.

TORRES (com voice)
Torres to Janeway. Captain, all the *men* have . . . disappeared. . . .

JANEWAY
(interrupting)
I'm aware of it, Lieutenant. Report to the bridge. Janeway out.
(to Q2)
Bring them back. Now.

Q2

Of course. Of course.

He waves his hand again. Nothing.

Q2

I'm just a little out of practice.

He waves again. Nothing. He frowns.

Q2

Well, that's that. I'm afraid they're . . . gone.

JANEWAY

Gone *where*!?

Q2

Just . . . gone. I apologize . . . for the . . . inconvenience. . . .

Before she can react verbally, with a sheepish look, he gives a slight frustrated gesture . . . and Janeway and Q2 DISAPPEAR in a FLASH. . . .

14 INTERIOR BRIDGE (OPTICAL)

And APPEAR with a FLASH here . . . Janeway sitting in her chair . . . Q2 standing beside her. . . . She bounds to her feet immediately. . . . Torres is there . . . a couple of other female supernumeraries . . .

Q2

Well, good luck to you. . . . I really have to be going now. . . .

JANEWAY

Return my crew!

Q2 sighs, shoulders sag, guilty . . .

Q2

I'm . . . I'm not sure how.

(apparently to himself)

Humans, humans . . . Who would have more recent experience with humans . . . ?

And on that cue, there is another flash, and standing there is our old friend Q (hereafter referred to as Q1) also dressed in Starfleet red. He looks annoyed at Q2. . . .

Q1

What have you done now, Q?

And on reactions . . .

FADE OUT.

ACT TWO

FADE IN:

15 INTERIOR BRIDGE—CONTINUOUS

Q1 shakes his head . . . sighs. . . .

Q1
(sarcastic)
Well now, isn't this just fine. . . . Humans are not supposed to be in this quadrant for another hundred years. . . .

Q2
I didn't bring them here. . . . It wasn't my . . .

Q1
(overlapping)
How did you get out, Q?

Janeway steps forward. . . .

JANEWAY
I'm afraid we're responsible for that.

Q1 reacts to her with disdain. . . .

Q1
Well, I guess that's what we get for having a woman in the captain's seat, isn't it . . . ? You know, I was betting that Riker would get this command.

JANEWAY
(reacts, cold)
May I assume you're the Q I've heard so much about?

Q1
You've heard of little me? Do tell.
(continuing)
Has Jean-Luc been whispering about me behind my back?
(realizing all the crew members are women)

Say, is this the ship of the Valkyries . . . or have human women finally managed to do away with their men altogether . . . ?

Q2

There was a slight accident. . . .

Q1

A slight accident. Let me guess. You were trying to commit suicide.

Q2 shrugs, acknowledging. Q1 just sighs, irritated. . . .

16 ANGLE (OPTICAL)

Q1 gestures with his hand; a FLASH, and all the men return. . . . Chakotay stands, alarmed . . . begins to move toward the intruders.

Q1

(reacting to Chakotay)

Facial art. How very . . . wilderness . . . of you.

CHAKOTAY

Captain . . . ?

Janeway holds up a hand to stop him.

Q1

All right then, Q, we should be going.

Q2

I'm not leaving. Captain Janeway, I demand asylum!

Q1

This is a joke.

Q2

I am officially asking you, Captain, to grant me asylum and give me protection from my enemies . . . which is him.

Q1

You would ask these puny humans to protect you from me? Fat chance . . .

Q1 begins to raise his arm in a gesture, but before he can, Q2 sweeps his arm in front of him; there's a flash . . . and Q1 disappears. . . . The ship begins to shudder. . . .

JANEWAY
What did you do to him?

Q2
Nothing. He's still there in the 24th century. I just took the rest of us to an old hiding place of mine.

The shuddering grows stronger throughout the scene. . . .

JANEWAY
Report.

KIM
Captain, there are no stars outside. . . .

Q2
That's partially correct. Actually, there's no universe outside.

JANEWAY
On screen.

17 INCLUDING THE VIEWSCREEN (OPTICAL)

To show the formation of the universe. . . .

CHAKOTAY
(off monitor)
I'm showing a large buildup of baryon particles. . . .

Q2
Perfectly normal . . .

TUVOK
Captain, based on our readings, it appears that we have been transported back in time to the birth of the universe. . . .

Janeway looks sharply at Q2, who smiles as he watches the viewscreen . . . acknowledging. . . .

Q2

Very old hiding place . . .

18 ANGLE (OPTICAL)

There's a flash, and Q1 appears near Torres. . . .

Q1

(beat, to Q2)

I know all the hiding places, Q. I hid here from the Continuum myself once.

TORRES

This ship will not survive the formation of the cosmos. . . .

Q1

But think of the honor of having your DNA spread from one corner of the universe to the other. . . . Why, *you* could be the origins of humanoid life. . . .

JANEWAY

Q! Either Q! Get us out of here.

19 ANGLE (OPTICAL)

Q1

(to Q2)

You heard the lady. Time for you to go back to your cell. . . .

He raises his arm, but before Q1 can do anything else . . . Q2 gestures and another FLASH . . . and Q1 is gone again, and now we're under attack. . . . The ship shakes with impact. . . .

PARIS

We're under attack. . . .

CHAKOTAY

By a ship . . . ?

PARIS

(off controls)

By . . . by . . . I'm not sure what they are. . . .

He hits a panel, looks up at the viewscreen . . .

20 ANGLE—INCLUDE THE VIEWSCREEN (OPTICAL)

To see we're surrounded by subatomic particles. . . . protons pummeling us. . . .

KIM
Captain, I don't believe this . . . but . . . according to my readings . . . we're being attacked by protons! We've been reduced to subatomic proportions!

Janeway reacts, turns to Q2 with fury in her eyes. . . .

Q2
He'll never find us here. . . .

JANEWAY
(exasperated)
Mister Tuvok, see if you can release a positive ion charge to repel them. . . .

Q1 APPEARS.

Q1
Ready or not, here I come.

Q2 reacts, waves his hand again in a defensive gesture . . . a FLASH . . . Q1 is gone. . . . The pummeling stops. . . . Janeway sags. . . .

JANEWAY
(to Paris)
Now what . . . ?

PARIS
Checking . . . We seem to be tethered to some kind of large . . .
(beat)
. . . plant.

JANEWAY
(exhausted)
Let's see it.

21 ANGLE—INCLUDE THE VIEWSCREEN (OPTICAL)

A fuzzy close-up of green . . .

JANEWAY

Computer, a wider angle.

22 NEW VIEWSCREEN ANGLE (OPTICAL)

To see we're an ornament on a Christmas tree. . . . The branches and other hanging balls and blinking lights are clearly visible. . . . Suddenly we're jolted . . . and everyone hangs on to keep from falling . . . and the picture on the viewscreen pans as a hand picks us up, and now we see Q1's face looking right into our viewscreen camera. . . .

Q1 (viewscreen)

You can't hide from me, Q.

Q2

And you can't take me by force. I'll stalemate you for eternity, if I have to.

JANEWAY

(angry)

The hell you will.

(to them both)

The vaunted Q Continuum. Self-anointed guardians of the universe. How dare you come aboard this ship and endanger this crew with your personal . . . tug-of-war.

Q1 (viewscreen)

(reacts)

Did anyone ever tell you you're angry when you're beautiful?

A flash, and Q1 is standing back on the bridge. . . .

PARIS

(off readings)

We're back where we started from, Captain.

Q2

It's doesn't matter. I'm not going into that cell again.

Q1

You could spend eternity as a Gorokian midwife toad.

Q2

Just try it. . . .

And just as they're about to resume their battle . . .

JANEWAY

Stop.

(to Q2)

You want asylum? Fine. We'll have a hearing.

Q1

A hearing . . . you would have me put his future in *your* delicate little hands?

(as he takes them in his)

So touchably soft. What is your secret, dear?

She disengages herself from him.

JANEWAY

When the captain of a Starfleet vessel receives an official request for asylum, there is a clear procedure to follow. I suggest . . . to end your deadlock . . . and save my ship . . . that we follow it to the letter.

Q1

(beat, thinking)

Well, this could go on for a millennium or two, I suppose. All right, I'll agree on behalf of the Continuum on one condition—if you rule in our favor, Q agrees to return to his confinement.

All eyes turn to Q2, who takes a beat to think and then announces—

Q2

I have a condition of my own. If she rules in my favor, the Continuum will grant me mortality.

Q1

Why? So you can kill yourself?

Q2

Exactly.

And now Q1 looks at Janeway, who considers this turn of events with concern. . . . Q1 smiles with amusement. . . .

Q1
(to Janeway)
Accepted. Well, this should make for an amusing diversion. Will you send him to prison for eternity or assist him with his suicide plan? My, my, that's a tough one . . . but then that's why they made you captain, isn't it . . . to handle the tough ones?
(beat)
I guess now we'll get to find out if the pants really fit. . . .

He grins and DISAPPEARS. Off Janeway's reaction . . .

FADE OUT.

ACT THREE

FADE IN:

23 INTERIOR TUVOK'S OFFICE (OPTICAL)

Tuvok is studying some Okudagrams on a monitor when Q2 APPEARS.

Q2

Am I interrupting anything?

Tuvok turns to see Q2.

TUVOK

I am curious. Have the Q always had an absence of manners? Or is it the result of some natural evolutionary process that comes with omnipotence?

Q2

What? Oh, you mean, just popping in when we feel like it . . .

TUVOK

That is one relevant example.

Q2

I apologize. At some point along the way, I guess we just stopped thinking about the little niceties. . . .

TUVOK

So it seems.

Q2

But you mustn't think of us as omnipotent. No matter what the Continuum would like you to believe. You and your ship seem incredibly powerful to life-forms without your technical expertise. It's no different with us. We may appear omnipotent to you, but believe me, we're not.

TUVOK

Intriguing. Just what . . . vulnerabilities . . . do the Q have?

Q2 laughs . . .

Q2

Always on the lookout for the tactical advantage, Mister Tuvok. Very good. As a matter of fact, that's why I've come to see you.

(beat)

In a way, our ''vulnerability'' is what this is all about. As the Q have evolved, we've sacrificed many things along the way. Not just manners. But mortality, a sense of purpose, a desire for change, a capacity to grow. Every loss is a new vulnerability, wouldn't you say?

TUVOK

Why are you telling me this?

Q2

I want you to represent me in the hearing . . .

TUVOK

Me. I have no legal expertise. . . .

Q2

I need someone who understands Federation asylum procedures. Besides, Vulcans approve of suicide. . . .

TUVOK

It is true that Vulcans who reach a certain infirmity with age do practice ritual suicides. Nevertheless, I fail to see how that fact would be meaningful in this circumstance.

Q2

I have the right to counsel, Mister Tuvok. Will you assist me?

A beat.

TUVOK

I will speak to Captain Janeway.

Q2

Thank you.

He begins to gesture with his hand to disappear. Then has a second thought . . . not wanting to be rude, he EXITS through the door.

24 INTERIOR READY ROOM

Janeway is deep in study with a variety of padds and her computer on. A chime.

JANEWAY

Come in.

Tuvok ENTERS.

TUVOK

Captain, the Q seeking asylum has asked me to act as his counsel in the hearing. . . .

JANEWAY

(reacts, then . . .)

Smart of him. Well, that's his right. You want to do it?

TUVOK

I feel it is my duty to accept.

JANEWAY

Very well.

(beat)

But I have to warn you, you're not going to have an easy job, Tuvok.

TUVOK

Is that an indication you are not entirely unbiased?

JANEWAY

I don't mind telling you I consider any kind of suicide abhorrent. For me to assist him in any way . . .

(beat, shaking her head at the thought)

I was just doing some research. Do you know that on Romulus attempted suicide is a crime . . . and helping someone commit suicide is considered homicide?

TUVOK

May I also point out that Klingons and Bajorans as well as Vulcans embrace suicide as an honorable way to end one's life.

JANEWAY

On my world, it's an almost forgotten practice. . . . And the rare times it occurs are very sad occasions. . . .

TUVOK

Sad, perhaps. But not illegal. And when one eliminates consideration of the survivors' emotional distress . . .

JANEWAY

I'm afraid I'm not capable of doing that, Tuvok.

TUVOK

(beat)

May I ask you to at least keep an open mind?

JANEWAY

Always, my friend.

He nods and EXITS. . . . We stay a beat on Janeway. . . .

25 INTERIOR HEARING ROOM

Janeway sits at a desk in the center. . . . Tuvok sits with Q2 on one side. Q1 sits on the other side. There is an empty witness chair near Janeway.

JANEWAY

Let me begin by stating clearly that I expect all parties to act appropriately and with respect for these proceedings. I will not have this hearing turned into a circus, is that clear?

(Q2 acknowledges, Q1 just looks at his fingers)

Is that clear, Q?

Q1 looks up . . . rises . . .

Q1

Madame Captain, we are dealing here with an issue of the greatest importance to the Q Continuum. I assure you we take this matter very seriously.

JANEWAY

Thank you. And please don't call me "Madame Captain."

(to Q2)
Since you've made it clear that your asylum would lead to suicide . . . you place me in a difficult position.

Q2
(sympathetic)
I understand, Captain.

JANEWAY
May I ask you *why* you want to commit suicide?

Q2
As difficult as it is for you to imagine, immortality . . . for me . . . is impossible to endure any longer.
(beat)
In the Continuum, an individual has an obligation to be responsible for the path his life will follow. . . .

Q1
(interrupting)
. . . His *life* will follow. Emphasize *life* . . .

Q2
(overlapping)
. . . I never yielded that obligation to the Continuum. If the path I choose leads to death, what right do they have to interfere?

Q1
He is putting his selfish wishes above the welfare of everyone else.

Q2
And if I don't agree with the majority, then I'm to be locked up for eternity.

Q1
You would not be confined if you weren't intent on harming yourself.
(beat)
With your permission, Captain, I would like to call an expert on the Continuum to discuss the implications of the decision to be made here.

JANEWAY

Proceed.

Q1

I call myself to the stand.

26 ANGLE (OPTICAL)

Another Q1 appears in the witness chair. (NOTE: Both appear simultaneously.)

Q1 (LAWYER)

Thank you for coming today. It's a rare honor to have someone of your reputation and accomplishment with us.

Q1 (WITNESS)

Thank you.

Q1 (LAWYER)

Tell me, what would be the impact of a Q suicide?

Q1 (WITNESS)

It would be an *interruption* to the Continuum. It would change the very nature of Q.

JANEWAY

Can you be more specific?

Q1 (WITNESS)

No, because we're not even sure what the end result would be. His suicide could have all sorts of unknown consequences to the Continuum.

Q2

Precisely! It would force the Q to deal with the unknown for the first time since the new era began. . . . They're not just afraid of me; they're afraid of the *unknown*. . . .

Q1 (LAWYER)

(to the witness, re: Q2)

How would you *characterize* his remarks?

Q1 (WITNESS)

No Q has ever tried to commit suicide. Immortality is one of the defining qualities of being a Q. By every measure of the Continuum, his remarks would have to be considered as mentally unbalanced.

Q1 (LAWYER)

(to Janeway)

Mentally unbalanced. And no civilized people in the universe, including the primitive Federation societies, would condone the suicide of a mentally unbalanced person.

He sits, satisfied. Tuvok rises, approaches the witness.

TUVOK

Can you offer any other evidence of mental instability on the part of my client?

Q1 (WITNESS)

What more do I need? He wants to kill himself.

TUVOK

In fact, until this issue arose, he was known in the Continuum as one of your great philosophers, is that not true?

Q1 (WITNESS)

Not anymore, it isn't.

TUVOK

So, your entire basis for judging him mentally unbalanced is his wish to commit suicide.

(beat, to Janeway)

I submit that is a faulty premise. In many cultures, suicide is acceptable, and in and of itself cannot be used as evidence of mental illness.

JANEWAY

I tend to agree with Mister Tuvok.

Q1 (LAWYER)

(frowns)

Vulcans.

Tuvok picks up a padd from his desk and consults the notes on it. . . .

TUVOK

Is it not true that on occasion the Continuum has executed Qs for certain crimes . . . ?

Q1

Rare occasions, yes.

TUVOK

Did not *their* deaths create an ''interruption'' to the Continuum?

Q1

Their *crimes* created the interruption. Their deaths ended it.

(beat)

I know where you're going with this, Lieutenant . . .

TUVOK

Do you . . . ?

Q1

. . . and it's not going to work. Our society, like any other, must control its disruptive elements. An execution may be undesirable, I'll grant you that, but on *rare* occasions it is warranted and necessary. And the decision to proceed is only made after great deliberation by the entire Continuum. You can't imagine the chaos that would be created if individuals, like Q here, had the ability to choose between life and death. This is a matter of social order versus anarchy.

TUVOK

I understand.

Tuvok takes a moment standing at his desk as though he's been beaten back by Q's verbal assault . . . glancing at his padd again . . . without eye contact. . . .

TUVOK

And you find nothing contradictory in a society that outlaws suicide but practices capital punishment. . . .

And now he looks at Q1 the witness evenly, and that catches Q1 off guard . . . there's a long beat of eye contact, and finally Q1 just says—

Q1

No.

Tuvok sits. . . . Q2 whispers feverishly to him. . . .

JANEWAY

Any other questions, Lieutenant?

TUVOK

(to Q1, the witness)

Just one other thing. Is it not true that you yourself were once accused by the Continuum of being mentally unstable? Were you not you disciplined for inappropriate behavior?

Q1 (LAWYER)

Objection!

JANEWAY

I'll allow the question.

Q1 (WITNESS)

My record has been expunged.

TUVOK

I will take that as a yes. Thank you. That is all.

JANEWAY

(to the witness)

You're excused.

The witness Q1 disappears. The lawyer stands.

Q1

May I beg the court's indulgence, I have other witnesses to call. . . .

JANEWAY

To what end?

Q1

Your Captain Honor, I am here to argue for the

majesty of life. What it means to us to be alive. A Q's life takes him to all corners of the universe. . . . This Q's life has touched and affected many, many others . . . including some on your own homeworld. With your permission, I'd like to call some of those people whose lives were changed by this Q. . . .

JANEWAY
(reacts)
You want to bring people here from Earth?

Q1
I promise you it will not impact the timeline, and no one will remember ever being here when I send them back.

JANEWAY
This is most unusual. Do you have any objection, Mister Tuvok?

TUVOK
I am as curious as you are, Captain.

JANEWAY
Very well. Proceed.

Q gestures with his hand . . . three people appear COMMANDER WILLIAM RIKER, SIR ISAAC NEWTON, and a '60s hippie with long hair, granny glasses, and a grungy beard, in flower-power shirt and bell-bottoms. He is MAURY GINSBERG. Riker immediately reacts . . . the other two, confused, look around trying to get their bearings. . . .

RIKER
Q! What the hell is this . . . ?

Janeway rises and approaches the witnesses. . . .

JANEWAY
My apologies, Commander. To you all. My name is Kathryn Janeway. . . .

RIKER
(reacts)
Janeway. The captain of *U.S.S. Voyager* . . . ?

JANEWAY
That's correct, Commander. You're aboard *Voyager*.

We're lost in the Delta Quadrant. As much as I wish you could tell them that when you get home, your memories will be wiped before you're sent back.

Ginsberg laughs *nervously,* incredulously . . . He might be stoned. . . . In fact, he might think that's what this is all about. . . .

GINSBERG
(praying)
God, if you let me live through this, I promise I'll clean up my act. I swear.

NEWTON
I demand an explanation.
(to Ginsberg)
Why are you dressed like *that?*

GINSBERG
Man, have *you* looked in a mirror lately?

JANEWAY
Allow me to . . . try . . . to explain, Mister . . .

GINSBERG
Ginsberg. Maury Ginsberg.

NEWTON
Sir Isaac Newton.

RIKER
William Riker.
(to Newton and Ginsberg)
Nice to meet you.

He shakes their hands. Janeway takes a moment to try and figure how to explain it to the prewarp fellows.

JANEWAY
Consider for a moment that it might be possible to travel forward in time . . . say to the 24th century . . . onto a starship . . . seventy-five thousand light-years from Earth. . . .
(long beat, off their faces; this isn't working . . .)
You're having a very strange dream. And in this

dream, you're seeing this man whom you've all met before. . . .

She indicates Q2. . . . He smiles, gives a slight wave. . . . Newton takes a step forward, eyes lighting up with recognition. . . .

NEWTON

But I *have* seen you before. . . . You were sitting under the tree the day. . . .

Q1

. . . the day the apple fell on your head?

NEWTON

Yes. That's right.

Q1

Quite a day, wasn't it? As a matter of fact, this man jostled the tree as he got up to leave. . . .

NEWTON

Just before the apple fell, yes.

Q1

And a new era of human science was born.

GINSBERG

(to Q2)

Wait a minute. Weren't you the guy in the jeep?

Q2 shyly acknowledges.

Q1

The "guy in the jeep" who picked you up after your own vehicle broke down one summer afternoon, isn't that so . . . ?

GINSBERG

Man, he was a lifesaver. . . . My van died and they dragged it off the road because of all the traffic. . . . It was backed up for miles. . . .

Q1

You were on your way to a job, weren't you . . . ?

GINSBERG

Yeah, I was supposed to be on the follow spot up on tower three. . . . I never would have made it in time if it weren't for him. . . .

(to Q2)

Hey, whatever happened to that groovy chick with the long red beads in the backseat . . . ? I've been looking for her ever since you dropped me off. . . .

Q2

(all-knowing)

You'll see her again; don't worry. . . .

Q1

To sum up, you were a spotlight operator at an outdoor concert of some sort . . . a concert that was put into jeopardy moments before it was to begin, when the entire sound system failed.

GINSBERG

(shrugs)

It was no big deal. . . . Somebody must've snagged an extension cord with one of the trucks, that's all. . . . I'm just lucky I noticed it. . . .

Q1

Yes, lucky you were at the right place at the right time, or it would have taken days to track down the problem . . . and there wouldn't have been a concert. . . .

RIKER

(to Janeway, re: Q1)

Well, I'm sorry to say I *have* met *him* . . .

(re: Q2)

. . . but I've never seen this man before in my life.

Q1

Are you sure?

TUVOK

Has it not been established that my client was in captivity during all of Commander Riker's lifetime?

27 ANGLE—AN EASEL (OPTICAL)

Holding a photograph appears with a flash. . . .

28 RESUME

Q1

Have you ever seen this photograph before?

Riker takes it and looks. . . .

29 INSERT—CIVIL WAR PHOTOGRAPH

Showing two Union soldiers . . . one of whom is recovering from wounds . . . on crutches. . . .

RIKER

Sure, I have. . . . That's Colonel Thaddius Riker after he was wounded at Pine Mountain. . . . They called him "Iron Boots." . . .

30 RESUME

RIKER

(continuing)

He was in command of the Hundred and Second New York during General Sherman's march to Atlanta. . . . This picture was taken in eighteen sixty-four, just after they let him out of the field hospital. . . .

Q1

And do you see the soldier beside him . . . ?

31 INSERT—THE PICTURE

Pushing in on the soldier. . . . It is Q2, half-turned away from the camera . . . but still recognizable. . . .

32 RIKER

RIKER

I'll be damned. It's him.

Q1

In fact, he carried your wounded ancestor two miles from the front line . . .

(to Q2)

Didn't you . . . ?

Riker looks over at Q2, who shrugs modestly: yeah, I did. Q1 goes to the witnesses and puts a hand on each's shoulder as he comes to them. . . . Each gives an appropriate reaction to what they hear about themselves. . . .

Q1

My point is, Captain, that Q has had a profound influence on these three lives.

(continuing)

Without Q, Isaac Newton would have died forgotten in a Liverpool debtor's prison, a suspect in several prostitute murders. Without Q, there would have been no concert at . . . uh . . .

(searching)

Q2

. . . Woodstock . . .

Q1

. . . wherever . . . and more importantly, Mister Ginsberg here would never have met his future wife, the groovy chick with the long red beads . . . and would never have become a successful orthodontist and settled in Scarsdale with four kids.

GINSBERG

Far . . . out.

Q1

Without Q, there would have been no William T. Riker at all. And I would have lost at least a dozen really good opportunities to insult him over the years. Oh, and lest I forget, the Borg would have assimilated the Federation too.

(turns to the witnesses)

Thank you.

Riker sighs, irritated. . . . Ginsberg gives a peace sign, which Newton looks at strangely. . . .

33 ANGLE (OPTICAL)

They disappear.

Q1
(continuing)
This is the life Q treats without respect. This is the life that he would give up so easily.

He sits. Tuvok rises.

TUVOK
May I remind this hearing and my learned colleague that for three centuries, my client has not been allowed contact with anyone. At this time, we would like to reproduce the environment in which he has been confined.

Q1
I object.

JANEWAY
No, I'll allow this.

Tuvok nods to Q2, who makes a gesture, and a FLASH and suddenly we find ourselves in—

34 INTERIOR Q CONFINEMENT (OPTICAL)

Inside the comet. A dark, very cramped environment surrounded by ice sheets. . . . All the people are close together. . . . It's very uncomfortable. . . .

TUVOK
These are the conditions that my client would be forced to live in for eternity if you deny asylum, Captain.

Q1
We just want him to have time to reconsider his position. . . .

Q2
I will never change my mind.

Q1
This is your own doing. You could live a perfectly

normal life if you were just willing to live a perfectly normal life.

JANEWAY

I've seen enough. Please return us to the hearing room.

Q2 waves his arm, a FLASH, and we're back . . .

35 INTERIOR HEARING ROOM

As before.

TUVOK

I would submit that the *quality* of life that my client will have to endure should be considered in this proceeding.

He sits. Janeway thinks for a beat . . . then addresses Q2.

JANEWAY

I don't like those conditions any more than you do, Mister Tuvok.

(to Q2)

And I wouldn't want to spend another day there if I were you, Q. . . .

A long beat as she looks down, is forced to confront internally what she's about to say—

JANEWAY

But I'm here to rule on a request for asylum . . . not to judge the penal system of the Q Continuum.

(motioning to Q1)

And he does have a point—you were confined only to prevent you from doing harm to yourself.

(beat, she picks up a padd)

I've been doing a great deal of research, studying a variety of cultural attitudes on suicide to help me frame the basis of a decision. Mister Tuvok, are you familiar with the "double effect" principle on assisted suicide that dates back to the Bolian Middle Ages?

TUVOK

I believe it relates to the relief of suffering, does it not, Captain?

JANEWAY

(acknowledges)

It states: "An action that has the principal effect of relieving suffering may be ethically justified even though the same action has the secondary effect of possibly causing death."

(beat, as she lets it sink in, to Q2)

This principle is the only thing I can find that could possibly convince me to decide in your favor, Q. And yet, as I look at you, you don't seem by our standards, aged, infirm, or in any pain.

(continuing)

Can you show this hearing that you suffer in any manner other than that caused by the conditions of your incarceration? Any suffering that would justify a decision to grant you asylum?

Q2 looks uncertain, glances at Tuvok. Q1 grins, sensing victory is near.

TUVOK

May I request a recess to consider our response, Captain?

JANEWAY

Granted.

And as the group prepares to leave . . .

TIME CUT TO:

36 INTERIOR MESS HALL

Tuvok and Q2 sit. . . . Tuvok eats sparingly . . . tries to think of a strategy. . . .

Q2

We're going to lose, aren't we . . . ?

TUVOK

I would say we have not yet convinced Captain Janeway of the validity of our argument.

Q2

(nods, a beat, with deep appreciation)

You're doing a fine job, Mister Tuvok. It's nice to know someone believes in me.

TUVOK

I am representing your position to the best of my ability. It is most definitely not my own.

(off Q2's surprised reaction)

I see no persuasive evidence that a life like yours should be wasted . . . simply because you are . . . disgruntled. Frankly, I see no logic to your position.

Q2

You . . . you surprise me, Mister Tuvok . . . which is a rare and lovely gift to a Q. Thank you.

(beat)

But may I say, if you only knew what life as a Q were like, you would see the logic.

Tuvok reacts, his mind working . . . a long beat . . .

TUVOK

Then, perhaps what we should do next—is take this hearing to see life in the Continuum itself.

Off Q's reaction . . .

FADE OUT.

ACT FOUR

FADE IN:

37 INTERIOR READY ROOM

Janeway paces, troubled, thinking . . . stops, takes a deep breath, hits her combadge. . . .

JANEWAY

Computer . . .

(it bleeps)

Is there any indication in our files about how to contact a Q?

COMPUTER VOICE

Negative. Qs traditionally contact humans. There is no known line of communication to the Continuum.

JANEWAY

Well, I have need to establish one. Do you have any suggestions?

COMPUTER VOICE

You might try yelling for him.

JANEWAY

Yelling . . . ?

COMPUTER VOICE

Or perhaps he already knows you want to see him.

JANEWAY

(realizing, overlapping)

38 ANGLE—TO SEE Q1 BEHIND HER

Continuing to talk in the computer's voice.

JANEWAY

I can't imagine how Captain Picard has put up with you all these years.

Q1

(normal voice)

I know you find this overwhelming, Kathy. And that's understandable. But trust me; in years to come, you will treasure our moments together.

He is uncomfortably close. . . . There is a definite tension. . . . She's as cold as ice. . . .

JANEWAY
I do not appreciate your flirtations.

Q1
(breaking the tension)
I always flirted with Jean-Luc too, but I never got the rise out of him that I get out of you.
(beat)
We really have to do something with your hair.

JANEWAY
Can we talk about the hearing . . .?

Q1
Talk about the case ex parte? Is that really appropriate?

JANEWAY
I'd like to get myself out of the middle of this, and you can make it easier for me.
(off his look)
Come to the next session of the hearing and announce that the Continuum is ready to reintegrate Q into your society. That you won't condemn him to that cell for eternity.

Q1
And you'd rule in our favor. . . .

JANEWAY
I would consider it a very meaningful gesture by the Continuum.

Q1
How would you know if I intended to keep my word?

JANEWAY

Based on my research, you have been many things—a rude—interfering—inconsiderate—sadistic . . .

Q1

. . . You've made your point. . . .

JANEWAY

Pest. And, oh yes, you introduced us to the Borg, thank you very much . . . but one thing you have never been . . . is a liar.

Q1

You've uncovered my one redeeming virtue. Am I blushing?

(beat, sighs)

I wish I could help you, Kathy. . . . I just can't. We're dealing here with the most dangerous man in the Continuum. I didn't tell you this, but one of his self-destructive stunts created a misunderstanding that ignited the hundred-year war between the Romulans and the Vulcans. No, he has to go back to his confinement.

(beat)

But I *would* like to make this easier for you.

(off her curious look)

The Continuum is prepared to do you a little favor . . . if we approve of your ruling. Look out the window.

She reacts, goes to the window . . .

39 ANGLE (OPTICAL)—HER P.O.V.

Out the window . . . she can see Earth. . . .

40 JANEWAY CLOSE-UP

JANEWAY

(whispering)

That's . . . Earth. . . .

Q1

Now you see it. Now you don't.

She glances away, toward him, and when she looks back to the window—

41 HER P.O.V.—NOTHING BUT STARS

42 JANEWAY

Reacts . . . turns back, but Q is gone.

43 INTERIOR HEARING ROOM (OPTICAL)

Tuvok rises. Move to reveal the session is under way, with all the players in position. . . .

TUVOK
We are prepared to illustrate the nature of Q's suffering, Captain. But in order to do so, we must show this hearing what life is like in the Continuum. . . .

Q1
And how do you intend to do that?

TUVOK
By going to the Continuum itself.

JANEWAY
Is this possible?

Q1
No. It's a ridiculous idea. You would never understand. . . .

TUVOK
My client has the right to ask for an inspection of the living conditions that lead to his suffering, Captain. . . .

JANEWAY
I would agree with that.

Q1 throws up his hands at the incredibility of this request—he looks over at Q2. . . .

Q1

I suppose you have some crazy idea how to pull this off?

Q2 acknowledges and moves over to Q1. . . . They huddle in a corner, discussing this in muted tones . . .

mostly out of earshot as Tuvok and Janeway exchange a glance. . . . At one point we hear Q1 say:

Q1

. . . only if . . .

Q2

. . . fine, fine . . .

And when they break, Q2 nods to Tuvok. . . .

Q1

We've agreed on a . . . format . . . for this sojourn. But I still believe it's ill-advised.

JANEWAY

I'll be the judge of that. Whenever you're ready, Mister Tuvok.

Tuvok nods to Q2, who makes a motion . . . a FLASH . . . and suddenly we find ourselves . . .

44 EXTERIOR DESERT ROAD—DAY (OPTICAL)

The wind whistling softly . . . the sky a red hue . . . Janeway and Tuvok react. . . .

JANEWAY

This is the Q Continuum? A road in a desert?

Q1

(to Q2)

I told you so.

Q2

This is a . . . manifestation . . . of the Continuum that we hope will fall within your level of comprehension. This way . . .

And as they trudge forward . . . we boom up to see the road stretch to the horizon in infinity. Up ahead is a single rustic building . . . sort of a roadside "grill" . . . or road stop. . . .

45 EXTERIOR ROAD STOP—DAY

A slow pan to show us the structure . . . a solid country feel, not dilapidated . . . a neon clock in the window has no hands . . . a sign next to it says, "Never Closes" . . .

on the porch where one man in a rocking chair smokes a corncob pipe as he reads a Biblical-looking book entitled "THE OLD". . . . An attractive young woman sits on the porch, leaning against a post as she reads a sexy magazine called "THE NEW," with a cover picture of a provocatively dressed couple in an embrace. . . . She laughs intermittently. . . . One man plays a pinball machine entitled "GALAXY" at the far end of the porch. . . . A young couple play croquet in front, except the balls seem to be miniature planets. . . . A scarecrow dressed in a Starfleet red uniform guards vacant fields. . . .

46 ANGLE—A HOUND DOG

Barks at the arriving visitors, retreats to the porch. . . . The country folk look with suspicion at the guests. . . .

JANEWAY

Good afternoon.

They don't speak. . . . At best, they glance up out of the corner of an eye. . . . Mostly they ignore them. . . . The woman cackles at her magazine. . . .

Q2

(embarrassed)

I apologize for their lack of hospitality, Captain. We are not used to visitors. . . . In fact you are the only ones who've ever come. . . .

TUVOK

Then what is the purpose of the road?

Q2

The road takes us to the rest of the universe . . . and then it leads back here . . . an endless circle. . . .

JANEWAY

This was your existence before your confinement?

Q2

(acknowledges)

I traveled the road many times. Sat on the porch . . . played the games . . . been the dog . . . everything. . . . I was even the scarecrow for a while. . . .

JANEWAY

Why?

Q2

Because I hadn't done it.

Q1

Oh, we've all done the scarecrow, big deal.

JANEWAY

I can't say I entirely understand what I'm seeing here. But these people don't seem to be suffering. . . .

Q1

Of course not. These are happy people. Happy people. What's there to feel sad about? Look at them. . . .

He tries to coax up some smiles with a look and hand gestures. . . .

Q2

They don't dare feel sad. If only they could, *that* would be progress.

Q1

(dismissive)

The philosopher speaks.

Q2

He's right, of course. When I was a respected philosopher, I celebrated the continuity . . . the *undeviation* of Q life. I argued that our civilization had achieved a purity that no other culture had ever approached.

And it *was* wonderful. For a while. At the beginning of the new era, life as a Q was one continuous dialogue of discovery and issues and humor from all over the universe . . . but look at them now . . . listen to their dialogue now . . .

TUVOK

I am afraid I cannot hear any.

Q2

Because it's all been said. Everyone has seen everything, heard everything. . . . They haven't had to speak to each other for ten millennia. . . . There's nothing left to say.

Q1

(defensive)

I don't know about you, but I appreciate a little peace and quiet now and again.

Q2 studies him. . . .

Q2

It is ironic, isn't it, Q . . .?

Q1

I don't know what you mean.

Q2

Of course you do. That you of all people should be arguing their case.

And that strikes home for Q. . . . He does his best to deny it. . . .

Q1

I believe in the ultimate purity of the Q. . . .

Q2

You who were banned from the Continuum and made mortal to pay for your crimes.

Q1

My penance has ended. I am a born-again Q. That life is behind me.

Q2

What a shame. Because in many ways, that life inspired me.

Q1

(caught off-guard)

It did? *I* did?

Q2

Oh yes . . . you never knew that, did you?

A beat as Q1, perplexed, studies Q2. After a beat, Q2 continues. . . .

Q2

You see, Captain, Q rebelled against this existence by refusing to behave himself—he was out of control, using his powers irresponsibly for his own amusement. He desperately needed amusement because he couldn't find any at home.

Q1

(trying to be the good Q)

I paid the price for my inappropriate behavior.

Q2

No, *we* paid the price when we forced you to stop. For a moment there, you really got our attention, *my* attention. *You gave us something to talk about!*

(beat)

But then you surrendered to the will of the Continuum like a good little Q. And may I say that you have become a fine, upstanding member of the Continuum.

(moving closer and speaking softer for emphasis, entre-nous)

But I miss that irrepressible Q . . . who forced me to think. . . .

Q1 looks away, trying not to be moved. . . . But in fact, he is deeply affected by this. . . . Q2 smiles after him, gently wise.

46A ANGLE

Q2 moves to the woman reading "THE NEW" magazine, takes the magazine out of her hands . . .

Q2

May I borrow this?

She glares at him. He hands the magazine to Janeway; Tuvok looks over her shoulder. . . .

Q2

This was the beginning of my fall from grace. . . .

47 INSERT—THE MAGAZINE ARTICLE (OPTICAL)

Shows a small photo of Q2 smiling . . . the regular column is titled "My Corner of the Continuum." The article is headlined: "I'm Ready to Die; How About You?"

Q2

It was the last edition, by the way. They "shut down the presses" after I wrote this. But they couldn't keep me silent. I continued to speak out in favor of self-termination.

Q1

That's when he lost his mind . . . and started trying to destroy himself. . . . Finally we had no choice but to confine him for his own safety.

Q2

Not for my safety. For *theirs.* I was the greatest threat that the Continuum had ever known. They feared me so much they had to lock me away for eternity. And when they did, they were saying that an individual's rights will be protected only as long as they're not in conflict with the state. And nothing could be more dangerous to a society.

(beat)

My life's work is complete. But they force immortality on me . . . and by doing so they cheapen and denigrate my life and all life in the Continuum.

(to the country folk)

All life.

(beat)

You are an explorer, Captain. What if you had nothing left to explore? Would you want to live forever under those circumstances?

(beat)

You ask me to prove to you that I suffer in terms that you equate to pain or disease. Look at us. When life is futile, meaningless, unendurable . . . it must be allowed to end. Can't you see, Captain? For us, the disease *is* immortality.

He locks eyes with Janeway, who understands completely. . . . Q2 waves his hand, and there's a flash and we're back. . . .

48 INTERIOR HEARING ROOM (OPTICAL)

As we left it. Tuvok rises.

TUVOK

We rest our case, Captain.

She looks to Q1, who seems affected by the day's proceedings. . . . He is thoughtful and introspective. . . . He shakes his head, uncharacteristically silent.

JANEWAY

(a beat)

Very well. I'll make my ruling in the morning. We'll be in recess until then.

She rises to EXIT . . . and as Q1 exchanges a look with Q2—we FADE OUT.

ACT FIVE

FADE IN:

49 INTERIOR JANEWAY'S QUARTERS (OPTICAL)

Dark. Janeway is in bed . . . but sleep will not come. . . . She stares at the ceiling . . . after a beat . . . her hair is down. . . .

Q1 (offcamera)

Trouble sleeping?

She reacts, turns to see Q in bed beside her in a Rip Van Winkle cap and gown. . . . He smiles. . . .

Q1

Ever try warm Kylerian goat's milk?

She leaps out of bed . . . puts on a robe. . . .

JANEWAY

Get out.

Q1

Did you think about our offer?

JANEWAY

You mean your bribe.

Q1

Merely an incentive to make the proper decision.

JANEWAY

It'll play no part in my deliberations.

Q1

(beat, quite serious)

No, I told them it wouldn't. That's why I talked them into giving you what you asked for. . . .

And it's important to note that Q has been touched by his encounter with Q2. . . . He genuinely cares for him at this point . . . OFF her curious look, low key, sincere—

Q1
(continuing)
I give you my word, he won't go back into the cell. We'll assign someone to look after him. Whatever it takes.

Janeway breaks eye contact, thinks about this new development. . . . It would have been easier yesterday . . . before Q2's plea to end his suffering. . . .

Q1
That is what you wanted, isn't it?

JANEWAY
(beat, thoughtful, still no eye contact, soft)
That's what I wanted.

Q1
So, you've won.

Janeway wonders if she has, silently.

Q1
Let's celebrate. You and me. Just the two of us.

Janeway does a take at that . . . breaks her thought pattern. . . .

JANEWAY
What?

Q1
I'll take you home. Before you know it, you'll be scampering across the meadow with your little puppies, the grass beneath your bare feet. A man, coming over the hill way in the distance, waves to you. . . . You run to be in his arms and as you get closer you see it's . . . *me*. . . .

JANEWAY
You . . .?

Q1
Forget Mark; I know how to show a girl a good time. How would you like a ticker-tape parade down Sri Lanka Boulevard . . . ? The captain who brought

Voyager back . . . a celebrated hero. I never did anything like that for Jean-Luc. But I feel very close to you. I'm not sure why. Maybe it's because you have such authority yet manage to preserve your femininity so well.

She stares at him for perhaps the longest silent beat in the history of film.

JANEWAY

Leave.

Q1

(undeterred)

We'll talk about it after the hearing tomorrow.

He DISAPPEARS. A beat on an incredulous Janeway and then . . .

50 EXTERIOR SPACE—*VOYAGER* (OPTICAL)

Time passage.

51 INTERIOR HEARING ROOM

Janeway at her desk . . . studies a padd with some notes on it . . . looks up, takes a deep breath and begins. . . .

JANEWAY

I've tried to find some way to reconcile all the conflicting emotions I've felt during this hearing. My own aversion to suicide . . .

(to Q2)

. . . my compassion for your situation, Q. It hasn't been easy.

(beat)

I've tried to tell myself that this is not about suicide, but about granting asylum. That I am not personally being asked to perform euthanasia. And as technically true as that may be, I cannot escape the moral implications of my choices.

(beat)

I've also had to consider that a decision to grant asylum and the subsequent suicide of a Q might have a significant impact on the Continuum. That such a decision could change the nature of an entire society, whether it be a favorable or unfavorable change, disturbs me greatly.

(beat)

But then there are the rights of the individual in this matter.

(talking directly to Q2)

I don't believe that you're mentally unbalanced. And I do believe you are suffering intolerably.

(continuing)

Under these conditions, I find it impossible to support immortality forced on an individual by the state. The unforeseen disruption that may occur in the Continuum is not enough, in my opinion, to justify any additional suffering by this individual.

(beat)

So, I hereby grant you asylum.

Reactions. Q1 rises.

Q1

Captain . . . may I see you in chambers . . . ?

JANEWAY

You've been in my chambers enough for one visit, sir. . . .

Q1

A sidebar, your honor. . . .

Q2

(to Q1)

She ruled in my favor. You made a promise. . . .

Q1 looks at him, frowns and sighs . . . snaps his fingers carelessly. . . . Q2 makes his "magic Q" gesture several times; nothing happens. . . . He glows. . . .

Q2

Nothing! Nothing happened. My powers are gone. I'm mortal!

Q1 looks at Janeway. . . .

Q1

Well, so much for ticker-tape parades.

JANEWAY

I'm not finished.

(to Q2)

Q, now that you're mortal, you have a new existence to explore . . . an entirely new state of being . . . filled with the mysteries of mortal life . . . pleasures you've never felt before. . . .

(beat)

I like this life, Q. You might too. Think hard before you give it up.

Q2 exchanges a long look with her, acknowledges.

JANEWAY

This hearing is adjourned.

She rises.

52 EXTERIOR SPACE — *VOYAGER* (OPTICAL)

JANEWAY (voice-over)

Captain's log, stardate 49301.2. We have assigned quarters to our new passenger, who has entered his name on our crew manifest as Quinn. I am eager to engage him in interesting ship activities as soon as possible.

53 INTERIOR READY ROOM

Janeway and Chakotay . . .

CHAKOTAY

How about Stellar Cartography?

JANEWAY

(shakes her head)

We could shut down Stellar Cartography with all the knowledge he would bring to the job. . . .

CHAKOTAY

Well, that's going to be a problem with just about everything we assign him to. . . .

JANEWAY
There's got to be something on board that will. . . .

DOCTOR (com voice)
Sickbay to Captain Janeway.

JANEWAY
Go ahead.

DOCTOR (com voice)
Captain, I think you should come down to sickbay. Mister Quinn is here. I'm afraid he's dying.

Janeway exchanges a look with Chakotay. . . .

54 OMITTED

55 INTERIOR SICKBAY

Tuvok is with the Doctor at Q2's bedside as Janeway ENTERS. . . .

JANEWAY
There's nothing you can do?

DOCTOR
He's ingested a rare form of Nogatch hemlock. There is no known cure.

She looks at him; he smiles weakly . . . takes her hand.

Q2
I'm sorry to disappoint you, Captain. But I would only be pretending to "fit in" to this mortal existence. This is my final gift to my people. Tell them those were my last words.
(beat)
I dearly thank you for making this possible.

And he's gone. Janeway looks down sadly and shakes her head and sighs.

TUVOK
Doctor, do you generally keep samples of fatal poisons in storage?

DOCTOR

No. . . .

TUVOK

The replicators will not produce them either.

JANEWAY

(catching on)

So how did he get his hands on Nogatch hemlock?

56 NEW ANGLE (OPTICAL)

To reveal Q1. . . .

Q1

I got it for him.

Reactions.

TUVOK

You assisted his suicide?

Q1

Illogical, is it, Tuvok? I don't think so. By demanding to end *his* life, he's taught me a little something about my own. He was right when he said the Continuum scared me back in line. I didn't have his courage or his convictions. He called me "irrepressible." *This* was a man who was *truly* irrepressible.

(beat)

I only hope I can be a worthy student.

JANEWAY

I imagine the Continuum won't be very happy with you, Q.

Q1

(smiles)

I certainly hope not.

He takes her hand and kisses it.

Q1
Au revoir, Madame Captain. We will meet again.

And he flashes away. Janeway takes a moment and then as a thoughtful expression begins to form, we . . .

FADE OUT.

STAR TREK: VOYAGER

The Q and the Grey

#40840-153

Teleplay by
Kenneth Biller

Story by
Shawn Piller

Directed by
Cliff Bole

STAR TREK: VOYAGER

The Q and the Grey

CAST

JANEWAY
KIM
PARIS
CHAKOTAY
TUVOK
TORRES
DOCTOR
KES
NEELIX

Q
FEMALE Q
COLONEL Q

Non-Speaking

N.D. SUPERNUMERARIES

Non-Speaking

N.D. Q

STAR TREK: VOYAGER

The Q and the Grey

SETS

INTERIORS

VOYAGER
BRIDGE
BRIEFING ROOM
CORRIDOR
ENGINEERING
HOLODECK/RESORT
JANEWAY'S QUARTERS
READY ROOM

MANSION/DRAWING ROOM

TENT

EXTERIORS

VOYAGER

MANSION
WOODS/CONFEDERATE CAMP
CLEARING

STAR TREK: VOYAGER

The Q and the Grey

PRONUNCIATION GUIDE

CYRILLIAN	seer-ILL-ee-n
DRABIAN	DRAY-bee-n
FORTE	FORT
THERINIAN	ther-INN-ee-n

STAR TREK: VOYAGER

The Q and the Grey

TEASER

FADE IN:

1 EXTERIOR SPACE (OPTICAL)

The quintessence of celestial serenity. CAMERA PUSHES slowly through the starfield, ambling toward a light that is brighter than the stars around it. As CAMERA MOVES closer, we see that the source of this light is also a star—a star PULSATING with incredible energy. As it occupies the center of FRAME, its core HEATS to a blinding white, and it suddenly IMPLODES. Then, just as suddenly, it EXPLODES in a dazzling fireball. . . .

2 OMITTED

3 INTERIOR BRIDGE—(INTERACTIVE LIGHT) (OPTICAL)
TO REVEAL a cheering audience: JANEWAY, CHAKOTAY, TUVOK, PARIS, KIM, TORRES, NEELIX, KES, THE DOCTOR, and N.D.'s—all either at stations or gathered around the viewscreen watching the spectacular light show, their faces reflecting the glow of the exploding star. The party atmosphere doesn't dissipate even after the applause dies down.

CHAKOTAY

Incredible.

JANEWAY

Absolutely thrilling.

NEELIX

All I can say is . . .

(bursting)

. . . Wow!

He turns to Tuvok.

NEELIX

What about you, Mister Vulcan? Wasn't that just . . .

(can't contain himself)

. . . *wow!*

TUVOK

Your inarticulate expression of awe notwithstanding, Mister Neelix, it was a fascinating spectacle.

Amused reactions. The ship SHUDDERS mildly. Kim reads off his monitor.

KIM

That's the edge of the shock wave. The pressure is over ninety kilopascals. . . . Thirty percent more than we predicted. . . .

JANEWAY

Tom, back us off at full impulse. I want to stay ahead of the brunt of that wave.

As Paris works, Janeway turns to the group.

JANEWAY

Congratulations, everyone. Only two other crews in the history of Starfleet have witnessed a supernova explosion.

Kim's still reading data off his monitor.

KIM

But neither one was this close. Less than ten billion kilometers.

(looking up)

Definitely a record.

JANEWAY

(smiles)

Who brought the champagne?

NEELIX

Champagne? Captain, if I'd known you wanted champagne . . .

JANEWAY

Relax, Neelix. It's a figure of speech.

KES

Thanks for inviting us to watch with you, Captain. It's

really gotten me interested in learning more about stellar phenomena.

The Doctor bristles slightly.

DOCTOR

Just remember, Kes. *Anyone* can stargaze on the bridge. But the *real* action will always be in sickbay.

Janeway smiles, as Kes and the Doctor head for the turbolift, then moves to Torres.

JANEWAY

How did those shield modifications hold up, B'Elanna?

She checks a console.

TORRES

Less than seven percent power drain.

JANEWAY

Good job. Chakotay, what do you say we get started analyzing those carbon-conversion readings?

CHAKOTAY

Captain, you've been on the bridge for fourteen straight hours. Don't you think you deserve a little rest?

Janeway hesitates.

CHAKOTAY

Harry and I will get to work on the astrometric analysis, and we'll give you a full report in the morning.

JANEWAY

You win. I'll see you at oh seven hundred.

As she heads for the turbolift . . .

4 INTERIOR CORRIDOR

As Janeway rounds the corner and approaches the door to her quarters. She hits the code on the panel, and the door SLIDES OPEN. . . .

5 INTERIOR JANEWAY'S QUARTERS (CONTINUOUS)

As she ENTERS, pulls up short, looks surprised.

6 HER P.O.V.

The lights are dimmed, candles burn, soft music plays, and in the middle of the room is a bed with a *heart-shaped* headboard. Next to it, in an ice bucket on a stand, is a bottle of champagne. She hits her combadge, speaks to com.

JANEWAY
Janeway to . . .

But before she can finish the sentence:

MAN'S VOICE (offcamera)
There's no need to call room service, Kathy. . . .

7 WIDER (OPTICAL)

TO REVEAL Q . . . wearing a silk bathrobe and a devilish grin.

Q
. . . I've already ordered.

JANEWAY
Q!

He moves to the ice bucket, pulls out the bottle, and begins pouring it into two glasses.

Q
You did say you wanted champagne?

JANEWAY
Janeway to security. Intruder Alert.

Q
It's no use. I've taken the proverbial phone off the hook. After all, we don't want any interruptions.

JANEWAY

What are you doing here?

He offers her one of the glasses.

Q

To us.

JANEWAY

There is no *us,* Q.

Q

(shrugs)

The night is young; the sheets are satin. . . .

JANEWAY

I want you out. But first, get rid of that bed.

Q

I have no intention of getting between those Starfleet-issue sheets. They give me a terrible rash.

JANEWAY

Since you won't be getting *in* the bed, I wouldn't worry about it.

Q

Oh, Kathy, don't be such a prude. Admit it: it *has* been a while . . .

JANEWAY

And it's going to be a while longer. Now get out.

Q

So tense. Why don't you slip into something more comfortable?

He snaps his fingers and POOF! When Janeway glances down at herself, she sees she's wearing a sexy negligee. Fuming, she looks back up at Q.

JANEWAY

If you think this puerile attempt at seduction is going to work, you're even more self-deluded than I thought.

Q

Oh, I see: you think I'm interested in some tawdry one-night stand.

(silly me)

That's because I haven't told you why I'm here yet.

As he moves in on her . . .

Q

(continuing, beat)

Out of all the females of all the species in all the galaxies . . .

(beat; smiles)

. . . I've chosen *you* to be the mother of my child.

OFF Janeway's stunned reaction . . .

FADE OUT.

ACT ONE

FADE IN:

8 INTERIOR JANEWAY'S QUARTERS (OPTICAL).

Moments later. Janeway's speechless.

Q

I know you're probably asking yourself: "Why would a brilliant, handsome, dashingly omnipotent being like Q want to mate with a scrawny little bipedal specimen like me?"

Janeway moves toward her sleeping alcove.

JANEWAY

Let me guess: no one else in the universe will have you.

Q follows.

Q

Nonsense. I could have chosen a Klingon tarq, the Romulan empress, a Cyrillian microbe. . . .

Janeway grabs a robe and starts to put it on.

JANEWAY

Really? I beat out a single-celled organism. How flattering.

Q

It is an overwhelming honor, isn't it? But I haven't been able to get you out of my mind. You're confident passionate, beautiful. . . .

JANEWAY

. . . and totally uninterested.

She starts for the door with Q in hot pursuit.

Q

Kathy, you can't leave. My cosmic clock is ticking. . . .

POOF! He suddenly appears in front of her.

Q

Besides, you don't know what you're missing. Foreplay with a Q can last for *decades.*

She advances. He backpedals.

JANEWAY

Sorry, but I'm busy for the next sixty or seventy years.

Q

Oh, I get it. This is one of those silly human rituals. . . .

(delighted)

You're playing "hard to get."

JANEWAY

As far as you're concerned, Q, I'm *impossible* to get.

Q

Oh, goody. A challenge.

(grins)

This is going to be fun.

He snaps his fingers and DISAPPEARS. Janeway breathes a sigh of relief, then turns to see that the heart-shaped bed is gone. She goes to her desk-top monitor, hits a control, speaks to com:

JANEWAY

Janeway to bridge.

This time the call goes through.

CHAKOTAY (com voice)

Chakotay here, Captain.

INTERCUT:

9 INTERIOR BRIDGE

Tuvok, Kim, and Chakotay examining data from the supernova. Chakotay studies a padd, speaks to com.

CHAKOTAY

I thought you were going to get some sleep.

JANEWAY (com voice)
I've just had a visit from Q.

Reactions.

JANEWAY (com voice)
He's gone now, but I want to be notified immediately if he reappears anywhere on the ship or if anything odd starts to happen.

CHAKOTAY
Acknowledged.
(concerned)
What did he want?

A beat.

JANEWAY (com voice)
Let's just say he had a *personal* request.

CHAKOTAY
Captain?

JANEWAY (com voice)
I'm not sure what he's really up to, but I have a feeling he'll be back. Janeway out.

As Chakotay and Tuvok exchange a glance . . .

10–10A OMITTED

TIME CUT TO:

10B EXTERIOR SPACE—*VOYAGER* (OPTICAL)

At impulse.

11 INTERIOR READY ROOM

Janeway works at her desk. The door CHIMES.

JANEWAY
Come in.

Chakotay ENTERS carrying a padd.

CHAKOTAY

I've got those carbon-conversion readings on the supernova.

JANEWAY

Thank you.

He hands her the padd, but doesn't leave. She looks up at him.

JANEWAY

Is there something else?

Chakotay tries to be casual, but we can tell he's covering something.

CHAKOTAY

Have you heard anything more from Q?

JANEWAY

No. I wish I could believe he's gone for good.

Chakotay hesitates. Whatever's on his mind, he's uncomfortable talking about it.

CHAKOTAY

I was wondering . . . just what you meant when you said he made a "personal request."

She gives him a quick look. They're on dangerous ground here, and she understands now why he was hesitant. She tries to be matter-of-fact.

JANEWAY

He wants to mate with me.

Chakotay reacts to this. It's irrational, as jealousy often is, but nonetheless it's a formidable emotion. His eyes bore into Janeway as he tries to keep a lid on his feelings.

CHAKOTAY

I see.

JANEWAY

Obviously, it's out of the question. And I suspect it's a smoke screen—knowing Q, he's probably got some hidden agenda.

CHAKOTAY

Maybe.

She looks at him. Goes to him. Hesitates, then puts a hand on his shoulder.

JANEWAY

Chakotay . . .

He shakes his head, backs off.

CHAKOTAY

I know I don't have any right to feel this way. But it bothers the hell out of me.

Q (offcamera)

I do believe . . . you're *jealous.*

12 NEW ANGLE

As they turn to discover Q. He addresses an irritated Janeway.

Q

Why didn't you tell me there's another man?

JANEWAY

Because there *isn't.* I'm just not interested in *you.*

Chakotay steps in between them, challenging.

CHAKOTAY

Any questions?

A charged moment as they continue to eye one another.

Q

I wonder, Kathy: what could anyone possibly see in this big oaf anyway?

(scrutinizing)

Is it the tattoo?

12A NEW ANGLE

As he turns to her, one half of his face now completely covered in a larger version of Chakotay's tattoo.

Q

Because *mine's* bigger.

Janeway shakes her head, dry . . .

JANEWAY

Not big enough.

And with that, she turns and EXITS. As Chakotay follows, OFF Q . . .

13–18 OMITTED

18A EXTERIOR SPACE—*VOYAGER* (OPTICAL)

At impulse.

JANEWAY (voice-over)

Captain's log, stardate 50384.2. Q's unannounced visits continue. Since I suspect he's up to something more than pursuing me, I've instructed the crew to take every opportunity to uncover his true motives.

19 INTERIOR HOLODECK/RESORT (OPTICAL)

While bikini-clad WOMEN rub their shoulders, Paris and Kim work on padds. Neelix polishes glasses behind the bar.

PARIS

Who says crew performance reports have to be a chore?

KIM

(agreeing)

It sure beats working on the bridge.

PARIS

Now if we could just convince the captain to start holding morning briefings in here . . .

KIM

(smiles)

That'll be the day.

Suddenly Q APPEARS in a seat near Harry and Tom. He's holding an "umbrella" drink in one hand. One of the women is now rubbing *his* shoulders.

Q

Nice program, Tommy.

Depressed, he glances up at the woman.

Q

But it's all just so much *holo* pleasure, isn't it?

PARIS

All right, Q. We'll bite. What do you want?

Q

(miserable)

I just don't understand your captain. I've tried everything: filling the bridge with roses, writing her Drabian love sonnets, serenading her in the bath. . . .

PARIS

(sarcastic)

I'll bet she loved that. . . .

Q sighs, genuinely despondent. . . .

Q

No matter what lengths I go to win her heart, she rejects me. *Me.*

(beat)

How, I ask, is that possible?

KIM

Did it ever occur to you that she just doesn't like you?

Q

Actually, no.

PARIS

Look, Q, we've been told about your appearances on the *Enterprise.* We know your little visits usually turn out to be more than meets the eye. So save the broken-heart routine and tell us what you're really after.

Q
(innocent)
I just thought you two might be able to give me some advice on how to break through Kathy's icy exterior. You know . . .
(conspiratorial)
. . . man-to-man.

PARIS
My advice is to give up before you embarrass yourself any more than you already have.
(to Kim)
Come on, Harry. We're not going to get a straight answer out of him.

They EXIT. Q shrugs, sucks on his straw. But he gets nothing but a loud slurp of air. Oh, the injustice of it all.

19A NEW ANGLE

As Q rises wearily, moves to the bar area.

Q
You . . . Bar rodent . . .

He holds up his glass.

Q
I want another one of these . . . fruity concoctions. . . .

Neelix scowls at him.

NEELIX
Not unless you tell me why you're bothering Captain Janeway.

Q
Ah, Captain Janeway. Just the subject I wanted to discuss. Tell me: what are a few of her favorite things?
(rattling it off)
Chocolate truffles, stuffed animals, erotic art . . . ?

NEELIX
You can't *bribe* Captain Janeway.

Q
Oh no? Isn't that what *you* do?

NEELIX
What are you talking about?

Q
I understand you acquire things for her . . . create amusing diversions . . . prepare her little taste-treats . . .
(with an edge)
Why else would she be so fond of that *fur*-lined face?

Neelix seethes.

NEELIX
You want to know what Captain Janeway likes about me? I'll tell you: I'm respectful, loyal, and most of all . . . *sincere.*
(in his face)
Qualities someone like you could never hope to possess.

OFF Q, pondering this . . .

20 OMITTED

21 INTERIOR READY ROOM

Janeway's sitting on the sofa working, when suddenly she hears a very faint sound. She looks up, listens for a moment, then goes back to work. But the sound comes again, louder this time.

It's someone or something—*whimpering.*

She gets up and moves toward the noise. And there, under her desk, she discovers an adorable Irish setter PUPPY. She knows where it's come from.

JANEWAY
This isn't going to work, Q.

22 NEW ANGLE

As she rises, turns to discover him standing there. He stoops down to pick up the dog, then holds the animal's nose inches from Janeway.

Q
How can you ignore that face?

She rises, moves away.

JANEWAY
He's adorable. But this has to stop.

Q
Please, accept him as a small token of my affection.

JANEWAY
No.

Q
(shrugs)
Suit yourself.
(gestures to the sofa)
May we talk?

She eyes him suspiciously. He holds up a hand in a sign of his innocent intentions.

Q
Just *talk.*

They move to the sofa and sit. Q puts the puppy down on the sofa between them. His attitude is noticeably different. Gone is his usual smugness.

Q
I'm afraid I haven't been *sincere.*

She gives him a questioning glance.

Q
When you asked me why I wanted to have a child
with you, I made jokes, bragged about my prowess,
engaged in sexual innuendo. . . .
(beat)
I was using all that to cover my true feelings.

JANEWAY

And I suppose you want to share your "true feelings" with me now.

Q hesitates, nods. This is difficult for him, or at least he would like Janeway to think so. Either way, he's convincing.

Q

I'm . . . lonely.

JANEWAY

Lonely?

Q

I know it's hard to believe, but . . . well . . . I've been single for billions of years. . . .

(not proud)

It was fun at first . . . gallivanting around the galaxy, using my omnipotence to impress females of every species. . . . But the truth is, it's left me . . . *empty*. . . .

(looks at his hands)

I want someone to love me . . . for *myself*. . . .

(beat)

I guess what I'm saying is . . . I want a relationship.

JANEWAY

(skeptical)

Uh huh.

Absently, she begins to pet the puppy.

Q

And I just thought . . . if you and I . . . had a child . . .

(looking up)

. . . it would give me the kind of stability and security I've been missing. . . .

JANEWAY

Sorry, Q. I'm not buying it.

Q considers for a moment, then tries a different tack:

Q

All right, let's see if you buy this.

He looks her right in the eye.

Q

(continuing)

You're stuck out here, thousands of light-years from home, and you're not getting any younger, are you? All your hopes for home . . . hearth . . . a family . . . grow a little dimmer every day.

(beat)

Admit it, Kathryn: you're lonely too. And you wonder if you'll ever have children. . . .

Janeway is silent. Q has obviously struck a chord.

JANEWAY

You're right. I would like to have a child someday.

(beat)

But not with you.

Q

Why not?

JANEWAY

I'm just not the right woman for you.

FEMALE VOICE (offcamera)

Truer words were never spoken.

23 NEW ANGLE

As they both look up to see FEMALE Q. She's bright, sexy, and every bit as sassy as the Q we've come to know. And though she'd never say it directly, she's jealous of Q's interest in Janeway.

Q

Q! How did you find me?

Q FEMALE

Never mind that. What are you doing with that dog?

Q looks down at the puppy, but the Q female turns to Janeway.

Q FEMALE

I'm not talking about the puppy.

OFF Janeway's dumbstruck expression . . .

FADE OUT.

ACT TWO

FADE IN:

24 INTERIOR READY ROOM

Moments later. Q addresses the Q female.

Q

Can't you see I'm busy here? Now stop *stalking* me.

Q FEMALE

You should be back in the Continuum.

Unamused, Janeway steps in.

JANEWAY

Excuse me, but who *are* you exactly?

Q

(exasperated)

Kathryn Janeway, may I present Q.

Q FEMALE

Not just any Q.

(pointed)

His Q.

Janeway reacts. Q shrugs.

Q

We were . . . *involved* for a while.

Q FEMALE

About four billion years.

She turns to Janeway and gives her a scornful once-over.

Q FEMALE

And now you desert me to pollute the Continuum with the DNA of this . . . *narrow* little being.

Q

I never said it was exclusive.

The Q female takes a threatening tone with Janeway.

Q FEMALE
Stay away from him.

JANEWAY
Look, Miss . . . Q . . . I'll save you a lot of trouble.
(points to Q)
I have *zero* interest in him.

Q
(to Q female)
Now look what you've done.
(re: Janeway)
I was finally making progress.

CHAKOTAY (com voice)
Bridge to Janeway. You'd better come in here, Captain.

JANEWAY
(to com)
On my way.
(to the Qs)
I'd really appreciate it if you took this . . . domestic squabble off my ship.

She turns to go, but the Qs follow. . . .

25 INTERIOR BRIDGE (CONTINUOUS) (OPTICAL)

As Janeway ENTERS from the ready room with the two Qs on her heels. Paris, Tuvok, Kim, Chakotay, and N.D.'s at stations.

JANEWAY
Report.

Chakotay reacts briefly to the presence of the two Qs, then responds.

CHAKOTAY
You're not going to believe this, Captain, but another star in this cluster just went supernova. It's point zero two light-years from our current position.

KIM

Correction, Commander. Make that *two* supernovas. I've just picked up another one at two-one-seven Mark four-seven. Estimated time of implosion . . .

(looking up)

. . . sixty-seven seconds.

JANEWAY

Get us out of here, Tom.

A beat as Paris works, then:

PARIS

I can't. The subspace shock wave from the star is collapsing the warp field.

JANEWAY

Red Alert. Tuvok, increase power to the shields. Tom, lay in a course away from that shock wave. Maximum impulse.

As they work, Janeway turns to the Qs.

JANEWAY

A star going supernova is an event that occurs once every century in this galaxy.

(continuing)

Now we're about to witness our third in less than three days—all in the same sector.

(beat)

Why do I suspect *you* have something to do with this?

Q FEMALE

(to Q)

She may be a member of an intellectually challenged species, but she's right. Your irresponsible behavior is continuing to have *cosmic* consequences.

Q

Oh, stop overreacting.

(to Janeway, re: Q female)

Always nagging. You can see why I left her.

JANEWAY

(impatient)

Are you causing these supernovas?

Q

Not exactly.

JANEWAY

What's that supposed to mean?

Before Q can respond, Paris urgently interjects:

PARIS

It's no use, Captain. The shock wave is too fast for us.

JANEWAY

Try evasive maneuvers.

TUVOK

I am afraid a course correction will be futile, Captain. There are now three distinct shock waves heading toward us on various trajectories. It will be impossible to avoid them all.

JANEWAY

Divert auxiliary power to the shields. Lieutenant Paris, plot the safest possible course.

Furious, she turns on the Qs again.

JANEWAY

You have the ability to get us out of here. So do it!

Q hesitates.

CHAKOTAY

Sixteen seconds to impact, Captain. I'm not sure if the shields will hold.

JANEWAY

Do something, Q!

Now even Q looks visibly distressed.

Q

All right. If you insist.

He snaps his fingers and POOF: he and Janeway DISAPPEAR from the bridge. The Q female reacts.

Q FEMALE

That two-timing toad!

She snaps her fingers, and she too DISAPPEARS. But the crew doesn't have time to react. . . .

TUVOK

Contact with the first shock wave in three seconds, Commander. . . .

CHAKOTAY

(to com)

All hands, brace for impact!

As everybody hangs on . . .

26 EXTERIOR SPACE (OPTICAL)

First one star, and then another in close proximity, EXPLODE in rapid succession. As the enormous double shock wave rumbles outward . . .

27 INTERIOR BRIDGE (INTERACTIVE LIGHT)

The crew is ROCKED violently. . . .

28 EXTERIOR SPACE—*VOYAGER* (OPTICAL)

Being BUFFETED by the edge of the first shock wave. The ship is HURLED past CAMERA, totally out of control. As the wave completely FILLS FRAME. . . .

29 EXTERIOR ANTEBELLUM MANSION—NIGHT (STOCK)

CLOSE TO ESTABLISH a pristine neoclassical structure that stands in stark contrast to the violent events occurring in space . . .

30 INTERIOR MANSION—DRAWING ROOM—NIGHT

A lavishly furnished parlor. (PRODUCTION NOTE: This could be a redesign of the Drawing Room set from Janeway's holonovel). Janeway, wearing a magnificent 19th-century gown, looks around in anger and confusion, calls out:

JANEWAY

Q?! Where have you taken me?

But there's no answer. She moves to the door, tries it, but it's locked. She goes to a window, but it too is sealed shut.

Q (offcamera)
I must say, Kathy, that gown is very becoming. . . .

31 NEW ANGLE

As Janeway turns to see Q entering. He's dressed in the strapping blue uniform of an American Union soldier circa 1861.

JANEWAY
I don't have time for your little fantasies. Return me to *Voyager.*

Q
This is no fantasy, Kathy.
(beat)
You're in the Q Continuum now.

JANEWAY
The Continuum . . . ?

Q
That's right. I'm simply allowing you to perceive it in a context your human mind can comprehend.

Janeway reacts, glances around at her surroundings, the dress.

JANEWAY
The last time you brought me here, it looked . . . like some sort of way station . . . on a desert road. . . .

Q
That *was* awfully drab, wasn't it?

He gestures around the room.

Q
But this . . . this is a much more colorful representation for a human of American descent, don't you think?

He's gestures grandly.

Q

An elegant manor house . . .

(indicating her)

. . . a beautiful southern belle . . .

(re: himself)

. . . a dashing Union officer determined to win her affections despite her hatred of Yankee interlopers . . .

JANEWAY

Enough. The only thing that interests me right now is the welfare of my ship and crew.

Q

I'm sure your first officer . . .

(racking his brain)

. . . *Chuckles,* is it . . . ?

(beat)

. . . I'm sure he's gotten everything under control for the moment.

JANEWAY

I'd like to make sure of that myself, if you don't mind.

He moves in very close.

Q

This has gone way beyond your ship, Kathy. It's even gone beyond you and me.

(beat)

This is about the future of the Continuum itself.

JANEWAY

Stop speaking in riddles. Tell me what's going on.

Q

I'll do better than that. I'll *show* you.

He moves to one of the windows, and as he throws open the shutters . . .

32 CLOSE ON JANEWAY

Turning to the window.

Q

The Continuum is burning, Kathy.

As Janeway, mesmerized, gazes outside . . .

33 HER P.O.V.—THROUGH THE WINDOW (OPTICAL)

In the distance, fires light up the night sky . . . Cities burn. . . . Forests flame. . . . We hear the far-off SOUNDS of cannons, whizzing bullets, and battle cries. . . . Q looks at her solemnly.

Q

The Q are in the middle of a *Civil War* . . .

OFF Janeway, the reflection of the flames dancing on her face . . .

FADE OUT.

ACT THREE

FADE IN:

34 INTERIOR MANSION

Moments later. Janeway turns from the window to Q.

JANEWAY

Start explaining.

Q

Remember our friend Quinn?

JANEWAY

The Q who committed suicide aboard *Voyager* . . .

Q

Do you recall what I said might happen if he were allowed to take his own life?

JANEWAY

You said it would represent an interruption to the Continuum . . .

(remembering)

. . . that it could have dire consequences . . .

Q

I'd say a Civil War is pretty dire, wouldn't you?

She gestures to the window.

JANEWAY

His death caused the conflict. . . .

Q

It created chaos and upheaval, because even though Quinn was gone, his calls for freedom and individualism continued to echo in the ears of those who believed in his teachings, myself among them. I sounded the trumpet and carried the banner. Naturally, others followed. The forces of the status quo tried to crush us once and for all. But we fought back. And now, there's a cosmic struggle for supremacy. Now, the battle is spreading and causing hazardous repercussions throughout the galaxy.

JANEWAY
(realizing)
The supernovas . . .

Q
You might call them "galactic crossfire."

A beat as Janeway tries to digest all this.

Q
It's terrible, isn't it?
(beat)
But it's also a wonderful opportunity.

Suddenly, an (offcamera) cannon blast RATTLES the windows. Janeway reacts.

JANEWAY
I fail to see anything wonderful about a war.

Q
War can be an engine of change. War can transform a society for the better. Your own Civil War brought about an end to slavery and oppression.

A beat as Janeway wraps her mind around this.

JANEWAY
But our Civil War came at a time before mankind had learned to resolve disputes without bloodshed. Surely, the Q have evolved to a point where you can find a nonviolent way to resolve a conflict.

Q
That's where you come in.

JANEWAY
What do I have to do with any of this?

Q

You're going to help me transform the Continuum in the way your Civil War transformed a nation.

JANEWAY

By *mating* with you?

Q

I know. It's brilliant, isn't it?

JANEWAY

I don't see how a *baby* is going to end a war being fought by a race of omnipotent beings.

Q

It's simple. It will create a new breed of Q that combines my omnipotence and infinite intellect with the best that humanity has to offer.

JANEWAY

(incredulous)

You believe human DNA is going to restore peace?

Q

Precisely. What the Continuum needs right now is an infusion of fresh blood . . . a new sensibility . . . a new leader . . .

(beat)

. . . a *Messiah.*

A beat. Janeway reacts to the sounds of (offcamera) SHOUTS and GUNFIRE. Q advances.

Q

Think of it, Kathy. Our child will be like a precious stone tossed into a cosmic lake . . . sending endless ripples of human conscience and compassion to wash up on every distant shore of the galaxy. . . .

(beat)

What greater contribution could a being of your limited power ever hope to make? What's more important to humanity than peace?

(beat)

I'm offering you the opportunity to be the *mother* of peace. . . .

Janeway is rendered momentarily speechless. Suddenly, a window SMASHES, followed by a HAIL of bullets.

Q

Kathy, get down!

Acting quickly to save her from the gunfire, Q tackles Janeway to the floor. Their faces are very close. Bullets WHIZ overhead.

Q

What's it going to be?

But before she can answer, Q suddenly winces, cries out, falls forward . . .

JANEWAY

Q!

He rolls off of her onto his side. She looks at the hand that was gripping his shoulder. It's covered in crimson.

JANEWAY

You're bleeding. . . .

As Q's eyes, maybe for the first time ever, fill with genuine fear . . .

35 EXTERIOR SPACE—*VOYAGER* (OPTICAL)

Adrift in the void . . .

36 INTERIOR BRIDGE

It's smoky, dark, consoles SPARK, as Chakotay regains consciousness. He picks himself up off the deck and staggers to his feet.

CHAKOTAY

Report.

Tuvok is pulling himself up to his console.

TUVOK

Shield strength is at twenty percent. Hull damage to Decks Nine through Fourteen. Minor injuries reported on all decks.

PARIS

Warp drive is off-line.

Kim is at his monitor now too.

KIM

Sir, according to these readings, the shock waves have knocked us sixteen billion kilometers from our previous position.

Chakotay suddenly spots the Q female struggling to her feet. She's bruised and dazed. He moves to her.

CHAKOTAY

I want to know what's going on here.

She starts to walk away from him, but he grabs her shoulder, turns her back around.

CHAKOTAY

Where's Captain Janeway?

She snaps her fingers . . . but nothing happens. She sighs.

Q FEMALE

Let me go before I hurl this ship and everyone on it into the Therinian Ice Age.

A beat as Chakotay eyes her, calls her bluff.

CHAKOTAY

I don't think you can.

Q FEMALE

Don't be ridiculous. . . .

CHAKOTAY

I don't know how or why, but something's affected your powers. Otherwise you wouldn't still be here. And you wouldn't have a bruise on your forehead.

(beat)

Now start talking before I hurl *you* into the brig.

OFF her defeated expression . . .

TIME CUT TO:

37 INTERIOR BRIEFING ROOM

Chakotay, Tuvok, and the Q female. Midscene.

CHAKOTAY

. . . and it's the war in the Continuum that's causing the supernovas?

She nods.

TUVOK

May we presume that this conflict is also responsible for the weakening of your powers and your inability to return to the Continuum?

Q FEMALE

The Vulcan talent for stating the obvious never ceases to amaze me.

CHAKOTAY

How were Q and Captain Janeway able to reenter the Continuum when you weren't?

Q FEMALE

I tried to return.

She gestures to the bruise on her head.

Q FEMALE

But I was wounded in the process.

Chakotay and Tuvok exchange a glance.

Q FEMALE

Don't try to understand it. It's far beyond your limited capacity to comprehend.

(beat)

What's important is that I'm stuck here with you mortals while Q is probably in the process of irreparably harming the Continuum with that . . . *woman.*

She shakes her head and says to no one in particular:

Q FEMALE
Tossed aside for someone five billion years younger.
(beat)
If it weren't so laughable, I'd cry.

CHAKOTAY
Look, we want our captain back, and you'd obviously like to get home. Why don't we help each other?

Q FEMALE
How could *you* possibly help me?

CHAKOTAY
There's got to be some way to get to the Continuum besides . . . snapping your fingers.

The Q female considers.

Q FEMALE
Well . . . there is *one* possibility. . . .

She glances at her surroundings.

Q FEMALE
. . . but somehow I don't think this rickety barge or your half-witted crew is up to the challenge.

TUVOK
May I remind you, madame, that this "rickety barge" and its "half-witted" crew are your only hope at the moment.

OFF the Q female.

38 INTERIOR MANSION—NIGHT

The siege has escalated. The house is being almost continuously rattled by CANNON FIRE and GUNSHOTS. Q and Janeway have taken cover behind an upended sofa. She's bandaging his wound.

Q
Ow! That hurts. . . .

JANEWAY

Sit still.

She continues working, trying to wrap her mind around what's happening.

JANEWAY

I never thought a Q could be injured. . . .

Q

Like I said, this is merely your *perception* of what's happening. I assure you those aren't cannon balls or lead charges being fired at us.

JANEWAY

So they're some sort of . . . Q weapons. . . .

Q

You'd be surprised what kind of innovative munitions can be created by one immortal being who's set his mind to killing another.

As she finishes bandaging him, an (offcamera) SHOUT is heard above the din . . .

SOUTHERN Q VOICE

Hold your fire, hold your fire. . . .

As Janeway and Q react, the noise dies down. . . .

SOUTHERN Q VOICE

You're surrounded, Q. Surrender now, and we'll be merciful. . . .

JANEWAY

Call a truce. Talk to them. Maybe you can resolve this peacefully. . . .

But he springs to his feet, pulls his pistol from its holster and goes to the window.

Q

I'll never surrender! You know that. . . .

He begins FIRING out the window, and within moments, bullets from outside are once again tearing into the walls. He grabs a rifle that's leaning in the corner, tosses it to Janeway.

Q

Take the other window. . . .

JANEWAY

This is your fight, Q. Not mine.

The wood SPLINTERS on the wall just above her head.

Q

If that's how you feel about it. But if their weapons can make me bleed, what do you think they'll do to you?

Before she can answer, there's a huge EXPLOSION of cannon fire. The whole house shakes. Plaster rains down from the ceiling. Q falls, a kerosene lamp tips over.

JANEWAY

Q!

As a spark from the lamp IGNITES the curtains, Janeway crawls toward Q on her hands and knees. He's barely conscious. She helps the groggy Q to his feet, throws his arm over her shoulder, and begins to pull him toward the door. As thick smoke rapidly fills the room . . .

FADE OUT.

ACT FOUR

FADE IN:

39 OMITTED

40 EXTERIOR CLEARING—NIGHT

A ravaged encampment. Exhausted, despondent Q SOLDIERS in tattered blue uniforms sit by the campfires. Some are on crutches, one or two may be missing limbs, others have wounds which are being tended by their comrades. CAMERA FINDS Janeway with Q's head in her lap. They're lit by the glow of a fire. He sleeps while she cools his feverish brow with a damp cloth. After a moment, his eyes flutter open, he squints. . . .

Q

Where . . . are we?

JANEWAY

One of your faction's encampments.

Q

How . . . ?

JANEWAY

I pulled you out of the mansion and managed to hide you from the enemy patrols. Then I spotted some of your people retreating from the battle. . . .

She takes a look around.

JANEWAY

From the look of them, I'd say you're not on the winning side.

He manages to sit up.

Q

You saved my life.

She lets this sink in for a moment.

JANEWAY

And now it's time to end all this.

Q starts to sit up.

Q

I knew you'd come around. . . .

JANEWAY

I've been thinking about what you said . . . that creating a new Q could bring an era of peace. . . .

Q

(heartened)

My wild, sweet Kathy . . . I promise you won't regret it.

JANEWAY

Oh, you're not going to have a child with *me.* You're going to mate with that charming lady friend of yours who appeared on my ship.

Q

Mate with another Q? Ridiculous.

JANEWAY

(shrugs)

It sounded to me like you and she had a *very* long-term relationship.

Q

Yes, but it was never . . . *physical.* The Q are way beyond *sex.*

(dismissive)

It's never been done.

JANEWAY

Really? Then how exactly did the Q come into existence in the first place?

Q

The Q didn't *come into* existence. The Q have *always* existed.

(beat)

I can only mate with a species capable of copulation . . . like you.

JANEWAY

But I don't love you, Q.

Q

What does that have to do with it?

JANEWAY

Everything. It's the foundation of a family. I could never have a child with someone I didn't love, much less give it up to the Continuum.

Q

Dearest Kathy, I wouldn't dream of having you give it up. Who would look after it? Who would raise it?

(shrugs)

I'm really not cut out to be a wet nurse. . . .

Janeway eyes Q pointedly.

JANEWAY

So you're not willing to do the hard work.

Q

(shrugs)

I'm an idea man. "Hard work" isn't exactly my forte.

JANEWAY

I'd change specialities, if I were you—because the kind of trouble you're in needs more than a quick fix. You can't just sprinkle a little human DNA into the Continuum and make everything all right.

Q

I can't?

JANEWAY

Those "best qualities of humanity" you talked about aren't a simple matter of genetics.

(beat)

Love . . . conscience . . . compassion . . . they're attributes that humankind has developed over centuries, values that are passed from one generation to the next, taught by parents to their children.

(beat)

Creating a new kind of Q is a noble idea. But it will take more than just impregnating someone and walking away. If you want your offspring to embrace your ideals, you've got to teach them yourself.

Q

That's exactly why I want you here—to nurture and guide the little tyke.

(beat)

Think of the opportunities here in the Continuum. The entire universe would be our child's playground . . . together, the two of you could explore dimensions you've never even imagined.

He gives her a sidelong glance, trying to gauge his impact on her.

Q

'Fess up, now, Kathy. . . . Don't you find that even slightly tempting?

JANEWAY

I'd be lying if I said no. What explorer wouldn't be intrigued by the idea of seeking out whole new dimensions . . . ? But I have other responsibilities—and *I* won't just abandon them.

Q

Ah, yes. The crew of the intrepid starship *Voyager.*

(beat)

Perhaps you'd be interested in sending them home.

She faces him firmly.

JANEWAY

You've tempted me with that prospect before. But frankly, your credibility is more than a little suspect. My crew and I *will* get home. We're committed to that. But we'll do it through hard work and determination.

(beat)

We're not looking for a *quick fix.*

Q is beginning to realize that she isn't going to be swayed.

Q
Even if I wanted to mate with Q, I wouldn't know how.
(beat)
It's totally *unprecedented.*

JANEWAY
I'm sure you'll figure something out. You are omnipotent, after all.

Q
I need time to think about this—

JANEWAY
(angry)
Time's up, Q. You've got to stop this war before it destroys the Continuum.

She tears a strip of white fabric from her ruffled underskirt, holds it up to him.

JANEWAY
Now I'm taking this white flag, and I'm going over to the enemy camp to tell them that you're ready to talk about terms for a cease-fire.

She rises.

Q
Kathy . . . don't be a hero.

JANEWAY
I'm going. So if I were you, I'd start working on a way to set that precedent.

OFF Q, as she EXITS . . .

41 EXTERIOR SPACE—*VOYAGER* (OPTICAL)

At impulse.

CHAKOTAY'S VOICE

First officer's log, stardate 50392.7. While we don't fully understand the astrophysics underlying her plan, we've laid in a course for a point in space where the Q female says we may be able to enter the Continuum and find the captain.

42 INTERIOR BRIDGE

Paris at the conn, Tuvok, Kim, N.D.'s at stations. Chakotay's in the captain's chair, the Q female next to him in the first officer's spot. She calls to Paris . . .

Q FEMALE

You, Helm Boy . . .

Paris turns, gives her a look: "*Excuse* me?"

Q FEMALE

Adjust course to heading two-three-five Mark zero-eight. Increase speed to maximum impulse.

Unamused, Paris looks to Chakotay, who nods his approval. Paris begins entering commands as Kim looks up from his monitor with concern.

KIM

Uh, Commander . . .

CHAKOTAY

What is it, Harry?

KIM

She's put us on a direct course for another star that's about to go supernova.

Chakotay turns to the Q female for an explanation.

Q FEMALE

You did say you wanted to get into the Continuum.

CHAKOTAY

Yes, but in one piece.

Q FEMALE

Try to wrap your minuscule mind around this: these supernovas are actually caused by spatial disruptions within the Continuum—a result of the war. Each time a star implodes, a negative-density false vacuum is created which sucks the surrounding matter *into* the Continuum.

CHAKOTAY

So *Voyager* will be pulled in too?

Q FEMALE

If we time it perfectly.

(matter-of-fact)

Otherwise, the subsequent explosion will blow you all into microfragments.

TUVOK

Commander, I need not remind you that close proximity to a supernova will crush us—whether or not we "time it perfectly."

Q FEMALE

(to Tuvok)

You're so *negative.*

CHAKOTAY

He does have a point.

The Female Q shakes her head derisively.

Q FEMALE

Humanoids . . .

(to conn)

Q to engineering . . .

INTERCUT:

43 INTERIOR ENGINEERING

Where Torres and N.D.'s work at stations. She speaks to com:

TORRES

Go ahead, Q . . .

Q FEMALE

Take warp drive off-line. Then, remodulate the shields to emit a beta-tachyon pulse and prepare to emit a series of focussed antiproton beams into the shield bubble.

CHAKOTAY

(to com)

B'Elanna, does this make any sense to you at all?

Torres works some complex calculations on a console.

TORRES

I'd be lying if I said I understood it completely . . .

Something on the monitor catches her eye. . . .

TORRES

. . . but if she's thinking what I *think* she's thinking, we'll increase power to the shields . . .

(amazed)

. . . by a factor of *ten.*

The Q female shoots Chakotay a look: satisfied?

TORRES

Of course, that's assuming the shield bubble doesn't ignite and burn us all to a crisp.

Paris turns from the conn to Chakotay. . . .

PARIS

We'll be reaching the imploding star in thirteen seconds. I still have time to change course. . . .

Crunch time. Chakotay makes a decision:

CHAKOTAY

Maintain your course. B'Elanna, take warp drive off-line, remodulate the shields, and get ready to emit the antiprotons.

44 EXTERIOR SPACE—*VOYAGER* (OPTICAL)

As it approaches a superheated star on the verge of imploding . . .

45 INTERIOR BRIDGE (INTERACTIVE LIGHT)

As everyone tenses, the light from the (off camera) star brightening their faces . . .

PARIS

Entering the star's corona in three seconds . . .

The Q female nods to Chakotay, who speaks to com . . .

CHAKOTAY

Antiprotons *now*, B'Elanna.

TORRES (COM VOICE)

Acknowledged . . .

46 CLOSE ON CHAKOTAY

As he squints from the intense WHITE LIGHT of the (offcamera) viewscreen . . .

47 EXTERIOR SPACE—*VOYAGER* (OPTICAL)

As it flies directly INTO the now-huge star, which IMPLODES! *Voyager* DISAPPEARS completely, and as the subsequent supernova explosion WHITES OUT the screen . . .

MATCH CUT TO:

48 A WHITE TENT FLAP

As it's pulled open to REVEAL Janeway, held at the arm by a grey-uniformed Q military AIDE. From offcamera comes a honeyed southern drawl:

MALE VOICE

Ah, Captain Janeway, I presume. . . .

49 NEW ANGLE—INTERIOR TENT

Lit by a kerosene lamp. The source of the voice is a gallant man in a Confederate officer's uniform. Call him Q COLONEL. Seated behind a portable writing table, he puts down the quill pen with which he's been scratching on a piece of parchment and rises. He gestures to a chair across from him.

Q COLONEL

. . . I'm sorry to have kept you waiting, madame. Please, sit down.

(to the aide)

. . . you're dismissed.

The Q aide salutes and EXITS. The Q colonel sits, regards Janeway. In the light now, the toll of her ordeal is more apparent: torn dress, dirty face, disarrayed hair. In spite of it, she maintains her dignity. His manner is correspondingly genteel.

Q COLONEL

I understand you walked into our camp alone and unarmed.

JANEWAY

That's right.

Q COLONEL

The Continuum is a dangerous place for all of us right now, not to mention a solitary human female.

(a nod)

I admire your bravery.

Janeway gets right to the point.

JANEWAY

I've come with an offer of truce from Q.

Q COLONEL

I'm afraid the time for diplomacy has passed, madame. If we don't end the war quickly, the damage to subspace will be irreversible.

JANEWAY

Then you agree the fighting has to stop.

Q COLONEL

Most certainly. That's why we intend to bring the war to a conclusion by the most expedient means possible.

JANEWAY

I'm relieved to hear you say that. May I ask how?

Q COLONEL

It's quite simple, really. Since Q is the ringleader of this so-called freedom faction, we shall have to execute him.

Janeway reacts with shock.

JANEWAY

With all due respect, sir, there are no chapters in the history of my own people more tragic than wars which set neighbor against neighbor. Q has an idea for a nonviolent way to bring this conflict to an end. I urge you to listen to what he has to say.

Q COLONEL

We are already resolved, madame. Now I'd be greatly in your debt if you'd tell me where we can find him.

JANEWAY

I won't do that.

Q COLONEL

I thought not.

As Janeway reacts. . . .

Q N.D. (offcamera)

Excuse, me sir . . .

50 NEW ANGLE TO REVEAL

The badly injured Q being brought in by the aide and another Q N.D. Confederate SOLDIER.

Q COLONEL

Fortunately, we won't be needing your assistance.

Janeway looks from Q to the colonel.

JANEWAY

I told you: he's willing to negotiate. Let him go.

Q

She's right. I've had a change of heart. . . .

The Q colonel rises, contemplates Q.

Q COLONEL

Grovel all you want, Q.

(smiles)

I've been waiting for this moment for an *eternity.*

Without taking his eyes off Q, the colonel addresses his aide:

Q COLONEL

Lock them both in the stockade.

The other Q takes Janeway's arm. She's indignant.

JANEWAY

What are you charging me with?

Q COLONEL

Collaborating with the enemy . . .

He turns to her matter-of-factly.

Q COLONEL

. . . which in the Continuum is a crime punishable by death.

OFF Janeway . . .

FADE OUT.

ACT FIVE

FADE IN:

51 EXTERIOR WOODS—CONFEDERATE CAMP—DAY

As Janeway and Q are led by two uniformed Q N.D.'s to a pair of tree-trunks standing close together. Q is still injured, but more alert than he was the last time we saw him. Janeway, never one to give up, tries to reason with her captors:

JANEWAY
You don't have to do this. I told your commander: we can resolve the situation peacefully . . .

But the Q N.D.'s don't answer; instead they begin tying Janeway and Q to the trees. Q turns to Janeway.

Q
If it's any consolation, Kathy, there are those in the Continuum who will remember us as martyrs.

JANEWAY
I'd rather skip that particular honor.

Q
Still . . . you have to admit there is something romantic about going to our deaths *together.*

Janeway just glares at him.

Q COLONEL (offcamera)
Do the prisoners have any last words?

52 NEW ANGLE

As Q and Janeway look up to see the Q colonel standing with a firing squad of six uniformed Q N.D.'s, in formation, rifles at their sides. There's also a Q DRUMMER. Janeway addresses everyone assembled, searching their eyes for anyone who'll listen.

JANEWAY
I won't plead for my own life. From your perspective, I know it seems insignificant.

(continuing)
What is *not* insignificant is the fact that the Q, as an omnipotent race, have the opportunity to be a positive force . . . to set a higher standard for other beings in the galaxy.
(beat)
I implore you all: don't go through with this. Don't allow yourselves to continue using violence to resolve your differences.

But her words go unanswered. The Q colonel turns to Q.

Q COLONEL
Q, do you have anything to add?

Puffing himself up, Q orates with all the dignity he can muster:

Q
Today, I sacrifice my existence for the principles of freedom and individuality that I have fought so long for. But *this* woman . . .

He turns to Janeway.

Q
(continuing)
. . . is *innocent.* What's more, she saved my life and has tried to save *us* from each other.
(with passion)
Kill *me* if you must, but let *her* go.

Visibly moved, Janeway looks at Q. The Q colonel, unfortunately, is not impressed.

Q COLONEL
That was a very touching speech, Q. But as usual, your rhetoric fails to compensate for your irresponsibility.

He nods to the drummer, who begins an ominous drumroll.

Q COLONEL
Ready!

The firing squad raises their rifles.

Q COLONEL

Aim!

As they obey . . .

53 CLOSE ON JANEWAY AND Q

As he turns to her, genuine regret in his eyes.

Q

I'm sorry.

JANEWAY
(nods)

I know . . .

They hold each other's gaze, bracing for what's coming:

Q COLONEL (offcamera)

FIRE!

SHOTS ring out! Q closes his eyes, slumps.

Q

I'm dying!

But Janeway is strangely unharmed. The (offcamera) GUNFIRE continues.

JANEWAY

Q!

Surprised, he opens one eye, looks at her.

Q

What?

JANEWAY

They're not firing at us.

Q

They're not?

As he follows her gaze . . .

54 NEW ANGLE—THEIR P.O.V. TO REVEAL
The firing squad, now engaged in a shoot-out with uniformed Union soldiers.

55 CLOSER TO REVEAL

That among the rifle-toting bluecoats are none other than *Kim, Paris, Tuvok,* and *Chakotay,* who fires off a couple of quick rounds, then ducks behind a tree. Also with them is the Q female, dressed in a 19th-century gown. Chakotay shouts to Kim . . .

CHAKOTAY
Harry, get to the captain!

Kim jogs off; the Q female follows. Tuvok, Paris, and Chakotay continue to engage the greycoats. . . .

55A–55B OMITTED

55C Q COLONEL

Spots Kim racing through the trees. He tries to pick him off with a couple of pistol shots. But . . .

55D TUVOK

Lays down covering fire, forcing the Q colonel to retreat . . .

56 NEW ANGLE

As Kim and the Q female arrive and begin untying Q and the captain. The sound of (offcamera) GUNPLAY continues.

KIM
Captain, are you all right?

JANEWAY
I'm fine.

Q
(to Q female)
Darling, I knew you'd come for me.

But she just folds her arms and glares at him.

Q

Aren't you going to untie me?

Q FEMALE

How do I know you won't run off with the next bipedal female that catches your eye?

Q

It just so happens I have a proposal that should reassure you of my devotion.

56A NEW ANGLE ON Q COLONEL

Firing at the bluecoats from a new position. Suddenly, a gun barrel ENTERS FRAME pointed at his head.

PARIS (offcamera)

Put down the gun. . . .

56B WIDEN TO REVEAL PARIS

The Q colonel has no choice but to let his pistol drop to the ground. . . .

56C RESUME

The group assembled by the execution site as Q finishes his pitch:

Q

. . . think of it, Q. We'd be visionaries, innovators, the *parents* of *peace*. . . .

Q FEMALE

(considers)

That does have a nice ring to it.

56D NEW ANGLE

Paris approaches with the Q colonel, whose hands are held high, as Kim unties Q.

PARIS

What should I do with him, Captain?

But the Q female, having made a decision, steps up to the Q colonel.

Q FEMALE
Q and I have a plan for ending the war. Tell your troops to hold their fire.

JANEWAY
Do as she says, and I'll call my people off.

The Q colonel hesitates. But the Q female issues a stern warning.

Q FEMALE
They may only be humanoids, but remember: they're using *our* weapons.

Realizing he's beaten, he calls out.

Q COLONEL
Cease fire! Cease fire!

As his soldiers begin to comply one by one, Janeway turns to Paris and Kim.

JANEWAY
Tell our people to stop shooting.

Kim and Paris jog off toward the others, shouting:

PARIS/KIM
Hold your fire! Put down your weapons!

Chakotay stops shooting, gestures to his men to do the same. Q turns to the Q female.

Q
So, darling, have you given any thought as to how we might accomplish this historic act of procreation?

Q FEMALE
I've thought of nothing else since you suggested it.

She whispers in his ear . . .

Q

Uh huh . . . uh huh . . . You will? *Really?* Oh . . .

(turned on)

. . . *OH* . . .

She steps back.

Q FEMALE

So what do you think?

Q

I love it when you talk dirty.

Janeway glances uncomfortably at the others.

JANEWAY

Uh, why don't we give you two some privacy. . . .

Q

What's the matter, Kathy? Don't you like to watch?

Before Janeway can respond . . .

57–58 OMITTED

59 NEW ANGLE (OPTICAL)

As Q turns to the Q female. With some trepidation, he extends his hand. She puts out her hand. Ever so lightly, *they touch fingertips,* producing a small SPARKLE. Then, they let their hands drop to their sides.

59A WIDE ANGLE

As the Q soldiers turn to one another in amazement—they've never seen anything like it.

59B RESUME

As the Q female and Q moon at one another.

Q

I was good, wasn't I?

Q FEMALE

Very good.

JANEWAY
(incredulous)
That was it?

Q
You had your chance. Don't go crying about it now.

He snaps his FINGERS. . . .

60 INTERIOR BRIDGE (OPTICAL)

. . . and POOF: Janeway, Chakotay, Tuvok, Paris, and Kim APPEAR, once again dressed in their Starfleet uniforms. After a split second to get their bearings, they immediately move to stations.

JANEWAY
Lieutenant Paris, what's our position?

PARIS
We're back on our original course.

Tuvok reads off a monitor.

TUVOK
All crew present and accounted for.

JANEWAY
Ensign Kim, any sign of supernovas?

KIM
(working)
No, ma'am. Nothing but calm space ahead.
(looking up)
Looks like the war's over.

JANEWAY
(smiles)
Mister Chakotay, run a series of standard diagnostics.
If everything checks out, take us to warp six.

CHAKOTAY
Aye, Captain . . .

JANEWAY
I'll be in my ready room.

As she heads for the door . . .

61 INTERIOR READY ROOM (CONTINUOUS)

As Janeway ENTERS, pulls up short.

JANEWAY

Q.

62 NEW ANGLE TO REVEAL Q (OPTICAL)

Seated on the sofa, bouncing a BABY on his knee. The child is dressed in a tiny Starfleet uniform. Like father like son. Q addresses Janeway without taking his eyes off the child.

Q

He's got my cheekbones, don't you think?

JANEWAY

He's adorable.

She looks from baby to father.

JANEWAY

I'd say fatherhood agrees with you.

Q

I'll admit, I look at the universe in an entirely different way now. I mean, I can't just go around causing temporal anomalies or subspace inversions anymore without considering what kind of impact it'll have on my son.

JANEWAY

(impressed)

I'm glad to hear you intend to set a good example.

Q

By the way, did I mention how smart he is? I've already taught him how to knock small planets out of orbit.

JANEWAY

I thought you were going to teach him about love and conscience.

Q

That's why we want Aunty Kathy to be his godmother.

(to the baby)

Don't we?

Janeway's a bit taken aback.

JANEWAY

I'm . . . honored.

Q

Just wait till we ask you to baby-sit.

(proud papa)

You can't leave the little guy alone for a nanosecond.

Q rises.

Q

Well, we've got to be going now. The old "ball and chain" really hates it when we're late.

He takes one of the baby's little hands and waves it at Janeway.

Q

Say "bye-bye" . . .

As father and son DISAPPEAR, OFF Janeway . . .

FADE OUT.

STAR TREK: THE NEXT GENERATION

All Good Things . . .

#40277-747

Written by
Ronald D. Moore & Brannon Braga

Directed by
Rick Kolbe

STAR TREK: THE NEXT GENERATION

All Good Things . . .

CAST

PICARD
RIKER
DATA
BEVERLY
TROI
WORF
GEORDI

COMPUTER VOICE

TASHA
O'BRIEN
Q
OGAWA, Nurse Alyssa
NAKAMURA, Admiral
JESSEL
CHILTON, Ensign Nell
TOMALAK
ANDRONA
GAINES, Lieutenant
ENSIGN Garvin
COM VOICE

Non-Speaking

N.D. SUPERNUMERARIES
CROWD MEMBERS
OGAWA'S N.D. HUSBAND

Non-Speaking

N.D. HUMANS
WORKMAN

STAR TREK: THE NEXT GENERATION

All Good Things . . .

SETS

INTERIORS

U.S.S. ENTERPRISE (PRESENT)
BRIDGE
CORRIDOR
TROI'S QUARTERS
SICKBAY
BEVERLY'S OFFICE
OBSERVATION LOUNGE
READY ROOM
ENGINEERING
RIKER'S QUARTERS

U.S.S. ENTERPRISE (PAST)
BRIDGE
OBSERVATION LOUNGE
ENGINEERING

U.S.S. ENTERPRISE (FUTURE)
BRIDGE
TEN-FORWARD
CORRIDOR
GUEST QUARTERS

MEDICAL SHIP (FUTURE)
BEVERLY'S READY ROOM
BRIDGE
TURBOLIFT

SHUTTLECRAFT (PAST)

SHUTTLEBAY (PAST)

DATA'S LIBRARY (FUTURE)

COURTROOM

EXTERIORS

U.S.S. ENTERPRISE

VINEYARD (FUTURE)
CAMBRIDGE (FUTURE)
MEDICAL SHIP (FUTURE)
TWO KLINGON CRUISERS (FUTURE)

PRIMORDIAL EARTH

STAR TREK: THE NEXT GENERATION

All Good Things . . .

PRONUNCIATION GUIDE

ACETYLCHOLINE	uh-seetl-KO-leen
CATARIA	kuh-TAR-ee-uh
DEVRON	DEV-ron
H'ATORIA	ha-TORE-ee-uh
IRUMODIC	ear-uh-MAHD-ik
LUCASIAN	loo-KAY-zhun
PERIDAXON	pair-uh-DAX-on
MEMP'HA	MEM-pah
RIGEL	RYE-jell
TERRELLIAN	ter-ELL-ee-'n
TERIX	TAIR-ix
TOMOGRAPHIC	toe-moe-GRAF-ik
TRIPAMINE	TRIP-uh-meen

STAR TREK: THE NEXT GENERATION

All Good Things . . .

TEASER

FADE IN:

1 INTERIOR CORRIDOR—PRESENT

WORF and TROI ENTER from the holodeck doors. They are dressed in casual clothing—it's late, and the mood is light and intimate. Troi is smiling, and even Worf is happy—it's clear they had a great time, wherever they were.

TROI
That was an incredible program.

WORF
I am glad you approve. I have always found the Black Sea at Night to be a most . . . stimulating experience.

Troi rolls her eyes at him as they begin to walk down the corridor.

TROI
Worf, we were strolling barefoot along the beach while balalaika music played in the air . . . ocean breeze washing over us . . . stars in the sky . . . a full moon rising . . . and the most you can say is "stimulating"?

WORF
(groping)
It was . . . *very* stimulating.

Troi smiles as they turn a corner . . .

CUT TO:

2 ANOTHER CORRIDOR—PRESENT

Worf and Troi walking towards her quarters.

TROI

The truth is, I don't spend nearly enough time on the holodeck.

(continuing)

I should take my own advice and use it to relax.

(beat)

Next time, *I'll* choose the program. If you like the Black Sea, you're going to love Lake Cataria on Betazed.

Worf frowns a little. They stop outside Troi's quarters. An awkward moment.

WORF

Deanna . . . perhaps before there is a "next time" we should discuss . . . Commander Riker.

TROI

(playful)

Why, is he coming along?

WORF

(awkward)

No . . . but I do not wish to . . . I mean, it would be unfortunate if he . . . If you and I are going to continue . . . I do not want to hurt his feelings. . . .

TROI

Worf . . . I think it's all right to concentrate on *our* feelings . . . yours . . . and mine.

She smiles affectionately at him, and Worf returns the smile. We can see that there is a genuine attraction between the two of them.

There is a beat as they look into each other's eyes. . . . The sexual tension rises a notch. . . . Will they or won't they? Finally, Worf takes the plunge—leans over to kiss her. . . . She lifts her lips to his, but just before they can kiss, the nearby turbolift doors OPEN and PICARD bursts out, wearing only his bathrobe—

PICARD

Counselor!

Worf and Troi look at him, startled. Picard rushes to them. He's wild-eyed; clearly something is wrong.

PICARD
(urgent)
What's today's date? The *date?*

WORF
Stardate 47988.

Picard thinks about this for a moment—trying to sort through something in his mind.

PICARD
(to himself)
47988 . . .

TROI
Captain, what's wrong?

Picard looks at her.

PICARD
I'm not sure. . . . I don't know how . . . or why, but . . .
(beat)
I'm moving back and forth through time.

OFF their reactions . . .

FADE OUT.

ACT ONE

FADE IN:

INTERIOR TROI'S QUARTERS—PRESENT

A short time later. Troi is handing Picard a cup of tea. Picard is pacing, trying to make sense of what's happening to him. Midconversation.

PICARD
It was as though I had physically left the ship and gone to another time and place. . . . I was in the past. . . .

TROI
Can you describe where you were . . . what it looked like?

PICARD
It's all slipping away so fast . . . like waking up from a nightmare. . . .

Picard concentrates.

PICARD
(continuing)
It was years ago . . . before I took command of the *Enterprise.* I was talking with someone . . . I don't remember who . . .
(beat, remembering)
But then—everything changed. I wasn't in the past any longer. . . . I was an *old* man, in the future. . . . I was doing something outside. . . . What was it?

He holds out a hand, rubs his fingers together as though remembering doing something with his hands . . . but what?

PICARD
I'm sorry. It's gone. I can't remember. . . .

TROI
It's all right. Have you considered the possibility that this was just a dream?

PICARD

It was more than a dream . . . the smells and the sounds . . . the way things felt to the touch. . . . It was all so real. . . .

Troi considers.

TROI

How long did you stay in each of these time periods? Did it seem like minutes . . . hours?

PICARD

I'm not sure.

(struggling to recall)

At first . . . there was a moment of confusion, of disorientation. I wasn't sure where I was. But that passed . . . and then I felt perfectly natural . . . as though I belonged in that time. But I can't remember how long I stayed there.

(frustrated)

I know this doesn't make much sense. . . . It's a feeling more than a distinct memory.

He looks down at his teacup—it's empty. Troi notices and picks up the teapot to pour him another cup.

TROI

Maybe we can identify specific symbols. Can you remember anything you saw, an object, a building perhaps—

As Troi talks, Picard extends his arm with his teacup, offering it to her. As he extends his arm, the SCENE SUDDENLY CHANGES TO:

3A ANGLE—CLOSE ON A VINE

4 EXTERIOR VINEYARD—FUTURE—DAY

We are now twenty-five years in the future. Picard is an OLD MAN, wearing civilian clothes and a hat to protect himself from the sun. He has a beard and longer hair. (But he should not look as old as he did at the end of ''The Inner Light.'' He is kneeling in a row of grape vines at his home in France (as seen in ''Family'').

He is reaching out for a vine with the same hand and in the same manner that we just saw him hold out his cup in Troi's quarters. As his hand closes around the vine, he hesitates. He seems disoriented, confused for a moment, just as he described to Troi. He looks around the vineyard in puzzlement. But the moment passes, and he accepts this time as the present.

He concentrates on examining the vine in his hand. He takes a pruning shear and snips off a few stray branches. There are gardening tools nearby. He works quietly for a moment. . . . Then we hear a voice shout across the vineyard.

GEORDI'S VOICE
(calls out)
Captain Picard to the bridge!

Picard reacts, a little surprised. He looks toward the sound of the voice, shielding his eyes from the sun. . . .

5 NEW ANGLE

Revealing GEORDI walking toward Picard. He is wearing civilian clothes, and he also has aged twenty-five years. His VISOR is gone and has been replaced by ARTIFICIAL EYES, which have a distinctive electronic look to them. Geordi is smiling broadly.

GEORDI
(with humor)
Sir, I think we have a problem with the warp core, or the phase inducers, or some other damn thing.

Picard stands up with some difficulty. He's old, and his voice and attitude should suggest advanced age and an eccentric, sometimes cantankerous demeanor.

PICARD
Geordi . . .

The two men approach each other and shake hands—these are two old friends who haven't seen each other in a very long time.

GEORDI
Hello, Captain . . . or should I make that ambassador?

PICARD
(snorts)
Hasn't been ambassador for a while either.

GEORDI
How about Mister Picard?

PICARD
How about . . . Jean-Luc?

GEORDI
(smiles)
I don't know if I can get used to that.

They look at each other for a moment, taking in the sight.

PICARD
Good Lord, Geordi. How long has it been?

GEORDI
Oh . . . about nine years.

PICARD
No, no . . . I mean, since you last called me captain? When was the last time we were all together . . . on the *Enterprise?*

GEORDI
Close to twenty-five years.

PICARD
Twenty-five years . . .
(looks him over)
Time's been good to you.

Geordi playfully pats his stomach.

GEORDI
It's been a little too good to me in some places.

He glances around.

GEORDI
(continuing)
Can I give you a hand?

PICARD
Oh . . . I'm just tying some vines.

Geordi kneels down and examines a vine.

GEORDI

Looks like you've got leaf miners. Might want to use a bacillus spray.

(off his look)

My wife is quite a gardener. I've picked up a little bit of it.

Geordi takes a tie and begins carefully tying the vines. Picard bends down with a little difficulty . . . and the two of them start to work on the vines.

PICARD

How is Leah?

GEORDI

Busy as ever. She's just been made director of the Daystrom Institute.

PICARD

And the little ones . . . Brett and Alandra? And . . .

GEORDI

And Sydney. Not so little anymore. Brett's applying to Starfleet Academy next year.

Picard shakes his head at the rapid passage of time.

PICARD

So what brings you here?

GEORDI

Oh . . . I just thought I'd drop by. I'd been thinking about the old days on the *Enterprise* . . . and I was in the neighborhood. . . .

Picard gives him a sharp look. The Picard of the future is a bit disgruntled, a cranky old man.

PICARD

Don't give me that. You don't make the trip from Rigel III to Earth just to . . . drop by.

Geordi knows he can't fool this man. The mood becomes a little more somber.

GEORDI

No.

PICARD

So. You've heard.

GEORDI

Well . . . Leah has a few friends at Starfleet medical . . . and word gets around.

Picard snorts and turns his attention to the vines. Grumpily—

PICARD

I'm not an invalid, you know. Irumodic Syndrome can take years to run its course.

GEORDI

I know. But when I heard I just . . . wanted to come by all the same.

Picard looks at him for a moment, and then some of the crusty exterior falls away . . . and we can tell that despite his protestations to the contrary, Picard is warmed by the moment. Picard finally breaks the moment.

PICARD

(softer)

Well . . . as long as you're here, you can help me carry in some of these tools.

Picard awkwardly and painfully gets to his feet.

PICARD

(continuing)

My cooking may not be up to Leah's standards, but I can still make a decent cup of tea.

Picard and Geordi both grab an armful of equipment and they start walking.

PICARD

(continuing)

By the way, I read your last novel. Not bad. I thought the protagonist was written a bit flamboyantly, but that's just my—

Picard's eyes trail off as he sees something offcamera . . .

6 PICARD'S P.O.V.

Standing in the vineyards are THREE scraggly looking HUMANS. They point at Picard, shouting and jeering.

7 RESUME PICARD

He reacts to this strange sight in the vineyard.

8 NEW ANGLE—INCLUDING GEORDI

Geordi follows Picard's look, but sees nothing. Picard is mystified—what's going on? We MOVE IN on Picard.

GEORDI

Captain, are you all right? Captain?

TASHA'S VOICE

Captain?

Picard turns at the sound of Tasha's voice, and as he does, the SCENE CHANGES TO:

9 INTERIOR SHUTTLECRAFT—PAST

Picard is sitting in the copilot's seat, wearing his OLD-STYLE UNIFORM as seen in the first season. TASHA YAR is sitting next to him. She looks exactly as she did in the series pilot.

TASHA'S VOICE

Are you all right, sir?

He looks disoriented and confused again. He is still not fully aware of what's happening to him. Then the moment passes.

TASHA

Sir . . .?

PICARD

I'm sorry, Lieutenant. My mind seems to have wandered for a moment. . . .

(beat)

What were you saying?

Tasha has that no-nonsense, military prickliness. These are two people who have just met a short time ago.

TASHA

I was asking if you'd ever been aboard a *Galaxy*-class starship before, sir.

Picard tries to focus his mind on the here and now, putting aside his strange feeling of disorientation for a moment.

PICARD

No. I'm, of course, very familiar with the blueprints and specifications . . . but this will be my first time aboard.

TASHA

Well then, sir, if I may be so bold—you're in for a treat. The *Enterprise* is quite a ship.

PICARD

I'm sure she is.

Picard gives her that strange stare again. For some reason, something about her troubles him slightly.

TASHA

Have I done something wrong, sir?

PICARD

No. You just seem very . . . familiar.

She nods, uncertain exactly what he's talking about. The console BEEPS. Tasha hits a control and we hear a com voice—

COM VOICE

Enterprise to *Shuttlecraft Galileo.* You are cleared for arrival in shuttlebay two.

TASHA

Acknowledged, *Enterprise.*

Tasha works the controls a moment, then looks out the window.

TASHA
(continuing)

There she is . . .

Picard looks out the window. . . .

10 NEW ANGLE (OPTICAL)

Through the windows of the shuttle we can see the *ENTERPRISE* sitting in its dock above Earth.

11 CLOSE ON PICARD'S FACE

As soon as Picard sees the ship, his feeling of disorientation is forgotten, and he can't help smiling at the beautiful sight. PULL BACK TO REVEAL WE ARE NOW IN:

12 INTERIOR TROI'S QUARTERS—PRESENT

Picard still smiling, staring, holding a cup of tea halfway to his mouth. *(NOTE: We will no longer be using the convention of Picard returning to the exact moment he left.)* Troi looks at him oddly.

TROI

Captain?

Picard glances around, momentarily disoriented.

PICARD

Tasha . . . I was just with Tasha, in the shuttle. . . .

Picard slumps back into a chair. He puts his hands to his head, clearly distraught. Troi can see that there's something very wrong with the captain. She hits a panel.

TROI

Troi to Doctor Crusher. Something's wrong with the captain. We're on our way to sickbay.

As Troi moves to the captain with concern on her face . . .

FADE OUT.

ACT TWO

FADE IN:

13 INTERIOR SICKBAY—PRESENT

Later. Picard is sitting on a bio-bed, still wearing his bathrobe. BEVERLY is finishing a scan.

Troi is standing with Picard as Beverly approaches with the results of a scan.

BEVERLY

I've finished the neurographic scan. I don't see anything that might cause hallucinations or a psychogenic reaction.

TROI

Is there any indication of temporal displacement?

BEVERLY

No. Usually a temporal shift would leave some kind of tripamine residue in the cerebral cortex. But the scan didn't find any.

(lightly)

Personally, I think you just enjoy waking everyone up in the middle of the night.

Picard smiles a little—grateful for Beverly's effort to lighten the mood.

PICARD

Actually, I just like running around the ship in my bare feet.

Beverly smiles at him. OGAWA walks over, holding a padd. She is visibly *pregnant*—around six months.

OGAWA

The biospectral test results, Doctor.

Beverly looks over the padd.

BEVERLY
(to Picard)
Your blood gas analysis is consistent with someone who's been breathing the ship's air for weeks.
(continuing)
If you'd been somewhere else, there would be some indication of a change in your oxygen isotope ratios.
(to Ogawa)
Thanks, Alyssa.

Ogawa smiles and withdraws. Beverly turns to Troi.

BEVERLY
(continuing)
Deanna . . . would you excuse us?

TROI
Of course.

Troi moves away and EXITS sickbay. Beverly turns back to Picard. She is solemn, troubled.

BEVERLY
Jean-Luc . . . I scanned for any evidence of Irumodic Syndrome, as you suggested. There wasn't any. But I did detect a small structural defect in your parietal lobe.

PICARD
A defect . . . that you've never noticed before?

BEVERLY
It's the kind of thing that would only show up on a level-four neurographic scan.
(beat)
It could leave you susceptible to several neurological disorders . . . including Irumodic Syndrome.

Picard absorbs this news.

BEVERLY
(continuing)
Now, it's possible you could have that defect for the rest of your life without developing a problem . . .
(beat)

. . . but even if you do . . . many people lead perfectly normal lives for a long time after the onset of Irumodic Syndrome.

PICARD
(smiles wryly)
Then why do you look like you've just signed my death sentence?

He's trying to lighten the moment, and she realizes he's picked up on her underlying feelings.

BEVERLY
Sorry.
(beat)
I guess . . . this has caught me off guard.

He takes a breath, squares himself—he's not going to waste concern over something he can't control.

PICARD
Well, let's not worry about it.
(beat)
Something tells me you're going to have to put up with me for a very long time.

BEVERLY
(trying to be light)
It won't be easy, but I'll manage.

They smile at each other in a friendly, intimate way. RIKER ENTERS.

PICARD
(to Riker)
Did Worf find anything?

RIKER
No, sir. His security scans came up negative. They're checking the sensor logs . . . but there's still no indication that you left the ship.

Picard gets up off the bed, thinks for a moment. He seems more sure of himself than he did earlier—the memories are still vague but he's sure that *something* happened.

PICARD
It wasn't a dream . . . something *did* happen.

Worf's COM VOICE interrupts—

WORF (com voice)
Worf to captain.

PICARD
(to com)
Go ahead, Lieutenant.

WORF
Sir—there is an incoming transmission from Admiral Nakamura. It is a priority one message.

Reactions.

PICARD
Beverly?

Beverly nods.

PICARD
(continuing, to com)
Mister Worf, route it through to Doctor Crusher's office.

Picard moves toward the office. . . .

14 INTERIOR BEVERLY'S OFFICE—PRESENT—CONTINUOUS (OPTICAL)

Picard ENTERS, sits down at the desk, and activates the desktop monitor. After a beat, ADMIRAL NAKAMURA appears on the screen.

NAKAMURA
Captain.

PICARD
Admiral.

NAKAMURA
I'm initiating a fleetwide Yellow Alert. Starfleet intelligence has picked up some disturbing reports

from the Romulan Star Empire. It appears that at least thirty warbirds have been pulled from other assignments and are heading for the Neutral Zone.

PICARD

Is there any indication why they would make such a blatantly aggressive move?

Nakamura looks disturbed.

NAKAMURA

Our operatives on Romulus have indicated that there appears to be something happening *in* the Neutral Zone—specifically, in the Devron system. Our own long-range scans have picked up some kind of spatial anomaly in the area, but we can't tell what it is.

PICARD

What are our orders?

NAKAMURA

This is a delicate situation. I'm deploying fifteen starships along our side of the Neutral Zone. I want you to go there as well—see if you can find out what's going on in the Devron system.

PICARD

Am I authorized to enter the Zone?

NAKAMURA

Not yet. Wait and see what the Romulans do. You can conduct long-range scans, send probes if necessary . . . but don't cross the border unless they do.

PICARD

Understood.

Picard turns off the monitor and stands. As he does, the SCENE CHANGES TO:

15 EXTERIOR VINEYARD—FUTURE—DAY

In the same motion, the older Picard rises to his feet—and in doing so, stumbles and nearly falls. Geordi grabs him by the arm, tries to help him up.

GEORDI

Captain . . . what's wrong?

Picard gets to his feet, looks around in confusion. Geordi is very concerned.

PICARD

This isn't my time. I belong somewhere else. . . .

GEORDI

What?

Picard stares at him, realizing he may not be making sense.

PICARD

I mean . . . I . . . I wasn't here a moment ago. . . .

GEORDI

What do you mean? You've been right here with me. . . .

Picard gropes for an answer, tries to concentrate . . . but his mental faculties in this time period have deteriorated. He's much less cogent than the Picard we're used to—it's hard for him to describe the experience.

PICARD

No, no . . . I was somewhere else . . . a long time ago. . . .

(beat)

I was talking to someone . . . *Beverly* . . . Beverly was there. . . .

Geordi's beginning to worry that the old man is starting to lose it.

GEORDI

It's okay, Captain. . . . Everything's going to be all right.

Picard pulls away from Geordi's grasp.

PICARD

(emphatic)

I'm not senile. It did happen. I was here, with you . . . and then I was in another place. . . .

(beat)

It was . . . It was back on the *Enterprise!*

(suddenly unsure)

At least, I think it was. . . . It seemed like sickbay . . . but maybe it was a hospital . . . or . . .

Picard trails off, frustrated. Geordi looks at him.

GEORDI

Captain, I think we should go back to the house . . . call a doctor . . .

PICARD

(louder)

No. I know what you're thinking. It's the Irumodic Syndrome—it's beginning to—to affect the old man's mind. Well, it's not that. And I wasn't daydreaming, either.

GEORDI

All right . . . all right . . . what do you want to do about it?

Picard thinks frantically for a beat, his mind trying to fasten onto a course of action. Finally, he seizes on something.

PICARD

I want to see *Data.*

GEORDI

Data . . . Why?

PICARD

I think he can help. . . .

GEORDI

Help—how?

PICARD

(angry)

I don't know! I don't know, but I want to see him!

Geordi takes a moment, not sure how to handle this situation, but finally agrees.

GEORDI

Okay . . . we'll go see Data. Is he still at Cambridge?

PICARD

Yes . . . yes . . . I think he's . . .

Picard trails off as he sees something offcamera . . .

16 NEW ANGLE

Revealing SIX scraggly HUMANS standing nearby around Picard and Geordi. They are jeering and pointing at Picard, as seen earlier. Picard looks at them in shock.

PICARD

(urgent, to Geordi)

Do you see them?

16A GEORDI'S P.O.V.

No one is there.

16B PICARD AND GEORDI

GEORDI

See . . . who?

PICARD

They're everywhere . . . laughing at me. . . . Why are they laughing?

Geordi doesn't know what to do—it looks like Picard has gone completely crazy.

GEORDI

Come on, Captain . . . let's go see Data.

17 ON PICARD

Who looks at Geordi, then looks back out at the vineyard. When he looks out, the humans are *gone.*

PICARD

Yes . . . Data . . . yes . . .

As they walk off . . .

CUT TO:

18 EXTERIOR CAMBRIDGE UNIVERSITY—FUTURE—DAY (MATTE)

The old school looks much as it always has over the centuries, with a few 24th-century touches.

19 INTERIOR DATA'S LIBRARY—FUTURE—DAY

A spacious and very comfortable room. The walls are lined with books. There is a FIRE roaring in the hearth. And there are about ten CATS wandering about or sleeping. (The mood and feel should remind us of the Sherlock Holmes Drawing Room set.)

Picard and Geordi are seated on a couch. DATA is standing nearby. He has not aged over the years, but there is a prominent streak of gray on one side of his head—it looks unnatural, as if someone has taken a paint brush to his head. He is wearing the 24th-century version of a smoking jacket. Data's struggle to become more human has progressed in the future. And although we will never spell out exactly how far he's come, we will see that he seems far more at ease with himself and others. He uses contractions, has a relatively sophisticated understanding of humanity, and seems to genuinely enjoy life.

PICARD

I know how it sounds . . . but it happened. It was real. I was back on the *Enterprise.*

Data and Geordi exchange a look.

Before they can comment, JESSEL, Data's English housekeeper, ENTERS with a tea service. She's a dour woman in her fifties with a heavy British accent.

JESSEL

(to Picard)

How do you like your tea?

PICARD

Tea? Earl Grey. Hot.

JESSEL

Of course it's hot. What do ya want in it?

PICARD

Nothing . . .

Picard shifts to another topic unexpectedly—another sign that his mind tends to wander occasionally. This will continue to happen throughout the script.

PICARD

This is quite a place you have here, Data. I see they treat professors pretty well at Cambridge. . . .

Picard laughs a little too loudly.

DATA

Holding the Lucasian Chair does have its perquisites. This house originally belonged to Sir Isaac Newton when he held the position. It has become the traditional residence.

Jessel brings tea to Data and Geordi.

JESSEL

(to Geordi, re: Data)

If you're really his friend, you'll get him to take that grey out of his hair. He looks like a bloody skunk.

Jessel moves back to the service, shoos a few cats off the furniture. Data gives Geordi a look.

DATA

(re: Jessel)

She can be trying at times.

(beat, smiles)

But she does make me laugh.

GEORDI

(smiles)

What is it with your hair, anyway?

DATA

I have found that a touch of gray adds an air of . . . distinction.

PICARD

Is this Earl Grey? I'd swear it was breakfast tea.

Data moves back to Picard.

DATA

Captain, when was the last time you saw a physician about your Irumodic Syndrome?

PICARD

A week ago. I was prescribed peridaxon.

(quickly)

And yes, I know it's not a cure. . . . Nothing can stop the deterioration of my . . . my synaptic pathways. . . .

(beat)

You think I'm senile . . . that this is all some . . . delusion.

GEORDI

No one said anything like that.

Data holds Picard's gaze steadily, not shying away from giving him the unvarnished truth.

DATA

In all honesty, Captain, it's a thought that has occurred to me.

(beat)

However, there is nothing to disprove what you are saying, either. So it's possible something *is* happening to you.

Picard looks hopeful! Data starts pacing, a human gesture that Data has obviously acquired.

DATA

(continuing)

The first thing we should do is give you a complete series of neurographic scans. We can use the equipment at the bio-metrics lab here on campus.

(to Jessel)

Jessel, ask Professor Rippert to take over my lecture for tomorrow and possibly for the rest of the week.

Picard is enthusiastic.

PICARD

That's the Data I remember! I knew I could count on you!

In his excitement, Picard spills some of his hot tea onto his lap. He yells out and JUMPS to his feet, and as he does, the SCENE CHANGES TO:

20 INTERIOR SHUTTLEBAY—PAST

Picard is JUMPING out of the shuttlecraft, which is now sitting in the middle of the bay. Picard hesitates for a moment, disoriented at first. A large group of CREW MEMBERS are lined up in several ranks next to the shuttle standing at ease. Visible at the front of the group are Troi, O'BRIEN, and Worf—all are wearing the uniforms and "look" of "Encounter at Farpoint." Tasha steps out behind Picard and calls out in a loud voice:

TASHA
(to all)
Commanding officer . . .
Enterprise . . . arriving.

At this command, an Ensign smartly brings an old-fashioned BOSUN'S WHISTLE to his lips and BLOWS it. At the sound of the whistle, everyone in the bay snaps to attention. Picard stares at the scene for a moment, silently orienting himself to where and when he is. He takes a beat, then moves to a nearby podium, sets the padd, on it and looks up at the crowd. There's a distracted look on his face—he's moving forward with the ceremony, but at the same time his mind is trying to assimilate all that's happened to him so far.

PICARD
(to all)
To Captain Jean-Luc Picard, Stardate 41148 . . .

Picard glances up from the padd. . . .

21 PICARD'S P.O.V.

We can now see three of the scraggly HUMANS standing on the catwalk. They are laughing at Picard.

22 RESUME PICARD

He reacts in surprise. . . .

23 PICARD'S P.O.V.

The figures are *gone.*

24 PICARD

Picard hesitates, jarred by the strange apparition . . . then recovers and continues reading from the padd . . .

PICARD
(reading)
. . . You are hereby requested and required to take command. . . .

Picard glances up again. . . .

25 PICARD'S P.O.V.

There are now *six* scraggly humans standing on the catwalk, laughing and jeering.

26 PICARD

Looks away from the crowd, tries to concentrate on what he's doing. There's an awkward silence. Tasha gives him a slightly puzzled look—what's wrong with him? Picard clears his throat and then continues . . .

PICARD
. . . to take command of the *U.S.S. Enterprise* as of this date. Signed Rear Admiral Norah Satie, Starfleet Command.

He turns off the padd, steps out from behind the podium, and looks at his crew. They stare back at him silently, waiting for his first words for them—the first words from the captain of the *Enterprise.*

27 PICARD'S P.O.V.—THE CATWALK

There are now ten of the humans standing there—all shouting at Picard with menacing looks.

28 PICARD

Reacts.

29 PICARD'S P.O.V.

The humans are *gone.*

30 PICARD

Takes a beat, then makes a decision—

PICARD
(yells)
Red Alert! All hands to battle stations!

There is a shocked and silent moment from the crowd. This is the last thing they expected. Tasha gives him a startled look, but recovers quickly—she barks at the crowd.

TASHA
You heard him—*move!*

The ship goes to RED ALERT. People rush out the shuttlebay doors to their duty stations. OFF the mad scramble to action . . .

FADE OUT.

ACT THREE

FADE IN:

31 OMITTED

32 INTERIOR OBSERVATION LOUNGE—PAST

Picard is staring out the windows as the crew of the past is filing in—Tasha, Worf, Troi. The room appears as it did in the FIRST SEASON, complete with gold ship models on the wall. Camera should FAVOR Tasha, to orient us that we're in the past.

PICARD (voice-over)

Personal log, stardate 41153.7. Recorded under security lockout Omega three-two-seven. I have decided not to inform this crew of my experiences. If it's true that I've traveled to the past, I cannot risk giving them foreknowledge of what's to come.

Picard sits as the others do. They eye him warily—these people don't know Picard and are not comfortable around him or each other.

PICARD

Report.

TASHA

We've completed a full subspace scan of the ship and surrounding space. We detected no unusual readings or anomalies.

WORF

With all due respect, sir . . . it would help if we knew what we were looking for.

PICARD

Noted.

(to Troi)

Counselor, do you sense anything unusual aboard the *Enterprise* . . . an alien presence that doesn't belong here . . . perhaps operating on a level of intelligence far superior to our own?

Troi pauses, thinks.

TROI

No, sir. I'm only aware of the crew . . . and the families aboard the ship.

Picard nods, takes a few step around the table. They watch him carefully.

PICARD

Mister Worf, I want you to initiate a Level Two Security Alert on all decks until further notice.

Worf looks surprised and gives an awkward glance to Tasha. Tasha takes a step forward. She keeps her voice level, but it's clear that Picard's order has rankled her for some reason.

TASHA

Sir, with all due respect . . . *I'm* the security chief of this ship. Unless you're planning to make a change . . .

Picard is taken aback . . . reorients himself, then presses on.

PICARD

No . . . no, of course not. Security Alert Two, Lieutenant.

TASHA

Aye, sir.

O'BRIEN (com voice)

Captain Picard to the bridge, please.

PICARD

(to com)

On my way, Chief.

Everyone EXITS to . . .

33 INTERIOR BRIDGE—PAST—CONTINUOUS.

Picard, Worf, Tasha, and Troi ENTER. Chief O'Brien is standing down in the command area. He hands a padd to Picard. There are N.D. crew members milling about on the bridge, working at opened panels . . . moving portable equipment around, etc. The ship is a mess—clearly, not ready for space travel yet.

O'BRIEN

Sir, Starfleet has just issued an alert. It appears that a number of vessels are moving toward the Neutral Zone between Romulan and Federation space.

TASHA

What kind of vessels?

O'BRIEN

Freighters, transports . . . all civilian. None of them Federation ships.

Picard reads the padd, and as he does, his frown deepens—what he reads rings a bell.

PICARD

(off padd)

It says a large spatial anomaly has appeared in the Neutral Zone . . .

(beat)

In the Devron system.

Worf reacts strongly—this is a younger, more outwardly aggressive Worf than the one we're used to seeing in the seventh season.

WORF

Perhaps it is a Romulan trick—to lure ships into the Neutral Zone as an excuse for a military strike.

O'BRIEN

(to Tasha, Worf)

Starfleet's canceling our mission to Farpoint Station and ordering us to the Neutral Zone as soon as we can leave spacedock.

Picard considers—his mind is racing, trying to figure out what to do next. He finally makes a decision.

PICARD

No . . . no, we'll proceed to Farpoint.

Shocked reactions.

TASHA

Sir?

PICARD

You heard me.

WORF

But Captain—the security of the Federation may be at stake!

Picard calmly looks at him.

PICARD

Man your station, Mister Worf.

Worf returns to the aft science station, bristling.

TROI

Captain, perhaps if we understood your thinking, if you could explain—

PICARD

I don't intend to explain anything . . .

(to all)

. . . to anyone. We will proceed to Farpoint Station, as originally planned.

A quiet, tense moment on the bridge . . . no one moves.

PICARD

(continuing, to O'Brien)

Now, if I'm not mistaken, Chief, we're having some problems with the warp plasma inducers.

O'BRIEN

(surprised)

That's right, sir.

PICARD

I think I know a way to get them back on-line. You're with me.

(to Tasha)

We'll be in main engineering.

Picard and O'Brien EXIT. Once they leave, people go reluctantly back to work. Worf moves closer to Tasha.

WORF

(quiet, to Tasha)

I do not understand. The Romulans may be planning an attack, and he does not seem to care.

(beat)

Are you certain this is the same man who commanded the *Stargazer?*

TASHA

As far as I know.

WORF

What are you going to do?

TASHA

I'm going to do what I'm told . . . prepare to go to Farpoint.

Worf looks frustrated by her response. As Tasha walks across the bridge, she moves past a WORKMAN, who is carrying a plaque toward the bulkhead next to the emergency turbolift. He stops, lifts the ship's DEDICATION PLAQUE, and begins to hang it on its familiar place on the wall. . . .

CUT TO:

34 INTERIOR ENGINEERING—PAST

Picard is in Geordi's office, sitting at a console, O'Brien standing next to him watching as the captain rapidly works the console. Several N.D.'s are working at various opened consoles and panels—they're getting the ship ready to go.

O'Brien is somewhat uncomfortable in the presence of the new captain. Picard finishes working and hands O'Brien a padd.

PICARD

Mister O'Brien, use these specifications to bypass the secondary plasma inducer.

O'Brien takes the padd, concern showing on his face.

O'BRIEN

You have to realize, sir . . . this isn't exactly my area of expertise. The chief engineer should be making these modifications.

PICARD

But the chief engineer isn't on board yet.

(beat)

Mister O'Brien . . . trust me. I know you can do this.

He smiles at O'Brien, whom he knows well and fondly.

PICARD

All those years you spent as a child . . . building model starship engines . . . were well worth it.

O'BRIEN

(surprised)

How'd you know that, sir?

PICARD

From . . . your Starfleet records.

O'Brien is amazed that this captain spent time scrutinizing the records so thoroughly . . . but it makes him feel more comfortable with this aristocratic man.

O'BRIEN

Yes, sir. I'll get right to the modifications.

O'Brien takes the padd and heads across the room. Picard continues to work in Geordi's office. *Stay on Picard* as O'Brien moves offcamera and begins giving orders to an offscreen ensign.

O'BRIEN'S VOICE

Fletcher—tell Munoz and Lee to get up here right away. We have to realign the entire power grid. We're all going to be burning the midnight oil on this one.

DATA'S VOICE

That would be inadvisable.

At the sound of Data's voice, Picard turns and looks—and we now reveal *Data,* who has just entered the room. Through the following conversation, Picard watches with a smile as he sees O'Brien encounter Data for the first time.

Data looks and acts as he did in the pilot. This is a less sophisticated, more naive Data than the one we're used to—he's the Data we knew seven years ago: more innocent and less comfortable with everyday human interactions.

O'BRIEN

Excuse me?

DATA

If you attempt to ignite a petroleum product on this ship at zero-hundred hours—it will activate the fire-suppression system, which will seal off this entire compartment.

O'Brien looks at him blankly.

O'BRIEN

Sir . . . that was just an expression.

Data reacts.

DATA

An expression of what?

O'BRIEN

(groping)

A figure of speech . . . I was trying to tell him that . . . we were going to be working late. . . .

DATA

Ah. Then "to burn the midnight oil" implies late work?

O'BRIEN

That's right.

DATA

I am curious. What is the etymology of that idiom? How did it come to be used in contemporary language?

O'Brien isn't sure what to make of this man.

O'BRIEN

I . . . don't know, sir. . . .

Picard finally comes to O'Brien's rescue.

PICARD

Commander Data, welcome aboard—it's good to see you.

Data turns and sees Picard for the first time. They shake hands. Picard smiles at him warmly, genuinely glad to see him and have someone he can completely rely on. Data isn't sure why this man he has just met is smiling so warmly at him.

DATA

It is . . . good to see you, too, sir.

PICARD

I could use your help with the infusor array.

DATA

Certainly.

They move to a wall panel near the warp core and open it. Picard points to a conduit.

PICARD

As you can see, we're having difficulty with the plasma conduits. . . .

Data eyes the panel.

DATA

(re: panel)

This will require a completely new field induction subprocessor.

(beat)

It appears that we will be required to . . . ignite the midnight petroleum, sir.

Picard glances at him, smiles slightly. Suddenly, we hear Beverly's voice—

BEVERLY'S VOICE

Jean-Luc . . . what's going on?

Picard turns, and as he does the SCENE CHANGES TO:

35 INTERIOR BEVERLY'S OFFICE—PRESENT

Picard standing in his bathrobe near the desk. Beverly and Riker are standing in the doorway, looking at him, puzzled. Picard is momentarily disoriented—tries to orient himself to the here and now.

PICARD

It happened again.

Beverly reacts.

BEVERLY

A time shift?

PICARD

Yes . . .

Beverly immediately grabs a tricorder and scans Picard's head.

RIKER

What happened?

PICARD

It's still a little vague, but I can remember more this time. I think the more I shift between time periods, the more memory I retain. . . .

(thinks)

First, I was in what appeared to be the future . . . years from now. Then I was in the past again . . . right before our first mission. . . .

Beverly reacts to the tricorder readings.

RIKER

(to Beverly)

What is it?

BEVERLY

(off tricorder)

I just scanned his temporal lobe and compared it to the scan I performed just a few minutes ago. There's a *thirteen* percent increase of acetylcholine in his hippocampus.

(to Picard)

Within a matter of minutes, you accumulated over *two days* worth of memories.

They all react . . . There's now real confirmation of what Picard's been saying. OFF Picard's reaction . . .

FADE OUT.

ACT FOUR

FADE IN:

36 INTERIOR OBSERVATION LOUNGE—PRESENT

Picard, Riker, Worf, Data, Troi, Geordi, Beverly. Midconversation.

PICARD
(to Troi)
Counselor, do you remember the first day I came aboard the *Enterprise?*

TROI
Yes.

PICARD
What happened after the welcoming ceremony?

TROI
There was a reception in Ten-Forward. . . . I introduced you to Worf and the other senior officers. . . .

PICARD
Do you have any memory of me calling for a Red Alert in spacedock? Do you remember Starfleet diverting us from Farpoint to the Neutral Zone to investigate a spatial anomaly?

TROI
No . . .

They consider this.

DATA
It would appear that there is a discontinuity between the time periods you have described. Events in one time period would seem to have no effect on the other two.

They try to make sense of this.

RIKER

And yet in both the past and the present—there's a report of the same anomaly in the Devron system. It's hard to believe that's a coincidence.

PICARD

For all I know, there may be one in the future, too.

GEORDI

Maybe the anomaly is some kind of . . . temporal disruption.

BEVERLY

(to Picard)

But how is all this related to your time shifting?

PICARD

These are good questions. And I suspect I might find some answers when I return to the past . . . but for now we're facing a potentially dangerous threat from the Romulans.

(beat)

All departments should submit combat readiness reports by oh eight hundred hours tomorrow. Dismissed.

Everyone rises to go and heads for the door. Riker catches Troi's attention.

RIKER

(to Troi)

Looks like it's going to be a late night. . . . Want to get some dinner first?

Troi hesitates, glances at Worf. There's an awkward moment. Riker looks a little puzzled, not sure what's going on.

TROI

Actually, I . . .

(re: Worf)

I mean . . . *we* have plans.

And in that moment, Riker suddenly realizes that Troi and Worf's relationship has progressed further than he ever realized. He's caught off guard here, but tries to respond casually and naturally.

RIKER

Oh . . . I see. Well then . . . see you tomorrow morning.

WORF

Goodnight, sir.

RIKER

Worf . . .

Worf and Troi EXIT to the corridor. Riker looks after them once they've gone. Clearly, the scene has disturbed him—he's not sure how he feels about this. Finally, he turns and EXITS to the bridge. . . .

37 INTERIOR BRIDGE—PRESENT—CONTINUOUS

Riker ENTERS. Beverly is standing near the aft console, watching Picard as he gives Data orders. The ship is at Yellow Alert.

PICARD

(to Data)

. . . and I want continuous subspace sweeps. We might detect a temporal disturbance.

DATA

Aye sir.

Riker and Picard move toward the command area.

PICARD

Wil . . . this time shifting . . . when it happens, I experience a moment of disorientation. If this should happen during a crisis, I want you to be ready to take command immediately.

Riker is still distracted by what just happened with Worf and Troi. He doesn't respond right away.

PICARD

Number One?

RIKER

Sorry, Captain. Be prepared to take command. Aye sir.

Picard looks at him, notes his distraction.

PICARD

Speaking of disorientation . . . are you all right?

Riker tries to shrug it off.

RIKER

Just a little distracted. I'm fine.

Picard doesn't quite believe this, but decides not to pursue the matter.

PICARD

You have the bridge. I'll be in my ready room.

Riker moves to sit down as Picard heads for the ready room.

38 ANGLE ON BEVERLY

She watches Picard exit, a look of concern on her face. OFF her expression . . .

CUT TO:

39 INTERIOR READY ROOM—PRESENT

Picard sitting at his desk. The door CHIMES.

PICARD

Come.

Beverly ENTERS, walks directly to the replicator.

BEVERLY

(to replicator)

Milk, warm—dash of nutmeg.

We HEAR the replicator work. Beverly takes away a glass of milk and hands it to Picard.

PICARD

What's this?

BEVERLY

A prescription. A glass of warm milk and eight hours' uninterrupted sleep.

PICARD

Beverly . . .

BEVERLY

Doctor's orders. You're exhausted. I don't know if you've slept in the past or the future . . . but I know you haven't slept in the present.

(lightly)

Get some rest, or I'll have you relieved and sedated.

PICARD

(lightly)

Yes, *sir*.

They exchange a smile. Beverly puts her hand on his in a friendly gesture, but then leaves it there a beat longer then necessary, and gives it a little squeeze. She looks concerned. He looks up at her with a little bit of surprise.

PICARD

(continuing)

What's wrong?

Beverly thinks, and for a moment, it seems as if she might say something . . . but she decides against it. . . . She turns and heads for the door. Picard stands up.

PICARD

(continuing)

Beverly.

She stops, takes a moment, then finally turns around and looks at him.

BEVERLY

As a physician, it's often my job to give people unpleasant news . . . to tell them that they need surgery or that they can't have children . . .

(beat)

Or that they might be facing a difficult illness. . . .

She breaks off, looks away from him. Picard moves to her, touched by her concern.

PICARD

You said yourself it's only a possibility.

BEVERLY

But you've been to the future . . . you *know* it's going to happen.

Picard takes a beat, then looks up at her again.

PICARD

I prefer to think of the future as something that is not written in stone. A lot of things can happen in twenty-five years.

She looks at him for a moment, smiles . . . then leans over and kisses him on the lips. They pull apart after a beat. She looks into his eyes.

BEVERLY

(quiet)

A lot of things can happen.

Beverly turns and EXITS. Picard watches her go, a thoughtful look on his face . . . then he picks up the glass of milk and takes a sip . . . moves to the couch and stretches out. He's exhausted. He closes his eyes. . . . His breathing deepens. . . . He begins to drift off. . . .

GEORDI'S VOICE

Sir? Wake up . . . sir?

The SCENE CHANGES TO:

40 INTERIOR DATA'S LIBRARY—FUTURE—LATE AFTERNOON

Geordi is gently waking Picard, who is sleeping on Data's sofa. Picard blinks open his eyes.

PICARD

Yes . . . yes, what is it? Have we reached the Neutral Zone?

GEORDI

The Neutral Zone?

Picard looks around, realizing what time period he's in. . . .

PICARD

Sorry . . . I was . . . in the past again. . . .

(beat)

What's going on?

GEORDI

Data's arranged for us to run some tests on you in the bio-metrics lab. We're ready to go if you are.

PICARD

No . . . no, we don't have time for that. We have to get to the Neutral Zone.

GEORDI

Why?

PICARD

In the other two time periods . . . Starfleet reported a . . . uh . . . some kind of . . . spatial anomaly in the . . . in the . . .

(beat)

. . . in the Devron system! The Devron system in the Neutral Zone!

Geordi sighs—the old man's ravings are starting to get a little out of hand.

GEORDI

Sir . . .

PICARD

(thinking)

If the anomaly was in the past . . . it might be here, too. We have to go find out. . . .

GEORDI

Just because you've seen it in two other time frames, doesn't mean it's going to be here.

PICARD

But if it is—that means something! Damnit, Geordi—I know what we have to do!

Geordi puts aside his own frustration.

GEORDI

Okay . . . but first of all, there is no Neutral Zone, remember?

Picard thinks.

PICARD

(struggling)

Right . . . right. Klingons . . . in this time period, the Klingons have taken over the Romulan Star Empire. . . .

GEORDI

And the relations between us and the Klingons aren't real cozy right now.

Picard struggles to his feet, irritated.

PICARD

I know that. I haven't completely lost my mind, you know.

Picard pulls up short at his own tone, tries to take the edge out of his voice.

PICARD

(continuing)

Sorry, Geordi . . . it's hard for me to concentrate . . . and remember things. . . . I don't mean to take out that frustration on you. . . .

GEORDI

It's okay. . . .

(beat)

Well, if we're going to the Devron system, we're going to need a ship.

PICARD

I think it's time to call in some old favors. . . .

(beat)

Contact Admiral Riker at Starbase Two-four-seven.

CUT TO:

41 EXTERIOR CAMBRIDGE—FUTURE—LATE AFTERNOON (MATTE)

As seen earlier.

42 INTERIOR DATA'S LIBRARY—FUTURE—LATE AFTERNOON (OPTICAL)

A short time later. Where the hearth and fire were seen earlier, there is now a large VIEWSCREEN and a computer console. Picard is talking to *Admiral Riker* on the viewer.

Riker is twenty-five years older, his hair almost completely gray. His attitude is now that of a seasoned and experienced Starfleet admiral . . . but there's something more. He's more brittle, less easygoing than the Riker we used to know. . . . Something's changed in him.

He regards Picard fondly but with a hint of tolerance. The power relationships have changed here—while Riker respects Picard, he is no longer beholden to him. Midconversation. Data and Geordi are standing nearby.

RIKER

Jean-Luc, you know I'd like to help . . . but frankly, what you're asking for is impossible. The Klingons have closed their borders to all Federation starships.

PICARD

Wil . . . if this . . . spatial anomaly really is in the Devron system . . .

RIKER

I saw a report from Starfleet Intelligence on that sector this morning. There's no activity. . . . There's nothing unusual happening in the Devron system.

PICARD

I don't believe that! Maybe their long-range scanners are flawed. . . . We have to *go* there, see for ourselves!

Riker is reluctant to turn him down flat . . . he looks for a way to ease out of it.

RIKER

Data, what do you make of all this?

Data considers. He no longer makes decisions based purely on logic, but compassionately takes feelings into account, too.

DATA

I am not certain. I cannot disprove what the captain is saying.

(beat)

And he is convinced he is traveling back and forth through time.

Riker eyes him. Clearly Data is siding with the captain. Riker feels he has to do something.

RIKER

Right.

(beat)

Look, I've got the *Yorktown* out near the border. . . . I'll have them run some long-range scans of the Devron system. . . . If they find anything, I'll let you know.

PICARD

That's not good enough.

RIKER

(firm)

It's going to have to be. I'm sorry. That's all I can do. Riker out.

The transmission ENDS. Picard steps back from the viewscreen, frustrated and angry. Data turns to the computer console.

DATA

(to computer)

Computer—restore holographic image.

The viewscreen and computer console VANISH and are REPLACED by the fireplace and roaring fire.

PICARD

(angry)

Damn him anyway. . . . After all we've been through together . . . he's been sitting behind that desk too long.

GEORDI

Well . . . I guess all we can do is wait to see if the *Yorktown* finds anything.

DATA

There is another option.

Picard looks hopeful, but Geordi is exasperated—he was hoping that Riker had put an end to all this.

DATA
(continuing)
We could arrange passage aboard a medical ship.

PICARD
Medical ship?

DATA
Yes. There was an outbreak of Terrellian plague on Romulus. The Klingons have been allowing Federation medical ships to cross the border.

PICARD
(excited)
Yes . . . yes . . .

Geordi is a little chagrined, but opts not to fight about it.

GEORDI
(resigned)
So now all we need is a medical ship.

PICARD
I think I can arrange that.
(to Data)
Find the *Pasteur.* I have some pull with the captain.
(beat, then concerned)
At least, I used to . . .

CUT TO:

43 EXTERIOR SPACE—MEDICAL SHIP—FUTURE (OPTICAL)

A small and sleek VESSEL with the 24th-century equivalent of "Red Cross" markings. The ship is orbiting Earth.

44 INTERIOR MEDICAL SHIP—BRIDGE—FUTURE

The bridge of a futuristic medical ship. Picard, Geordi, and Data (who's now dressed in travel clothes) ENTER from a turbolift. ENSIGN CHILTON is at the conn. Someone is sitting in the captain's chair and is turned away from them. The chair swivels to face them and we REVEAL—

Captain Beverly Picard. She smiles and rises.

BEVERLY

Well . . . this is a page out of the past. I never thought I'd see any one of you on a starship again.

(shaking hands)

Data, Geordi . . .

There is an awkward beat as Beverly and Picard look at each other—there is a tension in the air. At the exact same moment, Beverly moves to hug him, but Picard holds out his hand to shake hers. Then they both see what the other is doing, and they switch—Beverly starts to shake his hand and Picard moves to hug her. They both finally drop their hands and smile at each other, embarrassed and amused at their own awkwardness.

PICARD

Let's just . . . choose one.

They move toward each other and gently hug for a moment. There is a tenderness between them. . . . Then they separate and there's the awkwardness again.

PICARD

Well. Did you get my message?

BEVERLY

Yes. Jean-Luc . . . going into Klingon territory—it's insane.

(shakes her head)

But I never could say no to you.

PICARD

Ah. So that's why you married me.

She smiles at him. These are two people who still retain a fondness for each other in spite of not having been able to make marriage work.

BEVERLY

Now . . . the first order of business is to get clearance to cross the Klingon border.

GEORDI

What about *Worf?* Isn't he still on the Klingon High Council?

DATA

I'm not sure. Information on the Klingon political structure is hard to come by these days. However, at last report Worf was governor of H'atoria, a small Klingon colony near the border.

PICARD

Worf . . . yes, that's it . . . that's the answer. Worf. He'll help us. Let's make it so.

As Beverly considers this—

CHILTON

Captain Picard?

PICARD
(overlapping)

Yes?

BEVERLY
(overlapping)

Yes?

They give each other a look. Chilton addresses Beverly.

CHILTON
(beat)

Captain, Earth Station McKinley is signaling. They want to know when we'll be docking.

BEVERLY

Tell McKinley that we've been called away on a priority mission. We won't be docking.

CHILTON

Aye, sir.

Picard smiles at Beverly.

PICARD

Kept the name, eh?

BEVERLY
(smiling)
I've prepared quarters for you on Deck Five if you'd like some rest.

PICARD
I'm fine. I don't need any rest.

BEVERLY
(to Chilton)
Nell, please escort the ambassador to his quarters—

PICARD
I can find my way around a starship!

Picard addresses the group, building a head of steam.

PICARD
You're all treating me like an invalid, but I assure you I've got a few years left. I don't need to be led around and I don't want to be patronized.

BEVERLY
You're right. I'm sorry.

Disarmed, he starts for the turbolift.

PICARD
I'll go have a rest.

The doors close behind him. Once he's gone, Beverly turns to Geordi and Data with a slightly sad expression.

BEVERLY
How long since he's had a neurological scan?

GEORDI
I'm not sure, but don't waste your time suggesting it. He says he's not taking "any more damn tests."

BEVERLY
Do you believe he's moving through time?

Geordi looks down—it's clear he doesn't believe the captain.

BEVERLY
(continuing)
I don't know if I do, either . . . but—he's Jean-Luc Picard. And if he wants to go on one more mission, that's what we're going to do.

Beverly moves to the captain's chair.

BEVERLY
(to Chilton)
Ensign Chilton, set course for H'atoria.

CUT TO:

44A OMITTED

45 INTERIOR MEDICAL SHIP—TURBOLIFT—FUTURE

Picard standing in the moving lift.

PICARD
We'll find the anomaly. . . . I know we will. . . .

The lift stops. The doors open and Picard steps out. And as he does, the SCENE CHANGES TO:

46 INTERIOR BRIDGE—PAST

Picard walking out of a turbolift onto the bridge. He hesitates only for a moment, quickly orienting himself. He moves to the command area. Tasha, Worf, O'Brien, Data, and Troi at their stations.

PICARD
Report.

O'BRIEN
We're nearing the coordinates you gave me, sir.

PICARD
(to Data)
Is there anything unusual in the vicinity?

DATA
How would you define unusual, sir? Every region of space has unique properties that cannot be found anywhere else.

Picard thinks, remembers what happened originally.

PICARD

There should be a . . . "barrier" of some sort nearby. A large plasma field . . . highly disruptive.

Tasha works.

TASHA

Nothing, sir.

Frustrated, Picard looks down at O'Brien's console again.

PICARD

It's the right time . . . right place. . . . He should be here. . . .

O'BRIEN

Who, sir?

Picard straightens up and looks around the bridge.

PICARD

(calls out)

Q! We're here! This has gone on long enough! What sort of game are you playing?

There is no answer. The bridge crew exchange looks among themselves—they're definitely starting to wonder about this guy.

PICARD

(continuing, to Troi)

Counselor, do you sense an alien presence?

TROI

No, sir.

46A–46B OMITTED

47 ANGLE—WORF AND TASHA

WORF

(sotto, to Tasha)

What is a . . . "Q"?

TASHA
(sotto)
It's a letter of the alphabet, as far as I know.

48 PICARD

Is getting more and more frustrated.

PICARD
(quiet)
This is not the way it's supposed to happen. . . .
(to all)
Maintain position here. I'll be in my ready room.

Picard EXITS to the ready room. . . .

49 INTERIOR READY ROOM—PAST—CONTINUOUS

As Picard steps through the doors, the SCENE CHANGES TO:

50 INTERIOR COURTROOM (OPTICAL)

Picard is suddenly in front of the screaming crowd, as seen in "Farpoint." The crowd is looking down the hallway that leads into the courtroom. Out of the darkness, riding on his FLOATING CHAIR—Q appears, dressed in his judge's robes. The crowd ROARS in approval at the sight of him. Q holds up a hand and they fall silent. He looks toward Picard.

Q
Mon Capitaine . . . I thought you'd never get here.

FADE OUT.

ACT FIVE

FADE IN:

51 INTERIOR COURTROOM

Picard facing Q, as before.

PICARD
Q . . . I thought so. What's going on?

Q
It's *Judge* Q to you. And isn't it obvious what's going on?

Picard looks around at the courtroom, the unruly crowd.

PICARD
The last time I stood in this courtroom was seven years ago. . . .

Q
(mocking)
"Seven years ago . . . " How little you mortals understand time. Must you be so linear, Jean-Luc?

PICARD
(doggedly)
You accused me of being the representative of a barbarous species. . . .

Q
I believe my exact words were "a dangerous, savage, child-race."

PICARD
But we demonstrated that mankind has become peaceful and benevolent. You agreed, and let us go on our way.
(looking around)
Why do I find myself back in this courtroom?

Q

You'd like me to connect the dots for you. Lead you from A . . . to B . . . to C . . . so your puny mind can comprehend.

Q shakes his head wearily, vexed by man's limitations.

Q

How boring. They would be so much more entertained if you *tried* to figure this out. . . .

Q thinks for a moment.

Q

(continuing)

I'll answer any ten questions that call for a "yes" or a "no."

(beat)

Well?

Picard takes a breath, looks around the courtroom again. This is the only way he can get information.

PICARD

Are you putting mankind on trial again?

Q

No.

PICARD

Is there any connection at all between the trial seven years ago . . . and whatever's going on now?

Q

Hmmmmm . . . I would have to say . . . yes.

PICARD

The spatial anomaly in the Neutral Zone—is it related to what's happening?

Q

Oh, most definitely yes.

PICARD

Is it part of a Romulan plot? A ploy to start a war?

Q

No . . . and no. Five down.

PICARD

That's only four—

Q

(ticking on his fingers)

"Is it a Romulan plot?" "Is it a ploy to start a war?" Those are separate questions.

PICARD

Did you create the anomaly?

Q

(laughs merrily)

No, no, no. You're going to be so surprised when you realize where it came from—if you ever figure it out.

PICARD

(trying another tack)

Are you responsible for my shifting through time?

Q

I'll answer that if you promise you won't tell anyone.

(whispering)

Yes.

PICARD

Why?

Q

Oh, I'm sorry. That's not a "yes or no" question. You forfeit the rest of your questions.

He regards Picard with scorn.

Q

(continuing)

I expected as much. You're such a limited creature . . . a perfect example of why we've made our decision.

Picard gives him a questioning look.

Q

The trial never ended, Captain. We never reached a verdict. But, now we have: you're guilty.

PICARD

Guilty of what?

Q

Of being inferior.

Q looks at Picard with unconcealed contempt.

Q

Seven years ago, I said we'd be watching you. And we have been. Hoping your ape-like race would demonstrate some growth . . . give some indication that your minds have room for expansion.

Q's tone now is serious, threatening.

Q

And what have we seen instead? You spending time worrying about Commander Riker's career . . . listening to Counselor Troi's pedantic psychobabble . . . indulging Data in his witless exploration of humanity. . . .

PICARD

We have journeyed to countless new worlds . . . made contact with new species . . . expanded man's understanding of the universe. . . .

Q

In your own paltry, limited way. You have no *idea* how far you still have to go.

PICARD

We are what we are, Q—and we're doing the best we can. It's not for you to set the standard by which we're judged.

Q

Oh, but it is. And we have. Time may be eternal—but our patience is not.

PICARD
(tight)
Having rendered a verdict . . . have you decided upon a sentence?

Q
Indeed. It's time to put an end to your trek through the stars . . . to make room for other, more worthy species.

PICARD
We're to be denied travel through space? Q . . . even you could not be capable of such an act—

Q
I? There you go again, blaming me for everything. Well, this time I'm not your enemy. I am not the one who causes the annihilation of mankind.
(beat)
You are.

PICARD
Me . . .

Q
That's right. You're doing it right now . . . you've already done it . . . and you will do it yet again.

PICARD
What sort of meaningless double-talk is that?

Q sighs.

Q
He doesn't understand. I have only myself to blame, I suppose. I believed in you. . . . I thought you had potential . . . but apparently I was wrong.
(beat)
May whatever God you believe in have mercy on your soul. This court stands adjourned.

Q raises a hand and there is the crash of a GONG. The SCENE CHANGES TO:

52 INTERIOR READY ROOM—PRESENT

Picard *sits up* on the couch suddenly, the SOUND of the gong slowly fading away. He realizes what's happened.

He heads for the door of the ready room and EXITS to the bridge.

52A INTERIOR BRIDGE—PRESENT

Picard steps onto the bridge and addresses Riker.

PICARD
(to com)
Commander, assemble the senior staff and go to Red Alert.
(beat)
We have a bigger problem than we thought.

OFF his face . . .

FADE OUT.

ACT SIX

FADE IN:

53 EXTERIOR SPACE—THE *ENTERPRISE*—PRESENT (OPTICAL)

At warp.

54 INTERIOR OBSERVATION LOUNGE—PRESENT (OPTICAL)

Picard, Riker, Data, Worf, Geordi, Beverly, Troi. Midconversation.

GEORDI
I don't believe him. This has to be another one of Q's games. He's probably listening to us right now, getting a big laugh out of watching us jump through his hoops.

PICARD
I think that this time, we have no choice but to take him at his word . . . which means that in some fashion, *I* will cause the destruction of humanity.

BEVERLY
But didn't Q say you already *had* caused it?

TROI
And that you were causing it now . . .

DATA
Given the fact that there is an apparent discontinuity between the three time periods the captain is visiting, Q's statement may be accurate, if confusing.

A beat. Picard looks frustrated.

PICARD
So what should I do—just lock myself in a room in all three time periods?

RIKER
No. Maybe *not* acting is what causes the destruction of mankind. What if you were needed on the bridge at a key moment, and weren't there?

TROI

We can't start second-guessing ourselves. I think we have to proceed normally . . . deal with each situation as it occurs. . . .

PICARD

Agreed.

(beat)

I've been thinking about my conversation with Q. He admitted that he was responsible for my shifting through time . . .

The others listen carefully, wondering where the Captain is going with this.

PICARD
(continuing)

It occurred to me . . . that perhaps Q is giving me a chance to save mankind somehow.

Astonished looks all around.

RIKER

What makes you say that?

PICARD

Q has always shown a certain . . . fascination with humanity . . . and specifically with me. I think he has more than a casual interest in what happens to me.

DATA

That is true. Q's interest in you is very similar to that of a master and a beloved pet.

Picard shoots him a dirty look.

DATA
(continuing)

That was only an analogy, Captain.

PICARD

If I weren't traveling through time . . . I would never have realized that the anomaly in the Neutral Zone appeared there in the past as well.

(beat)

Assuming that's an important piece of a larger puzzle, my ability to shift through time may be the key to understanding what's going on.

COM VOICE

Bridge to Captain Picard.

PICARD

Go ahead.

COM VOICE

We're approaching the Neutral Zone, Captain.

Looks all around.

PICARD

On our way.

Everyone heads for the door. . . .

55 INTERIOR BRIDGE—PRESENT—CONTINUOUS

Picard, Riker, Data, and Worf ENTER and move to their positions. Beverly, Geordi, and Troi EXIT to the turbolift. The ship is still at Red Alert.

PICARD

All stop. Initiate a long-range scan.

DATA

(working)

There are four warbirds holding position on the Romulan side of the Neutral Zone, Captain.

WORF

The Federation Starships *Concord* and *Bozeman* are holding position on our side.

RIKER

Face-off. The question is, who's going to move first?

PICARD

We are. Mister Worf, hail the Romulan flagship.

Worf works.

WORF

The warbird *Terix* is responding.

PICARD

On screen.

56 ANGLE ON MEDICAL SHIP VIEWSCREEN (OPTICAL)

The image of an aged *Worf* appears on the viewer.

WORF

Captain Picard.

CUT TO REVEAL THAT WE ARE—

57 INTERIOR MEDICAL SHIP—BRIDGE—FUTURE (OPTICAL)

The older Picard is standing next to the captain's chair. Beverly and Chilton are at their stations. Data and Geordi look on. Picard blinks for a moment, steadies himself against Beverly's chair as he adjusts to the abrupt time shift.

BEVERLY

(to Worf)

Hello, Worf. It's been a long time.

WORF

Doctor . . . it is good to see you again.

BEVERLY

Did you have a chance to read our request?

WORF

Yes. But you must realize . . . I am no longer a member of the High Council.

BEVERLY

You *are* the governor of the H'atoria Colony.

WORF

(with contempt)

It is merely a ceremonial position given me when the House of Mogh was forced from power.

PICARD

Worf, surely you still have some influence. We must get into the Neutral Zone.

Worf hesitates.

PICARD

Can't you at least grant us permission to cross the border?

WORF

I must refuse. It is for your own safety—the Neutral Zone is extremely volatile.

(beat)

If Admiral Riker had given you a starship with a cloak, you would have been safe. I cannot believe he refused to help you.

PICARD

I don't care what kind of ship we're in—the important thing is to get to the Devron system—

WORF

I am sorry, but my first duty is to the Empire. I must adhere to regulations.

PICARD

Maybe I'm just an old man who doesn't understand . . . but the Worf I knew cared more about things like loyalty and honor than he did rules and regulations.

(beat)

But then, that was a long time ago. Maybe you're not the Worf I knew.

Worf suddenly explodes in a fit of rage. He throws everything off his desk with a powerful sweep of his arm.

WORF

(a curse)

Dor-sHo GHA!

His eyes flash, and he points an accusatory finger toward Picard.

WORF
(continuing)
You have always used your knowledge of Klingon honor and tradition to get what you want from me.

PICARD
(right back at him)
That's because it always works. Your problem, Worf, is that you really *do* have a sense of honor. . . . You really do care about things like loyalty and trust. Don't blame me because I know you too well.

Worf glares at him . . . then—

WORF
Very well. You may cross the border. But *only* if I come with you. I am familiar with the Neutral Zone.

Picard smiles at him.

PICARD
Terms accepted.

The transmission ENDS.

BEVERLY
(to Chilton)
Inform transporter room two to beam the governor aboard.

Beverly turns to Picard with a serious look on her face.

BEVERLY
I just want to make one thing clear, Jean-Luc. If we run into any serious opposition, I'm taking us back to Federation territory. We aren't well armed and we wouldn't last long in a fight.

CHILTON
Governor Worf is aboard, Captain.

BEVERLY
All right. Ensign, set course for the Devron system. Warp thirteen.

She raises her hand to give the order to engage, then pauses for a moment . . . looks to Picard and smiles.

BEVERLY
Once more, for old time's sake?

Picard smiles, knowing exactly what she means. He raises his hand in the old familiar way, and then the SCENE CHANGES TO:

58 INTERIOR BRIDGE—PAST

Picard sitting in the captain's chair, hand raised.

PICARD
Engage.

O'Brien turns around in his chair, a little confused.

O'BRIEN
Engage to where, sir?

Picard glances around, quickly orients himself.

PICARD
Set course for the Devron system and engage at warp nine.

TASHA
The Devron system is inside the Neutral Zone, sir.

PICARD
I'm aware of that, Lieutenant. Carry out my orders, Chief.

O'BRIEN
Aye, sir.

Tasha, Worf, and Troi exchange concerned looks.

TROI
(quiet, to Picard)
Captain . . . may I have a word with you in private?

PICARD
Of course.

(to Tasha)

Lieutenant, contact Farpoint Station. I want to talk to Commander Riker.

TASHA

Aye, sir.

They stand and head for the ready room . . .

59 INTERIOR READY ROOM—PAST—CONTINUOUS

Picard and Troi ENTER.

TROI

Captain, I just want to voice my concerns about the way the crew is responding to your . . . unexpected orders.

PICARD

They don't trust me. . . . They think I'm behaving erratically.

TROI

Some do. . . . Others are confused. . . . It takes some time for a new crew to get to know their captain, and for him to know them.

PICARD

I understand that. But I know what this crew is capable of, even if they don't.

TROI

I'm happy to hear you say that. It may do them good to hear it, as well. . . .

(beat)

It would also help if they knew what was going on.

Picard takes a moment.

PICARD

I know it's difficult operating in the dark, Counselor. But for now, I think it's the only choice.

Troi looks a little unconvinced.

TROI

Perhaps if you could at least indicate why—

TASHA (com voice)

Yar to Captain Picard. I have Commander Riker for you, sir.

PICARD

Put him through in here.

Troi reacts to Riker's name—and we see that this is a Troi who has not resolved her feelings about Riker. Picard sits down at the desk and activates the desktop monitor.

60 ANGLE ON MONITOR (OPTICAL) (STOCK)

The image of YOUNG WIL RIKER appears.

61 ANGLE ON PICARD

In the background, we can see that Troi reacts to the sight of Riker on the monitor.

PICARD

Commander. I just wanted to let you know we'll be delayed in picking you up at Farpoint Station.

RIKER (com voice)

I see. May I ask how long?

PICARD

I'm not sure. I'll keep you updated. Please inform Doctor Crusher and Lieutenant La Forge of our delay.

62 ANGLE ON MONITOR (OPTICAL) (STOCK)

YOUNG RIKER

Understood.

The transmission ends.

62A OMITTED

63 RESUME

Picard turns to Troi.

PICARD

Is there anything else, Counselor?

Troi doesn't answer right away—something is clearly troubling her.

TROI

Actually . . . there is, sir. I've been debating whether or not to mention it . . . but perhaps . . .

(becomes more resolute)

It's about Commander Riker.

Picard, of course, knows all about their relationship. . . . He even knows how it will run its course in the future. But he plays it out as if this is the first he's heard of it.

PICARD

What about him?

TROI

Well . . . I think you should know that we . . . have had a prior relationship.

PICARD

I see. Do you anticipate this interfering with your duties?

TROI

No, sir. It was several years ago. And it's well behind us both. But I thought you should know. . . .

Picard takes a beat.

PICARD

I appreciate your telling me . . . but I'm sure the two of you will find a way to . . . deal with the situation.

Picard says this with confidence . . . but Troi isn't so sure. Picard moves to the replicator.

PICARD

(continuing)

Tea. Earl Grey. Hot.

COMPUTER VOICE

That beverage has not been programmed into the replication system.

Picard reacts. He turns to Troi with a smile, as if to make a remark . . . and as he does, the SCENE CHANGES TO:

64 INTERIOR BRIDGE—PRESENT (OPTICAL)

Picard standing in front of the viewscreen. TOMALAK, the Romulan Commander, is on the viewer.

TOMALAK

So, Captain . . . how long shall we stare at each other across the Neutral Zone?

PICARD

There is another alternative, Tomalak. We're both here for the same reason. We could each send one ship into the Neutral Zone to investigate the anomaly in the Devron system.

Tomalak considers this.

TOMALAK

Has Starfleet Command approved this arrangement?

PICARD

No.

TOMALAK

(smiles)

I like it already.

(beat)

Agreed. One ship from each side . . . but I warn you—if another Federation starship tries to enter the Zone . . .

PICARD

You needn't make threats. I think we're all aware of the consequences.

TOMALAK

Very well. I'll see you in the Devron system.

The transcription ENDS.

PICARD
(to conn Officer)
Set course for the Devron system. Warp five. Engage.

CUT TO:

65 EXTERIOR SPACE—THE *ENTERPRISE* (OPTICAL)

The ship at warp.

66 INTERIOR BRIDGE—PRESENT (OPTICAL)

A short time later.

DATA
Sensors are picking up a large subspace anomaly directly ahead.

PICARD
All stop. On screen.

The viewscreen now shows the SPATIAL ANOMALY—a large mass of color and light. There is an ethereal quality to the anomaly . . . it's beautiful and frightening all at once. They all react to the sight.

PICARD
(to Data)
Full scan, Mister Data.

DATA
Aye, sir.

Data begins to work his console.

67 ANGLE ON OPS CONSOLE

As Data's HANDS work the console. MOVE TO REVEAL WE'RE IN:

68 INTERIOR BRIDGE—PAST (OPTICAL)

Data is working his console, O'Brien is at conn.

DATA

We are approaching the Devron system, Captain. Sensors are picking up a large subspace anomaly directly ahead.

Include Picard in the command area. Tasha, Troi, and Worf at their stations. Picard adjusts to the time shift.

PICARD

All stop. Put it on screen.

The viewscreen now shows the distinctive SPATIAL ANOMALY as seen before. But this time, it's much BIGGER on the screen. Picard reacts to this.

PICARD

(continuing, to himself)

It's bigger in the past. . . .

TROI

Sir?

PICARD

Nothing. Full scan, Mister Data.

DATA

Aye, sir.

Picard stands and moves to the viewscreen, peering at the Anomaly.

69 OMITTED

70 INTERIOR MEDICAL SHIP—BRIDGE—FUTURE

Another angle. Picard glances around, orienting himself. Beverly in command, Chilton at conn; Data and Geordi are working at an aft console. Worf is looking on.

PICARD

On screen! On screen! Let's see it!

The others react as though he's saying something very strange.

70A ANGLE ON VIEWSCREEN (OPTICAL)

Nothing but the starfield.

70B INTERIOR MEDICAL SHIP—BRIDGE—FUTURE

DATA

As you can see, sir—there's nothing there.

Beverly and the others exchange a look. . . . They expected this all along. OFF Picard's frustrated and perplexed expression . . .

FADE OUT.

ACT SEVEN

FADE IN:

71 INTERIOR MEDICAL SHIP—BRIDGE—FUTURE

A few minutes later. Beverly looking over Data's shoulder at the aft science station. Picard nearby. Chilton at conn. Worf is working at a nearby console. Geordi looking on.

DATA

Still nothing, Captain. I've conducted a full sensor sweep out to one light-year from the *Pasteur.* No temporal anomalies, no particle fluctuations . . . nothing.

PICARD

Have you scanned the entire subspace bandwidth?

GEORDI

Yes. The subspace barrier is a little thin in this region of space, but that's not unusual.

PICARD

I don't understand. I've already seen it in the other two—the other two time periods. Why isn't it here?

Worf suddenly looks up from his console with concern.

WORF

(to Beverly)

Captain. I have been monitoring Klingon communication channels. . . . Several warships have been dispatched to this sector to search for a . . . renegade Federation vessel.

Reactions. Picard looks at Beverly.

PICARD

You're not thinking about leaving?

BEVERLY

Jean-Luc, there's nothing here. . . .

PICARD

There should be—there *has* to be!

(to Data)

Data, there must be some other way to scan for temporal disturbances . . . something that's not covered in a normal sensor sweep.

DATA

There are several methods of detecting temporal disturbances, but we're limited by the equipment on the *Pasteur.* This ship is designed primarily for medical emergencies.

BEVERLY

Jean-Luc, we've done all we can. . . . We should head back to Federation territory.

DATA

(still thinking)

However, it may be possible to modify the main deflector to emit an inverse tachyon pulse, which could scan beyond the subspace barrier.

PICARD

Very good! Make it so!

BEVERLY

Wait a minute. . . . Data, how long would this take?

DATA

To make the modifications and search the entire Devron system will take approximately fourteen hours.

Beverly thinks for a moment.

BEVERLY

All right. Data, begin modifying the tachyon pulse. Ensign Chilton, lay in a course back to the Federation. If we haven't found anything in six hours, we're heading back at maximum warp.

CHILTON

Aye, sir.

PICARD

Six hours may not be enough. We have to stay here until we find it—no matter how long it takes!

BEVERLY

(to Chilton)

Carry out my orders.

(to Picard)

May I see you for a moment?

Beverly heads for her ready room. Picard follows. . . .

72 INTERIOR MEDICAL SHIP—READY ROOM—FUTURE CONTINUOUS (OPTICAL)

Beverly and Picard ENTER.

PICARD

Beverly, I can't believe you're not willing to stay here until—

Beverly turns to him, her eyes flashing with anger.

BEVERLY

Don't you *ever* question my orders on the bridge of my ship again!

Picard is taken aback for a moment, but blusters a response.

PICARD

I'm just trying to . . . there are larger concerns here . . . don't you understand that—

BEVERLY

I understand that you would never have tolerated that kind of behavior back on the *Enterprise*—and I won't here. I don't care if you're my ex-Captain *or* my ex-husband.

Picard looks flustered and angry for a beat . . . but finally has to back down and concede the point.

PICARD

You're right. . . . I was out of line. . . . It won't happen again. . . .

(beat)
But you have to understand. . . . The stakes here are enormous. Q has said all of humanity will be destroyed. . . .

BEVERLY
I know. And that's why I'm willing to stay here a while longer and keep looking.
(beat)
But I also want you to consider the possibility that none of what you're saying is real.

PICARD
What . . . ?

BEVERLY
Jean-Luc, I care for you too much not to tell you the truth. You have advanced Irumodic Syndrome. I have to consider the possibility that all of this is in your mind.
(beat)
I'll stay here six hours . . . and then we're heading home.

She moves to him, softens her tone.

BEVERLY
And I want you to remember, if it were anyone but you . . . we wouldn't be here at all.

Beverly turns and EXITS. Picard thinks for a moment . . . realizes that he's pushed his friends about as far as he can. After a beat, Q APPEARS. He's a parody of an OLD MAN—bags under the eyes, scraggly gray hair, baggy ill-fitting clothes. He's leaning on a cane and holding a hearing trumpet to one ear.

Q
(aged voice)
Eh? What was that she said, sonny? I couldn't quite hear her. . . .

Picard turns and reacts to the sight in irritation.

PICARD
Q . . . what's going on here? Where's the anomaly?

Q
(''mishearing'')
Where's your mommy? I don't know. . . .

PICARD
Stop this foolishness and answer me!

Q
There is an answer, Jean-Luc. But I can't hand it to you. Although you do have help . . .

Picard realizes Q may be telling him something important.

PICARD
What help?

Q
You aren't alone, you know . . . what you were . . . and what you will become . . . are always with you.

PICARD
My time shifting . . . the answer does lie there . . .
(beat)
Just tell me one thing. . . . This anomaly we're looking for . . . is that what destroys humanity?

Q
You're forgetting, Jean-Luc. *You* destroy humanity.

PICARD
By doing what? When? How are you—

Suddenly, the SCENE CHANGES TO:

73 INTERIOR BRIDGE—PRESENT

Picard standing near the ops station, leaning on the same cane we just saw in Q's hand. Riker and Worf at stations. Picard glances at the cane and tosses it aside.

PICARD
(to Data)
Report, Mister Data.

DATA

(off console)

The anomaly is two hundred million kilometers in diameter. It is a highly focused temporal energy source which is emitting approximately the same energy output as ten G-type stars.

PICARD

What is the source of that energy?

DATA

I am uncertain. Sensors have been unable to penetrate the anomaly.

Picard thinks, remembers something from the future time period.

PICARD

What if we modified the main deflector to emit an . . . inverse tachyon pulse. That might scan beyond the subspace barrier . . . give us an idea what the interior of this thing looks like.

Data thinks for a moment, a little surprised.

DATA

That is a most intriguing idea, Captain. I do not believe a tachyon beam was ever put to such use. I had no idea you were so versed in the intricacies of temporal theory.

PICARD

I have some friends who are quite well-versed in the matter. Make it so.

DATA

Aye, sir.

Data stands.

DATA

I believe we can make the necessary modifications in main engineering.

Picard nods. As Data heads for the door . . .

CUT TO:

74 INTERIOR ENGINEERING—PRESENT

Later. Data and Geordi working at consoles.

GEORDI

We can get more power if we reroute the primary EPS taps to the deflector array . . .

DATA

Agreed.

Data works.

DATA

Initiating tachyon pulse . . .

75 EXTERIOR SPACE—THE *ENTERPRISE*—PRESENT (OPTICAL)

A thin, oscillating BEAM emits from the deflector dish and begins SCANNING the anomaly.

76 INTERIOR ENGINEERING—PRESENT

As before. Data and Geordi watch the monitors.

GEORDI

Okay . . . the pulse is holding steady. . . . We're starting to receive data from the scan. . . .

DATA

It will take the computer some time to give us a complete picture of the anomaly's interior. I suggest we—

Geordi reacts to a sudden stab of *pain* in his VISOR.

GEORDI

(in pain)

Whoa . . .

DATA

What is wrong?

GEORDI

I'm not sure . . . oh . . . it's like somebody put an ice pick through my temples . . .

(beat)

My VISOR's picking up all kinds of electromagnetic distortions.

Geordi staggers a little.

DATA

(to com)

Data to sickbay. Medical emergency in main engineering.

CUT TO:

77 INTERIOR SICKBAY—PRESENT (OPTICAL)

A while later. Geordi sitting on a bio-bed with his VISOR off.

Beverly and Picard are looking at Geordi's eyes. They're not as they usually appear; the iris shows faintly. Data is working on a monitor in the background.

BEVERLY

Look at his eyes. . . . You can see the difference yourself.

PICARD

(peering)

Yes . . . I can see the iris. . . .

Beverly picks up a scanning DEVICE and scans his eyes.

BEVERLY

(off scanner)

This is amazing. The DNA in his optic nerves is being regenerated. . . .

She lowers the device and looks at Picard.

BEVERLY

It's as if he were growing new eyes.

GEORDI

I guess that's why I started to feel pain. . . . My optical cortex was falling out of alignment with my VISOR.

PICARD

How is this possible?

BEVERLY

It shouldn't be possible at all. There's no medical explanation for the spontaneous regeneration of an organ.

Ogawa, still pregnant, approaches holding a padd.

OGAWA

Doctor . . . we've just gotten reports from two crew members who say they have injuries . . . which are healing themselves.

Picard reacts to this bizarre news. Data looks up from his monitor.

DATA

I believe I may have a partial explanation, Captain.

They move to where he is working. The monitor shows a complex Okudagram of the ANOMALY with various pieces of sensor information.

DATA

(continuing)

I have completed my analysis of the anomaly. It appears to be a multiphasic temporal convergence in the space-time continuum.

BEVERLY

In English please.

DATA

It is, in essence, an eruption of . . . *anti-time*.

PICARD

Anti-time?

DATA

A relatively new concept in temporal mechanics. The relationship of anti-time to normal time is analogous to the relationship of antimatter to normal matter.

PICARD

(catching on)

So if time and anti-time were to collide . . .

DATA

They would annihilate each other . . . creating a rupture in space. I believe this is what has happened in the Devron system.

(continuing)

The rupture may be sending out waves of temporal energy which are disrupting the normal flow of time.

BEVERLY

Then it's possible the DNA molecules in Geordi's optic nerves aren't regenerating themselves. . . . They might be reverting to their original state.

PICARD

You mean his eyes are getting . . . younger?

DATA

For all intents and purposes, yes.

Picard considers this for a moment.

PICARD

So the temporal anomaly has certain . . . rejuvenating effects. It certainly doesn't sound like the destruction of humanity.

(beat)

Data, what could have caused this collision between time and anti-time?

78 ANGLE ON DATA

Who is sitting in his chair at ops, looking confused.

DATA

Anti-time, sir?

MOVE TO REVEAL WE'RE IN:

79 INTERIOR BRIDGE—PAST

Picard is standing on the bridge, talking to Data. Picard quickly moves to Data's console and begins entering information rapidly. Tasha, Worf, O'Brien, and Troi at their stations.

PICARD
(to Data)
I believe that if we modify the deflector to send out an inverse tachyon pulse, you'll find that the anomaly is a rupture between time and anti-time.

Data watches Picard work the console for a moment.

DATA
That is a fascinating hypothesis. . . . How did you formulate—

PICARD
It would take too long to explain. Begin the modifications and send out the pulse. Once you've done that, start working on a theory as to what could have caused this rupture.

DATA
Aye, sir.

Data begins working. Picard thinks for a moment.

PICARD
Mister O'Brien . . . how big is the anomaly?

O'BRIEN
(works)
Approximately four hundred million kilometers in diameter, sir.

PICARD
I still don't understand why it's larger *here.* . . .

O'Brien gives him a puzzled look—he doesn't know what the Hell Picard is talking about, but decides not to pursue it. Worf suddenly reacts to something on the aft console.

WORF
Captain . . . there are five Terrellian transport ships holding position in the Devron system.

TASHA
We're being hailed by the lead ship.

PICARD
On screen.

80 INCLUDE VIEWSCREEN (OPTICAL)

Which now shows a Terrellian pilot named ANDRONA.

ANDRONA
Enterprise, you are a welcome sight. We've been receiving threats from the Romulan Star Empire ever since we entered the Neutral Zone. I'm glad to see you're here to protect us.

PICARD
Why have you come here?

Androna's expression brightens a little.

ANDRONA
We heard about the Light . . . from a merchant ship who told us about the power it has to heal illness . . . to rejuvenate the elderly . . . and we *had* to come here.

The others on the bridge look a little confused. . . . They've never heard about any of this.

PICARD
We can't really be certain that the . . . Light . . . has this power. And there may be dangers, side effects we're not aware of. . . .

ANDRONA
I have five ships full of sick and dying people, Captain. If there's even a chance it's true, I can't turn back now.

PICARD
It would be safer for all concerned if you left the Neutral Zone . . . and let us investigate the phenomenon more fully.

ANDRONA
No. I've come too far.

Picard is frustrated, but has no authority to order them away.

PICARD

I warn you that if the Romulans should decide to intervene, I may not be able to protect you.

ANDRONA

I understand. We'll take that risk.

(beat, then smiles)

Good luck, Captain.

The transmission ENDS. Picard thinks for a moment, then heads for the ready room.

PICARD

(to Tasha)

You have the bridge, Lieutenant. I'll be in my ready room.

TASHA

Aye, sir.

Picard EXITS briskly to the ready room.

Picard is moving briskly toward the door. The ship suddenly SHAKES, and Picard is nearly knocked off his feet. The ship goes to RED ALERT and Picard heads for the bridge.

82 INTERIOR MEDICAL SHIP—BRIDGE—FUTURE—CONTINUOUS

Beverly in command, Chilton at conn. Worf, Data, and Geordi working aft consoles. Picard ENTERS from the ready room.

PICARD

What's going on?

BEVERLY

We're under attack.

The ship is ROCKED again.

CHILTON

(off console)

Shield strength down to fifty-two percent. Minor damage to the port nacelle.

WORF

Two Klingon attack cruisers have decloaked to port and starboard.

They all react to this grim news.

83 EXTERIOR SPACE—MEDICAL SHIP AND KLINGONS—FUTURE (OPTICAL)

The *Pasteur* is surrounded by TWO KLINGON ATTACK CRUISERS.

FADE OUT.

ACT EIGHT

FACE IN:

84 INTERIOR MEDICAL SHIP—BRIDGE—FUTURE

As before, ship at Red Alert. The ship is ROCKED again.

BEVERLY
(to Chilton)
Warp speed—get us out of here!

Chilton works.

CHILTON
Warp power is off-line, sir.

Another JOLT.

BEVERLY
(to Chilton)
Heading one-four-eight Mark two-one-five.

85 EXTERIOR SPACE—MEDICAL SHIP—FUTURE (OPTICAL)

The *Pasteur* is trying to get away from the two Klingon attack cruisers, which continue to fire on the medical ship.

86 INTERIOR MEDICAL SHIP—BRIDGE—FUTURE

The ship is ROCKED more violently.

CHILTON
(off console)
Impulse power is fluctuating . . . shields down to thirty percent.

PICARD
(to Worf)
Weapons status?

WORF
These phasers are no match for their shields.

BEVERLY

Geordi, we need warp power—*now.*

Geordi works a console.

GEORDI

Sorry, Captain, they're just too much for us. I can't keep the phase inducers on-line—

Another JOLT.

CHILTON

(off console)

Shields down to nine percent. One more hit and they'll collapse.

BEVERLY

Open a channel.

(beat)

This is Captain Beverly Picard. We're a medical ship on a mission of mercy! Break off your—

The ship is ROCKED again. A grim moment.

BEVERLY

(continuing)

Worf, signal our surrender.

Worf works a console for a moment.

WORF

(to com)

Tos Vah'cha Worf, do'lo jegh! (This is Governor Worf; we surrender!)

The ship is ROCKED violently. Chilton's console EXPLODES, throwing her BACKWARD to the ground. Picard rushes to her, but it's too late—she's dead. Picard reacts.

WORF

(off his console)

Our shields have collapsed. We're defenseless.

Beverly and Picard exchange a look. Beverly sits back in her seat, steels herself. They all wait for what seems to be certain death.

DATA

(off console)

Captain, there's another ship decloaking—bearing two-one-five Mark three-one-oh . . .

(beat)

It's the *Enterprise*!

87 EXTERIOR SPACE—FUTURE (OPTICAL)

Suddenly, the *ENTERPRISE*-D DECLOAKS—the ship is travelling *vertically*. FOLLOW it as it swoops up towards the medical ship and the two Klingon attack cruisers.

87A INTERIOR MEDICAL SHIP—BRIDGE—FUTURE (OPTICAL)

DATA

They're hailing us.

The group looks up at the viewscreen to see Riker.

RIKER

I had a feeling you weren't going to listen to me. Stand by while I try to get the Klingons' attention. . . .

87B EXTERIOR SPACE—*ENTERPRISE* AND KLINGON SHIPS—FUTURE (OPTICAL)

The *Enterprise* FIRES on the attack cruisers with a furious volley of PHASERS and TORPEDOES. One of the Klingon ships EXPLODES.

88 INTERIOR MEDICAL SHIP—BRIDGE—FUTURE (OPTICAL)

As before. The shaking has STOPPED.

WORF

The *Enterprise* is drawing their fire.

BEVERLY

Damage report.

GEORDI

Our warp core's badly damaged. . . . There's a breach in progress.

Picard reacts to this with a look of sudden dread.

PICARD

Warp core breach . . . that may be it. We have to stop it!

Picard moves to look at Geordi's console.

DATA

The Klingon ship is disengaging.

(beat)

Admiral Riker is hailing us.

They look at the viewscreen.

RIKER

Our sensors indicate your ship has a warp core breach in progress. Prepare for emergency beam-out.

Suddenly, the entire bridge crew DEMATERIALIZES.

CUT TO:

89 INTERIOR *ENTERPRISE*—BRIDGE—FUTURE (OPTICAL)

Riker in command, Gaines at tactical. The *Enterprise* has seen a few technological updates over the years. The captain's chair is now slightly higher than it used to be, and there are other changes in evidence. Picard, Beverly, Worf, Data, Geordi, and other N.D.'s from the *Pasteur* MATERIALIZE on Bridge.

GAINES

(to Riker, off console)

All the *Pasteur* crew is safely aboard, Admiral.

RIKER

Raise shields. Where are the Klingons?

GAINES

They're still moving off, sir—half a light-year away.

RIKER

They'll be back. . . .

Riker turns to the others, a look of irritation on his face.

RIKER
(to Picard)
As I said—I figured you weren't going to take no for answer.
(then to Worf)
But I thought *you* would have more sense. I can't believe you let a defenseless ship cross into hostile territory without an escort.

Worf won't take this from Riker. Angrily—

WORF
If you had not turned down the captain when he came to you for help, none of this would have happened. Unlike you, *I* still have a sense of loyalty and honor. . . .

Picard steps in before this can escalate any further.

PICARD
We don't have time for this. The *Pasteur*'s core is going to breach.

RIKER
(to conn officer)
Move us away. Full impulse.

89A EXTERIOR SPACE—*ENTERPRISE* AND *PASTEUR*—FUTURE (OPTICAL)

The *Enterprise* backs away from the *Pasteur.* After a beat, the medical ship EXPLODES.

89B INTERIOR *ENTERPRISE*—BRIDGE—FUTURE

Everyone reacts.

RIKER
All right. Let's get out of here.

PICARD
No . . . we can't . . . we have to save humanity. . . .

RIKER
(to Gaines)
Engage cloak.

GAINES
(off console)
Our cloak isn't functioning. We took a direct hit to the starboard plasma coil. Engineering reports seven hours until we can cloak again.

RIKER
We'll have to do this the old-fashioned way. Lay in a course back to the Federation. Warp thirteen.

Picard reacts strongly to this. As he argues with Riker, we see Beverly move to a COMPARTMENT in the background and take out a medical kit . . . prepare a hypospray. . . .

PICARD
(to Riker)
Wil, don't leave! We have to stay here—find the cause of the temporal anomaly . . .

RIKER
Captain, we can't stay. . . .

Picard is frantic to convince Riker to stay—but his mental condition is getting worse and his desperation sounds almost like hysteria.

PICARD
We have to! Everything depends on this! We can't leave now—please listen to me!

Beverly moves up behind him and applies the hypospray. And as Picard collapses into Riker's arms, the SCENE CHANGES TO:

90 INTERIOR CORRIDOR—PRESENT

Picard nearly bumps into a crew member as he turns a corner. Picard hesitates for a moment, then continues walking towards sickbay. . . .

91 INTERIOR SICKBAY—PRESENT

Picard ENTERS. Beverly is tending to Ogawa, who is lying on a bio-bed. Ogawa is wearing a patient's gown and no longer appears to be pregnant. She looks distraught—she's been crying. Ogawa's N.D. HUSBAND is standing by her, holding her hand, trying to comfort her. Geordi is in the background, lying on another bio-bed.

BEVERLY
Jean-Luc.
(to Ogawa)
I'll be right back, Alyssa.

Ogawa nods as Beverly takes Picard aside and speaks to him quietly.

BEVERLY
(sotto)
Alyssa lost the baby.

Picard reacts.

BEVERLY
I think it's the same thing that happened to Geordi. Somehow, the temporal energy from the anomaly caused the fetal tissue to revert to an earlier stage of development. It was as if the unborn child began to . . . grow younger . . . until finally the DNA itself began to break down.

Picard looks over at Ogawa.

PICARD
How is she?

BEVERLY
Physically, she's fine. For now. But if this temporal reversion continues, I don't think any of us are going to be fine for much longer.

PICARD
So this is affecting the entire crew. . . .

BEVERLY
(nods)
Our cellular structures appear to be coalescing . . . reverting to earlier structures. In some cases, this has caused old injuries to be healed . . . but that's only a temporary effect. Eventually, this could kill us all.

OFF Picard's reaction . . .

CUT TO:

92 EXTERIOR SPACE—THE *ENTERPRISE*—PRESENT (OPTICAL)

The ship holding position near the ANOMALY. We can still see the ENERGY BEAM scanning the anomaly.

93 INTERIOR OBSERVATION LOUNGE—PRESENT

Picard, Data, Riker, and Troi at the table. This is the end of a staff meeting.

PICARD
We also have to find out how widespread this effect is.
(to Troi)
Send an inquiry to Starbase Twenty-three—they're the nearest outpost—have them begin checking their personnel for any signs of temporal reversion.

TROI
Aye, sir.

PICARD
Mister Data, how long until we've completed the tachyon scan?

DATA
Approximately one hour, forty-five minutes.

PICARD
Good. Once it's completed, I want you to find a way to dissipate the anomaly without making things worse. Give me a risk analysis on whatever solution you come up with.

DATA
Aye, sir.

PICARD
Dismissed.

Everyone except Picard EXITS. Picard moves to the table and picks up a padd from the many scattered on the table. He walks to the window, taking a few steps as he reads the padd. From offcamera, we hear Q's voice—

Q'S VOICE
That's a pretty big decision, Jean-Luc. . . .

Picard turns to see that Q is standing in the room. He is dressed in his Starfleet uniform.

Q

Tinkering with an anomaly you know nothing about . . . trying to collapse it . . . isn't that risky?

PICARD

Why? Will that cause the destruction of mankind?

Q

(pondering)

Maybe . . .

(beat)

On the other hand, maybe leaving it *alone* would be the wrong thing to do. . . .

He approaches Picard, intense, intimidating.

Q

It's a big decision, all right. . . . Perhaps it would help to get a different perspective. . . .

Abruptly, the scene CHANGES to:

94 EXTERIOR PRIMORDIAL EARTH—DISTANT PAST (OPTICAL)

Picard and Q are standing on a craggy ledge overlooking a vast expanse of LAVA, VOLCANIC GASES, and CHURNING SEAS. Picard reacts, looks around for a moment. (NOTE: Picard still in present-day uniform; Q in his Starfleet uniform).

Q

Welcome home.

PICARD

Home?

Q

Don't you recognize your old stomping grounds? This is Earth—France. About . . . oh . . . three and a half billion years ago. Give or take an eon or two.

(sniffs the air)

Smells awful, doesn't it. . . . ? All that sulfur and volcanic ash . . . I really must speak to the maid.

PICARD

Is there a point to all this?

Q smiles and points to the sky.

Q

Look—

Picard looks up—

95 NEW ANGLE—THE SKY (OPTICAL)

Instead of a starfield, the sky is FILLED with the SPATIAL ANOMALY seen throughout the show. But here it is HUGE—filling the entire sky from horizon to horizon.

96 RESUME

Picard reacts.

PICARD

The anomaly is here, at Earth . . . ?

Q

At this point in history, the anomaly has filled this entire quadrant of your galaxy.

Picard considers this, thinking aloud.

PICARD

The further back in time . . . the larger the anomaly.

Q

(suddenly sees something)

Oh, oh—come here, there's something I want to show you!

Q kneels down, and Picard comes over to see what he's looking at. Q is peering down into a small muddy POND. The water is murky, but there should be no suggestion of algae, fungus, or anything living.

Q

(re: pond)

See this? This is *you.*

Picard looks annoyed, thinks Q is toying with him.

Q

(continuing)

I'm serious. Right here, life is about to form on this planet for the very first time. A group of amino acids is about to combine and form the first protein. The building blocks of what you call "life."

Despite himself, Picard is a little intrigued. He can't help but peer closer into the pond.

Q

(continuing)

Strange, isn't it, Jean-Luc? Everything you know . . . your entire civilization . . . it all begins right here in this little pond of goo. It's appropriate somehow, isn't it?

(beat)

Too bad you didn't bring a microscope—this is quite fascinating.

They look into the water.

Q

(continuing)

Here they go. . . . The amino acids are moving closer . . . closer . . . closer. . . .

(reacts)

Ohhhh! Nothing happened!

(to Picard)

You see what you've done?

Picard thinks for a moment, then looks up at the sky.

PICARD

You mean I caused the anomaly . . . and the anomaly . . . in some way . . . disrupted the beginning of life on Earth.

Q's eyes bore into Picard.

Q

Congratulations.

The SCENE CHANGES TO:

97 INTERIOR BRIDGE—PAST

Picard in command. Off his reaction . . .

FADE OUT.

ACT NINE

FADE IN:

98 INTERIOR BRIDGE—PAST

Picard, Tasha, Worf, Data, and O'Brien at their stations. Troi ENTERS, looking very concerned.

TROI

Captain, I've just spoken to Doctor Selar. . . . She said that twenty-three children on board have contracted some kind of illness. Their tissues appear to be . . . reverting to an earlier stage of development.

(beat)

She thinks it has something to do with the anomaly.

Picard turns to Tasha.

PICARD

Inform Starfleet Command that we believe the anomaly has toxic effects. Tell them I'm ordering the Terrellian ships back to Federation territory, but that we're staying here.

TASHA

We are?

PICARD

Yes. We have to find a way to collapse this anomaly.

(to Troi)

Counselor, prepare to evacuate all civilians and nonessential personnel to the Terrellians ships.

TROI

Aye, sir.

PICARD

Data, O'Brien, you're with me.

Picard, O'Brien, and Data head for a turbolift.

CUT TO:

99 EXTERIOR SPACE—THE *ENTERPRISE*—PAST (OPTICAL)

The ship near the LARGE ANOMALY. The tachyon pulse is scanning the anomaly.

100 INTERIOR ENGINEERING—PAST

Picard, O'Brien, and Data working at the pool table.

PICARD
Let's concentrate on how this anomaly was initially formed. Speculation?

DATA
Temporal ruptures in the space-time continuum are rarely a naturally occurring phenomenon. It is therefore most likely that this anomaly was caused by an outside catalyst.

O'BRIEN
Like a warp core explosion . . .

PICARD
I think I can rule out a warp core explosion.

DATA
Our tachyon pulse has been unable to penetrate the anomaly completely. If we had information about the center of the phenomenon, we might have a basis for speculation.

PICARD
Can you find a way to scan the interior?

O'BRIEN
I've tried everything I know of . . . there's just too much interference. There's nothing on board that'll do the job.

PICARD
Do you know what could?

Data thinks.

DATA

In theory, a tomographic imaging scanner capable of multiphasic resolution would be able to penetrate this much interference.

(beat)

The Daystrom Institute has been working on such a device, but it is still only theoretical.

Picard looks down at a screen on the pool table. . . .

101A ANGLE ON OKUDAGRAM—PRESENT (OPTICAL)

A graphic showing various sensor information. CUT TO REVEAL WE'RE IN:

101B INTERIOR BRIDGE—PRESENT

Picard is looking at a graphic at one of the aft stations. Data is sitting nearby.

PICARD

Data . . . do we have a tomographic imaging scanner on board?

DATA

Yes, sir.

PICARD

Can you use it to scan the interior of the anomaly?

DATA

Possibly.

Data works for a moment.

DATA

(continuing, off console)

There is a great deal of interference . . . but I am getting some readings.

(beat)

This is very unusual. . . .

PICARD

What is it?

DATA

It appears that our tachyon pulse is converging with *two other* tachyon pulses at the center of the anomaly. The other two pulses have the exact same amplitude modulation as our own pulse. It is as if all three originated from the *Enterprise.*

Picard suddenly has a revelation.

PICARD

Three pulses . . . from three time periods . . . all converging at one point in space.

DATA

Captain, what are you suggesting?

Before Picard can answer, THE SCENE CHANGES TO:

102–103 OMITTED

104 INTERIOR GUEST QUARTERS—FUTURE

Old Picard suddenly sits up in bed. He's wearing nightclothes. He looks around the room for a moment, orienting himself. He gets out of bed, taps a control on a nearby table.

PICARD

Computer, where's Admiral Riker?

COMPUTER VOICE

Admiral Riker is in Ten-Forward.

Picard heads for the door, a determined and driven look on his face.

104A INTERIOR CORRIDOR—FUTURE—CONTINUOUS

Picard steps out into the corridor in his nightclothes. He takes a step down the corridor . . . then stops, looks back the other way . . . is he heading in the right direction? He turns around and goes the other way down the corridor.

CUT TO:

105 INTERIOR TEN-FORWARD—FUTURE (OPTICAL)

Riker, Beverly, Geordi, and Data are at a table. Worf is sitting alone at a separate table on the other side of the room. Midconversation.

Geordi looks around the room.

GEORDI
The ship has held up pretty well over the years.

RIKER
They were going to decommission her about five years ago . . . but one nice thing about being an admiral is getting to choose your own ship.

Beverly glances over at Worf.

BEVERLY
(to Riker)
Wil . . . how long is this thing between you and Worf going to go on?

RIKER
It's been going on for twenty years now . . . doesn't look like it's going to end any time soon.

DATA
I suspect the last thing Counselor Troi would have wanted is for the two of you to be alienated.

BEVERLY
I agree. It's time to put this behind you.

RIKER
I tried—at Deanna's funeral. He wouldn't talk to me.

GEORDI

Might have been tough for him then. . . . He took her death pretty hard.

RIKER

Yeah, well . . . he wasn't the only one.

BEVERLY

I know. But in his mind . . . you were the reason he and Deanna never got together.

RIKER

I didn't do anything to stand in his way—

BEVERLY

(beat)

Didn't you, Wil?

Riker looks at her, regretful.

RIKER

Did I?

She doesn't answer. He looks down, acknowledging. Okay, maybe he did.

RIKER

(continuing)

I just . . . never could admit it was over. I kept thinking one day we'd get together again . . . and then . . . she was gone.

(beat)

You think you've got all the time in the world, until. . . .

Riker stares down at his drink. Deanna's death is still with him, too.

RIKER

Yeah.

But he doesn't trust himself to say more.

CUT TO:

106 INTERIOR CORRIDOR—FUTURE

Picard is walking through the ship with a slightly confused expression. He pauses at an intersection . . . isn't sure which way to go . . . he's drawing curious looks from passing crew members. . . . Picard finally chooses a direction and goes down the corridor. He stops outside a set of doors and then OPENS them. We can see the transporter room inside. Picard stops . . . turns and looks panicked and despairing. . . . He's lost on his own ship.

Follow Picard as he tries to find his way . . . but it's no use. . . . He's completely lost. Finally he stops a passing ENSIGN.

PICARD

Ensign. How . . . do I get to Ten-Forward?

ENSIGN

Two decks up, sir. Section zero zero five.

PICARD

Thank you.

Deeply embarrassed, Picard heads for a turbolift.

CUT TO:

107 INTERIOR TEN-FORWARD—FUTURE (OPTICAL)

Riker, Beverly, Data, and Geordi at their table as before. Beverly suddenly reacts to something offcamera.

BEVERLY

Oh, my god.

She stands and we MOVE TO REVEAL that Picard has just ENTERED the room in his nightclothes. He moves directly to Riker's table.

PICARD

Wil! I know what's happening . . . I know what causes the anomaly . . . we have to go back!

Riker reacts in surprise.

RIKER

Jean-Luc . . . the only place you're going back to is bed.

PICARD

Damnit, Wil, I *know* what's happening. *We're* causing the anomaly . . . with a . . . with the tachyon pulse . . . it happened in all three time periods. *We do it in all three time periods!*

BEVERLY

Jean-Luc, you better come with me.

Beverly tries to take his arm, but Picard jerks away from her.

PICARD

Leave me alone! I'm not crazy. The tachyon pulses . . . they —they were used in the same spot— in all three time periods . . . don't you see? When the tachyon pulse used the —I mean, when the *Pasteur* used the tachyon pulse, *we* set the—you know— we . . . started everything . . . we set it in motion.

Words fail Picard . . . his mental faculties preventing him from giving them a clear picture.

PICARD

It's like . . . the chicken and the egg! You think it started back then . . . but it didn't. . . . It started here in the future . . . that's why it gets larger in the past. . . .

DATA

I think I understand what the captain is saying. If I'm not mistaken, he is describing a *paradox*.

PICARD

Yes! Yes, exactly!

Data takes a beat, thinking of the possibilities.

DATA

Intriguing . . . it is possible we could've created the very anomaly we have been looking for.

Data begins to pace . . . he's the very image of a professor at work.

DATA

Let us assume, for the moment, that the captain has indeed been traveling through time. Let us also assume he has initiated an inverse tachyon pulse at the same coordinates in space in all three time periods.

(beat)

In that case, it is possible that the convergence of three tachyon pulses could've ruptured the subspace barrier and caused an anti-time reaction.

Geordi is beginning to catch on.

GEORDI

I see where you're going. And because anti-time operates in the opposite way *normal time* does, the effects would run *backwards* through the space-time continuum.

PICARD

Yes! That's why the anomaly was larger in the past. It was growing as it traveled backward through time.

A beat as they absorb this.

RIKER

All right . . . let's say, for the moment, you're right. What do we do about it?

PICARD

Go back. Go back to the Devron system.

DATA

He may be right. If we return to the Devron system now, we might see the initial formation of the anomaly.

Everyone looks at Riker . . . waiting to see what he'll do. After a long beat, Riker hits his combadge.

RIKER

Riker to bridge. Set course for the Devron system. Maximum warp.

GAINES (com voice)

Aye, sir.

Riker stands. Everyone except Worf heads for the doors. Riker stops and looks back.

RIKER

Worf . . . we could use a hand.

Worf takes a beat . . . considers . . . then decides to help out, but it's not clear if there has been a reconciliation. They EXIT.

FADE OUT.

ACT TEN

FADE IN:

108 EXTERIOR SPACE—THE *ENTERPRISE* —FUTURE (OPTICAL)

Coming out of warp.

109 INTERIOR BRIDGE—FUTURE (OPTICAL)

Riker, Picard, Beverly, Data, Worf, Geordi, Gaines. Gaines at tactical; N.D.'s man the other stations. Data and Geordi at aft stations. Picard is back in his travel clothes.

GAINES

Entering the Devron system, sir.

RIKER

All stop.

DATA

(off console)

Sensors are picking up a small temporal anomaly off the port bow.

Reactions.

RIKER

On screen.

The VIEWSCREEN now shows a *very small version* of the ANOMALY seen throughout the show. Picard looks vastly relieved.

PICARD

I was right. . . .

GEORDI

(off console)

It's an anti-time eruption. It seems to have formed in the last six hours.

PICARD

We've got to stop it here . . . so it won't be able to travel back through time. . . .

RIKER

All right, Data—we need a solution and we need it fast.

DATA
(off console)
The anomaly is being sustained by the continuing tachyon pulses from the other two time periods. I suggest they be shut down.

PICARD
(serious)
The next time I'm there, that's the first thing I'll do.

RIKER
Isn't there more we can do *here* . . . seal the rupture somehow?

DATA
(still working)
I am investigating the options.

As Picard MOVES toward Data, the SCENE CHANGES TO:

110 INTERIOR BRIDGE—PRESENT

Picard MOVING toward Geordi and Data at the aft consoles, as in Act Nine. (Note: Picard is at different locations in all three time periods, allowing for straight-cut transitions during the fast pace of Act Ten.)

PICARD
(quickly)
Data, disengage the tachyon pulse.

DATA
Sir?

PICARD
Just do it. The convergence of tachyon pulses from the three time periods is what causes the anomaly.

DATA
Aye, sir.

Data works.

111 EXTERIOR SPACE—THE *ENTERPRISE*—PRESENT (OPTICAL)

The ship holding position at the anomaly. We see the tachyon beam TURN OFF.

112 INTERIOR BRIDGE—PRESENT

As before.

PICARD
Report. Is there any change in the anomaly?

113 ANGLE ON DATA—PAST

Sitting at ops.

DATA
No, sir.

MOVE TO REVEAL:

114 INTERIOR BRIDGE—PAST

Picard in command. Data, Tasha, Worf, Troi, O'Brien at their stations.

PICARD
Disengage the tachyon pulse.

The others exchange a look.

O'BRIEN
We haven't finished the scan, sir.

PICARD
I know that. But it's imperative that you disengage it immediately.

DATA
(works)
Aye, sir. Disengaging.

Picard stares at the viewscreen (not seen).

PICARD
Why isn't the anomaly affected?

O'BRIEN
(puzzled)
Why would it be, sir?

THE SCENE CHANGES TO:

115 INTERIOR BRIDGE—FUTURE

Picard sitting in the command chair. Everyone else as seen before.

PICARD
(to all)
I've shut off the tachyon pulses in the other time periods—but the anomaly didn't change.

This draws a few curious looks from the others—but everyone now accepts that Picard is indeed traveling through time.

DATA
(off console)
It remains unaffected here as well.

BEVERLY
What do we do?

GEORDI
The only way to stop this thing is to repair the rupture at the focal point where time and anti-time are converging.

RIKER
How do we do that?

DATA
It would require taking the ship *into* the anomaly itself. Once inside, we may be able to use our engines to create a static warp shell.

GEORDI
(onto the idea)
Yeah, yeah . . . and the shell would act like an artificial subspace barrier —separating time and anti-time. . . .

DATA
Collapsing the anomaly and restoring the normal flow of time.
(turns to Picard)
But this would have to be done in the other two time periods, as well.

Picard considers.

PICARD

That could be a problem. . . . The anomaly's so much larger in the other time periods. . . .

THE SCENE CHANGES TO:

116 INTERIOR BRIDGE—PAST

Picard finishing his sentence—

PICARD

(continuing)

. . . It could be dangerous to take the ship in.

Everyone looks at him.

O'BRIEN

Take the ship in where, sir?

Picard takes a beat, then makes a decision.

PICARD

Into the anomaly, Chief. Lay in a course to the exact center. Transfer all available power to the shields.

Shocked reactions around the bridge.

TASHA

Sir . . . can you give us some explanation?

PICARD

No. I cannot.

TASHA

Captain, so far we've obeyed every order—no matter how far-fetched it might have seemed. But if we're to risk the safety of the ship and crew . . . I think we have to ask you for an explanation.

Picard looks around at the crew, which is staring intently at him, waiting to see how he'll handle this.

PICARD
(continuing)
I know all of you have doubts about me . . . about each other . . . about the ship. All I can say is that even though we've only been together for a short time . . . I know that you are the finest crew in the fleet . . . and I would trust each of you with my life.
(beat)
I'm asking you to make a leap of faith—and trust me.

A quiet beat on the bridge . . . then suddenly everyone starts working. The team has come together at last.

TASHA
Shields up, maximum strength.

WORF
Boosting field integrity on the warp nacelles. We may encounter shearing forces once we enter the anomaly.

DATA
I am preparing to initiate a static warp shell.

O'BRIEN
Course laid in, sir.

TROI
(off armchair console)
All decks report ready, Captain.

Picard looks at his crew—he's proud of them and it shows.

PICARD
Chief . . . take us in.

THE SCENE CHANGES TO:

117 INTERIOR BRIDGE—PRESENT

Picard at aft console command—everything as before. Data turns to him from the aft console.

DATA

Captain, I have an idea. If we take the ship to the center of the anomaly and create a static warp shell . . .

PICARD

(overlapping)

. . . a static warp shell, it could repair the barrier and collapse the anomaly.

DATA

(surprised)

Yes, sir.

PICARD

Mister Data, you're a clever man—in any time period.

Picard moves down to the command area with Data and Geordi.

PICARD

(continuing)

Lay in a course to the center of the anomaly. Prepare to initiate a static warp shell.

As Picard moves, the SCENE CHANGES TO:

118 INTERIOR BRIDGE—FUTURE

As before.

PICARD

The other two *Enterprises* . . . they're on their way.

RIKER

Very well.

(to conn)

Ensign . . . take us in.

119 EXTERIOR SPACE—THE *ENTERPRISE*—FUTURE (OPTICAL)

The ship begins moving towards the anomaly . . . closer . . . closer . . .

120 INTERIOR BRIDGE—PAST (OPTICAL)

As before. Tense. The crew is watching the ANOMALY on the viewscreen—it's getting *closer.*

O'BRIEN
We're entering the anomaly, sir.

PICARD
All hands brace for impact!

The ship ROCKS violently. The lights FLICKER.

TASHA
The temporal energy's interfering with main power. Switching to . . .

Another JOLT carries us to:

121 INTERIOR BRIDGE—PRESENT (OPTICAL)

The ship is ROCKING. The anomaly has almost FILLED the viewscreen. Lights flickering on and off here, as well. People hanging on.

GEORDI
. . . auxiliary power. I'm having trouble keeping the impulse engines on-line! I've got power fluctuations all across the board!

PICARD
Maintain course and speed!
(to Data)
Mister Data, how long until we reach the center?

DATA
Another thirty seconds at least, Captain.

The SCENE CHANGES TO:

122 OMITTED

123 INTERIOR BRIDGE—FUTURE

The ship is SHAKING.

GAINES
We've entered the anomaly.

The SCENE CHANGES TO:

124 INTERIOR BRIDGE—PAST

As before—the ship SHAKING.

DATA
We have reached the center, sir.

PICARD
Initiate warp shell!

Data works. SCENE CHANGES:

125 INTERIOR BRIDGE—PRESENT

As before—the ship SHAKING.

DATA
(working)
Initiating static warp shell—*now.*

SCENE CHANGES:

126 INTERIOR BRIDGE—FUTURE

As before—ship SHAKING.

RIKER
Is it having any effect?

SCENE CHANGES:

127 INTERIOR BRIDGE—PAST

As before—shaking.

DATA
(off console)
Something is happening. . . . A new subspace barrier appears to be forming—

TASHA
(urgent)
Captain! Sensors are picking up . . . two other *ships* . . .

Everyone looks at the viewscreen—

128 VIEWSCREEN—PAST (OPTICAL)

Which is filled with the roiling anomaly. But faintly through the energy, we can see the GHOSTLY IMAGES of TWO *ENTERPRISES.* The ships are drifting in the anomaly very close to each other—in fact, they appear to be moving *through* each other. It's a startling sight.

129 INTERIOR BRIDGE—PRESENT (OPTICAL)

The crew watching the exact same image on their viewscreen—two *Enterprises.*

130 INTERIOR BRIDGE—FUTURE (OPTICAL)

This crew watching the same image on their viewscreen. It's an awesome moment.

131 INTERIOR BRIDGE—PAST (OPTICAL)

As before.

DATA
Captain, it appears to be working. The anomaly is beginning to collapse. I think that—

TASHA
(suddenly)
Sir—the temporal energy is rupturing our warp containment system!

WORF
We must eject the core!

PICARD
No. We have to maintain the static warp shell for as long as possible!

The ship SHAKES *harder.*

TASHA

We're losing containment! I can't stop it; it's going to—

Suddenly, the bridge is ENGULFED IN A BLAST OF FLAMES AND DEBRIS—

132 INTERIOR BRIDGE—PRESENT (OPTICAL)

On the viewscreen, one of the ghostly *Enterprises* EXPLODES—destroyed. Reactions.

PICARD

(quickly, to Geordi)

Transfer emergency power to the antimatter containment system!

The ship starts SHAKING more violently than ever.

GEORDI

(working frantically)

I'm trying, sir . . . but there's a lot of interference. . . .

DATA

(off console)

The warp shell is definitely having an effect, sir. The anomaly is collapsing—

GEORDI

The containment system's going—I can't hold it—

PICARD

Maintain position! Mister La Forge—

Scene CHANGES TO:

133 INTERIOR BRIDGE—FUTURE (OPTICAL)

As before—shaking out of control. On the viewscreen, we see the second *Enterprise* EXPLODE. Reactions to the sight.

DATA

Both of the other ships have been destroyed.

At this moment, Q APPEARS standing next to Picard. He's wearing a GRIM REAPER's outfit, complete with scythe and hourglass.

Q

(to Picard)

Two down . . . one to go.

PICARD

(to Data)

Data, report!

DATA

The anomaly is nearly collapsed. . . .

GEORDI

We're losing containment. . . .

The ship ROCKING, ROLLING!

Q

(calm)

Good-bye, Jean-Luc. I'll miss you. You did have so much potential. But I guess . . . all good things must come to an end.

GEORDI

Containment field at critical! I'm losing it—

134 EXTERIOR SPACE—THE *ENTERPRISE*—FUTURE (OPTICAL)

The anomaly COLLAPSES INWARD on top of the *Enterprise*—the SCREEN WHITES OUT—

CUT TO:

135 INTERIOR COURTROOM (OPTICAL)

Silence. Picard standing alone in a now *empty* courtroom. He's dressed normally, present-day age. Picard is a little disoriented by the sudden silence. After a moment, Q's floating chair drops down into frame. Q is dressed in his judge's robes again. He studies Picard.

Q

The Continuum didn't think you had it in you, Jean-Luc . . . but I knew you could.

Picard looks at him.

PICARD

Are you saying it worked? We collapsed the anomaly?

Q

Is that all this meant to you? Just another spatial anomaly . . . just another day at the office?

PICARD

Q, did it work?

Q

You're here, aren't you? You're talking to me, aren't you?

PICARD

What about my crew?

Q

(mocking)

"The anomaly . . . my crew . . . my ship." I suppose you're worried about your fish too. Well, if it puts your mind at ease, you've saved humanity once again.

Picard regards Q briefly.

PICARD

Thank you.

Q

For what?

PICARD

You had a hand in helping me get out of this.

Q

I was the one who got you *into* it, Jean-Luc. That was the directive from the Continuum.

(beat)

The part about the helping hand . . . was my idea.

Picard looks around the courtroom.

PICARD

I sincerely hope this is the last time I'll find myself here.

Q shakes his head.

Q

You just don't get it, do you, Jean-Luc?

(leans in to him)

The trial never ends.

He smiles patronizingly.

Q

(continuing)

We wanted to see if you had the ability to expand your mind and your horizons . . . and for one brief moment, you did.

PICARD

When I realized the paradox . . .

Q

Exactly. For that one fraction of a second, you were open to options you'd never considered. *That's* the exploration that awaits you . . . not mapping stars and studying nebulae . . . but charting the unknowable possibilities of existence.

The chair begins to MOVE AWAY from Picard.

PICARD

What are you trying to tell me, Q?

Q touches his hat in a half-salute. His chair is almost fully withdrawn.

Q

You'll find out.

(beat)

In any case, I'll be watching . . . and if you're lucky, I'll drop by to say hello from time to time.

(beat)

See you out there.

And he's gone. The SCENE CHANGES TO:

136 INTERIOR CORRIDOR—PRESENT

Picard stepping out of the turbolift, dressed in his bathrobe. Troi and Worf are standing there, looking at him in surprise. *We are back at the exact same moment we saw in the Teaser.* Picard stares at them, then looks down at himself, sees his bathrobe . . .

TROI

Captain, are you all right?

PICARD

Worf . . . what's the date?

WORF

Stardate 47988.

Picard smiles . . . overwhelmed with relief . . . he *laughs.* Troi and Worf exchange a puzzled look.

TROI

Is something wrong, sir?

PICARD

No, no . . . in fact, I think I'll go back to bed. I could use some sleep.

Picard steps back in the lift. Troi and Worf exchange a look. . . .

CUT TO:

137 EXTERIOR SPACE—THE *ENTERPRISE* —PRESENT (OPTICAL)

At impulse.

PICARD (voice-over)

Captain's log, supplemental. Starfleet Command reports no unusual activity along the Neutral Zone, and there is no sign of a temporal anomaly. It would appear that I am the only member of the crew to retain any knowledge of the events I experienced.

138 INTERIOR RIKER'S QUARTERS—PRESENT

Riker, Data, Beverly, Troi and Geordi sitting at the table, playing POKER. Troi is raking in her winnings with a big smile. Beverly pushes back her chair and gets up.

BEVERLY
That's it for me.

TROI
There's always next time.

Beverly smiles and moves to an empty chair off to one side of the table.

GEORDI
That's four hands in a row. How does he do it?

RIKER
I cheat.

Data's head snaps up in shock.

RIKER
(continuing)
I'm kidding.

Data collects the cards and begins shuffling at normal speed. Beverly looks thoughtful.

BEVERLY
I've been thinking . . . about all the things the captain told us about the future. The way we changed and drifted apart . . . why would he tell us what's to come?

GEORDI
It sure goes against everything we've heard about not polluting the timeline. . . .

DATA
I believe, however, that this situation is unique.

They all look at him.

DATA
(continuing)
Since the temporal anomaly did not occur, there have already been changes in the way this timeline is unfolding. The future we experience will undoubtedly be different from the one the captain encountered.

RIKER
Maybe that's why he told us. Knowing what that future could bring . . . gives us a chance to change things *now.*

He gives Worf a meaningful look.

RIKER
(continuing)
So that some things never happen.

Worf nods in understanding.

The door CHIMES.

RIKER
Come in.

Troi ENTERS.

TROI
Am I too late?

RIKER
Not at all. Have a seat.

Troi sits, and Riker begins giving her chips.

TROI
What's the game?

DATA
Five-card draw, deuces wild.

The door CHIMES.

RIKER

Come.

The doors open and Picard ENTERS. Everyone reacts in surprise, sits up at attention.

RIKER
(continuing)

Captain. Is there a problem?

PICARD

No. I just thought I might . . . join you this evening. If there's room. . . .

Surprised but pleased looks go around the table.

RIKER

Of course.

Picard takes a seat at the table. Data gives him the deck of cards.

DATA

Would you care to deal?

PICARD

Oh . . . thank you.

Picard starts to shuffle the cards.

PICARD
(continuing)

I should have done this a long time ago. I was quite a card player in my youth, you know.

TROI

You were always welcome.

Picard nods. His experience has left him with a new appreciation of his feelings for these people . . . his crew . . . his family . . .

PICARD

So. Five-card stud, nothing wild. The sky's the limit.

As Picard continues dealing, we PULL BACK for one final look at this family of characters. . . .

CUT TO:

139 EXTERIOR SPACE—THE *ENTERPRISE* —PRESENT (OPTICAL)

The great ship moving off into the distance . . .

FADE OUT.